In the Father's Hands

J.E. SOLINSKI

AMOC
PUBLICATIONS™

In the Father's Hands
by J.E. Solinski

J.E. Solinski books may be purchased through booksellers, www.jesolinski.com, or amazon.com.
Cover illustration and design by Dusan Arsenic.
Interior book design by Pamela Lee.

ISBN: 978-0-9989096-6-0(sc)
ISBN: 978-0-9989096-7-7(hc)

Library of Congress Control Number: 2017908601

Printed in the United States of America

First Edition
September 2017

Dedication

To all the Christian students, teachers, staff, and administrators in the public school system. Continue to be a light in a dark world by speaking truth in love and being God's hands and feet on earth.

Acknowledgments

The importance of others reviewing one's work cannot be overstated, but it is even more important with a sequel as continuity must be achieved. Therefore, I would like to thank my three readers—Janice Millar, Linda Taylor, and Michael Lee—for making sure the story was faithful to the first book but took on a life of its own. I also need to give a huge thank you to my editor, Genevieve Healey, for her critical eyes and attention to detail. The book is tighter, clearer, and more consistent because of her. Thank you, once again, to my marketing and creative director, Pamela Lee. This endeavor never would have made it to print without her.

Dear Reader,

Though the story takes place in Detroit, Michigan, and some real street names and locations are used in the book, all buildings, churches, and places of business are fictional and do not exist. Thank you.

J.E. Solinski

"For I, the Lord your God, will hold your right hand, saying to you, 'Fear not; I will help you.'" Isaiah 41:13

Chapter 1

Travis leaned against the brick building, his right foot up behind him flat against the wall and his arms crossed in front of him. He took a long, deep breath, then slowly released it as he surveyed the scene in front of him from behind the protection of his Ray-Bans. Various groups had gathered according to kind, some glancing his way every so often, others purposefully keeping their eyes and activities hidden from view, most intent on their cell phones. A wry smile crossed his lips, and he let out an abrupt laugh. They thought they had him fooled, that their actions were discreet and sly, that their intentions could not be read. But he had been reading the lines of this neighborhood for years now, and very little got past him. He dropped his foot to the ground, stood straight up, and uncrossed his arms. It was just about time.

"Good morning, Mr. Johnson!"

Travis glanced to his left as a fifteen-year-old girl passed in front of him smiling.

"Good morning, Sharmayn," he said returning the smile. "Hannah," he added to her friend.

"Good morning, Mr. Johnson," Hannah replied.

Travis started toward the groups in front of him.

"Morning, Mr. Johnson," came a call from the right.

"Jimmy," he returned with a nod.

"Did you have a good summer, Mr. Johnson?" a third asked as the two crossed paths.

"I did," he remarked. "And you, Parker?"

"The best," came the reply. "But I'm ready for the school year!" he added enthusiastically.

And so am I, thought Travis. *So am I.*

Several more students passed by offering him their greetings, and he returned each with the appropriate name, but he continued toward the group that had gone to great lengths to keep its activity hidden from him. The jackets were a dead giveaway. Even though lightweight, jackets were the last thing you needed in Detroit's September humidity. Funny, he thought, that they had chosen to stay out here in the open. Brazen, in fact. And even more astonishing was the fact that they weren't making any attempt to move as he approached. He didn't recognize any of them and that explained a lot.

"Gentlemen," he said once he reached their group. Four pairs of eyes, all shielded by their own sunglasses, turned toward him. Travis saw that their mouths were set, and their attitudes already hardened and sealed. The whole vibe threw him back fifteen years. Though he didn't recognize the boys standing in front of him, he knew them all by heart. He could have been any one of them. Heck, he *had* been one of them.

* * * *

"Gentlemen," he said again. "Let me introduce myself. I'm Mr. Johnson, and I'm the principal of Montgomery High School, and *WE*," he emphasized the word and looked at all four of them, "need to talk. Shall we go to my office?"

He held out his right arm, palm open, and gestured toward the building in front of them. They didn't move. One licked his lips. Another's head made a slight movement to the left. The third cleared his throat a bit nervously. The fourth did nothing at all. Travis took it all in and in one sweeping second knew immediately the hierarchy within this group. Number Four was the leader. Number Four would be his challenge. He looked straight at Number Four. Finally, Number Four gave a brief nod and stepped out toward the building. The other three fell in line behind him, and Travis followed. Then the doors swallowed them up just as the bell rang, signaling the start of a new school year.

* * * *

Martha Richards heard the bell ring, took a deep breath, and glanced one final time around her classroom just as the students for her first period Freshman College Prep English class began entering. She smiled and greeted each one. Some beamed in response, others grunted a reply, and a few chose to ignore her completely. She couldn't help but smile to herself and shake her head a bit. *Same song, different verse,* she thought. In fact, it was the thirty-sixth verse for her, for this was her thirty-sixth year of teaching at Montgomery High School.

She watched the students claim their seats, each selection giving her a bit of insight about that student. Those who chose the front row were either eager to learn or eager to get her attention. Back-row students were all about keeping out of the line of fire. Out of sight, out of mind, and hopefully out of question range. Middle-row students ... they were a mixed bag. Those who chose the middle of the middle were saying, "I will be engaged, but I like my space." For those who migrated toward the walls, they were saying, "I like learning, but I like to experience it from a distance." Of course, this educational personality assessment wasn't perfect because of one fatal flaw. If the student just happened to be among the last third of the class to come in, then there was a strong possibility that their preferred seat of choice was already taken, so they had to make do with what was left. It was easy to see which students fell into this last category. The minute they walked into the room, they would head to a particular spot only to come up short when they saw someone else sitting there. Freshmen weren't good at hiding their disappointment or their fear, especially if the open seats moved them closer to the front.

Martha watched the students as they settled in. It was the first period of the first day of high school for the students in front of her. Whereas sophomores, juniors, and seniors might be whooping it up in other rooms as they saw each other for the first time since school let out last spring or already bent on disrupting the teacher's carefully planned lesson, these students shuffled around the class in relative silence—a mixture of anxiousness and excitement all rolled into one.

The bell rang again, signaling the beginning of class and what little noise there had been vanished immediately. All eyes stared straight at her, and Martha once again felt the burden of responsibility, for as the first teacher these students encountered on the first day of high school, she could set the tone for their next four years. Martha looked around the room. Each young student, both the eager and the quasi apathetic, looked up at her and waited expectantly.

"Good morning," she said brightly.

A weak "good morning" twittered across the room.

"We can do better than that," she said and repeated her greeting a little louder, leaning toward her charges. Her eyes shone bright and intense, her smile broad. "Good morning," she repeated.

"Good morning!" they—even the back row—replied in a much healthier fashion.

"Much better," she said and relaxed. "Welcome to room 372— Freshman *College Prep* English." She emphasized the middle two words. "Is everyone in the right place?" Her eyes swept the room. Some students nodded. All sat very still.

"Excellent," she said as she walked between the rows of students. The students twisted their bodies to follow her progress. "Then let's get started."

And so in room 372 another verse of English under the watchful tutelage of veteran teacher Martha Richards began. For Martha, it was a bittersweet start of the year. For after thirty-six years of teaching, this would be the last verse, her swan song. She was retiring in the spring.

* * * *

Danny Richards silently observed the young man sitting across from him. The young man feigned indifference and boredom. He heaved heavy sighs and reshuffled his legs every few seconds. His eyes flittered around the room anxiously, landing briefly first on the file cabinet, then on the framed diploma on the wall, then on the pencil holder on the desk, and finally on the clock on the wall. All the while, Danny carefully watched him.

A proper middle-class twenty-year-old college student. The classic button-down dress shirt and slacks. The conservative haircut. And that river of fear and anxiety running just below the façade of confidence and bravado. The young man hid it well, but every so often the eyes would let down their guard, and a flash of uncertainty would appear. Danny still waited. The young man began to fidget in his chair.

"Well, aren't you going to ask me any questions?" he finally blurted.

"Like what?" Danny responded.

"Like am I doing drugs or something?" he said.

"Are you?" Danny asked.

Now it was the young man's turn to stare at him.

"Humph!" he finally ejected. "Some counselor *you* are. Don't even know how to weasel a confession out of someone."

Danny smiled.

"I've always found the direct approach pretty effective," he said. "So are you doing drugs?"

The young man smirked, shook his head dismissively, and

released another sigh of contempt.

"What do you think?" he challenged. "You're the shrink. See if you can figure me out."

Danny didn't take the bait.

"Sorry, I'm not your shrink," Danny countered. "Wrong office. And I hate to tell you, but it really doesn't matter one iota what I think. What matters is what you think. However, if I were a betting man, I would say that since you chose to spend time with me, a *drug* counselor, rather than spend two years in jail, I would let a few dollars ride on the notion that said you have taken a drug or two."

Danny gave his little speech without malice or sarcasm. His soft reply was without condemnation or reproach. The court had already done that, and Danny was sure that this young man had condemned himself multiple times in the solitude of his own bedroom. Most of the people he saw were first offenders or those who chose option A—seek drug counseling—rather than option B—go to jail. Some had no intention of giving up the drugs. The good times were good enough to make up for the downers, but they would rather sacrifice *some* of their freedom to attend counseling sessions than all of their freedom sitting in jail. Plus, they might be able to continue the habit if they could keep from getting caught and pass the drug tests. Most had turned to drugs as an answer to some sort of pain, only to discover that the drugs didn't deliver them from pain, they only produced more pain. Many felt duped and cheated, and now they wanted out.

Danny knew all about that, which was why he was sitting

on *this* side of the desk now. Fifteen years ago, he had been the fidgety, anxious, frightened, and confused college student who had turned to drugs to regain control of his life only to find that control wrested from him, and his life spinning wildly awry. Fifteen years ago, a man had sat across from him, just as he was sitting now with this young man, and had slowly helped him take his life back. Fifteen years ago, the downward spiral had stopped for him, and ever since then he had dedicated his life to helping others right their own sinking ships.

Chapter 2

"Straight down this hall," said Travis, nodding toward the far end of the corridor, when boy Number One turned to look at him questioningly. Number Four never turned around, never looked at Travis, and never took his hands out of his pockets, but confidently walked straight ahead while his companions followed behind him. Travis watched them intently, sizing up the four, especially Number Four. Travis knew the street. He knew gangs, he knew pockets, and he knew he should probably have Number Four keep his hands where he could see them. But something here didn't quite ring true to gang behavior. Sure, Number Four held his head high and walked with a strong purpose, but Travis couldn't help but notice that every so often Number Four's head would move ever so slightly to the right or to the left. Without seeming to take his eyes off the boys, Travis quickly scanned each portion of the hallway that caught Number Four's attention—the trophy cases, the photos, the banner sporting the school motto:

Dream Big. Then Work Hard.

The three boys following Number Four were oblivious to their surroundings and merely marched forward, dutifully following their leader, without incident or comment. All a bit strange, thought Travis, for gang boys, but then they looked young, and he didn't know them, so they were probably no more than fourteen years old and perhaps young recruits.

By the time they had reached the principal's office, he had moved forward to even himself with boy Number Four. He ushered them past the secretary and into his office, pulling two chairs from against the wall up next to the two already facing his desk, and gestured for the boys to sit. They did, and Travis pulled off his sunglasses. The three looked at Number Four to see what he would do. After a moment's hesitation, he took his off as well, and the other three followed suit.

Under the guise of settling himself behind his desk, Travis looked at Number Four discreetly, making a quick assessment. Without his sunglasses, he looked extremely young. Though his face was firmly set, it wasn't hard or cold. His clothes were neat and clean but not new or expensive. His hair though clean looked like it hadn't been cut in a while, an anomaly for the first day of school. Travis took in the other three in almost the same glance. Their clothes were newer; their hair, recently cut. Travis noticed Number Four trying to look straight ahead but saw his eyes take in the office when he thought Travis was looking elsewhere. Travis cleared his throat. It was time to open up the dialogue.

"Good morning, boys," he said with a slight smile. "Welcome

to Montgomery High School. Once again, I'm Mr. Johnson, the principal here, and I make it my business to know all of my students. And, since I don't know your names, I assume you are new to Montgomery High. Is that true?"

Three pairs of eyes shifted toward Number Four, who dipped his head in a slight nod.

Travis nodded back. "Freshmen?" he asked.

Again, the deference to Number Four. Again, the barely perceptible nod.

"And your names?" Travis asked, turning toward Number One.

The boy glanced toward Number Four, who never moved his head, leaving him to fend for himself.

"Thomas," he said. Travis nodded and turned toward Number Two.

"Charles."

A nod toward Number Three.

"My name's Curtis," he said.

Travis smiled. The boy was true to his name, courteous even in this situation. Finally, Travis turned back to Number Four.

"And you?" he asked.

Number Four looked at him squarely.

"Gabriel," he said proudly.

* * * *

As soon as he had seen the man drop his foot from the wall and start walking their way, Gabriel had felt his heart stop, then stutter start, then pound uncontrollably in his chest. He knew who the man was.

Everyone knew who he was. He was Mr. Johnson, the principal, and he had a reputation of no nonsense. He had wondered why Mr. Johnson had singled them out. What had they done? The last thing Gabriel wanted was to get noticed.

Now as he sat in the man's office, he tried to keep his legs from shaking. And when Mr. Johnson asked him his name, he took his time and swallowed hard to keep the quiver out of his voice before answering proudly, all the while hoping to give the illusion of confidence.

As they had entered, before he had taken his sunglasses off, and then again while the principal was asking the others their names, Gabriel had taken a quick survey of the room. It was a spacious, pleasant room, with large windows that let in an ample light. The walls were the color of a robin's egg and there were bookcases, filled to saturation, lining every wall—floor to ceiling. Where there wasn't a bookshelf, large oil paintings filled the wall space. Though each included scenery of some kind, the sky and clouds were the main subjects in most. One in particular caught Gabriel's attention, mostly because it was right in his line of sight behind the principal's desk, but also because of its colors. The scene was obviously set just before sunrise because all he could see was the outline of a mountain range with one mountain rising a bit higher than the rest. The mountain range was black, but the sky above it was the most intense blue Gabriel had ever seen, and the underbellies of the clouds were the color of ripe cantaloupe. The clouds themselves were either like shredded cotton balls or stretched out in long strands. It was the most overwhelmingly beautiful picture he had ever seen and by far the most peaceful. He felt himself sigh inwardly. It was a peace he wished he had.

* * * *

Nothing the boys did escaped Travis's notice, especially Gabriel's interest in his paintings, and particularly in the one behind his desk. Having learned their names, he rose, moved to the front of his desk, and sat on its front edge, facing the boys.

"Montgomery High School is a safe, *clean* place," he told them, and his slight emphasis on the word "clean" let them know that drugs would not be tolerated. "I have every intention of keeping it that way."

The boys didn't move. Three of them had their eyes on him. Number Four just looked straight ahead. Travis continued.

"I don't like to do this on your first day with us," he began, but I am going to ask you, one at a time, to empty your backpacks and pockets and put the contents on my desk."

Now all four pairs of eyes looked at him at once, questioning him.

"Why?" asked Gabriel. The question was asked without malice but did have a hint of rebellion, and Travis immediately knew the boy was hiding something. He nodded toward their clothes.

"Well, for starters, it's ninety degrees outside with eighty percent humidity, and you four are wearing jackets." Curtis squirmed. "Second, you were taking great care not to let anyone see what was being passed between you." Charles swallowed hard. "So, Thomas, let's start with you."

Thomas looked over at Gabriel who had pulled his lips into a hard line and was staring straight ahead but for the first time that morning looked angry. Travis had hit a nerve.

Thomas stood up and pulled the lining out of his jacket and pants pockets, revealing nothing but a few dollars—lunch money most likely. Next, he opened and emptied his backpack. Books, pencils, and notebooks. Nothing else. Travis checked the lining. Nothing. Charles and Curtis did the same with the same results. Travis was becoming more and more baffled as the procedure continued. What was going on here? he wondered. Why all the secrecy if they had nothing to hide? Finally, it was Gabriel's turn.

He stood up and looked straight into Travis's eyes, and Travis saw what could have been hatred if it hadn't been for the flash of hurt behind it. Gabriel pulled out the lining of his pants' pockets to reveal nothing—not even lunch money. He hesitated when he got to his jacket, but, finally, he reached into one and pulled out a banana and laid it on the table. Then into the other, pulling out an apple followed by a granola bar. Then he pulled out the lining of both pockets to show they were empty. Gabriel had no backpack.

Travis worked hard to suppress any indication of his surprise. He was confused here, but without wavering for a second he said, "And now, what do you have in your right sock."

Gabriel's head jerked up slightly, and Travis knew he was right. He had noticed as the boys were walking that Gabriel's right pant leg bulged ever so slightly when his leg was extended. Gabriel didn't move.

"Your right sock, Gabriel," Travis said softly but firmly.

Gabriel didn't move for what felt like a minute. Finally, he reached down, slid his right pant leg up and his sock down, then pulled out the final item and laid it on the desk.

Travis stared at the object. It was a four-inch spring-loaded knife.

* * * *

Travis stood at the window and looked out over the empty inner courtyard of Montgomery High. All the students were in first period now... even the four boys. After he had found the knife, he had sent Charles, Thomas, and Curtis back to class and kept Gabriel behind. A student bringing a knife on campus was subject to suspension—even expulsion—but Travis was loath to pursue either. First, what was the point of sending a student home for five days on the first day of school? Too much would be lost. Second, the knife seemed out of place on Gabriel. Sure, the boy knew where to put it to conceal it, but Gabriel did not fit the mold of a gang member. No, the knife was for some other reason.

Instead, Travis had decided to take the direct approach. He explained to Gabriel the school's policy and told him that if he brought a gun or another knife to school, he would be suspended immediately and up for possible expulsion. The boy didn't blink. Travis then told him that he was going to call home and tell his parents the same thing. *That* brought an immediate reaction. Slight though it was, Travis noticed the flash of fear followed by concern register in Gabriel's eyes. Then the firm, tight line of Gabriel's drawn lips returned.

"What's your phone number?" Travis asked him.

Gabriel gave it to him. "But it's been disconnected for about a month now," he added.

Travis looked at the boy as he dialed the number and listened to the familiar recording he heard so often when dealing with many of Montgomery's students: "The number you are trying to call has been disconnected." Travis hung up the phone and looked back at Gabriel.

He would double check the home phone number with Gabriel's student records, but he hadn't a reason to doubt the boy. He sighed inwardly and looked back at Gabriel.

"Cell?"

Gabriel shook his head.

Travis stared at the boy sitting before him who was trying hard to play tough. His gut told him that this young man may not be battling it out on the streets becoming gang tough but that he was fighting a battle somewhere. But where?

Chapter 3

Martha had opted to stay in her room for lunch today. The faculty lunch room would have just as much adrenaline and hyperactivity on the first day of school as the classrooms did, and she wanted to relax, take a lot of deep breaths, and have a few moments of peace. Tomorrow she would dine with the others.

She unwrapped her sandwich and looked out at the rows of desks in front of her. When had she changed from that teacher full of energy into this one, just trying to make it through the day? She remembered herself as a young, energetic teacher, shaking her head sadly and in righteous condemnation at the older teachers who seemed just to go through the motions, who didn't seem to engage with their students anymore, and who didn't want to try new techniques or strategies. She let out a small chuckle. Now she understood. It wasn't that they didn't care about their students anymore; it was that their teaching world and the students they taught had changed so much. Not at the core, perhaps, as teenagers were teenagers, and English was English—or whatever the subject was—but everything else had. Now kids were wired twenty-four seven. Connectivity and availability at all times was nonnegotiable as students deemed their cell phones their best friends. They were also the students' greatest distraction and a teacher's greatest curse.

Teachers were asked to embrace technology, and while Martha enjoyed what computers offered, she didn't have the energy to learn how to use new devices and then test them to see if they generated the same desired results. So she had now become that teacher who was set in her ways and would carry her archaic teaching style and system to her retirement day. There were a few her age who could embrace the changes, and she admired them for it, but she couldn't do it herself. She let out a heartier laugh this time. Teaching's Circle of Life.

It was time. Time for her to move over and move on. Though she might have years of experience in her camp, it was time to let the younger teachers with their energy, enthusiasm, and new ideas have their turn, and Martha was ready. She was emotionally spent and physically tired. Thirty-five years of solving multiple problems in the five minutes before class started, learning more than 150 names within the week, grading stacks upon stacks of papers, and adapting lesson plans to suit each individual class on a daily basis had drained her. She would find her nerves frayed at the end of one week and experience a sense of anxiety at the beginning of the next.

Martha finished her sandwich and glanced up at the clock. Five minutes before the bell rang. She looked at her grade book to remind herself which class was coming next. Junior College Prep English. Until three years ago, she had taught drama after lunch, and that had been a wonderful way to end the day. But the demands became too much, and knowing that she would retire in three years, she knew she needed to hand the reins of the department she had so successfully built over to the heir apparent who had assisted her with classes for three years and was chomping at the bit to take over. The young lady had stepped in seamlessly and was doing a marvelous job, and while Martha had felt an initial pang of jealousy at her success, she had also felt a sense of relief knowing that the future of the theater department was in good hands.

The bell rang, and she stood to welcome the students as they drifted in from lunch. She felt herself warm to the task at hand until a girl whom she had never seen before powered through the door and looked squarely at Martha. Her eyes were easy to read. They said, "I hate you."

* * * *

Claire Middleton crossed the threshold of yet another Montgomery High School classroom, only this time to be abruptly met by a smile and a welcome. In no mood for either, she released a scathing look toward the offender. The sudden look of surprise she received in return gave her a sense of satisfaction and superiority, though deep within she felt a sharp pang of guilt, for what had this lady ever done to her? She quickly moved away from the woman and headed toward an empty seat near the window, dropped her books on the desk, and slumped unceremoniously into the seat. If she was looking or hoping for a reaction from those around her, she got neither. Her classmates were busy talking and laughing with each other.

Claire's bad mood deepened, and her anger intensified. Montgomery High stunk. Detroit stunk. Life stunk. Heck—*God* stunk. Her breathing came in shorter and shorter bursts, and her eyes narrowed until they were laser sharp and staring straight ahead but at nothing and no one in particular. She crossed her arms, let out an audible sigh of disgust, and slid further down in her chair, letting anyone who cared to look her way know that this was the absolute *last* place on earth she wanted to be. Unfortunately for Claire, no one looked.

Chapter 4

"So how was the first day?"

The question came from behind him and to his left, forcing Travis to turn around, but as he did, a large smile spread across his face.

"Good … Interesting," he replied, extending his hand toward the good looking man standing there.

The man smiled, took his hand in return, but then pulled Travis toward him and gave him a big bear hug before releasing him.

"Still stingy with your words, I see," the man quipped.

Travis grinned.

"Selective," he corrected. "Here to see your mom?

The man nodded. "See how her *last* first day went… and see when you might want me to start."

Travis looked at the man standing before him—a man with whom he had a *lot* of history: Danny Richards—Martha's son—

and a constant reminder to Travis of who he had been and who, by the grace of God, he was not now.

Fifteen years ago, Travis had been a student, of sorts, at Montgomery High. But more importantly, he had been a player on the streets—drug dealer, gang leader, murderer. Danny, a freshman at Wayne State, had been drowning under the weight of self-imposed expectations and had sought out Travis for some "relaxation aids." Travis, as always, was more than willing to assist.

However, God had other plans for Travis, the cold-blooded murderer, and soon Travis found himself alone, scared, and completely unsure of what to do or where to turn. On a night when Travis didn't know if an innocent little four-year-old girl was going to live or die because of his actions, God had made himself known to Travis, and Travis had found a peace he had never experienced. Then, in a manner and speed that only God could orchestrate, Travis and his siblings were moved out of their abusive home situation within three weeks.

From there, his life took one ironic twist after another. He had turned himself in to the police, confessing to the murders he had committed. But with no one willing to corroborate his testimony, a backlog of unsolved murders, and his being a minor, the authorities were reluctant to waste time and precious resources on a thread that they thought would go nowhere, so the district attorney had chosen not to prosecute. But the juvenile court judge had no such qualms and slapped Travis with two years in a juvenile detention center until he was eighteen. However, after nine months of exemplary behavior, the judge commuted his sentence, placing him on probation and into Martha and Graydon Richards's custodial care for the remainder of his time. Travis and Danny were now "brothers," and with his past behind him, Travis was able to pursue a real future, one with promise. He graduated from Montgomery High and was accepted to Wayne State, majoring in English and minoring in art. After graduating, he pursued his teaching certificate.

But the classroom was not a good fit for him. Though he loved his subject, he hated being cooped up. When he was in the gang, he had always opted for the streets, not the warehouse. He needed space and wanted to see the big picture.

It was Martha who had suggested administration, believing that his time on the streets had helped him develop the qualities necessary for leading a school: strength, vision, and a very tough skin.

So he had obtained the necessary certification, and four years later he was the principal of Montgomery High School. Now in his third year, he couldn't be happier.

He turned back to Danny, who was waiting for some sort of reply from him.

"Soon," he said.

* * * *

Danny smiled slightly. Would Travis *ever* put more than six or seven words together in a sentence?

Travis, the man who had metamorphosed from his drug dealer to his brother, definitely had a story films were made of, but Danny's journey was no less worthy of the big screen. As with many high school graduates, he had set his eyes on a career replete with fame and fortune. He wanted to be a doctor. True the earnings and lifestyle it afforded were enticing, but he really *did* want to help people. He had an altruistic streak a mile long, and medicine seemed the best way to exercise it. He had been a strong high school student, making mostly As with a few Bs, and so had entered college with a confidence that soon took a severe beating. In a matter of months, he learned that college was nothing like high school, and as he struggled to get Cs in his science classes, he saw his dreams slip away and his self-esteem crumble.

As an only child, he had believed that his parents' expectations matched his own, so when the troubles with school began, not only did he see his self-worth evaporate, but he also knew he had failed his parents. His failure had been too much, and when he had unwittingly witnessed Travis making a drug deal on the college campus, he gathered the courage to approach him and secure something to relieve his own stress: marijuana first and, when that failed to satisfy, he had moved on to heroin.

The drugs let him escape temporarily, but the price tag was heavy indeed: lies, conflict, anger, more depression. Had his father not courageously stepped in, who knew where Danny might have wound up. So the plan changed, and Danny followed a new pursuit—counseling, specifically drug counseling—and loved it. Now he worked for the city as a drug counselor and volunteered to help Travis at the high school.

As principal, Travis had made it his mission to rid the school of drugs. Knowing that they would be supported and that actions would be taken, teachers no longer threw a blind eye at suspicious behavior, but they reported it instead. Travis enforced strict discipline and, when needed, called the police in. After the first year, fewer students congregated in the shadows and corners. The second year, a weight seemed to have been lifted from the school. Students were happier and more carefree.

However, it was one thing to create the environment, but it was quite another to help free someone from their own bondage of addiction. That was where Danny came in, working one on one with students. Travis was the macro-manager; Danny, the micro. Together they made a formidable team.

* * * *

Slipping into her desk chair, Martha let her body collapse. *What had happened?* The day had been going so well. Two periods of freshmen in the morning followed by a nice leisurely prep period. Then the seniors before a relaxing lunch. And then that *girl* had entered the room. Claire. Claire Middleton. That was one name that was now, on the very first day, forever etched into her memory, and it didn't require any clever mnemonic device.

Hatred pure and simple. From the moment she had passed through the door, till the second she had exited, Claire Middleton had systematically poisoned the class environment—or was it more like a quiet asphyxiation? Whatever it was, it was amazing how insidiously and quickly it had changed the dynamics in the room. The first day excitement was there until Martha had started taking roll. Enthusiastic replies until … Claire Middleton. Her response was sullen, sarcastic. It caused the others to look at her in surprise and a bit of shock, and the playful banter disappeared. The rest of the class period was a slow deterioration as every student was now cognizant of Claire's critical spirit and wary of a potential retort. By the end of the period, Martha could hardly get anyone to say anything. A perfectly good class was now going to be a struggle.

For a while, she thought sixth period, her final period of the day, would follow suit, for it had taken her a full ten minutes to get her feet back under her and her positive attitude front and center, but the students warmed up after her rocky start, and the day ended on a high note. But Martha knew in her heart that this was not a good omen. It was only the end of the first day, and already she wondered if she would survive her last year.

Chapter 5

"So how was your first day?"

The question was packed with anxiousness as Mrs. Middleton waited apprehensively for her daughter to reply. She hoped beyond hope that the answer would be positive, but she had no reason to believe it would. Nothing about the move to Detroit or the events leading up to it were reasons for celebration, so why should the first day at a school so foreign in every way be any different?

Claire looked up at her mother, disgust written all over her face.

"What do you think?" she sneered and then turned on her heel, walked down the short hallway and into her room, and slammed the door shut.

Rachel Middleton just watched her daughter turn her back on her and felt the heartbreak once again.

Lord, why? Why did this all have to happen? What did I do wrong? she silently asked.

Four months ago, she was living the dream, or so she had thought. The wife of a prominent neurosurgeon at the UC San

Juan Medical Center, she and her husband had built a wonderful life for themselves and their one daughter, Claire. Dr. John Middleton was respected both in the medical world and at their church, where he was a member of the board and she, Rachel, was part of the women's ministry's leadership team. Claire had been active in the children's and junior high department and was all set to step into the high school group when she announced she didn't want to go to the local high school but instead to a very elite and expensive private school set in the beautiful San Jacinto Mountains of Southern California: Fieldbrook Arts Academy in Fieldbrook, California.

The school catered to students focused on pursuing the arts, from creative writing to dance to theater to music. Claire wanted to study film. Ever since she was a young girl, her parents hadn't been able to keep a camera of any kind out of her hands. Everything she saw, she framed in her mind's eye. Every mission trip to Mexico the junior high group took, Claire memorialized on film, both still and video, and the results mesmerized and moved the congregation. There was no doubt she had a gift. And there was no doubt her parents would indulge her in her pursuit. Though Rachel didn't work, John's salary could easily handle the annual price tag of $57,000 to have Claire board there.

At first her parents had worried that Claire would feel homesick, out of place, and bored. Over one hundred miles away from home at a school that served only three hundred students in a small mountain village seemed a far cry from the fourteen hundred students who attended San Juan High School. Though San Juan city itself boasted only forty-two thousand residents, San Juan County had over three million. How would their daughter survive?

But survive she did. In fact, she thrived. She loved the classes: cinematography, directing, producing, screenwriting. She was a duck to water and she was happy, incredibly happy. They all were—until four months ago. That's when the bombshell hit. That's when John's affair with one of his medical assistants was uncovered. Three months later when the messiness and hostility of it all had become too much for her, Rachel had packed up and headed to her mother's home in Detroit, bringing Claire with her.

Claire had begged to stay at Fieldbrook. She would be a junior. She was having fun. She was making progress and meeting important people. She could see her future. But even if Rachel had wanted to indulge her daughter, she couldn't. The courts had locked up all the money because of the impending divorce. No spending until the lawyers had hammered out every last decimal.

In the meantime, Rachel Middleton—née Poplawski—had returned to Hamtramck, where her father had worked in the Ford plant, to hole up, wait out the storm, and hopefully heal her badly bruised and broken heart. She looked down the hallway at the door closed not only to her but also to the world and wondered if Claire's heart would ever heal as well.

* * * *

Claire threw her backpack on the floor and herself on her bed. As the tenseness of the day began to wane, the trembling began, then the shaking, then the moisture in her eyes until finally she was convulsing in tears, her face planted in her pillow, hoping her mother wouldn't hear her. The last thing she needed was to have to explain her day, and even more so, her feelings, though that part wasn't difficult. She was mad. Pure and simple. At her father for having the affair. At her mother for yanking her out of school and moving her clear across the country to some godforsaken city. At God for letting it all happen. And, if the truth be told, she really didn't think she believed in God anymore. What kind of God would let life get this messed up, especially by and to people who claimed to be Christians.

Claire let out a snort. Christian. She couldn't remember a time she hadn't been in church. It was as much a part of her life as breathing. She had made plenty of friends there, had been involved in the activities and mission trips, but she had never really embraced the whole "Jesus is the Son of God and Savior" bit. Too weird. Too difficult to wrap one's mind around. Too ... out there. Claire was all about the here and now. The tangible. What you can see—especially through the lens of a camera. For her, though church was a great social club, it was full of naive and gullible people willing *and* wanting to believe something because it made them feel good. And now, thanks to her dad, she could add hypocritical to that list. How many times had he spoken of making choices that pleased and honored God? How many times had he said that God would honor and bless those who lived their lives righteously? So Claire had toed the line ... for the most part. She had sipped a few drinks here and there when her parents were away, told a few lies in order to hang with friends. Nothing that would harm anyone or land her in jail or warrant God's wrath ... or so she had thought, but look at her now. If this wasn't hell, it was certainly the next worse thing. The way she saw it, there were only two options: either God was really, really mad at her, or there was no God at all, and this Christianity stuff was a complete sham.

She rolled over on her side and stared at a wall devoid of anything. Though her grandmother had said the room was now hers and she could decorate it any way she wanted, she had refused to put up so much as a postcard. Was it denial that she was really here ... for good? Was it her way of rebelling, of being passive-aggressive and making her mother pay for putting her through so much pain? Was it just her way of playing the martyr, which she could be pretty good at? Probably all of the above, but she really didn't care. There was no way this was home, and she wasn't going to pretend it was.

She heaved a huge sigh and rolled over on her back, now staring at the ceiling and pursing her lips. Day one—over. Only 449 to go—two school years and a summer—before she was free to leave. She lay there a moment more until a slight smile slid across her face, and then she rolled back on her side, opened her end table drawer, pulled out a Sharpie, and stood up on her bed. Her grandmother wanted her to make this room her own? Okay, she would commence with the decorating. She took the top off the Sharpie and pushed off her tiptoes, trying to balance herself on the moving mattress. She managed to touch the ceiling with the tips of the fingers of her left hand and steady herself. Then, with her right hand, she extended the Sharpie and made a two-inch line above her. She relaxed, lay back on her bed again, and looked up at the line she had drawn. Like a prisoner marking time in his jail cell, she would mark the time she had to spend in this awful city. If she survived it, then she could leave Detroit for good, get back to her life, and never look back.

* * * *

As she neared the half mile mark, Destiny Williams felt her muscles begin to relax, her breathing become more rhythmic, and her pace settle into place. The weather wasn't ideal. It was hot and humid, pure and simple, but this particular route, along the Detroit RiverWalk, was one of her favorites and offered an occasional gust of cool air from the river. Starting at the Joe Louis Arena, it ran 3.5 miles along the Detroit River, ending at Gabriel Richard Park. Because it was basically a flat course, the cross-country team used this route to work on distance, as it was seven miles round trip, but a detour over to Belle Isle would add about another three. Though the whole team was out running now, Destiny liked to pace herself in the early practices, so she had opted to get ahead of the rest of the team. She needed to keep herself on task and on pace. She had a state championship to win.

She had come within a hair's breadth of winning the Division I Michigan State Girls Cross-Country Championship last year. In that race, she had kept pace with the leader, clocking a 5:15 first mile, which was a bit faster than normal for her. She was usually a moderate starter, gaining speed each mile, and then kicking strong to the finish. Though the 5:15 hadn't felt bad at all, it had been her undoing. She had kept up a strong pace through the second mile, clocking a 5:30 and had taken the lead outright. But whereas normally she would have another 5:30 for her final mile, she had tapped the tank dry a bit too early and had closed with a 5:50. The winner had slid by her at the very end, posting a 5:47 third mile. Her opponent's 17:19 wasn't the all-time record, but it was close. Her own 17:22 was more than respectable but had left a bitter taste in her mouth. Too close. She had prepared enough; it was just that mental lapse of not running her own race that had cost her the title. Had she run her planned 5:40-5:35-5:30 race, she would have come in with a 16:45—well ahead of the winner and very much a new state record.

Destiny's body was at full speed by the time she hit William G. Milliken State Park and Harbor, and she could feel her legs extend full length, her arms relax as they pumped rhythmically, and her heartbeat actually settle back down. Though focused on her run, she still enjoyed seeing a hint of the autumn colors. Belle Isle would be beautiful. She smiled. Hence the name.

Her own name seemed to be just as prophetic. As a junior, she had already caught the attention of plenty of college coaches with her times, and the Trinity Western coach had tied the two together.

"Destiny," he had said. "Perfect name for you, for you indeed have a great future ahead of you."

She had listened politely, but she had no intention of going to Trinity Western. Sure they had a respectable cross country program, but she had her eyes set on number one—Michigan State—just an hour and a half up I-96. It had been her dream ever since she started running in the sixth grade. As for her name, she loved it. Destiny. That said it all. God had given her a gift and a destiny, and she was living to prove it.

She reached the bridge to Belle Isle and hung a right. Because it was only two weeks into the season, the rest of the team would just do the seven miles, but she would run all ten. She felt a slight breeze wash over her from the river as she crossed it and then fell into the cool of the trees lining the roadway. She checked her sports watch. Six minute miles. Right on schedule. Exactly as she had planned.

Chapter 6

Gabriel turned left and headed down the alley, his emotions vacillating from anger to worry. He was biting mad at Mr. Johnson. There was no reason for the man to pull his friends and him into the office on the very first morning of the first day of his first hour of high school. Talk about paranoid. That man obviously saw a drug dealer lurking behind every bush and pillar of the school. But Gabriel was scared as well. The threat of suspension and expulsion, and then the call to his house. At first he was afraid all his well laid plans were going to unravel until he remembered that their phone had been disconnected because of overdue bills. That was lucky. Still, when all was said and done, what did Mr. Johnson get for his troubles besides the knife? A banana, granola bar, and apple, which to his credit he had given back.

The thought of the food items made Gabriel's stomach growl, and he reached into the pocket of his jacket (the jacket that got him into this fix in the first place) to make sure they were all still there. His stomach growled again, and he was tempted to pull out the banana and eat it, but he would wait.

He slowed his pace as he approached a garbage can, and then glanced around cautiously to see if anyone was watching. Satisfied the alley was free of curious eyes, he removed the lid and peered inside. He was behind a ribs takeout and was pleased to find, after minimal searching, a couple of intact, uneaten ribs. He pulled them out, located some partially used napkins, wrapped the ribs up, put them in his jacket pocket, and then moved on.

That was a good find. He passed up the dumpster, having learned through experience that they created more problems than they were worth. Not only did he have to hike himself up to the lip, but then he also had to drop down into the dumpster just to see what it offered, and that was usually messy. Plus, this particular dumpster belonged to a Chinese restaurant. He may be hungry, but he drew the line at loose rice and slimy vegetables.

Two more trash cans provided some fried chicken (slightly eaten) and a couple of biscuits, while a third one offered some French fries and a partially eaten ham sandwich. Each time, he found some newspaper or fairly clean wrapping of some sort to secure his finds before shoving them into his pockets. It might be ninety degrees out, but his jacket was proving invaluable.

He would have checked one more can but the back doors to a couple of the buildings opened and he now had an audience. He would just have to be content with this for today. Tomorrow, he would check an alley off of Grand. He shoved his hands into his coat pockets like it was the most natural thing to do on a humid September day in Detroit. When he reached the end of the alley he stepped into the bright sunshine and bustling activity of Gratiot Avenue. He involuntarily stiffened, his eyes and ears on high alert. He was not familiar with this part of town yet, so he didn't know what was safe, what was marginal, and what was downright dangerous. He unconsciously flexed his right ankle against his boot expecting the familiar feel of cool steel when he remembered again. His knife was gone.

He looked at the activity of the street. He would just have to find another knife somehow because he couldn't—he wouldn't—survive in this neighborhood without some sort of protection. He continued down Gratiot. He would also have to figure out another place to meet up with Charles, Thomas, and Curtis. He didn't need Mr. Johnson keeping an eye on him. What he wanted was just to fade into the background where no one would notice him.

He turned right off of Gratiot and onto Bellevue. Then two blocks up, he glanced around before heading down another alley. Two buildings in, he stopped, made one more check to see that no one was watching, pushed a dilapidated door open, and then closed it quickly behind him. He was now in semidarkness, but he had been here often enough to know his way around.

He ran his hand along the wall until he felt the opening to the stairwell and then climbed the stairs, counting them out. Twelve, and then a landing. Turn around, twelve more, and then a landing. He did this for three flights. At the end of the third, he pushed open the door and was met with a sliver of light coming through a window at the end of the hall. He headed toward it until he came to the last door on the left. He opened it slowly and peered in.

The room was partially lit with the diffused light coming through two grimy windows on the right. Gabriel struggled to adjust his eyes but when he did a huge smile broke across his face.

"Hi, Gabriel," called a female voice from across the room. Gabriel's smile never left his face.

"Ruthie," he responded.

* * * *

Gabriel quickly crossed the length of the room and gave the girl, who had risen to greet him, a huge hug.

"How was your first day of school?" he asked when he finally released her.

"Fun," she said. "I think I'm going to like third grade." Gabriel smiled.

"How was your first day, Gabriel?" The smile faded as he looked down into his sister's expectant face. How much should he tell her? None, he decided.

"It was good, too," he said, forcing the smile back on his face. "And look what I brought you for dinner." He pulled out the ribs and the chicken, fries, sandwich, and biscuits. Ruthie's eyes grew wide, but her stomach didn't rumble. "Aren't you hungry?" he asked. She shook her head.

"They gave me lunch at school," she said and then suddenly remembered something, "but we need to fill out this form for me to continue to get it." She turned to the folder she had on the ground, picked it up, and pulled out a blank form. Gabriel looked it over. It was the Free and Reduced Lunch form. His heart quickened, then plummeted, and then steadied. He had forgotten about the lunch program. The upside was he and his sister would have something hot to eat during the day. The downside was it required the signature of a parent, and they hadn't seen their mother for two weeks, which was why they were here ... in an abandoned building ... with no air, heat, plumbing, or supervision.

Their mother had done this before ... left for a few days or even a week at a time whenever she needed a fix or met a man or just forgot where she was and who she was responsible for. But, in the past, she had always come back, apologetic, and with gifts for the kids, courtesy of whichever guy she had been with. This time, however, she hadn't, or at least hadn't yet, and Gabriel would have stayed in their home except that the neighbors had begun to get concerned and, when that happened, Gabriel knew what came next. The authorities were called and the children hauled away.

All Gabriel had was Ruthie, and he was all she had. They had no idea who their father or grandparents were. They had no idea if they had aunts or uncles or cousins. They only had each other. If the authorities decided to split them up, then they wouldn't even have that. Gabriel couldn't face losing her. So, one week ago, he spent a day scouring the neighborhoods for a place the two of them could live.

He needed to stay in their same school district. Moving to a new one would require new paperwork and a parent's signature, and he didn't want to raise any suspicion. So he started early. There were plenty of abandoned buildings in this part of Detroit. Heck, half of Detroit was abandoned, but he had certain requirements. He needed access to running water; he needed to have access to a bathroom; and he needed a way to get into the building that was hidden from view.

By four that afternoon, he had found this place. The building was far enough down the alley and the alley access was recessed enough that they could hide from anyone just walking past on the main roads. Directly across from them was the back entrance to a restaurant, which had a water spigot outside for cleaning grease traps, and just inside the door was a bathroom, which if they were careful and hurried, they could use without getting caught. It wasn't ideal, but it would have to do for now. He had found two old, discarded buckets; he used one to carry up water, and he placed the other in one of the far corners for emergencies. He himself would carry that bucket down, wait till the coast was clear, and dump it in the bathroom toilet when no one was looking. Then he would wash out the bucket and hightail it back up the stairs.

So far it was working, but it was stressful. Not only were they living secretively, but they also were living hand to mouth in one of the poorest and possibly most dangerous parts of Detroit. And that thought brought back another pang of worry. He now had no knife.

The knife hadn't been his to begin with. One of his mother's many "boyfriends" had inadvertently left it behind, and when he never came back for it, Gabriel had grabbed it. He had tried the release mechanism to make sure it worked. The knife was well cared for and opened effortlessly. Gabriel had no idea if he would be able to use it when the time came, but, all the same, he felt safer just having it. Now he didn't—didn't have it—and didn't feel as safe.

He looked down at Ruthie, who was still looking at him expectantly, as he held the lunch form in his hand. The form wouldn't be a problem. He had signed his mother's name to most of their forms since he could remember. No, his worries were real, more immediate. Could he keep his sister safe? And would they be able to survive on their own?

Chapter 7

*M*artha opened Claire Middleton's student records folder on the counter and gazed at her transcript. It didn't take her long to connect the dots. Dot number one: Claire hadn't gone to Montgomery High School her freshman and sophomore years. Dot number two: Only one parent was listed in the box marked parent or guardian. Martha had seen this pattern before; ninety-nine percent of the time it meant that there had been a major disruption in the family—a death, a divorce—something forcing the other parent to make an abrupt change in living situation.

Martha took another look at the transcript, pursed her lips, and furrowed her brow: Fieldbrook Arts Academy filled the space marked "school." She had never heard of Fieldbrook Arts Academy but made a mental note to look it up that night on the internet. She glanced down at the courses under each semester. Though there were the traditional college preparatory classes listed—math, English, social science, foreign language—all the electives Claire had taken were in the arts, primarily in film—cinematography, directing, screenwriting. Martha checked Claire's grades: stellar— all As. The girl was not a slacker. She was bright, but she was definitely angry. Martha flipped through the rest of the folder until she found what she was looking for—the address of Fieldbrook Arts Academy.

The fact that Martha had never heard of Fieldbrook, California, meant that it had to be small. The mere title Arts Academy meant it had to be private ... and expensive. Martha now understood the root of Claire's anger. Whatever the reason for the move, it had been abrupt and hurtful and not of Claire's choosing. She had been a victim, ripped out of a rich environment where she had been flourishing and abruptly dropped into an inner city Detroit school that from the outside looked anything but flourishing.

Martha pulled her lips and brows tighter together in concentrated thought. Already forgotten was the ruined morning, the fatigue of the first day, and the final year countdown. Martha's mind was working. Somehow she had to engage this young lady and engage her fast if she was going to save Claire and her own class. Mentally, she flipped through the week's lesson plans and slowly shook her head. No, they wouldn't do. They wouldn't break down the barrier that was already so forcibly built to keep everyone out.

Martha took a deep sigh. Though she had always tweaked lessons each year to meet the needs of individual classes and sometimes students, she had never had to stray far from the order of major units or projects. Her yearly strategy, which had proven effective in providing a solid foundation for her students, pretty much remained intact. However, she could already see that this year—her final year—would require major change, and Martha knew how to do it.

* * * *

Travis turned out the light, locked up his office, walked past the vacated desk of his secretary and out the main office doors, and into an empty hallway. He heard the echo of his own footsteps as he walked down the empty hallway, a small smile playing on his lips. Overall, the day had gone well ... except for his before school conference with the four boys, an encounter that still baffled him. He shook his head, and as he did he caught the white of a football jersey displayed behind two rows of athletic trophies: #84 ... Alex Kowalski's jersey.

Travis stopped and stared at the jersey, taking a deep breath. Though Travis never really knew Alex, Alex had been a pivotal, albeit tangential, player in Travis's life, and Alex's retired jersey brought back a flood of memories: a football game, a near fatal shooting, and a close encounter that changed his life.

Travis glanced at the jersey again and then at the picture next to it: Alex Kowalski in a Detroit Lions uniform. Alex had always dreamed of playing for Michigan State and then the Lions, and now he was living that dream. After a stellar collegiate career at Michigan State and then four years of playing backup for the Lions, Alex had finally come into his own, earning the starting wide receiver spot for the Lions and never looking back.

Travis continued down the hallway until he came to another glass showcase. He smiled, and his eyes softened with affection.

There, in a large frame, was a photograph of Reba Washington, caught on stage and mid-action. Though she never grew past five feet four inches, Reba could fill a stage with her energy and create any atmosphere she desired through the inflections and dynamics in her voice and her exaggerated expressions. But it was always her eyes, too big for her petite frame, that captivated an audience and drew them right into the soul of her character.

Travis felt his heart do an uncharacteristic flipflop. The Washington family held a special place in his life as he first met the love of Christ through the love and selflessness of that family who had nothing but was willing to share every bit of it. Travis especially loved Reba. At some point in his adult life, he had realized that he had always loved her, not romantically, but deeply in his soul, for she had a pure heart, one that had prayed for his salvation and had seen her prayer answered at what could have been a costly price—the death of her younger sister Jocelyn.

Now Travis's mood turned somber. Fifteen years ago, little four-year-old Jocelyn Washington had taken a stray bullet that had been meant for him. That one moment had ripped the arrogance and self-sufficiency right out of him, catapulting him into a chaotic night of terror and remorse—a night, however, that would not end in despair but in his deliverance. For almost three weeks, little Jocelyn had teetered on the brink of death. But through God's divine mercy on both the family and Travis, coupled with the prayers, faith, and strength of her family and friends, little Jocelyn, after months of recovery, was healthy again. Only a severed facial nerve left any telltale sign of her ordeal: the left side of her otherwise beautiful face drooped like the faces of those permanently suffering from Bell's palsy.

The scars left on Travis, however, were much deeper. For years, though he was saved and forgiven, he wrestled with the guilt of his responsibility, until Jocelyn finally, at age seventeen, sat him down. With the wisdom of Joseph, and in her own quiet spirit, she held his hand and told her twenty-nine-year-old principal and friend that what man might have meant for evil, God had meant for good. She smiled serenely and then told him she was going to study to be a pediatric nurse when she graduated, all because of her weeks in the hospital. The memory of the love and attention and care she received from the nurses stayed with her all these years, and her one desire ever since was to be that person for someone else. Now at nineteen, she was enrolled in the nursing program at Wayne State.

Reba, on the other hand, had continued to follow her love of acting and the theater. She, too, had attended Wayne State but pursued a degree in theatre and like Alex had enjoyed success in college. But she struggled for years in New York at the professional level, surviving like most aspiring actors by working odd jobs at odd hours and living in cramped and Spartan conditions. However, for Reba, this was no sacrifice, for not only did she enjoy acting so much that any sacrifice was worth it, but she also had grown up in similar meager conditions.

Though Mr. and Mrs. Washington still lived in one of Detroit's poorest neighborhoods, the rest of the Washington children had moved on. Willie's love of and expertise in basketball had landed him a teaching and coaching job at a neighboring high school. Jake, though still an avid singer, had decided that engineering might be a more stable route to take, and young Chris, now a senior at Montgomery High, was toying with the idea of a career in law enforcement.

Travis sighed deeply. This impromptu trip down memory lane made him feel much older than his thirty-one years. But then, he reasoned, everyone who grew up in the ghettos grew up fast.

Chapter 8

"So how did the last first day of your teaching career go?"

Martha looked at the beautifully set table and the lit candles. She could smell the rich aroma of garlic and rosemary emanating from the kitchen.

"Am I to expect this kind of treatment every night?" she asked with a sly smile. "After all, each day is the last day of something."

"Doubtful," Graydon said playfully. "I don't think I could keep it up. But we will celebrate the milestones, and the last first day of school is definitely one of those milestones." He paused, walked over to the couch, and motioned for her to sit next to him. When she had, he asked his question again. "Now, how was the last first day of your teaching career?"

Martha leaned back on the couch and sighed deeply.

"Not quite what I was hoping for," she answered honestly.

Graydon's eyebrows rose in question. "What happened?"

Martha gazed off into the corner of the room as though the rerun of the day was playing there. Then she turned back to look at

Graydon. "Claire Middleton happened," she said simply.

"Tell me all about this Claire Middleton," he encouraged.

Martha took a deep breath and then dove into the events of the day, beginning with the almost picture perfect morning, the relaxing lunch, and then the human smart missile that just about took out both afternoon classes. She shared what she had learned by reviewing Claire's student records and transcript, and Graydon could already sense that his wife had turned the corner of Frustration Boulevard and was now driving down Concern Avenue.

His eyes twinkled as he watched her. She was looking first one way and then the other, which meant her mind was already working on a solution. His heart warmed as he listened to her throw out possible approaches she might try to engage Claire and at the same time allow the girl to show off her talents. His wife was not going to get that gentle coast to the end of the year she had anticipated. Nor would Claire Middleton. *Claire Middleton,* he thought, smiling inwardly, *you don't know what you just got yourself into.*

* * * *

"So how was the first day of school?"

The dinner dishes had been cleared, and Cecile Johnson handed her husband a large glass of iced tea, took one herself, went over to the sofa, sat down, and patted the seat next to her. Travis smiled softly, his tie and shoes long gone, and sat down next to her but didn't say anything for a few minutes. The silence didn't bother Cecile. She knew her husband too well to expect him to immediately dive into his day.

She had known him ever since she could remember as they had grown up in the same ghetto neighborhood of Detroit. Though he never knew it, she had always had a crush on him, which was the primary reason why she had joined the Marauders. There were the other typical reasons as well: money, sense of belonging, protection, but Travis had been the main pull, and though she had to loan herself out to other gang members, she always tried to be there for Travis when he "needed" her. But she had mistaken sex for love, and even though Travis seemed to prefer her over any of the other girls, he only used her to satisfy his physical need. His emotions were turned off, they had to be, she soon learned, just as hers had to be if she wanted to maintain any self-respect or dignity while humiliating herself.

Travis was nine when he had joined the Marauders, and he took his young duties with the seriousness and skill of a seasoned pro. He seemed to be on a mission, for what, no one ever really knew. All they knew was that at an early age, he was hardened, meticulous, and careful. He had the respect not only of his own gang but of rival gangs as well.

Cecile joined when she was fourteen. Though there were duties young girls could perform as well, like running drugs or being lookouts, Cecile never really wanted to be a part of the gang culture; she just wanted to be near Travis, so she had waited until she was "woman" enough to join. The gang life hardened them both, and she could remember thinking at age sixteen, when Travis would come to her but not really know her, that life was meaningless, and she really wouldn't care if it were short. She saw no way out, no future, no hope. Until ....

Until ... that day ... both awful and wonderful at the same time. Little Jocelyn Washington had been hit by a bullet meant for Travis, and in a twenty-four-hour period, Travis went from hardened gang lord to penitent sinner to saved son of God. Cecile thought the change was instantaneous, but as the years unfolded, Travis had shared, bit by bit, his unnerving journey, not the least of which was leaving the gang.

No one just leaves a gang. But Travis did. And she remembers it clearly. It was a Sunday afternoon, the very afternoon after the shooting. She was there because there was nowhere else to be. Travis showed up at the warehouse in dress clothes and the few members lying around, stoned or working off a hangover, took one look at him and laughed. Travis didn't. His eyes were icy and his jaw set.

"Get the word out that we're having a meeting tonight—seven sharp," he said. "I want everybody here." And then he left. The word got out fast, and when seven o'clock rolled around that night, there wasn't a Marauder missing. *No one* defied Travis. He stood before them, his jaw still firm, his eyes staring bullets at each one of them individually. When he looked carefully at the other lieutenants, she remembered seeing him briefly run his tongue across his lips, the only time she ever saw a sliver of hesitation or nervousness on his part.

"I'm leaving," he said succinctly. "I'm leaving the Marauders, and I'm leaving the gang life." Two of the lieutenants started to rise, but Travis nailed them back down with his stare. "Don't try to stop me. My mind is made up. I know what you are afraid of ... that I will turn on you, turn you in, but I won't. And if there is one thing you know about me, it is that I keep my word."

Travis knew better than to preach to the members about his newfound faith, but he wasn't about to leave until he had whet their appetite and piqued their curiosity. "I'm leaving because I have found something better. I have found all those things I thought I could find here: significance, importance, meaning, love. But none of those exist here ... not really ... we just play at them. We just make ourselves important, we just give ourselves meaning and significance, and we don't even know what love is."

Cecile had watched in stunned silence. It was the most Travis had ever said, not just at one time, but ever, and she had found herself glued to his words and wondering at their meaning. And she had felt an emptiness she had never known before. She had only joined the Marauders because of him and now he was leaving. What would she do now? How could *she* leave? She didn't have long to think about it though, for as Travis turned to leave, knowing full well he could have a bullet in his back in an instant, he had come over to her, taken her hand, and said, "You're coming with me." Never had she been so willing to obey.

* * * *

Travis stretched out his legs before him, took a long drink of iced tea, and felt himself begin to relax. How was his first day?

"Interesting," he said, and stopped, but Cecile didn't prod him or sigh in exasperation. He would say more when he was ready. They had known each other too long to have secrets. Raised in the same neighborhood. Two years together in the Marauders. Two terribly lost and damaged souls. Seven years of dating and now eight years of marriage. They knew each other well.

Travis glanced over at his wife. He loved her so much but his heart always ached when he saw her curled up on the end of the couch, iced tea in hand, patiently waiting to hear about his day. She would have been such a wonderful mother, but the two years in the Marauders had cost her the ability to have children.

He remembers the day they had left the Marauders' warehouse. He had wondered two things: would someone put a slug in his back to assure his silence and would he be able to share his new faith with Cecile in a way that she would both understand and want it. He shouldn't have worried. God had his back in the warehouse, and Cecile was so hungry for real meaning, significance, and love, that she hung onto every word he said. But he was a day-old Christian and didn't trust himself to explain his salvation completely or correctly, so that night he found himself back at the Washington house and, while Mr. Washington watched over little Jocelyn at the hospital, Mrs. Washington explained the steps of salvation to Cecile, who was saying yes way back at step one. From that day on, they had built their faith together.

Cecile had also found an outlet for her mothering nature. While Travis was busy pursuing his degree in English and art, she was earning a degree in early childhood education and now ran one of the most innovative Head Start programs in the city. He was extremely proud of her.

"Interesting," he said again, and then began sharing his day and by ten that night, all had been recounted, Cecile was content, and Travis, renewed. Then together, they prayed over day two.

* * * *

"So did you see your mother?" Grace Richards asked as she set two plates of chicken parmesan at the ends of the table and two plates of mac and cheese at the sides. Both, however, had plenty of vegetables.

Danny looked up from the floor where he was wrestling with his five-year-old son, Matthew, while his three-year-old daughter, Abigail, climbed on his back.

"I did," he replied.

"And?"

"And she has 179 more days to go," he said with a smile. "She looked tired and a bit shell shocked. I think her anticipated easy final year got a huge shake up by an unexpected student." Grace raised her eyebrows, but Danny only shrugged. "She didn't elaborate. You know Mom. Nothing revealed until a plan is in place."

Grace smiled. Yes, she knew Martha, and even though every potential retiree claims to be looking forward to a breeze of a final year, Grace knew Martha would never have survived that kind of year. She thrived on challenges. If there weren't any in her own life, then she made sure there were plenty in her students' lives.

Grace checked over the table, realized the bread was missing and went back to the kitchen. Danny's eyes followed her. *I am one happy and lucky man*, he thought.

He and Grace had met in biology, when Danny had entertained dreams of becoming a doctor before flaming out and doping up, but they didn't start dating until the second semester when both were taking psychology. Danny's adjusted self-expectations and new major put him in a much healthier state, which created a much stronger dating relationship. Grace had continued on the pre-med track and had become a successful pediatrician, opting to work at the Children's Hospital rather than open her own practice.

He looked back down at his son, who had stopped wiggling while Danny and Grace were talking, but the minute his father and he locked eyes, the battle was on again: Danny tickling, Matthew struggling to escape, and Abigail trying to hold her daddy's arms down to help out her older brother. Matthew was a strong boy with a gentle nature while Abigail had a bubbly, happy nature but with a streak of the devil every so often.

"Dinner's ready," Grace announced upon her return, and in one fluid motion, Danny was on his feet, had reached behind him, pulling Abigail off his back and under his left arm, and then lifting Matthew up off the floor with his right. The two squealed in delight as he plopped each in their respective chairs before taking his own seat. He stretched out his arms as did each of his family members until all were holding hands around the small table.

"I say grace, I say grace," Abigail announced, and Danny nodded toward her.

"Okay," he said.

Little Abigail bowed her head low, and the other three followed suit.

"God is good," she said. "Amen."

Danny smiled. *He is very good indeed.*

* * * *

For over an hour, Martha stared at her calendar that outlined all her major lessons for the year. Mentally she moved and adjusted units and discarded and created lesson plans. *All in order to engage one very angry and hurting student,* she mused and for a moment wondered if it was worth it. But that thought was fleeting. Of course it was worth it. Not merely for Claire but for the other students as well. If she didn't take the venom out of Claire's bite soon, the class would die, and everyone would lose.

She penciled in her changes, noted her rationale in the margin to satisfy the questions that would come from the more astute students, turned to her computer to type up the new lesson she would use for tomorrow, and then printed it out. She would run off the copies in the morning during her prep.

She leaned back in her chair, let out a contented sigh, and felt the familiar twinge of excitement and spark of fire. She glanced at the clock: ten forty-five. She had been at this for the last two and a half hours. She shook her head. What had she been thinking when she thought that the best final year of teaching was one that just slid serenely into the sunset with a "whimper" like T.S. Eliot's "The Hollow Men." No, the best final year was one that went out with a bang! She just hoped it was one of celebration.

* * * *

Struggling to get to sleep, Gabriel lay on top of the mattress in only his undershorts and listened to the soft breathing of Ruthie next to him. It was hot and muggy and sticky outside and even worse inside. One of the windows wouldn't open, but the other had been broken, allowing some air in, but it was anything but fresh.

He rolled over on his side away from Ruthie, hoping to find a fresh patch of cool, but it was more than the heat keeping him awake. They had been on their own for almost a week now, and what had started out as an adventure was now turning into a lesson in reality. For one, they had run out of clean clothes. That was something Gabriel hadn't taken into account. He didn't know how or where to do laundry or how much it would cost. Perhaps he could just find another bucket and do it himself here in the room. Possibly, but there was more than just the laundry. He couldn't keep his sister fed just by scrounging through garbage cans. He needed to get some fresh fruits and vegetables too. And he needed another knife. He could not protect himself or Ruthie unless he had something. His mood sobered as one of life's little truths was becoming clearer and clearer: you need money to survive.

His mind started working overtime as he wrestled with his dilemma. Where could he get work? Who hires fourteen-year-olds? And how would he work *and* go to school *and* take care of his sister. The weight of the world grew heavier and heavier as he pondered his problem until a cold sliver of an answer sliced through him, and he felt the blood drain from his face. Drugs. Gangs. The chills turned to sweat. He didn't want to go there. He had worked so hard all his life to keep himself and Ruthie clear of the gangs, but now he was understanding why guys joined: money and protection. The two things he was in dire need of right now.

He sighed as he rolled over again. He was learning that the easy part was running away. The hard part was staying alive.

Chapter 9

estiny stood just inside the cafeteria doorway and scanned the room. Each table was packed with friends squeezing together as they tried to catch up on three months of summer. Multiply that by forty tables and the atmosphere was loud and frenetic. As a senior, she recognized the various groups: band members, aspiring actors, athletes, goths. The football players were the biggest and loudest. Though the cafeteria tables should seat twelve normal high schoolers comfortably, the football players managed only about eight, which meant there was a lot of shouting across tables. Not that the players minded, as that drew them more attention. The freshmen were easy to spot. Being only the second day of school, they still looked unsure of themselves, but Destiny knew within a month they would find their footing and then watch out—immaturity unleashed.

She glanced across the room and saw Mr. Joseph, the assistant principal, against the far wall, and smiled. He already looked miserable, and rightly so. There wasn't much to look forward to in lunch duty. The only reason he was there was to avert potential problems, which meant all he had to look forward to was one potential disaster after another. *And he went to college for that job,* she thought and grinned. *To each his own.*

She looked over the crowd more carefully, hoping to pick out her three friends: Carla, William, and Jason. Not that she wanted to sit with them. They had met up yesterday at lunch … for a planning meeting. The four of them, all seniors, went to the same church, Calvary Christian, and two years ago decided it was time for them to put some feet to their faith. So once a month, during lunch, each would look for a student sitting alone and try to befriend him or her. If they could engage them, then they would spend the month with them and gradually pair up with one of the other twosomes. Finally, all eight would join up, so the four newbies could get to know each other and, hopefully, begin their own friendships, allowing Destiny and her friends to go trolling again for new students, outcasts, or loners. The "project" had worked out pretty well overall. Though some of the kids were determined to keep their distance from everyone, most had made at least one new friend.

Destiny caught a glimpse of a black fedora, Jason's trademark attire, on the right side of the cafeteria, so she knew the others were somewhere in the masses, which meant she needed to turn her attention to the task at hand. She let her eyes sweep over the tables, knowing that even in the very middle of the room at a full table, someone could still be very much alone.

It took four passes of the room before Destiny saw her, but

it was obvious that she was both alone and new. Alone because the two people on both sides of her were looking the other way, and there was no one directly across from her. New because ... well, because she was white. And at Montgomery High only about twenty percent of the students were white, so it didn't take long for the rest of the student body to get to know them.

Her target now determined, Destiny took a deep breath and began working her way toward the middle of the cafeteria. Project Rescue was underway.

* * * *

"Is this seat taken?"

Claire looked up at the tall, black girl smiling down at her.

"Does it look like it is?" she stated sarcastically and saw the girl wince slightly and the smile fade. Claire felt a slight pang of regret. She really shouldn't have said that. The girl hadn't done anything to her, but Claire's inner pain and loneliness were too raw to be too sorry. However, the girl seemed to recover quickly, and the smile returned.

"Do you mind if I sit here?" she asked.

Claire shrugged. "Suit yourself."

Destiny sat down, and Claire went back to her sandwich, thinking the black girl just wanted a place to sit.

"My name's Destiny," the girl said, extending her hand.

Claire was taken completely by surprise, and not knowing what else to do, took the extended hand and shook it.

"I'm Claire," she returned, and the girl nodded in acknowledgement.

"Glad to meet you," Destiny replied, pulling out her own sandwich from a paper bag. "I'm going to ask the obvious here," she continued, "but are you new to Montgomery High?" She asked it with a rueful smile on her face, which threw Claire even further off her misery train, and she managed to return a weak smile of her own.

"Is it that obvious?" she asked.

Destiny nodded and then leaned in conspiratorially. "You're white," she whispered and then sat back, raised her eyebrows, tilted her head, and nodded as if that said it all.

Now Claire couldn't help but release a small laugh. "Yeah, I guess I do stick out, don't I?"

Destiny leaned into the table, looked left, then right, then up over the top of Claire's head at the sea of tables behind her, then twisted around to look behind her. Satisfied, she leaned back.

"Yep," she answered succinctly. "You definitely stick out. So what brings you here to Montgomery High?"

The brief, carefree mood was broken, and Claire felt a vacuum just suck the air out of her lungs, allowing all the pain to rush back in. "Family," she answered simply and looked back down at her sandwich with renewed interest. She had no desire or intention to elaborate, and she hoped her dismissal of the subject, and the girl across from her, would put an end to any more conversation. There were things far worse than sitting all by yourself at lunch, and one was having someone pry into your personal life.

But the girl didn't continue that line of questioning. Instead she returned to her own lunch and took a bite out of her sandwich. After a couple of minutes, before the silence became *too* awkward, she asked another question.

"What year are you?"

Still a bit on edge, Claire took her time answering, feigning great interest in her apple slices. "Junior," she finally answered, and she could see Destiny nod slightly.

"What classes do you have?"

By this point, Claire really would have been fine sitting in silence and just eating her lunch, but the questions were safe enough, so she figured she would count this lunch period a loss and just get on with it. At least the conversation took her mind off of the more depressing problems plaguing her. She recited her classes, during which Destiny would ask her who the teacher was, and if Claire didn't remember, would go to great lengths to describe the various instructors and their mannerisms until by the end of lunch, Claire was laughing again.

The bell rang and the mass of students all moved as one, climbing out of bench seats, sweeping up litter, and gulping down the last of their drinks. Claire pulled her legs out from under the table, slid around, and stood up, grabbing her own garbage.

"See you tomorrow, perhaps?" Destiny asked, and again Claire was caught by surprise.

"Sure, I guess," she managed, not able to come up with an excuse not to.

Destiny smiled at her. "Great!" she said with genuine enthusiasm. "I look forward to it!" Then walked away.

Claire watched her go, sensing an old feeling wrestling with her despondency, trying to break through. Anticipation.

* * * *

Martha heard the bell ending lunch ring and her heart involuntarily began to race while her hands grew clammy. *It's like I'm a first-year teacher all over again,* she thought. *Nervous, unsure.* She took a deep breath and braced herself for the next fifty minutes.

She greeted each student as they entered, but her stomach was churning inside her as she waited for Claire's arrival. When she saw the blonde hair break through the threshold, Martha felt her heart stop and her smile tighten as she readied herself for the encounter.

"Claire," she said as the girl approached. Claire looked up with brooding eyes, said nothing, and continued toward her seat. Martha's smile faded as she watched the girl pass by. *More wounded than weapon today,* she thought, and continued to greet the remaining students. Once all were in their seats and the tardy bell had rung, Martha quickly checked her seating chart to see who was missing, breathed a sigh of relief that no one had opted to take day two off, and then addressed the class.

"Well," she said with a smile, "Day one is over, so let's get right into learning something. No reason to waste time." The announcement was met with a few stunned faces from those hoping for a day or two more of the "let's get to know each other" exercises or even a bit more of "this is how the class is going to run" lecture—anything but work—but most seemed content on actually using their time productively. Martha glanced at Claire who continued to look off in the distance, her mind obviously somewhere else today. *Day one, animosity. Day two, apathy,* she thought. *Well, let's see if we can change all that by day three.*

"I'm going to number you off and put you into groups," she continued, "and then I will explain the assignment." The numbering process was to make the students think that the groups were going to be randomly selected, but Martha had perused her seating chart last night, hoping she knew enough of the juniors in this class so that she could put Claire with a positive and engaging group. It took her awhile to figure out a way to connect those students without drawing suspicion to the entire process being overtly manipulated, but she had finally settled on an approach.

"Let's start in the back," she suggested, and then proceeded to work her way around the classroom of thirty-two, giving out numbers from one to eight in order to create groups of four. When all students were accounted for, Martha called out each group number, having the students raise their hands so they could identify the other members of their group. When group five, Claire's group, was called, Martha was relieved to see that only one of the group looked a bit disappointed when Claire raised her hand. Obviously, the other two either didn't remember her caustic responses from yesterday or didn't care.

"Okay, now," Martha instructed. "I want you to get into your groups and introduce yourselves. I will come around with the assignment sheet, and then we will go over it together as a class."

The natural leaders raised their hands and called out for their group members to join them in a certain area. Occasionally, two students would take the lead role, forcing their other two teammates to decide which one they were going to follow. The rest just picked up their books and backpacks, worked their way to the designated spot, picked a desk, and sat back down, while a select few added suggestions of their own, such as to how to arrange the desks, in order to assert a bit of their own authority into the proceedings. Martha was always amazed at how quickly a classroom hierarchy was set as students' learning styles and personalities emerged.

Out of the corner of her eye she watched what was happening with Claire's group. She had handpicked Claire's three partners, having had all as either freshmen or sophomores. Violet was the organizer. This group would definitely get the project done. By the end of this period, Martha was sure, Violet would not only have divvied out the assignments, but would also have a calendar of due dates already in place. Claire had no choice but to be successful on this first project. Blake was the natural leader, the idea man, and was never deterred by pessimism or naysayers. If he thought it could be done, it would get done, even if he wasn't the one who could actually do it. He was always thinking outside the proverbial box. Sometimes he didn't have the ability or talent or skill to see that idea through to production, but his ideas were always original. He was also a very good writer, so between him and Violet, who was a stickler for accuracy, the written portion would be strong.

That left Quintin. Of the group, Quintin was the average student. He would get his work done in a fashion and with occasional prodding, but it wouldn't be stellar. Martha smiled to herself. She could already hear Violet's sigh of exasperation as she proofread Quintin's portion of the project. "Don't you remember *anything* about commas?" she would ask him, to which he would just shrug and let her have her way with his portion. Easier to let her do it than take the time to try and remember all those rules himself. No, Quintin's value came in a different area. Quintin was a people person. While Blake was concerned with the grand ideas, and Violet with the product itself (it had been Violet whose face fell in disappointment when Claire's name was called), it would be Quintin who would be concerned about the group dynamics. Quintin would care about Claire, and, right now, Martha deemed that attribute of major importance. And Claire made the fourth. She would be the creative partner, and Martha was hoping she had created the assignment in a way that would let Claire shine.

Blake had managed to gather his little group to his side of the room. Violet had already arranged four desks into a square, two facing two, and Quintin was already looking for their fourth. Only Claire had been slow to start moving, but once her area had been taken over by another group, she had no choice but to join her own. She let her books fall unceremoniously onto one of the desks before plopping herself into the attached chair. Blake didn't take any notice, Violet gave her a stern look, but Martha could already see that Claire's hurt echoed in Quintin's eyes as he slid right into the seat next to her. Martha sighed. So far, so good.

* * * *

"Hi, I'm Quintin."

Claire glanced over at the good looking black boy who was looking at her with kind eyes. He was smiling, but not one of those fake, overpowering smiles that said, "I am trying to be uber friendly." His was a soft, genuine smile, and Claire could not sum up the strength to create some sarcastic response. Her guard had already suffered some direct hits from Destiny's kindness at lunch, and now Quintin's sincere approach weakened her defenses even more.

"I'm Claire," she responded. "I'm new," she added just to save him the trouble of asking.

Quintin grinned. "I kind of guessed that," he said.

"'Cause I'm white?" Claire asked with a slight grin herself. Quintin nodded.

"That, plus I kind of know most of the juniors," he added.

Violet had been pulling out paper from her binder, putting the date on the front page, and organizing and readying herself for the task even though one hadn't been given yet.

"And most of the seniors," she added matter-of-factly, without looking up. "Quintin knows just about everybody." Quintin shrugged but gave Claire a sly smile. "I, on the other hand," confessed Violet, "know about half. Hi, I'm Violet, and I'm afraid, while Quintin is busy meeting and greeting everyone, I have to make sure the tasks get done." She threw Quintin a semi-judgmental look, which Quintin chose to ignore. "Not sure why we always get paired up together."

"But it always seems to work out," Quintin added congenially. "We always get a good grade." Violet's look now turned to full judgment, and Quintin realized he needed to curry some favor. "Thanks to Violet," he admitted. "She really knows her grammar and is super organized, so we will not get off task." Violet threw him a mock smile of thanks and turned back to receive the papers Mrs. Richards had just handed her. *Even if we wanted to,* he mouthed to Claire, and Claire had to work hard to suppress a laugh.

"I'm Blake," the last member of the team inserted, finally introducing himself. "Not sure what I bring to the team, but I love group projects. Much better than just a straightforward essay or test. Lots of latitude and opportunity for creativity. Anything out of the norm is what I want to do."

Claire looked from group member to group member and felt herself relax. Quintin would be easy to be around, Blake would be fun, and even Violet, with her nothing-but-business attitude, was nice underneath it all. This project might be okay—whatever it was. She didn't have long to wait. Mrs. Richards had finished distributing the assignment and was calling for everyone's attention as she made her way back to the front of the room. It took a few seconds for the room to quiet down.

"I think most of you know that during this year we will be studying American literature." The announcement was received with blank stares, which meant either none of them knew that or none of them cared. Whether the lack of interest bothered Mrs. Richards, Claire couldn't tell because she just continued with the explanation. "The most obvious approach would be to start with the earliest American literature and move to the most recent." Again, no reaction. "However, I am starting *in medias res*. Who can tell me what that means?"

In the middle of things, Claire said to herself.

A hand appeared from the left. Mrs. Richards acknowledged it.

"It means 'in the middle of things.'"

Mrs. Richards nodded. "Anyone want to elaborate on that?" she asked.

It means to start a story or a movie or a novel in the middle of the story, Claire thought.

Another hand got the nod, this time from the right.

"It means to start a story in the middle of it."

"And why would someone choose to do that?"

Despite knowing the answers to all the questions, Claire sat on her hands and bit her tongue, refusing to get involved. Though life was a little better today, there was still enough bitterness stored up to last her a lifetime—well at least a school year.

"Well," Mrs. Richards continued, when no one ventured a guess, "we are going to start our study of American literature *in medias res*, right in the middle with the transcendentalists. Can anyone tell me who they were?"

Claire didn't know anything about the transcendentalists, but even though she loved literature, she feigned indifference, leaning her head apathetically on her hand. However, she listened intently as Mrs. Richards provided a basic definition and description, before summing the movement up with its belief in the inherent goodness of man and nature and the corruptive influence of society on man's purity. She concluded by introducing Henry David Thoreau and *Walden*.

With that, Mrs. Richards detailed the project written on the paper each of them now had. Just as Thoreau had spent two years away from society to be alone and commune with nature, each group was tasked with three objectives. First, to find the natural settings in the Detroit area and try and commune with nature; second, to look for that inherent goodness in man and nature; and third, to see how society corrupts both the purity of nature and man. Just as Thoreau had written about his findings, they, too, must have a written component of twelve pages (three pages per each group member) and some sort of visual, artistic component to share with the class. They would take three weeks both to read the book and complete the project. Week four would be the presentations.

* * * *

"So any ideas?" It was Quintin who posed the question.

Violet sat poised to take notes, looking from group member to group member. Blake stared at the far corner, rubbing his chin and grunting occasionally. Claire looked at the others and felt a budding sense of excitement building for the first time. She waited for someone to contribute. Finally, Blake spoke.

"We could create a PowerPoint," he suggested. Quintin nodded in affirmation, Violet scribbled the idea on her piece of paper, and Claire grimaced. PowerPoints had been done to death. *EVERYONE* does PowerPoints.

"Or a rap?" Quintin threw out. "That's sort of creative." Violet's pencil had the idea down in a flash. Blake pursed his lips but didn't say what Claire knew he was thinking—*NO!* Claire waited for Violet to offer her suggestion. She didn't have long to wait.

"What about a collage?" she said. All three looked at her. *Old school,* thought Claire.

"What's the difference between that and a PowerPoint?" asked Blake. "I mean the PowerPoint shows pictures, too, and the screen is bigger. People can actually see them."

"Just an idea," she responded defensively, and Claire felt

slightly sympathetic toward the girl. She had at least offered an option. Violet decided to give it a second try. "A collage allows you to give an overall presentation rather than just one or two pictures at a time, and anyway PowerPoints have been done to death, and I don't think a rap will cover everything we need."

Claire was surprised at Violet's assessment. The girl was exactly right. She felt herself relax a little more. Blake, Violet, and Quintin sat in silence until Quintin finally looked over at Claire. "Any ideas?" he asked her hopefully. The other two looked toward her as well. Claire nodded her head slowly.

"Actually, I do," she said, "and it might incorporate all of your ideas into one."

She wasn't sure if it was the fact that she had a new idea or that each of their suggestions had been validated, but all three perked up.

"Well," said Violet, pencil poised and anxious to get the decision making over and move on to the nuts and bolts.

"How about a movie," Claire suggested. The three smiles froze and then slowly began to fade.

"It's a great idea," Quintin said supportively, "but—"

"But how do we do that?" Violet inserted, getting straight to the point.

"I guess we could use our phones somehow," Blake said, "but—"

"I have a camera," Claire said. "A real movie camera, well one that a lot of amateurs use, from when I was at my last school. My parents bought it for me."

Now three jaws dropped open. Blake was the first to recover. "You do?"

Claire nodded.

Blank stares from all three.

"What does that mean?" Violet asked.

"It means I can take what looks like professional film footage. I have a computer program I can use to edit it too. There is also a way to incorporate still pictures as well through what's called the Ken Burns effect."

"I've seen that," said Quintin. "The pictures kind of move around the page, don't they?"

Claire nodded, holding her breath, watching the owners of three furrowed brows and pursed lips consider her suggestion. Blake was the first to respond, as a smile began to slowly spread across his face.

"Man, we would be awesome," he said enthusiastically. "No one would have something like that."

"Bet we would get an A just for originality," Violet added.

Quintin just smiled and gave Claire a wink, and Claire could feel a bit of the icy membrane around her heart begin to melt. Just slightly.

* * * *

"What are you looking for, honey?"

Mrs. Middleton had heard her daughter out in the garage shuffling boxes around, opening some and pulling out their contents, so she had come to investigate.

"Where is it?" Claire exploded and, exasperated, released a

swear word.

"CLAIRE!" her mother responded in surprise. "That's not nice. Where did you learn to say things like that?"

In my head and as long ago as I can remember, Claire thought cynically, halfway wanting to admit to her mother that while she and Dad were playing Christian, at least Claire wasn't trying to be something she wasn't. Besides, everyone swore. What rock had her mom been living under? But she didn't say any of that.

"Sorry," she responded but never looked up to see her mother's concerned look.

Her mother sighed but decided not to pursue the issue. "Now, what are you looking for?" she asked again.

Claire straightened up and looked down at the latest offending box. "My camera!" she replied with impatience. "I know I packed it. I just don't know what—." She stopped herself before she let out another offensive word. "—what box it's in." The reality was that when she had been forced to leave Fieldbrook, she had packed that camera away securely because she hadn't ever wanted to find it again. She was going to make them all pay by showing them how miserable she was and how unfair they were. She was going to let her talent dry up and go to waste, and the world would miss out on its next big filmmaker.

"That box is over in this corner," her mother said and started walking.

"What's it doing over there?" Claire asked irately. "Why isn't it with all my other stuff?"

Her mother paused and turned, her face tightening as she

gathered herself to square off with her daughter. "Because *this* is the box that has things I thought you might need or want. While, those," she said pointing to the ones Claire had manhandled, "didn't and could be hidden away."

Claire caught herself as she looked at her mother's face. It was a composite of pain, impatience, anger, compassion, and concern, and Claire felt a sharp pang of guilt and shame over her behavior and selfishness. How must her mother be feeling to be completely blindsided by her father's affair and then have her daughter snap at her as well? As angry as Claire was with her father, how much more devastated must her mother feel having invested twenty years of her life to a marriage and a man who had ended up betraying her.

"Thanks," Claire said softly and moved to the corner to open the box. She wasn't sure what to say next and felt the heaviness of the silence. Fortunately, her mother saved her.

"So what do you need the camera for?" she asked.

Claire let out a slow, thankful breath. Safe ground again.

"An English project," she replied, as she started pulling out the contents of the box. The box was small but had many of Claire's photography and film books and pictures. Finally, near the bottom, she pulled out the camera case that held her Canon and immediately relaxed as she felt the weight of it. As strange as it sounded, this was home for her … this camera. When it was in her hands, she felt secure and sure of herself. With her camera she could create any world she wanted, and right now, any world but this one sounded very good.

Chapter 10

Travis headed down the hall, peeking in open classroom doors, stepping through others, and then nodding at the teacher before heading to the back of the room to watch the lesson. Now in his third year, the teachers were used to him popping in unannounced, but during his first year these impromptu arrivals had created an undercurrent of fear and anxiety. Teachers felt threatened and suspicious and, within a week, Travis sensed something was wrong. He had finally sought out Martha to find out what the issue was.

"For one," Martha explained, "you look like a gang leader checking out the territory or turf or whatever it is called. You might want to drop the stern look and crossed arms. It's pretty intimidating."

Travis scowled but didn't say anything.

"More importantly," Martha continued, "teachers aren't used to people being in their classrooms. It is their own little world, their domain, to do with as they like. Behind those doors they have complete autonomy, and they don't like to be questioned or challenged. Now bring a principal into the mix, especially in a culture where administrators rarely set foot in a room except for the mandatory one period evaluation every three years, and you have a recipe for paranoia. They think you are there only to critique and evaluate them. It makes them nervous."

Travis tried not to show his surprise. Actually, that was *exactly* why he was there. He liked to know the lay of the land, who all the major players were, what their strengths and weaknesses were, and what the classroom dynamics were. Plus, he absolutely *hated* sitting in his office. And Martha inadvertently hit on another commonality. Travis did look at Montgomery High as his turf ... the one major difference, however, was that on the streets, it was all about power and money at the expense of lives, while here in the school it was all about lives but sometimes without the benefit of power and money. So at the next faculty meeting he apologized to the teachers for not informing them ahead of time that he would be coming into their classes, but that he wanted to help however he could.

And he really *did* want to help. Detroit schools were struggling— with finances and morale. There wasn't enough money to meet needed repairs let alone buy necessary equipment. Even so Travis would talk with the teachers after class or at the end of the day and ask them what they needed or wanted that would make their lessons go even smoother.

Then Travis had used the summer to implement many of the teachers' ideas. It took work and a lot of community contacts. Since the district didn't have the money, he needed to find it elsewhere, so he started forming alliances with neighboring businesses, convincing them that a strong school environment and a quality education were the best weapons against gangs, drugs, and violence in their neighborhoods. As much as he wanted to add, "and the saving grace of Jesus," he didn't. A public school principal walked a fine line. Build relationships in public but pray in private. And pray he did, along with working his tail off. He enlisted the help of some of the local fathers, and all summer the men along with the custodial staff worked on transforming Montgomery High from a tired shell to a beautiful facility that he, the staff, and students could be proud of.

When everyone came back in the fall for year two, the reaction was palpable. Students and teachers alike gawked at the new signage, which made it easy to find one's way around. They admired the handcrafted display boxes, which showcased past and present students; and they tried to hide their enthusiasm for the new motto, "Dream Big. Then Work Hard," which came from Travis's favorite Langston Hughes's poem, "Dreams." In addition, toilets had been fixed, walls painted, and floors shined.

A new sense of pride seemed to be born right then, and Travis noticed students reminding other students to pick up their trash, berating them for even *thinking* about etching something into one of the desks or scribbling graffiti on the walls. The beautiful, refurbished facility was growing into a living, healthy organism.

Now his popping into classrooms was routine and welcomed. Math instructor Jim Gregory's door was wide open, so Travis took a right and walked in. The students were already in groups of four with sets of manipulatives before them working through a problem. Jim nodded to Travis in acknowledgement as Travis moved toward the rear of the room, leaned against the back wall, and watched the students diligently working together, their heads bowed toward one another. A few noticed him and followed his movements with curiosity, but most were heavily absorbed in their work. Travis glanced around the room, rehearsing names he had just learned when his eyes landed on one student whose back was to him, preventing him from seeing Travis enter. The boy was deeply engrossed with the activity, talking with his peers, offering suggestions, rearranging some of the manipulatives. Travis watched him curiously. Boy Number Four—Gabriel—was becoming quite a paradox.

* * * *

Claire waited anxiously at her seat in the cafeteria while all around her the table was filling up. Yesterday, she wanted nothing to do with anybody, and though today she still had no intention of embracing Montgomery High, she wasn't as determined to shut everyone out. Quintin, Blake, and even Violet had made one class tolerable, and meeting Destiny meant that she wouldn't have to look like a pathetic loner during lunchtime. She wasn't even considering being friends yet because she didn't even know the girl, but if being even slightly courteous meant she didn't have to eat by herself, then she was willing to make an effort.

However, it was five minutes after the start of lunch, and Destiny hadn't arrived. Had she decided not to return? Had Claire been taken for the fool and abandoned yet again? She felt that familiar mixture of dread, sadness, and anger settling in the pit of her stomach and an unaccustomed wetness in the corner of her eyes, which she hastily and angrily blinked away. There would be *no* tears.

This is ridiculous, she thought. *I'm stronger than this. I don't need any stupid girl befriending me.* She stared at her unopened lunch in front of her, rallying her resolve and feeling her heart harden just a bit more in defense and defiance. When she finally felt her emotions were under control, she looked up, just in time to see Destiny walking toward her, and she felt the newly constructed wall come tumbling down and her heart quicken in relief.

* * * *

Destiny walked through the cafeteria doors, glanced up, took a quick survey of the room, and headed straight for the middle. She could already see Claire, seated right where she was yesterday. It was a positive sign. If the girl hadn't wanted her around, then she would have moved in order to avoid her. She finally managed to get to Claire and was surprised not only to see Claire give an effort at a smile but also to slide her backpack back across the table.

"Someone wanted to sit there, so I had to save you a seat," Claire explained.

Destiny smiled. "Thanks. I appreciate it. Hope you weren't waiting long."

Claire shook her head. "Just got here myself," she lied.

Destiny settled herself across from Claire and pulled out her lunch. Then she silently bowed her head and gave a quick blessing.

Claire just stared. Destiny's head soon came back up, and she gave Claire a big smile.

"So, how has everything been going? Classes okay?"

It took Claire a moment to regain her composure. Destiny's praying had caught her off guard and created an immediate wariness and suspicion. Was this girl some religious freak? Was she out to "save" Claire? Was that why she had befriended her? All of Claire's defenses went into overdrive, the walls rapidly rebuilt, the heart carefully shielded, and the cynicism pulled out of storage.

"Fine," she replied, offering no more.

Destiny could immediately sense the difference and decided to address it head on.

"I hope I didn't offend you by blessing my food," she said.

Claire shrugged. "Do what you like, doesn't bother me," but then decided to add, "but you didn't do it yesterday. Just wondered why you decided to do it today?"

Destiny now knew that Claire was sensing an ulterior motive, and if Destiny were honest with herself, she would have to admit the girl was not far off. Though the four friends did want to include those who seemed outsiders and provide some friendship, ultimately they did hope to demonstrate God's love to them. Destiny nodded slightly.

"Yesterday I prayed before I came into the cafeteria."

Claire eyed her warily. "Why?" she asked.

Destiny hesitated a moment before answering but decided to be frank. Claire was astute and would pick up quickly if she were being played with. She was already defensive and suspicious.

Destiny needed to be honest. If Claire rejected her, then that was that. She would move on.

Destiny took a deep breath, said a quick, silent prayer, and dove in.

"Because yesterday it was more important that I meet the right person, so I prayed that God would show me someone I could befriend. I asked him to bless my food, perhaps subconsciously so I wouldn't put anyone off."

Claire chewed on this. "So you thought I was the right person, huh?"

Destiny nodded.

"Why, because I looked so pathetically alone?" she asked, her biting sarcasm having now returned in full vigor.

Destiny shook her head. "No, because the minute I finished praying you were the first person I saw who I didn't know."

Claire's smile was now dripping with irony. "I thought you said I was hard to miss, being the only white girl in a wave of chocolate."

Destiny winced slightly at the derogatory comment but didn't comment. Instead she replied quietly, "I think that was by design."

Claire shook her head. "So are you one of those people who thinks everything happens for a purpose?"

Destiny nodded. "I am."

Claire shook her head. The pain of her parents' divorce, the sudden move halfway across country, her loss of friends, school, and dream all still fresh.

"Well, I'm not," she replied.

Destiny nodded again. "Fair enough." The two sat in awkward silence for what seemed like an eternity. Finally, Destiny broke the silence. "Would you like me to leave?"

Claire pressed her lips together in a hardened line. Yes, she wanted the girl to leave. She embodied everything Claire currently had no use for: friendliness, hope, religion, purpose. No, she didn't want this girl around, but the thought of being alone again pressed against her just as hard. If she were to admit it, she was a mess of conflicting emotions. In the end, she decided it took less effort to give in than to fight. She shook her head.

"No, just don't try to preach to me. I've been to church. Christianity doesn't work so don't waste your time on me."

Destiny listened to the deep pain behind the words and felt for the girl. Something very hurtful had definitely happened in her life.

"Deal," she said. "We will just be friends then ... as long as you are okay with me still blessing my food before I eat."

Claire shrugged again. "Fine. To each his own."

"Good," Destiny said with finality before returning to her initial question. "Now, how have your first couple of days been?"

Chapter 11

Gabriel walked down the hall at the end of the day, a light spring in his step. Life was looking up. He had turned in the paperwork for the free lunch program without a hitch and had received his card and had enjoyed a wonderful lunch—the first time he had been full in over two weeks. He was enjoying all his classes, but especially geometry. He could already tell he would be good at it because after only three days, while others seemed confused by theorems and proofs, he was grasping them easily, so easily, in fact, that Mr. Gregory had kept him after class and asked him if he would like to test to be a tutor.

"It's two hours a day, but you don't have to work every day, and you would be paid," he added, and Gabriel's heart leaped.

Money, he thought. Just what he needed. But there was a problem.

"I watch my sister after school," he said with concern. "I can't leave her at home alone."

Mr. Gregory nodded, as this was not uncommon since many of the tutors had younger siblings in tow. "She is more than welcome to come to the tutorial room if she is quiet."

"Oh, she will be, sir," Gabriel replied politely. "She loves to read."

Mr. Gregory smiled. "Alright then. If you come in after school tomorrow, I will give you the test to see if you qualify. Your sister can come with you."

His mind lost in the myriad of possibilities, Gabriel headed out the front doors and started turning toward home ... his old home, not his new makeshift one. He stopped abruptly, corrected himself, and headed down the road that would lead to the alleyway. So engrossed was he in his own thoughts that he failed to notice another student watching him carefully, camera in hand.

* * * *

Claire watched the young black boy heading down the street make a startled and abrupt stop, jerk his head up to take note of his surroundings, and then make a one-eighty and head in the opposite direction. Curious, she decided to follow.

During class, Mrs. Richards had given the groups today's class period to finalize the approach they wanted to take on their projects. Any other discussion would have to be on their own time, she had emphasized, so students were instructed to make the most of it.

Though Claire could offer general suggestions as to the types of photos and videos they could use, she was at the mercy of the other three to tell her places where she would find them. They all agreed they needed pictures of nature, the goodness of man, and then the corruption of the city environment—all transcendental ideas. Blake, Quintin, and Violet had no problem coming up with a list of places around Detroit that were beautiful examples of nature, and the corruption of the city was almost everywhere else.

"Just walk out the front doors of this school and turn in any direction you please," Quintin had said, "and you'll end up in a ghetto. No better example than that." The others had solemnly agreed. But they were stumped on not only where to find man's innate goodness but also how to capture it, and so the three had left that one to be hammered out later.

Claire had brought her camera to show her group what it could do. Quintin was the most complimentary.

"Man, that thing has so many buttons, dials, and functions, it makes my graphing calculator look like an abacus."

Blake had just kind of whistled his way around it as he held it up and scrutinized it from all angles. "This thing must've cost a fortune," he said, and, despite her initial sense of superiority, Claire had felt herself redden.

Violet had just narrowed her eyes, furrowed her brow, and pursed her lips, and then had looked from the camera to Claire and then back to the camera again. Claire knew Violet was calculating the cost of the camera as well and was now trying to make sense of how this white girl from California with a very expensive camera ended up at Montgomery High.

Once school was out, Claire had decided to do what all good photographers did—take advantage of the unexpected—so she had taken her camera out, put in some general settings, and waited to see what she came across on the way home. She decided not to think about the list today but just capture what she fancied. Perhaps something might fit. She had taken a couple of pictures of the school's chipped exterior as well as a few candids of some of the students loitering outside, and she was on her way home when the erratic actions of the young black boy had caught her attention.

At the first corner, he turned left, and Claire hustled to catch up. She stopped before turning, not wanting to give herself away, and peeked around the corner, her camera held at the ready. What she saw gave her such a start that she almost forgot why she had followed him.

Having glanced around to see that no one was watching, the boy began foraging through the garbage can. His back was toward Claire, and she quickly changed her setting to multi shot, brought her camera into position, zoomed in, and began firing off photos. Gabriel turned ever so slightly, scrutinizing something he had pulled from the trash, and she was able to capture him in profile. But when he turned even further her way, she ducked quickly back around the corner and waited.

When she thought enough time had passed, she peeked back around the edge of the building and saw that he had moved farther down the alley and to another garbage can. There was no way she could follow as he would see her, and since he was just about out of lens range, she decided to capture another series of shots. Again, he examined his finds, discarding some and stuffing others into his pockets. Satisfied he had exhausted this can as well, he looked around circumspectly, walked to the end of the alley, and turned right. Claire hurried after him, but when she arrived at the end of the alley, she was blinded by the stark sunlight. Shielding her eyes with her hand, she looked both ways but failed to find him. She stuffed her camera into her backpack, released a sigh, and leaned against the building.

After a couple of minutes, her eyes, having adjusted to the blinding sun, now took in the rawness of the street life. Tattooed young men in thin tank undershirts loitered in doorways, trying both to stay cool and, more importantly, look cool. In front of them, parading up and down a twenty-foot stretch of sidewalk were the girls, sporting tattoos of their own along with multiple piercings, and their provocative clothing provided little protection from the ultraviolet rays and left even less to the imagination. The air was riddled with lewd stares, rude catcalls, and coarse profanity.

Claire desperately wanted to take some pictures, but every eye was suspiciously looking her way. A white girl with an expensive camera would definitely not go unnoticed. She realized that she had stepped into a world that was not only outside of her comfort zone but also her safety zone, and she slowly stepped back into the alley, always keeping her eyes on her surroundings.

Once safely in the shadows, she let out a huge breath and realized she was shaking. She turned and walked quickly back the way she had come, praying no one was following her. Not wanting to turn around, she listened intently for approaching footsteps but only heard the fierce pounding of her own heart. When she arrived back at school, she stopped, took a huge breath, and felt her whole body shake. Scared as she was, she knew she would be back—but not without backup.

* * * *

Destiny shook out her arms, hands, and shoulders while she ran in place catching her breath, before starting back down the stadium steps. Below her, the football team was running through a series of plays, and all around her were her fellow cross-country teammates sprinting up the stadium stairs, jogging in place, and then jogging back down the stairs to do it all over again.

Hill training was tough in Detroit, which was pretty flat. The school's weight room had one treadmill, but one wasn't adequate for team workouts, so Coach Kastner had partnered with a local fitness center and managed to get them to donate four old, soon to be discarded treadmills that had an incline feature. However, the only place he could find to house them was an old storeroom, which had no ventilation except the open door, and not until the temperatures cooled a bit would he begin using them. Sometimes the team would head out to Auburn Hills or one of the other suburbs, but that was always dependent on transportation. Parents who were able offered to carpool the students to various locations, but that was not a daily option, so today the stairs and the track would have to do. Twenty-five sets of stairs, two miles of recovery running on the track, then back for another twenty-five stairs, then a final two miles of recovery on the track.

Destiny finished her first set of stairs and headed for the track, dodging an errant pass by a quarterback hopeful. Some schools had two separate facilities for track and football, but the Montgomery teams had to share, which brought two vastly different athletes together in a sort of forced camaraderie.

She started her first two mile recovery run, singing Jason Gray's "Good to be Alive" softly to herself to keep her pace slow. She smiled as she rounded the first curve. It was good indeed.

* * * *

Travis sat at his desk and stared at the pile of paperwork in front of him. This was the part of the job he enjoyed the least—sitting at a desk and working his way through the timely but tedious demands of the job. He enjoyed the problem solving that came with it but never the paperwork.

He enjoyed people, too. Even though he wasn't a talker, he learned early that if he asked the right questions, people were more than willing to talk about themselves, and he could glean a lot of valuable information if he remained patient and waited out the insignificant or self-serving portions of the conversation.

Travis's desk was large but bare. He didn't like clutter of any type—verbal or physical, so besides the pile in front of him and his calendar, there were only three other items on his desk. A picture of Cecile, front and center, a framed copy of the poem "Dreams" by Langston Hughes on his right, and a framed Bible verse on his left.

Cecile was his compass and when his day got tough what he wanted and needed most was to see her face.

The poem he had first read his junior year of high school while sitting on the lawn at Wayne State waiting to make a drug deal. At the time, he had scoffed at the words, thinking Langston Hughes to be ingenuous. But when his life changed so drastically after he became saved, so had his outlook, and now the poem echoed the feelings of his heart. He read it again silently, though he had it committed to memory.

Dreams
Hold fast to dreams
For if dreams die
Life is a broken-winged bird
That cannot fly.

Hold fast to dreams
For when dreams go
Life is a barren field
Frozen with snow.

—Langston Hughes

Travis knew how important dreams were, especially to these kids who were nearsighted by poverty, crippled by dysfunctional families, and imprisoned by the drugs and gangs that surrounded them. They needed to dream past their current situation, past their ignorance, past their ghetto. That's what he *wanted* them to do. That's what they *needed* to do. But he also knew that dreaming wasn't enough. That's why he had created the school motto, the one top-down move he had made without asking anyone else's opinion. "Dream Big. Then Work Hard." When the teachers had first seen the huge banner hanging in the hall over the entrance to the auditorium, they had just stared. Then he saw heads nod, smiles develop, and the energy build, and he knew they agreed.

The Bible verse was one sentence written on top of a picture of the universe—Psalm 147:4: "He counts the number of the stars; He calls them all by name." This one verse had impacted him more than any other because it had been nights of staring at the stars that had revealed to him his own insignificance and aloneness in a vast universe. But it also showed him that if God cared that much for the stars, then surely God cared about *him*. Psalm 147 also inspired Travis to learn every one of Montgomery High School's students' names and many of their meanings.

That left only his calendar and the pile on his desk.

He checked his calendar. No meetings today, so he turned his attention to the pile of paperwork and began sifting through it: test scores, budget requests, enrollment discrepancies that meant scheduling adjustments, dropout rates, parent meeting minutes and agendas. He put the pile back down for a moment and looked up at the clock: three forty-five. He needed to address some of these today. It was going to be a long afternoon.

Chapter 12

*D*anny scanned the busy tutorial room. School had been in session for only two weeks now, but already the tutoring program was in full throttle. "Room" was a bit of a misnomer because this was actually Montgomery High's original gymnasium. Located at the end of the main building, it had provided ample space for the boys basketball games in the early 1900s. On one side, bleachers rose ten feet above the gym floor. The sidelines were barely four feet from the walls, and the end lines enjoyed only one more foot of space. Pity the poor player who had more forward than upward momentum going in for the layup, for he was bound to come to an abrupt halt when body met concrete.

However, as women's sports began to take hold, and other indoor sports started finding their own footing, a bigger, more modern gym had to be added. Finally, with the advent of Title IX in 1973, the old relic lost all favor and a second new, albeit small, gym was built. The discarded gym went through a series of metamorphoses of its own. First, it became the biggest discarded equipment storage area on campus, but Martha had quickly put an end to that.

"You are supposed to be getting rid of all that stuff," she had chided the principal at the time. "This space should be used for kids," and she quickly asked board approval to use it for her drama program. It had been wonderful. Space galore, and she never would have given the place up if a windfall of state money for the arts hadn't provided underprivileged schools filled with underrepresented student populations with new facilities and equipment for certain programs. Martha had volunteered to write the grant, and two years later an old Quonset hut was removed from the school property, and a new arts building was raised, equipped with kilns and wheels for ceramics, small stages for the drama classes, and a large room with risers for the choir, band, and orchestra classes. Instead of building a new theater, the original, a beauty beneath its weary and weathered veneer, was refurbished. Montgomery High was an anomaly in an otherwise financially starving district.

So that left the old gym up for sale again. That was fifteen years ago, and this time it was math teacher Jim Gregory who stepped up at a faculty meeting and suggested a tutorial center.

Martha had been one the biggest supporters of Jim's idea but hadn't been surprised when Principal Smith had balked at paying a teacher a stipend for running the lab.

"Just call it a coaching position, Bob, and the board will be sure to pass it," Carol Myers, one of the science teachers, suggested sarcastically. The whole room laughed, and Big Bob Smith reddened, but it was Carol's suggestion that Principal Smith took to the board, calling the position an Academic Coach. The board not only unanimously approved the position but also "found" some money to remodel the building just a bit. A local business donated some tables and chairs, and Jim Gregory applied for an after school grant to purchase computers.

Except for the set of elevated bleachers, where more than a few students sat reading or studying together, any remnants of a gymnasium were long gone. The space was divided into four major sections—one in each corner: math, science, English, and social science. In the center were two more sections, one for foreign language and the other for the smaller disciplines. Then in the spaces between the corner groups and all along the walls were the computers.

Montgomery High's policy was to have teachers act quickly and refer students as soon as they started falling behind. The early intervention had proved to save many students from reaching the point of no return. Danny's reasons for starting at the lab were twofold. First, students who had drug or alcohol problems usually had academic issues as well, and second, those who actually showed up were crying for help.

* * * *

Gabriel slid his right leg under him on his chair to hike himself up a bit, then rested his forearms on the table and leaned toward his tutee to look at his answer.

"That's right!" he said enthusiastically, and the student smiled. "Do you understand how you got the answer?" Gabriel asked, and the boy nodded.

"For the first time," he said. "Thanks."

"No problem," Gabriel answered. "Algebra is actually pretty easy once you get the basic concepts down. Now try these next two problems and see if you can get them. If you can, then it means you really do understand, and we can move on."

He slid the piece of paper in front of the boy and then turned to look for Ruthie. He saw her and gave a sigh of relief. She was right where he had left her, at one of the tables in the middle of the room with some other younger siblings. She was busy doing something, he wasn't sure what, since he didn't think third graders had that much homework. When he had told her about his new job as a tutor and that she could come with him, she bubbled with excitement.

"I will be so good," she promised. "You won't even know I am there."

"Well, you don't have to be *that* good," he teased before turning serious. "You know what this means, don't you?" he asked. Ruthie shook her head. "It means I will be making money and then we can buy things." He saw Ruthie swallow.

"Like new clothes?" Ruthie asked, and Gabriel felt his stomach drop. He had been thinking more along the lines of food and soap and laundry. Though they had a place to sleep and almost enough to eat, he was learning very quickly that there was much more to living and a whole lot more to living cleanly and safely.

Even though he was managing to get a bucket of water up to their hiding place each evening, the cold water was not enough to keep them clean, and he was already detecting dirt lodging itself deep into their skin. Fortunately for him, he had PE, and though showering was not mandatory at Montgomery, Gabriel had swallowed his inhibitions and fear and opted for a shower every day, the only student to do so. He had taken a bit of teenage abuse for a couple of days, but when he didn't respond, the ribbing had ceased.

Ruthie, however, was a different matter, so he encouraged her to wash as much as she could at school.

"See if you can scrub your neck and elbows, too," he suggested, but he knew she didn't know how to rub hard enough to really make a difference. He would need to do that. And then their hair. Thomas had sneaked him a quarter bottle of shampoo, and Gabriel had washed Ruthie's and his own hair twice already, but both needed trimming. Their tight locks were beginning to show an unevenness.

Plus, after two weeks, he was already growing tired of emptying the bucket that served as their toilet. As much as both of them tried to relieve themselves at school, or sneak into the back of the restaurant across the alley, there were just too many hours between when they got home and when they went back to school to not have to use the bucket. Sometimes it would sit there a whole day, the odor filling the room, but even that they had become accustomed to.

Finally, their clothes. There was no good way to wash them. The first weekend he used some of Thomas's shampoo and did laundry in their washing bucket, but it had been hard to get the shampoo out once it was in the bucket and the clothes. He had finally waited until the alley was clear and took their clothes down and rinsed them there, then hung them to dry over nails poking out of the walls. Even with all his efforts, he could tell they were beginning to smell and show signs of ground in dirt.

No, he needed this job, and he needed to get paid—soon. Living was expensive.

* * * *

Claire sat in her bedroom reviewing her pictures and video on her computer. She had convinced Quintin to go back with her down the alley to the main street and then form a human blind from behind which she could take pictures. At first he was reluctant, but when she said it was for the good of the project, he had relented.

Now reviewing them, she saw that she had captured some stellar shots and live footage. She needed the weekend to go through all of them, cull out the best, and put them into a rough presentation to show the others on Monday. She slowly clicked through the images. The young boy rummaging through garbage cans came up, and she paused. She had tried to locate him again in order to follow him, but he had never reappeared, so she had given up.

She scrolled through the candids. They were good. The facial expressions captured both the contempt, despair, and weariness dished out by the big bad city and the hope and happiness of the children not yet tainted. Perfect transcendentalist stuff.

She worked her way through the nature scenes. At Violet, Blake, and Quintin's insistence, the four of them had met at Belle Isle and Claire had fallen in love with it. The island offered all kinds of beauty from parkland to lakes. It was an oasis from the heat and busyness of the city. And it provided one more surprise for Claire. Destiny was a runner. Though they had been having lunch together for a couple of weeks, Destiny had never told her she ran cross country. Claire discovered it through the lens of her camera.

The four had met up at Belle Isle on a day that the cross-country team was practicing. Claire had seen some runners in the distance and had moved into position to capture them as they ran past her. Not until she had clicked the picture did she realize the runner looked familiar, and she looked up just as Destiny ran past her. Claire frantically looked across the width of the island to try and guess the route the runners would take. Quintin watched her, made the intuitive leap, grabbed her gear lying on the ground, and started hoofing it across the park, yelling for her to follow. Claire hustled after him and once settled, quickly set up her camera in video mode. She could see Destiny and a couple of other runners in the distance, and she started shooting.

She makes it look so easy, Claire thought.

Claire hated running. Actually, she hated most things that required physical activity, preferring to stay close to cameras and computers, though occasionally the first did require her to be in some uncomfortable weather conditions, but other than that she preferred the indoor life.

Claire questioned Destiny the next day.

"Why didn't you tell me you were a runner?" she asked.

Destiny shrugged. "You never asked," she replied. Claire had taken offense at first, wondering how in the world she was supposed to know to ask Destiny if she ran cross country, but then she felt herself grow red. She had never asked Destiny *anything* about herself. In all their lunches together, Destiny asked all the questions while Claire divvied out answers as she saw fit, keeping the girl at bay.

"How long have you been running?" Claire asked, hoping to remedy the situation immediately.

"I can never remember a time when I wasn't," she answered with a smile. "I can remember my mother always yelling, 'Don't run in the house!' so I must have started very young."

Claire smiled. "You're good," she said and realized it was the first time she had ever paid anyone a sincere compliment. "Not that I really know what good is, but from my point of view, you look really good. So are you?"

Destiny smiled. "Thanks," she replied, then continued, "I think so. I came close to winning the state championship last year and hope to win it this year."

Claire struggled to think of appropriate questions to ask. "So can you? I mean, do you have a lot of competition out there?"

Destiny nodded. "Always, but the girl who won last year has graduated, so if I keep up my current pace, I should be in contention. Of course, I hope to improve on my personal best by the time state comes around."

As the conversation continued, Claire was both amazed by all Destiny had accomplished and embarrassed by how self-absorbed she had been. But she could change that. As she left the lunch table and headed toward class, Claire developed a plan for learning more about Destiny, never realizing that her decision was part of a much bigger plan.

Chapter 13

"Are you sure you don't want to go with us?"

Claire stared at her mother in disbelief. She was more than sure. She had no desire to spend an hour or more with a bunch of religious hypocrites, and she certainly couldn't understand why her mother would want to either. Hadn't her father professed to be a Christian and then cheated on her? And then her Christian mother had been so naive. Trusting her father when he had said he had to work late. If that was what it meant to be a Christian, then no thank you. She wanted nothing to do with it. The sudden reminder of the divorce brought back a flood of unwanted emotions: pain, anger, hurt.

Her first impulse was to let some snide, sarcastic remark slide from her mouth, but she caught herself. What good would that do? It would only hurt her mother more and what *really* had *she* done? She also realized, for the first time, that her sarcasm was her way of masking her own pain. Maybe if she made someone else hurt, she would feel better or at least know someone else was hurting as badly as she was.

She swallowed all her words and thoughts, managed a weak smile, and offered a lame but plausible excuse. "Sorry, Mom," she said, "but I have this project due in a week, and I need to finish the first version today so I can show my group tomorrow."

Her mother just looked at her with kind eyes for a few moments, opened her mouth as though to say something, thought better of it, and offered a smile instead.

"Alright, darling," she said softly. "You work hard, and Grandma and I will see you in a couple of hours."

She turned and exited Claire's room. Claire watched her leave and in her absence a palpable emptiness not only filled the room but Claire as well. An emptiness so profound that all Claire could do was cry.

* * * *

Destiny joined the rest of the congregation as they sang Darlene Zschech's worship song "Shout to the Lord." She loved the song. God had been very good to her, and she wanted to worship, serve, and praise Him. And she had much to praise Him for. Her senior year had started off well. Classes were good, her cross-country workouts were going well, and she was meeting her weekly goals. Her hours of running during the summer were definitely paying off. And then the "project" was going strong. Claire had been a bit of a challenge at first, but the two had actually warmed to each other, and Destiny had been pleasantly surprised to find that Claire had shown some interest in her running. The next challenge would be to get her to meet the others at the end of the month and see if she could make some new friendships, thereby freeing Destiny at lunchtime to go in search of another lonesome heart.

The music director started on the second verse, and Destiny let her mind wander. One thing about black churches, or churches with primarily black members, such as Calvary Christian, is that you could expect to sing every verse of every song. There were no shortcuts here, so Destiny knew she had a couple of minutes to sing on autopilot before she had to move to a new song. She let her mind drift to where it always did—running.

Mentally, she took her current time as of Friday and calculated how many seconds she would need to drop each week to reach her desired goal by the time state finals rolled around. Once she knew that figure, she silently whistled: three seconds a week was a lot to sustain. That meant additional weight training, speed workouts, and distance. She really didn't *need* to drop that much time. Just a few seconds off last year's time should be enough to take first, but Destiny wanted more than just to win the state championship; she wanted to make sure she secured a scholarship to Michigan State, and the best way to do that was to blow the top off of the state record.

The song came to an end, and the organ began the intro into the old hymn "Blessed Assurance," another song Destiny knew by heart, and so once again, she let her mouth sing the words while her mind returned to tomorrow's workout. *The weight room opens at six thirty,* she told herself. *I could put in an extra half hour of weights and agility before school and even add some treadmill work.*

Her new plan formulated, Destiny put cross country out of her mind just in time to put Jesus back in before the sermon started.

* * * *

"Do you want to go to the park today?" Gabriel asked. It was Sunday afternoon, and Gabriel's stomach was growling. He could hear Ruthie's stomach rumbling as well, but she wasn't complaining, and that made his insides knot up and his throat contract in a tight swallow. He licked his lips. He was supposed to be taking care of her, but he wasn't doing a very good job of it. Weekends were hard. No friends bringing a free apple or granola bar. No free lunch. Even the garbage cans seemed to have less on Sunday mornings than on other days.

Plus there was a lot more gang and drug activity on Saturdays and, suddenly within a few weeks, both groups had found their way to Gabriel and Ruthie's empty building, realizing it offered them some privacy for their activities as well. Last night, Gabriel could hear them thudding through the building, stomping up stairs, bumping into the walls, shouting out obscenities, and singing raucously. He held his breath while his heart pounded in his chest. What if they came into *their* room? What if they found him and Ruthie? What would he do? He had never found a replacement for the confiscated knife, and he silently cursed Mr. Johnson.

Ruthie had heard the noises and voices as well and had looked up at Gabriel in the darkness with wide eyes. He knew he had to look strong for her. He had smiled at her and put his arm around her, hoping she wouldn't feel him shaking.

"Don't worry," he said. "They're not coming in here." And they hadn't, but they had come close. Gabriel had waited in their little room till long after noon, listening for the exodus of feet. Finally, he ventured out, telling Ruthie to stay put until he came back.

He was amazed at what he found. On both sides of him and across the hall was evidence of last night's activities. Why no one had chosen *their* room was a mystery to him. In fact, no one had even tried their door. He felt himself start to shake all over when he realized how close they had come to being discovered ... and then what?

The building had six floors, but when Gabriel was house shopping, he had stopped his search on the third, thinking that would be high enough. Now he wasn't sure. He carefully checked all the rooms on the two floors below him. No sign of previous activity. Then he checked the three floors above him. Nothing. For some reason, only the third floor. He hurried back to Ruthie.

"We need to move further upstairs," he said, beginning to gather up their makeshift bedding. Ruthie didn't argue, but picked up the few items that remained. She stared at the bucket in the corner.

"I'll come and get that later," Gabriel said, and thought of how many stairs he would now have to climb to empty the bucket and get fresh water. A heaviness fell on his young shoulders, but he took a deep breath and shook it off. He needed to stay strong.

"Follow me," he said and led Ruthie up three more flights of stairs, but all the while he was thinking. Distance alone would not keep them safe. He had to think of something else. As they rounded corner and headed for the landing on the sixth floor, he felt one of the treads creak and give under his weight, and his mind clicked into gear.

He now put pressure on the first stair, found it strong, but the second one gave just a bit, as did the third. A smile began to spread across his face. Perhaps there was a way to keep safe after all.

* * * *

"What are you doing, Gabriel? How are we going to get back?"

Ruthie stood watching her brother pull two boards from the landing before moving down the stairs and removing the loose tread from its hold. Then he repeated the process on the tread below it and one more for good measure. Fortunately, they had rotted away from the wall. Gabriel could feel his muscles bulge and was proud of his burgeoning strength, but still it was a struggle for a fourteen-year-old. He opened a nearby door and slid the boards into the empty room.

"This will keep anyone from trying to come upstairs," he told her. "It will keep us safe."

Ruthie dared to look over the edge and into the gaping yawn of space that disappeared into blackness. She didn't know how far the darkness went before it hit something, but she knew it was far enough that it scared her. She looked back at Gabriel with worried eyes.

"But how are *we* going to get up and down?" she asked.

"We'll lay the boards back down one by one and walk very carefully. Then I will remove them again and take them to our room at night."

His explanation did little to calm Ruthie's nerves.

"But won't it be dark when we come up here?" she asked. Gabriel was caught short. He hadn't really thought of that. Of course it would be dark, at least darker. There were no windows on the stairwell, and only one small one on the landings. Even now, in midafternoon, it was only marginally light, and he knew that as the year progressed, and it got darker earlier, they would be trying to maneuver their makeshift stairwell in pitch dark.

"Curtis is bringing me a flashlight," he lied. "I'll get it tomorrow."

This revelation seemed to mollify Ruthie, and the two went down the remainder of the stairs and out into the sunlight.

Ruthie had wanted to go to the park near her school, but Gabriel had insisted they go in the other direction. He didn't need parents from the neighborhood seeing the two of them and start asking questions about where they've been.

No, they would go in the opposite direction.

* * * *

Danny followed Abigail as she ran toward the swings. Though he didn't know many young children, he swore there wasn't one out there that loved the sense of flying as much as Abigail.

She's going to by a fighter pilot for sure, he thought, for not only did she love heights, but she was also a daredevil. Once, she had almost let go of the swing at the top of its arc, wanting to sail through the air on her own. He had seen it happening in slow motion and yelled at her to stop. The tone and strength of his voice shocked her, and she regripped the chain, but once she swung back by him, he stopped her abruptly, pulled her from the swing, and stood her before him while he kneeled down to eye level.

"Don't you *ever* let go from up there," he said to her sternly, looking her straight in the eye and feeling his own arms shaking as his heart pounding frantically. "You could have been hurt very badly."

She looked back at him curiously. Though she didn't know she was witnessing controlled terror in her father, she did know that she had never seen him like this, and it scared her.

"I won't," she said sincerely. Still, Danny couldn't help but have a latent fear regarding his daughter, and, after that, he never let her out of his sight if he could help it.

Matthew, on the other hand, was as conservative as an old lady. He no more wanted to take a risk than he wanted to take a bath. He cared nothing for swings or merry-go-rounds or death drops off of bars. (Danny feared the day when Abigail learned how to do a death drop.) All Matthew wanted to do was play soccer, and as soon as he was out of the car, he ran with his soccer ball to the middle of the park and waited for some of the other boys and girls to join him. Though only five, he could compete with those a couple of years older. Danny watched his son out of the corner of one eye, but kept one and a half eyes on Abigail.

Grace was back at the picnic table with Martha while Graydon, with two proud eyes focused on his grandson, had started to walk toward the pickup game. Until Matthew had discovered a soccer ball, Graydon had no use for soccer.

"Sissy game," he had commented when he and Danny were watching the World Cup, the only time they watched soccer. "No hitting, and a bunch of whining, melodramatic actors."

That was all before Matthew had found a soccer ball at two-

and-a-half and started kicking it, and kicking it well. From that point on Graydon was on the soccer bandwagon. He searched out all the possible youth soccer programs in the Detroit area, checked out books and DVDs from the library, and almost became a nuisance until Danny informed his father that he and Grace just wanted Matthew to enjoy kicking the ball around and that they weren't going to put him into any structured program until he entered school. Graydon had backed off—a bit—but every once in a while Grace, Martha, or Danny would catch Graydon giving Matthew a free tip here and there.

Martha watched two of the men in her life as she helped Grace lay out the picnic lunch. She smiled as she saw Graydon trying so hard to restrain himself from interfering in his grandson's game. Then she glanced over at Danny who was pushing Abigail in the swing, but not too high, much to Abigail's dismay, and Martha's smile turned a bit sad.

You can't protect her forever, she said silently to her son. *At some point, good or bad, she will make her own choices.*

Chapter 14

By the time Gabriel and Ruthie arrived at the park, Gabriel realized his stomach had stopped rumbling. He hoped Ruthie's had as well.

Ruthie glanced around the park, a much bigger one than their old neighborhood park, and her eyes lit up. "Wow!" she said slowly, and Gabriel felt a bit of his burden lift. His sister was happy.

"What would you like to do?" he asked. Ruthie surveyed the park, considering all her options.

"Swing," she said and looked up at him expectantly. "Can I?"

Gabriel smiled broadly. "Go for it," he said. "Do you need me to push you?"

Ruthie straightened abruptly and gave him a "get real" look. "I'm eight years old, Gabriel! I know how to swing!"

Gabriel threw his hands up in defense. "Sorry. I'll stay out of your way. Go on."

Ruthie turned and ran toward the swing without any more

encouragement. Gabriel watched her go, find a swing, and then pump away until she was soaring so high that the chains became slack at the top of each ascent, and he began to worry about her. He started to head her way to caution her to be careful and not go so high, but he hadn't seen his sister so carefree since they had left their mom's house, so he stopped himself.

"Not now," he told himself softly. "Not today."

Anyway, he saw a man pushing his own daughter say something to Ruthie as she swung past him and noticed Ruthie slow herself just a little.

"Good," Gabriel murmured under his breath and then looked around the park for some diversion of his own. He noticed the pickup soccer game and headed toward it. He could already tell he was too old to play in this game, but he loved soccer so much perhaps they would let him act as referee. That would be fun.

He stood on the sideline watching. When the ball careened off a foot and rolled toward him, he picked it up, secured it under his arm, put his fingers to his lips, and let out a shrill whistle before pointing toward the opposite end of the field.

"Blue ball!" he yelled, only because he saw a young boy in a blue shirt running toward him, obviously knowing it was his team's ball. The young boy skidded to a halt and stared up at him.

"Are you a referee?" he asked.

"Maybe," Gabriel responded. "Why?"

"Would you be our referee?" the young boy asked excitedly.

"I would be glad to," Gabriel replied. "Just show me who is on whose side."

The boy turned and waved all the players toward him, giving a quick explanation to his playmates, and then the two sides sorted themselves quickly so that Gabriel could tell who was who. Fortunately, the blue boy was not the only one in blue, and the other team had more white than anything else."

"Okay," Gabriel said. "This is the *blue* team," he said pointing to the first team, "and you," he added nodding to the other team, "are the *white* team. Any questions?"

The kids shook their heads, anxious to get on with the game.

"Okay, then, BLUE BALL!" he shouted, and he handed the ball to the young boy in the blue shirt who then held the ball over his head before executing a perfect throw in. The game was back on, and Gabriel was all in.

* * * *

Graydon watched the interchange in awe: first he looked at his grandson and then at the young teen who had stepped in so easily and ingratiated himself into the younger kids' game. There was a striking similarity there. Both were willing to take charge, each had a sense of humble confidence, and both had no trouble getting the others to follow their directives. Graydon let a smile form on the corners of his mouth. Both were natural leaders.

He watched the teenager interact with the younger ones. He was smart. He didn't call all the infractions or the game would never get played, but he did call the most blatant offside offenses and fouls. He was also patient and instructive. Every so often when the ball would careen away, or there would be a corner kick, or a free kick, he could hear the boy offer just a sliver of advice as the player lined up or got ready to start the play, and then he could see the player make the slight adjustment. This kid was not only a natural leader, but he was also a capable teacher and coach. Graydon was learning a lot. Too many parents wanted to correct every misstep and coach every play as he himself was so tempted to do, but now he saw that this boy's approach was much better. Let them play, let them enjoy the game, and when the opportunity arises, then offer some instruction. The kids were only five or six for heaven's sake.

The game might have gone on for another half hour or so, but Graydon could see that some of the kids were tiring. He glanced back at the picnic table where Martha and Grace were sitting, and they nodded. They had been watching as well. Now was a good time to eat. Graydon nodded back and then looked at Martha again, and after thirty-seven years of marriage, she knew what that look meant. She nodded back. Graydon smiled, let out a contented sigh, turned back toward the game, and let out a whistle of his own.

"TIME!" he yelled, and the ball dribbled to a stop. Gabriel looked over at the older man who had yelled. Graydon tapped at his watch. "Time to rest a bit and get some lunch," he called to one of the players, and the young boy in blue ran to grab his ball.

"I gotta go," he told the others. "We can play again later."

A few groaned, but most were fine with stopping, and some of the other parents took their cue from Graydon and called their own children back for lunch as well. Gabriel just stood where he was, watching the others scatter to their various families, and he felt a hollowness that wasn't caused by lack of food. He turned around to see where Ruthie was, but she wasn't on the swings anymore, and he felt a flash of panic. The game had gone on quite a while, and he had forgotten all about his sister. His eyes panned the park in search of her, and the panic rose, but he soon found her on the merry-go-round, oblivious to his concern.

"Is your family here?"

The voice was right behind Gabriel startling him, and he wheeled around to find himself looking up into the face of the tall man who had called the game to an end. Gabriel looked around him to see if the man was actually talking to him. The man smiled and repeated himself, "Are you here with your family?"

Gabriel shook his head. "No, sir, just my sister and I," a little worried as he was not quite sure what the man was after. Graydon nodded, impressed by the boy's politeness.

"Then would you like to join my family and me for lunch? I watched you playing with the children. You were really good with them, and my grandson is quite taken by you. I think he would be thrilled if you ate with us."

Graydon had tilted his head backward, indicating where his family was. Gabriel looked past him at the picnic table and saw the boy in blue watching his every move. He had completely forgotten about food during the excitement of the game, but the mention of lunch inadvertently caused his stomach to rumble. He hoped the man hadn't heard it. He licked his lips and tried not to look too anxious.

"I have my sister with me," he confessed to the man, "so it might inconvenience your family." He hated to say it. He was really hungry.

Graydon turned around. "Is that your sister?" he said, nodding toward Danny, Abigail, and a young girl already seating themselves at the picnic table. Gabriel's eyes widened.

"Yeah, I mean, yes," he said embarrassed.

"Then I think she has beaten us to the table," Graydon replied smiling, "and in answer to your question, no, it won't inconvenience us at all." He held out his left arm and lightly touched Gabriel's shoulders. "Come on," he encouraged, "before that son and grandson of mine eat all the fried chicken!"

* * * *

Earlier

Danny watched the young girl next to him swinging freely, lost in the enjoyment of the moment. She looked somewhat familiar, and as he pushed Abigail, he glanced around the park, looking for the father or mother who had their eye on her, but he couldn't see anyone looking this way. How did he know her? He slowed down his pushing a bit more and took a more careful look first at the girl, then around the park for the parents.

"DADDY! PUSH!"

Danny brought himself back to his daughter. "Sorry, baby," he said and began pushing her again in earnest, but he realized after his second survey that the girl was indeed alone. He glanced over at her again and realized that she had propelled herself higher and higher to the point where the chain was going slack at the top. As she swung back by him, he called to her.

"Not quite so high," he warned. "That can be dangerous."

Ruthie looked over at the man on her next pass, and saw that his face wasn't angry, just concerned, and very kind. He reminded her of Gabriel. She voluntarily slowed down. Danny smiled as she went by.

"Thank you," he said. "That's much better."

Danny had push-started Abigail again, and the two girls swung together, laughing, but never going too high. After about fifteen minutes, they both began to slow to a stop. Danny stepped in as Abigail jumped out of the swing. Ruthie stayed where she was, watching with a pang of envy as father and daughter moved toward each other.

Danny turned toward her.

"Are you here with your family?" he asked.

She nodded. "My brother's over there," and pointed to where Gabriel was playing referee. Danny squinted to get a better look at the boy. He had seen him somewhere before too.

"How about your mother and father?" he asked.

Ruthie hesitated, a look of concern crossing her face, which Danny caught, but then shook her head. "They couldn't come," she answered simply, and Danny didn't press.

"Well, then," he said cheerfully, "would you like to join my daughter Abigail on the slide and the merry-go-round? She seems to really enjoy your company."

Ruthie's face broke into smile, and she nodded vehemently, and Danny laughed.

"Well, I hope you have energy," he said, "because she is going to keep you running."

Ruthie didn't say anything, and Danny soon found out why. Ruthie had Abigail's energy and daredevil tendencies times two.

* * * *

"For what we are about to receive, may the Lord make us truly thankful. Amen."

Gabriel stared at the tops of the heads of the people around him. After the introductions, the prayer had happened so fast, and he was so confused by what was happening that he never bowed his head. But Ruthie had. She had never taken her eyes off of Mrs. Richards, the young one, from the moment the two of them had sat down, so when Mrs. Richards bowed her head, Ruthie did too. When her head came back up, she turned to Gabriel.

"Isn't she pretty?" she said, and he looked down to the end of the picnic bench at the lady Ruthie had been staring at and had to agree. Mrs. Richards was indeed beautiful, but he shushed his sister.

"She might hear you," he said, but Ruthie didn't see a problem with that.

"So," she countered. "I'm going to tell her." Gabriel was mortified and panicked. He didn't know these people, but he also didn't know what to do. Before he could stop her, Ruthie had displayed her feelings.

"I think you're beautiful," she said emphatically toward the woman. Grace Richards smiled kindly.

"Thank you," came the reply. "And I think you're beautiful as well." Though it sounded sincere, Gabriel thought it was just a kind thing to say in response, but Ruthie couldn't care less.

"Thank you," she replied, genuinely pleased, and then continued to compliment the woman. "The food looks wonderful."

Gabriel just stared at his sister. *Where had she learned this stuff? Was etiquette just in a girl's genetic makeup?* He hadn't even *thought* of complimenting anyone on the food. He thought he was showing good manners just by refraining from grabbing it and gulping it down. He was so hungry.

"Thank you again," Grace responded. "My mother-in-law is responsible for a lot of it." To which Ruthie turned and now smiled at the older woman. Gabriel shook his head in more amazement.

He watched the platters of food being passed around and turned to his right to receive the plate full of fried chicken. He could feel his mouth water ... and the eyes of the young Mr. Richards on him. He glanced up into his eyes, and the man smiled, looked away, and then looked back curiously. Finally, he put the dish he was holding down and looked right at Gabriel.

"I'm sorry," he said, "but you look very familiar. Where do you go to school?"

Gabriel felt his whole body go cold. How would this man know him? Gabriel had never seen him in his life. He swallowed hard, thought about lying, but knew he couldn't. Especially, since Ruthie was sitting right there.

"Montgomery," he said simply. He had thought this park was still in Montgomery's school limits, but maybe it wasn't. Maybe his being here was suspicious. He could feel his stomach tighten.

The older Mrs. Richards now joined in the conversation.

"I teach at Montgomery. Who do you have for English?" she asked.

Gabriel looked over at her. "Mr. Vincent," he said, and he could see her nod in approval.

"Very good teacher," she said. "You will learn a lot."

Gabriel smiled weakly and returned his attention to the man. He could tell the young Mr. Richards was mulling this answer over as his lips were pulled together and his nose was wrinkled up.

"Hmmm," he said to himself and then looked at Ruthie.

"You look familiar, too," he said to her with a smile. "Do you go to Montgomery High School as well?"

Gabriel could feel his skin begin to prickle despite the heat. Why was this man asking so many questions?

Ruthie nodded, and everyone, even Gabriel, looked at her in surprise.

"I go after school while Gabriel helps people with their homework," she announced, and then the light went on in Danny's head.

"That's it!" he said excitedly, and Gabriel could see and feel the man's relief. "That's where I've seen you. I help out in the tutorial center as well and came in last Friday to take a look around. You were helping in the math section, and you, young lady," he said, and he leaned toward Ruthie with a big smile, "were diligently working on something very important at one of the tables in the middle."

Ruthie smiled in glee. "That was me!" she said excitedly and then turned serious, her brow furrowed in concern. "I was practicing my cursive writing. It is very hard you know."

The table laughed, and the conversation turned to other things, but Gabriel felt he had aged a lifetime in those few minutes, and the hunger that had plagued him minutes before was gone. All he felt now was fatigue.

Chapter 15

*D*estiny pressed the button on the treadmill that raised the incline another degree. She could hear the machine whine as the elevation increased, and she could feel her legs adjust to the difference. She had been working out only fifteen minutes, but already she was dripping with sweat. No one was at her end of the weight room. All the football players were down at the free weights doing squats and the bench press.

She kept her pace at this level for another ten minutes, considered raising the incline one more notch, but then thought better of it. *No reason to rush*, she thought. *Slow and steady wins the race.* She depressed the elevation button three times, bringing the treadmill back to level and then dropped the speed to half, allowing herself to cool down. Another five minutes, and then she brought her pace down to a walk for the last two.

She smiled at her decision to start adding early morning workouts to her routine. She was sure the extra effort would help her shave off those seconds a bit quicker.

She glanced at the clock. Seven thirty. She should stretch, but she didn't have time if she wanted to get a shower and eat something before classes started. She would have to leave earlier tomorrow. No later than six.

* * * *

Claire waited outside the tutorial center for her three group members. Her stomach twisted a bit in anticipation. Though she hated to admit it, she was excited. She loved what she had created and just knew ... well, hoped ... the other three would as well. Would they know how much work she had put into it? Would they appreciate the skill it entailed? She hoped so.

She glanced at her watch and then decided to go in. She could be setting it up on one of the computers while she waited so that it was ready to view when they arrived.

She pushed the door open and stepped into the large room and was taken aback by the state of the art technology. She smiled in appreciation and let her eyes pan the room, taking in everything and everybody. Suddenly, her eyes did an abrupt halt. There, no more than ten feet away from her, was who she had been looking for the past few weeks—the boy from the alley.

* * * *

Claire watched the tutorial center begin to wind down. Her group had left an hour ago, more than impressed with what she had created. Once again, Quintin had been the most effusive.

"We are *so* going to get an A," he said repeatedly. "We are *so* going to get an A."

Blake had been a bit more subdued but just as impressed.

"How did you make those transitions between categories?" he asked, and Claire had beamed. Not many people would have noticed that subtle change, but Blake had, and she had explained the process to him. "Sweet," he concluded with a nod.

Only Violet had thrown a fly into the ointment—one that Claire had anticipated but hoped the others wouldn't catch.

"It's kind of shy on 'the goodness of man,' isn't it?" she voiced. "I mean, you have a few shots of people helping other people or talking to people, but do you think that will be enough?"

Claire shrugged a reply. Probably not, she thought, but, if the truth be told, trying to capture the innate goodness of man was tough, not because it was difficult to photograph, but because she was beginning to think there wasn't much of it. Oh, there were nice and kind people: Destiny and her friends as they worked to befriend the new and the lonely. Quintin, since he was always trying to make her feel good. And some others. But most people had to work to be good. It wasn't often their first response. Though Blake was complimentary, his first reaction was always the grade. Violet was unduly cautious. And Claire had already seen people cheat, and though she was tempted to attribute this deplorable behavior to Montgomery High, she had to remind herself that the cheating and self-serving behavior, the backbiting and jealousy had been even more prevalent in the wealthy and supposedly cooperative environment of Fieldbrook Arts Academy. She had also learned that people everywhere swore, bullied, and gossiped. She had determined that age obviously had nothing to do with it because many adults she knew displayed those same attributes. Isn't that why she was now living in Detroit? In a little house with only her mother and grandmother?

Then as she was writing her portion of the paper, she had further realized that she had only to look at herself. Her basic go to mode *definitely* didn't start at kindness. She was filled with bitterness and sarcasm and self-pity. Even when life had been going well, and she had been living the cinematic dream at Fieldbrook, she realized that she really hadn't been happy. She had always been comparing herself to others, hoping others would fail so she would win, envying someone else's new camera or equipment.

She had written her paper and talked about how the transcendentalists believed man was a self-reliant and independent thinker, and pure, but she wasn't sure she bought it. Fortunately, Mrs. Richards had asked for a personal response—backed up with a strong rational argument, and Claire had tried to make her opinions sound clear and logical.

She briefly explained her thoughts to Violet, and surprisingly, the other girl nodded in approval.

"I thought it was a bunch of hogwash all along," she said. "No one starts out good." And Claire thought she was going to leave it at that when Violet added the clincher. "I have too many younger sisters and brothers to buy that line. Everything is 'Mine!'" And the other three laughed.

But it was what Violet said next that really impacted Claire, probably because it came from Violet.

"You're a really good filmmaker, you know," she said. "You are *really* good. You should just make more movies even if there isn't a class assignment."

And that was why she was still sitting in the tutorial center—an hour after her classmates had left—pretending to be working on her video. She was watching and waiting for the boy from the alley to leave. There was a story there, a good one she was sure, and she was going to discover it, film it, and publish it.

* * * *

Gabriel reached down and took Ruthie's hand as they turned into the alley. Though only late September, the evenings were beginning to shorten, and the alley was growing dark faster. He took a deep breath, pulled back his shoulders, puffed out his chest, and headed down the alley with a purposeful walk. He couldn't let Ruthie know he was scared. She needed him. She trusted him.

"Gabriel, I'm hungry," she said softly.

Gabriel felt a sharp pang run through his own gut, but his wasn't hunger. It was shame and guilt for letting his sister go hungry. He gave her hand a squeeze.

"I get paid this Friday," he said, "and then we can buy some peanut butter and some crackers and fruit to keep in our room. Won't that be nice?"

She nodded. "But what about tonight?"

A second pang slashed his middle. He hated to dig through the trash cans when she was there, but what could he do? He saw his go-to can up ahead, but one of the workers was outside washing a pan. He couldn't stop there, so he passed it by.

"I'll get us something," he promised, and he felt his own stomach rumble. They passed a recessed doorway and Gabriel thought he saw something move in the shadows, and he stiffened slightly. Ruthie felt him and glanced up at him, worried. He smiled down at her.

"All okay," he said. "Got a chill."

That seemed to satisfy her, and she turned her attention back to the dim alley, holding Gabriel's hand calmly. Gabriel, however, was anything but calm as each darkened doorway brought a potential threat. They closed in on another trash can and Gabriel glanced behind and around him. No one. He pulled the lid, and silently hoped that something to eat would be right on top, so he wouldn't have to dig around. He glanced down. Newspaper. He felt his heart sink as he pulled the newspaper aside. Still nothing. He bit his bottom lip, not wanting to embarrass himself in front of his sister. Ruthie just watched him. He couldn't do it.

"I'll get us something tomorrow," he vowed. "Will you be okay tonight?"

Ruthie looked up at him with big eyes, and he could see the hunger and hurt in them, but she just nodded. Gabriel felt like someone had slammed a fist into his gut, and he wanted to cry.

I will get us food, he vowed. *No matter what it takes.*

* * * *

Claire had the camera rolling from the minute the boy and little girl left the school, zooming in and out. Only once, when the boy had stopped at the trash can and looked around, had she pulled back into the shadows to avoid detection. Otherwise, it was easy. Well, the following and videoing was easy. The area was scary.

She followed the pair through the alley. When the two hit the main street, she sprinted to the end, not about to lose him again. She peeked around the corner just in time to see them make another right. She prudently stuffed the camera into her backpack then ran to the next corner, trying not to think about what those watching might conclude about a white girl following two black children. She was puffing hard when she got there.

This is the most exercise I've had in years, she thought but made no vow to rectify that in the future.

She looked around the corner and once again was rewarded with perfect timing. The two were turning into one of the buildings. She headed down the new alley toward the door, surprised that there wasn't anyone around, but then as she looked closer, she realized that the buildings were empty as well.

When she got to the doorway, she pushed it open slowly; a sweet smell greeted her.

Marijuana, she thought, and stepped in as quietly as she could, closed the door behind her, and found herself almost in the dark. Her heart began to race. What was she getting herself into? She swallowed hard and listened. She could hear footsteps on the stairs above her. Did they belong to the boy and his sister? Or someone else? If someone else, what would they do when they found her snooping around? She listened again. Just two sets. It had to be them.

She started up the stairs slowly, trying not to make the boards creak, and winced, stopped, held her breath, and listened every time one did. Only when she was sure she hadn't been detected did she continue. Now other smells mingled with the marijuana—

stronger, more acrid smells—and Claire found herself wrinkling her nose in distaste. How could they live here?

She was breathing heavily, having climbed four flights, when she heard the boards, first sliding, then plopping, then sliding again. She cocked her head to listen more closely. What was going on? Finally, the sliding and plopping stopped, and the footsteps resumed. Then a door opened and shut, and all was quiet.

Claire waited a few minutes and then took the steps as quickly as she dared to in the darkness and approached the next landing only to stop right before she put her foot into a gaping hole where the next step should be. She stared at the stairwell, breathing a sigh of relief at the little light the landing had. She could have been at the bottom of that abyss. She looked at the stairway again. Curious. The steps were missing, but the supports were still there. All she had to do was just step on the braces and put her hand against the wall, and she could easily navigate herself up. But the boy was going to a lot of trouble to make it seem difficult. Claire scratched her head. Something was definitely going on here, she thought, and she would be back when there was more light to see what it was. For now, though, the shadows were creeping in, and her anxiety rising. She turned and hightailed it out of there.

Chapter 16

"I need a flashlight."

"We have one at home," Charles offered. "How long do you need it for?"

"Forever," Gabriel replied. Charles looked alarmed.

"I can't give you our flashlight to *keep*," he said.

Gabriel looked at the others.

"I don't even know if we *have* one," Thomas confessed.

Curtis just shrugged. "Don't know, but I could check. When do you need it?"

"Today."

All three looked at him.

"Well how would we get it to you today anyway?" Thomas asked.

"You could go home and bring it back," Gabriel suggested.

The three friends looked at each other, and all three came to the same conclusion: it wouldn't work. Thomas was the one to break the news.

"Sorry, Gabe, man, but we can't be late to school. Plus, we

can't be giving you our parents' flashlights."

Gabriel knew this was true, but the urgency of the situation stifled any logic and only fueled his anger.

"Fine," he said sharply. "I'll just take care of it myself."

"If you can wait till tomorrow, I might have an extra one at home," Curtis said, trying to appease his friend. "An extra one is easier to loan you."

But Gabriel wouldn't be placated. He wanted it tonight. He had made it a week without a flashlight, but now it was getting darker in those stairwells, and it was getting harder to get the boards for the stairs back into place. The whole situation was getting harder. He worried every morning as they came down the stairs that one of the new occupants would see them. He worried they would find the hidden treads and wonder what that was all about and come up and discover them. He worried that he couldn't get a full bucket of water up the stairs before dark or the full toilet bucket down the stairs in the middle of the night without a flashlight. He worried he would run into someone coming out of one of the other rooms. He worried … well, he worried *a lot*, and it was beginning to show. He was more nervous, more volatile.

"I need it today," was all he said by way of explanation.

The three looked at each other again. Curtis nodded, and Charles spoke up.

"Gabriel, why don't you just go home?" he asked. "All they will do is put you in a foster home, but at least then you will have food, and you won't have to worry about all of this other stuff."

Gabriel turned on his friend. "I can take care of myself!" he said, his eyes blazing. "All those foster people would do is separate Ruthie and me. All I need is a stupid flashlight, and everything would be okay." He paused for a moment to catch his breath when a new thought crossed his mind, and he moved toward Charles. Charles took a step back. "You'd better not tell anyone how I'm living," he threatened.

Charles' eyebrows rose in surprise at his friend's anger. He had never seen Gabriel this upset. "I won't," he promised. "It was just a suggestion. Just an idea."

"Well, it's a bad one," Gabriel replied, and the others fell silent not knowing what to say next.

"I gotta get to school," Thomas said, breaking the silence and heading down the street.

"Yeah, me too," said Curtis, following right on Thomas's footsteps.

Charles just looked at Gabriel and then shook his head.

"You're blowin' it man," he said. "You're blowin' it big time." And he too headed toward the school, leaving Gabriel standing on the corner.

Gabriel watched them leave and felt a ball the size of a cantaloupe lodge itself in the pit of his stomach while a shiver ran down his arms. That was exactly what he was afraid of.

* * * *

Gabriel couldn't concentrate all day. He had too much on his mind, too many questions, and no answers. First, he couldn't let Ruthie go hungry again. He had to get food. He would get paid on Friday, but that was still three days away. And he needed a flashlight. Now.

At lunch, he had eaten his salad and fruit but wrapped his piece of pizza in a napkin to take home. Now, on his way to his last period, his stomach was growling, but he tried not to think about it. Better his than hers.

A couple of the janitors were already working the hallway, getting a jump start on the afternoon cleaning, but they had left their cart in the middle of the hall, making it difficult for students to maneuver around and get to class. Gabriel could see the bottleneck ahead of him and silently swore. He was in no mood for more problems; his patience was running thin. But there was little he could do but wait and push his way through.

He grumbled every time an elbow jabbed him. He was just about to throw an elbow of his own when he saw it. His heart skipped a beat and his breath caught. There on top of the janitorial cart was a flashlight. Not just any flashlight but one of those big, long, heavy black ones like the police used.

Gabriel kept his eye on it as he inched closer with the crowd. He could feel his mouth go dry. Was he really thinking about taking it? That was stealing. He licked his lips, and his heart beat faster. If he planned to bring it back though, wouldn't that just be borrowing? The bottleneck lessened, and the crowd started moving faster. Gabriel had to think fast, so he slowed down. Someone bumped into the back of him.

"Hey! What are you doing stopping in the middle of the hallway?"

"Sorry, sorry," Gabriel apologized and stepped out of the way. "Dropped something."

"Well, find it and move on," came the sharp reply.

Gabriel pressed himself against the wall while the others passed and looked down the hall in both directions, trying to see the janitors. Nothing, but he knew they would be back shortly for their cart, so he had to act quickly. He waited till the last student went by and then fell into line. The cart was right in front of him. He took one more look behind and to the side, and when he saw that the coast was clear, he reached out with his left hand, pulled the flashlight toward him, then slid it inside the right side of his jacket, holding it in place with his right hand. Too obvious, he thought, and took his coat off, careful to keep the flashlight concealed. Then he rolled his jacket up and casually slid it under his arm, trying to look calm and carefree.

* * * *

Claire worked her way back down the alley, stopping at the corner. She felt her heart quicken and kind of wished she had asked Quintin to come with her again, just for security. But that would have led to too many questions. *How did you find this place? Why this place?* And if she had led him right to the room, he would have been even more suspicious. No, despite the foolishness of her actions, she would have to go it alone.

She did take precautions though. She had dressed in black today, long sleeves and loose jeans, and then had found an old baseball cap in the garage and shoved it into her backpack—an old backpack that didn't have anything feminine about it. Her camera was buried at the bottom of the bag as well. Hopefully she would just blend in.

She surveyed the activity, took a deep breath, made a right, walked nonchalantly to the next alley, and hung another right. She counted the doorways until she got to the fifth. This was the door. She cautiously pushed it open and stepped in. The same sweet, stale smell of marijuana was still lingering in the air. She headed up the stairs slowly, listening for any indication that someone was in the building. On the second landing, she heard some shuffling and quickly backed down and waited until it quieted, her heart pounding in her chest. Then she started up again, placing her feet carefully in the dimness. When she neared the top of the fifth set of stairs, she was once more met by the absence of three treads.

She pulled out her camera and took a few shots, then gingerly worked her way up the skeleton stairs and partial landing and into the hallway, which was lighter now, since it was midafternoon. She had checked the tutorial center to make sure the boy and his sister were there before heading out. Now, she found herself staring down a hallway of ten closed doors. She would have worried about pushing open a wrong door, but figured with all the trouble the boy was going through to keep others away, that only he and his sister were living up here. Logic took her to the far end of the hallway. She pushed open the door and immediately the smell of urine assaulted her. She involuntarily stepped back outside.

She caught her breath and stepped back in, steeling herself for the strong odor. Once inside, she just stared. Despite the smell, there was some semblance of order. An old blanket was on the floor in the corner, carefully folded over to look made up. An old pillowcase was filled with newspapers forming a makeshift pillow.

Two cinderblocks spanned by a warped board held up a glass and chipped mug, a couple of old rags, and half a bar of soap. A half bucket of water stood next to it. Every attempt at cleanliness had been made but had fallen dismally short. She could see another bucket over in the corner but didn't approach it. She knew what it held.

Instead, she walked over to a small pile of girls clothes and a smaller pile of boys. They were nicely folded. She bent down and picked one up, and when she smelled it, she could tell there had been an attempt to wash it, but the dirt was ground in.

She licked her lips, caught up in the emotions of the moment and temporarily forgot why she had come. But then she felt the weight of her camera in her backpack and slowly pulled it out. She adjusted the settings and started filming.

Chapter 17

"Three sandwiches?" Mrs. Middleton asked.

Claire stared at the six pieces of bread lined up, the peanut butter spread across three of them.

"I'm staying after school to do some filming and might not make it home in time for dinner, so I thought I would take some extra."

Mrs. Middleton watched her daughter carefully as she made the sandwiches and knew this wasn't the total truth.

"You're spending a lot of time after school filming," she said. "Another group project?"

Claire shook her head but didn't look at her mother. "No, this is a personal project. I really don't want to talk about it yet, but I'll show you when I'm through." Now she looked up, and Mrs. Middleton knew this part of the story *was* ringing true.

"Well, I'm glad to see you have your appetite back," she said with a smile, and gave Claire a quick hug. "And I look forward to seeing your film."

Claire watched her mother leave the room and breathed a sigh of relief. She knew her mother would approve of what she was doing, which was probably why she didn't want her to know. She would approve *too* much, and Claire didn't want her getting the wrong idea.

She placed the sandwiches in a paper bag, added three apples as an afterthought, then put the bag in her backpack and smiled in satisfaction. As she headed for the door, her heart skipped a beat, and Claire realized that for the first time since she left home for Fieldbrook Arts Academy over two years ago, she was excited about something.

* * * *

Claire spent the first hour and a half after school filming. She caught the football team and some of the students waiting to audition for the fall play; she took some footage of the trophy and display cases. She even filmed the janitorial staff working in one of the wings. She was pleased with some of the angles she used and the diffused lighting through the upstairs windows.

However, a half hour before the tutorial center closed, she packed up her camera, grabbed her backpack, and headed for the alley. She knew she was early, but she wanted to find a spot where she could watch.

She looked up and down the alley and saw it was empty. That was good. She went to the first trash can and placed the paper bag, with the three sandwiches and apples, on top. Though she had made one for herself, she had decided on the way to school that she would give all three to the boy and the girl. She could buy something at the snack bar. But then she had changed her mind. She wanted to see what it felt like to be hungry, so she didn't eat anything all day. She didn't like the feeling. Her stomach gnawed in her belly, she felt irritable and light headed, and she was tempted to pull her own sandwich out, but she gritted her teeth and resisted. Eventually, the rumbling had gone away, only to return later.

At first she had been curious as to why the boy hadn't rummaged through the trash can yesterday when he clearly had done so before. But it didn't take her long to figure it out. Though his body language suggested he wanted to, his hesitation said it all. He didn't want his sister to see.

Claire came back out of the alley and found a grassy area across the street that gave her a clear vantage point of the trash can. She pulled out a book and some notebooks and spread them around her, making it appear like she was deep in studious pursuit. Though her head was buried in a book, her eyes were peering over the top, keeping a watchful eye. Finally, coming toward her down the walkway were the two siblings. She ducked her head and hoped she didn't look too obvious as they came to the corner and crossed the street. Once they were across, she could breathe again and brought her head up just enough to watch their progress. The trash can was only ten feet away.

* * * *

Gabriel walked silently next to Ruthie. She hadn't said a word about food today, but he could hear her stomach rumbling, and he cursed himself for not saving another piece of pizza for her. He looked up at the garbage can ahead of him, wishing he could search it and find something, but he had already decided he wasn't about to humiliate himself in front of her.

About ten feet from it, though, he stopped short. A neat, clean brown paper bag was just resting on the lid. He bit his lower lip.

That's strange, he thought and moved closer. When he was right next to it, he didn't touch it, just looked at it ... from all angles.

"What's wrong, Gabriel?" Ruthie asked.

Gabriel shook his head. "Not sure," he replied. "Just wondering why this bag is just sitting on top of the trash can."

"What's in it?" she asked.

Good question, he thought and bit his lip again. Why was he so hesitant to look in it?

"Not sure," he said again. "But I guess we can look and see," he continued with a little smile. "Shall we?"

Ruthie nodded her head vigorously. Gabriel set his books down on the other half of the garbage can lid, freeing his hands, and then carefully unfolded the lip of the paper bag. Why was he so nervous? He pulled the edges back and peeked in, and his heart stopped then flutter started, and he swallowed hard.

"What is it?" Ruthie asked and moved in to look. Gabriel quickly closed the mouth of the bag and jerked his head up and looked quickly around. His heart was beating fast. No one. Well, the girl across the street studying on the grass, but she was more than a hundred feet away.

Gabriel grabbed the bag in one hand, his coat and books in the other, and pushed Ruthie forward with his forearm.

"Let's go home," Gabriel replied, "and I'll show you there." He continued to hurry Ruthie along despite her protests. His breath was coming in short spurts, and he was now chewing hard on his bottom lip. The sandwiches were not there by mistake. They were too neatly packed and too perfectly placed. Though his stomach was rumbling enthusiastically, his mind was in a quandary, for the sandwiches could only mean one thing: somebody knew about him and Ruthie.

* * * *

Claire's heart was pounding in her chest so hard she was sure the boy and girl could hear it. The boy had reacted so suddenly when he saw the sandwiches that she had almost been caught unaware staring at them. Only at the last second had she ducked, so quickly that she wasn't sure if he had caught her or not. But when she finally dared to peek again, after what seemed like half an hour, she was pleased to see the bag missing and the two kids gone. They had taken it.

A rush of pent up air escaped, and she realized she was shaking. The sense of satisfaction had been replaced by emotional fatigue. She was happy they would be able to eat tonight, but what about tomorrow, and then the next day, and then the one after that? She couldn't keep up the pretense of staying late every night after school. Plus, she had just given all three sandwiches away, and she was starving, yet she couldn't go home and fix something as that would raise her mother's suspicions.

Suddenly she realized that her one good deed might not have been such a good idea after all.

Chapter 18

*D*anny finished helping his last student with a history assignment, stood up, stretched, and looked at his watch. Four forty-five. He glanced around the room at the students. Some were hard workers who struggled in a subject or two. Danny admired them, but those weren't the ones he was here to help. He was here to flush out the drug users.

He looked around the room more carefully. Students were beginning to pack up their books, and the tutors were cleaning up the tables. Danny could see Gabriel helping put the math manipulatives and calculators away and headed toward him. He waited until Gabriel was packed up and ready to go before he spoke.

"Would you and Ruthie like to join my family at the park this Sunday for a picnic?"

Gabriel looked at Mr. Richards in surprise. The man had appeared out of nowhere.

"Uh, I'm not sure," Gabriel replied honestly. The invitation had thrown him off guard. Two surprises in two days. He was still trying to figure out who had left the bag on the garbage can yesterday and if it was *indeed* intended for him and Ruthie. Now, this invitation to the park for lunch. Just thinking about it caused Gabriel's mouth to water.

"Is your family doing something already?" Mr. Richards asked.

Gabriel had to catch himself from letting a smile escape. His family *doing* something? That was a bitter joke. His friends gave him a weekly report, and even after a month and a half, his mother had yet to make an appearance back at the apartment. She could be dead for all he knew. That was common for drug addicts in the hood. They leave in search of the next hit only to wind up dead somewhere. No, the only real family he had was Ruthie. And no, they weren't doing anything this weekend.

"No, nothing planned," he replied straight faced, and then added, "Mom works on Sundays, so I have to watch Ruthie."

Danny smiled. "Abigail has been asking for 'Bee-bee' for the past couple of weeks," he said smiling and Gabriel smiled at the nickname. Abigail obviously could not get her mouth around "Ruthie," so she had just improvised. He liked the name "Bee-bee." It was cute.

"Okay then," he said. "Uh, what time?"

"Well, we get home from church around noon, get changed, get packed up ... say about one o'clock?"

Gabriel listened to Mr. Richards tick off his Sunday routine activities, none of which coincided with Gabriel's Sunday mornings. Church? Nope. Get changed? Into what? Pack up? He caught himself, and a small frown formed on his lips. He licked them and then asked.

"Is there anything we can bring?" It was a question he knew he should ask, but waited in fear for the answer. What if Mr. Richards said yes and then gave him an item that took up most of his first paycheck? He unconsciously prayed that the answer would be no.

Mr. Richards laughed. "Maybe next time," he said, "but this time, just bring yourself and Ruthie. That will be perfect."

Gabriel breathed an inward sigh of relief. Another bullet dodged.

* * * *

Gabriel stared at the bag, and the bag stared back at him. Then he looked all around him as his feet stayed planted in one spot. This time there was absolutely no one around, not even the student studying on the grass. He tentatively reached for the bag while Ruthie watched, waiting for him to take a peek.

"Do you think it's more sandwiches?" she asked. Gabriel shrugged. The situation was unnerving. Obviously someone had seen him rummaging through the trash cans and felt sorry for him. The thought sparked a flame of anger in him. He didn't need anyone's pity, but, at the same time, he felt grateful someone cared *and* wasn't interested in sticking his nose into their business. If it was a him. Gabriel thought for a moment. No, it wasn't a guy. Guys didn't do things on the sly. They came right out and confronted you. They asked you what you were doing. If you wanted any help. Guys got into your business. No, it had to be a girl. Not a woman. Women were worse than men. They got into your business and never let go. They followed through. They kept an eye on you. They wanted to mother and smother you. No, it had to be a girl. Old enough to care but too young to feel comfortable enough to stick her nose too far into someone's business.

"Aren't you going to look, Gabriel?" Ruthie asked. "I'm getting cold ... and hungry."

Gabriel brought himself back to the present and smiled weakly at his sister. She was right. The evenings were getting cooler and there was no reason just to stand here getting colder when both of them knew there was going to be food in the bag. He took a deep breath, looked around one more time, then picked up the bag and looked inside. His eyebrows rose. Pizza. He looked closer. School pizza. His heart started pounding in his chest. That meant it was someone from the school.

Mr. Richards immediately flashed before Gabriel's eyes and his breath caught in his throat. Was it him? He had just convinced himself that it couldn't be a man, but it sort of fit. He was asking him and Ruthie to have lunch with his family on Sunday. Maybe he did that because he knew they were hungry. But Gabriel had never seen Mr. Richards anywhere near this side of the school as he was leaving, and he had been pretty careful to keep an eye out. He chewed on his bottom lip until it hurt.

"Well?" Ruthie's impatience was growing.

"Oh, sorry. It's pizza."

Ruthie's eyes grew in delight. "I love pizza!" she exclaimed, and she started to do a little fidgety dance in excitement. Gabriel smiled down at her.

"Then I suggest we get a move on," he said enthusiastically.

"Before it gets cold," Ruthie added, to which Gabriel had to smile. If the pizza was from lunch then it was already cold, but—and a shiver of fear ran down his back—someone was definitely hot on their trail.

* * * *

Claire didn't know how long she should wait before she headed toward the alley to see if the boy had picked up the bag. Really, she didn't need to check at all. There were only three options. He had, he hadn't, or someone had got to it before him. She hoped the third option hadn't happened, but how would she know if it had? She had tried hard to get the bag in place right before they would get there, but she also had to give herself enough time to get out of sight. From her hiding place, she had watched the two head down the alley. She hadn't seen anyone else enter before them, so she felt confident they would be the first to find it.

After about ten minutes, she slid from behind the tree, crossed the street, and moved along the side of the building toward the alley. If the boy decided to come back and check out the street to see if anyone around was watching, she would be caught, unless she improvised quickly enough. Her heart was pounding.

When she reached the end of the building, she peeked around the corner, trying hard to keep herself hidden. The boy and girl were just standing there staring at the bag. Claire pulled her head back quickly, her heart racing. They should have picked it up and kept going by now. What was the problem? She could feel the rhythmic thud of her heart move her whole body, and her mouth went dry. What if he came back toward her? She waited, barely breathing. She looked around, suddenly aware that someone might be watching *her* and wondering what *she* was doing, but the students from the tutorial center had left quickly, and the athletes wouldn't be leaving for another half hour. Claire reminded herself to be more careful in the future.

She waited what she thought was another ten minutes and then peeked around the corner again. This time both the bag and kids were gone. She felt her whole body relax, and a slight smile involuntarily escaped. Then she recognized a feeling she hadn't experienced in a long time. Satisfaction.

Chapter 19

$\mathcal{T}$ravis sat at his desk and just stared at the letter in his hand. Then he turned it over to see if anything was written on the back—nothing. He flipped it back over and read it again.

Dear Principal Johnson:

This is to inform you that because of declining enrollment in the Detroit School District, one of the zoned high schools will be closed at the end of this year. Though it is difficult to close any of our schools, fiscal responsibility requires that we make this move. Because Montgomery High School has been suffering declining enrollment, it is one of the schools being considered for closure. We would welcome and appreciate anything you might have to offer that would give us reason to keep Montgomery High School open. We will be discussing the matter at the November board meeting and look forward to hearing your thoughts before then. Thank you.

Sincerely,
Jacob Mitchell
School Board President

Travis read the letter again … and again, but the words never changed. Montgomery High School was on the chopping block. He turned the letter over once more and then looked in the envelope, hoping to locate the names of the other schools in danger. He wanted to know how many schools were being considered and which ones were his competition, but there was nothing. He pursed his lips. The district had eleven comprehensive zone high schools and additional optional schools, which specialized in either technology or the arts. In fact, there were more optional schools than comprehensive high schools. Were any of those up for elimination? Travis checked his watch. Ten thirty. Then he checked his calendar. Nothing pressing till after lunch. Good.

He stood up, straightened his tie, and grabbed his jacket. This wasn't something he wanted to do on the phone. He didn't want to be put on hold or passed around. He wanted to see someone face to face. He walked out of his office.

"I'm headed to the district office until lunch," he told his secretary on his way out. "You can reach me on my cell if you need me."

"Yes, Mr. Johnson," she said, knowing immediately that something major was happening. Travis *never* left the school site during the day.

* * * *

Claire looked around at the seven other students sharing her table.

What a motley looking group we are, she thought. Never in a million years would she have imagined herself with such a gathering of misfits. Well, three at least.

There was Destiny, of course, and she wasn't a misfit or motley looking. Then there were Destiny's three friends from church—Carla, William, and Jason—who also befriended loners and losers like herself during lunch. She chided herself for her ungrateful and sardonic attitude. She shouldn't think that. Though Destiny had picked her out of the cafeteria lineup because she was alone, she had never treated Claire like a loser. If anything, after that second day when Claire had questioned Destiny on her motives, Destiny had been very open and honest about what she and her friends were doing: befriending the new or the shy or anyone who seemed to need a friend. Destiny had also told Claire that the eight of them would be getting together mid October to meet each other in hopes that the newbies might strike up a friendship or two. That would free up the four friends to go out and "save" some other poor souls. Claire's words, not Destiny's.

Claire shook her head clear and berated herself again. When had she become so sarcastic and negative? She would like to think it was since the start of her parents' nasty divorce, but she knew her biting comments and snippy remarks had been developing long before that. She wasn't being fair to Destiny or her friends. Destiny had been nothing but nice to her, and the two had the start of a nice friendship. Destiny had wanted Claire to know that she was not abandoning her but just seeking out others who might need friends.

Claire was actually fine with it. She and Quintin had struck up a friendship, and he had joined her and Destiny for lunch a couple of times. However, right now it looked like she might, out of courtesy, have to have lunch with this brood for a couple of days. Claire sized up each one of them and knew instantly why they had been selected.

Courtney was five feet high and three feet wide. That right there made her an outsider. High school was no place for fat people. High school was all about fitting in: same body style, same haircut, same clothes, same jokes, same slang, same worldview. Any deviation from *any* of those, and you could kiss having friends and escaping ridicule goodbye. Though most outsiders seemed to gravitate to each other and form their own little clans, that didn't save them from the contempt or deprecating jokes of the "in" population.

Colton was all about being punk, which seemed odd to Claire. First, because punk was a little out of style, kind of like grunge, but maybe it was making a comeback. But what Claire didn't realize until she saw Colton was that all the punkers she had ever known were white kids. She couldn't even remember seeing a black punker on MTV, in the movies, *or* in a magazine. They must be out there because here was Colton, but ... and she screwed her mouth up in thought ... black punk just didn't seem to work, meaning that Colton really *did* want to be an outsider.

Then there was Mason. A kid couldn't look geekier. He was right out of classic TV, the spitting image of Urkle from *Family Matters* minus the suspenders: from the dorky shoes to the high water pants to the buttoned up shirt.

So that's the group, she thought, *minus me.* She complimented herself on being the odd man out, the normal one, the one *they* were looking at and wondering how they got so lucky to eat with someone like her. Why was someone so normal looking a part of this group? But her own thoughts made her pause. *I wonder what they* do *think of me?* she thought. *I wonder if they're trying to guess what's wrong with me?*

Her initial thoughts didn't please her. She knew she rarely smiled anymore, so by this time her face had probably frozen into a perpetual scowl. That wasn't good. What else? She looked down at her clothes. They were okay, but she hadn't taken the time to iron a few of the wrinkles out because lately she hadn't cared how she looked. Whom did she have to impress? And her hair ... hmmm. More of the same ambivalence there. So maybe she did fit in with this group. Bummer. What a thought. The conversation caught her attention.

"I'm from Louisiana," Courtney was telling the others. "Moved here this summer because my parents divorced." Claire's eyes narrowed as she watched and listened to the other girl. The story had a familiar ring to it.

"I didn't want to move," she confessed. "This is my senior year. Some of my friends said I could live with them this year, but my mother said no. A family stays together. What a laugh that is. *Our* family didn't stay together." Claire recognized the pain hidden behind Courtney's sarcastic veneer. Claire could have been saying those words. She looked at Courtney more closely. She had a pretty face.

"So what did you do?" Punker Colton asked the question, which surprised Claire. She didn't think punkers were interested in anyone but themselves and their counterculture—in this case a counterculture of one. *No, that was just you who thought that, Claire,* she reminded herself. Now she studied Colton more closely. Beneath all that punk makeup and that weird purple, spiked mohawk was a very young face. He tried to look hard, but there was a vulnerability to it, and obviously a sensitive heart.

"I ate," Courtney confessed. "Then I ran away. Then I came home. Then I ate some more. Don't let me kid you. I was never skinny, but I also wasn't this fat. This was my revenge on my mother for making me move here."

Colton nodded. "Yeah, I get ya," he said, "just moved here this year myself." And Claire suddenly realized that his punk attire was born out rebellion as well.

Two birds of a feather, Claire thought. *They just chose different feathers.* She turned her attention to Mason. *Okay, little man. What's your story?* She didn't have to wait long. "What about you, Mason?" William prodded. "What's your story?"

"Well, I've lived here my whole life," Mason confessed, "and I have friends, but they are still in eighth grade. I got moved ahead in the fourth grade, but never really fit in with those kids. They thought I was trying to be better than they were, so I'm just riding this year out until my friends get here next year."

Claire listened to the ring of another too familiar story. "And you, Claire?" Jason asked. "What brings you to Montgomery High and our little group?"

Claire looked at the others who were waiting expectantly. What should she say? She hated thinking she fit in with this group of misfits, but ....

"A divorce," she said, looking straight at Courtney, "rebellion," she added, nodding toward Colton, and then focused on Mason, "and a desire just to 'ride a couple of years out' until I can get on with my life. So it looks like I fit in just fine."

* * * *

"Now *that's* what I'm talking about."

Quintin held the sheets of paper up to his chest so that all could see and pointed to the large A printed on the bottom of the page, all the while nodding his head in approval. As soon as Martha had handed them their group project back, Quintin had snatched it up and flipped right to the final page to see their grade. It was all that he had hoped for.

Violet pursed her lips and squinted, trying to read the fine print under the grade. "What did Mrs. Richards write below the grade?" she asked.

Quintin turned the paper around so he could see it, read through the lines, and then flipped it back around. "Nothin' important," he said, shrugging. "Anyways, it doesn't matter. We got an A."

Violet reached for the papers and pulled them out of Quintin's hand.

"It *does* matter," she said and then lowered her voice to a grumble, "and there's no such word as 'anyways.'"

Claire glanced at Violet in surprise. "There isn't?" she asked.

Violet shook her head. "Lazy high school English." She flipped to the page that had the grade and read the writing aloud. "Overall a very well written and thorough understanding of the transcendental period. Also, each section showed original thought regarding man's innate goodness and the negative influence of the city. There were periods of loose writing and a few too many grammatical errors in parts—," Violet paused briefly to look up at Quintin who chose not to engage eye contact, "but overall extremely well done. Your visual component surpassed all expectations."

Claire felt herself redden at the last comment, remembering the day the class had seen their presentation. Complete silence, and then low murmurs followed by lots of looks. Claire knew the reactions were mixed. Some were in awe, others discouraged because now their efforts would be measured against hers, and a few downright hostile, thinking she was showing off and showing them up. Her own group didn't mind and chimed in now.

"Knew it was going to be a hit," Quintin said, smiling and throwing her a wink.

"It was excellent, Claire. I don't think anyone had ever seen anything so professionally done," Violet said sincerely, and Claire felt her blush deepen.

"Always good to think outside the box on these things," said Blake. "Always pays off. Good job team."

Blake turned away and headed back toward his desk, catching Claire by surprise.

"Don't mind him," Violet said. "He always does that. Once a project or assignment is over, he is on to the next one and new people, so don't take it personally." Claire shook her head to let Violet know she hadn't. "I, on the other hand," Violet continued, "will work with you on *anything*!"

* * * *

"Ten. Twenty. Thirty. Forty. Fifty. Sixty. Seventy. Eighty."

Gabriel watched as Mr. Gregory counted the ten-dollar bills into his hand. He had never seen so much money at one time. He knew he was going to be paid five dollars an hour for two hours a day and four days a week. He also knew he would be paid every two weeks, so he *knew* how much money he was going to earn. Heck, he was a math whiz! Still, once he saw it in his hand, his hand began to shake, and he clutched the money a bit tighter to steady it. Eighty dollars. All at once. A smile played on the corner of his lips until he couldn't hold it back, and then he broke out in a big grin.

"Thank you, Mr. Gregory," he said.

The teacher smiled. "You're welcome. You've done good work. I'll see you next week."

"Yeah, see you," he said and moved away.

Gabriel stared at the money clutched in his fist and slowly open his fingers. He went over to a desk, laid the money down, and slowly smoothed out each bill. Wow! What he could do with this money! First, he would get Ruthie and him some food, maybe even go out and eat somewhere. That would be neat. Then he really needed to wash their clothes in a real washing machine. He had passed a couple of laundromats but hadn't paid attention to how much it cost to wash clothes. Plus, he had never washed clothes before, but he couldn't imagine it was that hard.

But he needed to wash all their clothes, so what would they wear? His eyes suddenly widened in excitement, and he looked down at his money. He would buy them each one new outfit. He was sure eighty dollars would be more than enough, and wouldn't Ruthie be surprised. That's it! he thought, caught up in his own excitement. He would take her shopping tomorrow to buy new clothes.

Gabriel folded the money carefully and shoved it into his pants' pocket when one more thought hit him. Maybe he could even buy a flashlight and then he could return the one he "borrowed." He pulled his lips into a thin line of determination. He had a plan.

* * * *

Martha leaned back in her desk chair and let out a long breath. She could hardly believe school had been in session for over a month. Though it hadn't gone quite the way she had planned, leisurely and uneventful, it had gone quickly and had already had its fair share of successes, one being the apparent change of attitude in Claire Middleton.

Martha knew better than to perform a victory dance just yet. She had been in teaching long enough to know that early success could turn sour without warning. She had also been a Christian long enough to know when to step back, let go, and let God take over. Though she had rearranged her curriculum and manipulated the groups in order to somehow engage Claire and make her feel welcomed, that was all she was going to do. After that, it was up to Claire, and so far, the young woman seemed to be responding. Martha was ready for a bit of rest now, but she was taking no chances. Claire would continue to be on her radar and her prayer list until the last bell of the school year rang.

Chapter 20

*D*estiny stood at the starting line, taking deep breaths to steady her heartbeat. She was ready. She had been training hard these past two weeks, and she could sense the added strength in her legs. She took another deep breath, shook out her arms, and stretched her neck muscles left, then right, then in a three-sixty. She was already loose and warm. These moves were just to calm her nerves. Though this was just the first league race of the season, already there were college scouts wandering the course ... and they were here to watch her. Central did not boast of a strong team, so Destiny wasn't going to be pushed, but they had come anyway. They wanted to see how she started the season. She was also sure they were curious to see how much she might improve by the season's end.

She heard the horn, and the runners moved in and readied themselves.

"Take your marks!"

Destiny leaned forward, her body taut and ready to explode.

"Beeeeep!"

Destiny was off. It was important in this first hundred-yard straightaway across the open field that she get ahead of the pack and get some distance between her and the others before the course narrowed. Once a runner got caught up in the middle of the pack, she could lose precious time and end up a significant distance behind the leaders. By the time Destiny reached the trail, she had already put the field a good fifty feet behind her. She kept up this pace for another hundred yards, and then she dropped back into what felt like her first-mile pace. She wanted to run a 5:39 for this mile, one second faster than the end of last year.

By the half mile mark, her breathing had become regular as she moved from anaerobic to aerobic running, her lungs expanding and contracting easily. She went up the small rise and then rounded the corner taking her toward the mile mark. She saw people lining the course, and she knew some of them were cheering for her, but the voices faded into the background. All she heard was her own breathing and self-talk, taking her through the run.

Cross country was a strategically individual sport. A runner had to stay within herself. Teams did play all sorts of head games, hoping to draw another runner out of her comfort zone and then capitalize on that mental error. Some teams would sacrifice a runner by having her be the rabbit. Her job would be to set an unbelievably fast pace for the first mile, hoping to force the top runners to keep up with her, thereby having them burn more energy that first mile than they normally would and consequently burn out or be so exhausted by the last half mile that they wouldn't have any kick left. Destiny had fallen for such a ploy last year, but she wouldn't this year. She had worked hard on her mental approach all summer, and this was the perfect race to practice. No one was around her, no one would be pushing her, and she could run the race she had penciled down on paper and committed to memory. She would soon find out.

"FIVE THIRTY-NINE!"

Destiny heard her coach yell the time as she crossed the mile mark and gave a slight smile. Mile one was in the books and right on time. Only two more to go.

* * * *

"What kind of camera is that?"

Claire, though used to the question by now, sighed wearily. "A Canon D Mark III."

"Nice."

"You familiar with it?" Claire asked.

"Yup. Used an older version of it at my old school."

The response surprised Claire, but she didn't have time to question Colton just now. She had parked herself at the two mile mark because it gave her a great view of the runners coming toward her, and through her lens she could see the first runner round the bend and come into view.

Has to be Destiny, she thought. Destiny had said Central didn't have a strong team. She focused her lens on the runner and zoomed in as much as she could. Fortunately, she had the camera mounted on a tripod, so she didn't have to worry about the tiniest of movement causing a blur. She followed the progress of the runner up the next incline before she lost her. She stood up, grabbed the camera and tripod and repositioned herself to catch Destiny coming straight toward her.

"Whacha gonna do with the video?" Colton asked. Claire silently prayed he would shut up. She was trying to concentrate and really didn't want to discuss her personal projects with anyone, especially someone she had known for less than a day.

"Haven't decided," she answered vaguely.

"Hmmm. Gonna put music to it?"

Claire swore under her breath and didn't answer. Maybe then he would get the hint that she was busy. Colton waited, not repeating the question, while Claire filmed Destiny coming toward them and then whizzing past. Claire swung the camera with her, hoping she had moved it smoothly enough not to blur.

"Wow. She's fast," Colton said under his breath. "You gonna try and get her at the finish line?"

"I would like to," Claire replied.

"If I carry your bag for you, we might make it," he said.

Claire's initial reaction was to stubbornly refuse, but she really did want the finish and Colton was just trying to help.

"Thanks," she said smiling as she reduced the tripod legs so she could carry it and the camera more easily. Colton grinned and grabbed her bag.

"RUN!" he said and started jogging across the open field toward the finish.

Claire moved her legs into a fast walk and then into her best effort of a run, trying to keep up with the purple mohawk.

* * * *

"FIVE THIRTY-FOUR!"

Destiny couldn't believe it. She had run two perfect miles. One more and she would have successfully shaved off three seconds from her best time last year in this her first meet.

She had seen Colton first. Who could miss that purple mohawk? Then she had seen Claire with her camera, and she had warmed inside. Claire was turning into a good friend. But that was a thought for another time. Right now, she had a third mile that needed to be run in 5:29, and she couldn't see why she shouldn't do it. Her legs still felt strong, and she knew she had a kick left. She shifted into a half gear higher, turning up the speed one more notch.

*   *   *   *

Colton reached the finish line first. That was a no brainer. Claire hadn't run since freshman PE and was carrying a camera on a tripod. By the time she arrived at the finish line, she was gasping for air. From the corner of her eye she could see worried looks cast her way, but she refused to acknowledge them. She set to work telescoping the tripod legs back out, securing them, and then swinging the camera into position. Perfect. Destiny was just coming out of the trees and toward the finishing chute.

*   *   *   *

Destiny broke out of the trees and onto the open field. One hundred yards stood between her and the finish line and a new personal best. She knew she had run a good race and felt she was right on track, but she still had a bit more in the tank. She might be able to shave off one more second if she tried.

The waving banners of the finishing shoot were a blur as

she sped by them. The ribbon was quickly approaching. Destiny extended her stride, straining forward until fifteen yards later she leaned forward and broke the tape. A broad smile broke across her face as she decelerated.

She heard the snap before she felt it. Then her whole leg gave way, and she collapsed to the ground, grabbing her ankle in excruciating pain. She rolled back and forth, clenching her teeth yet screaming through them. What had happened? What had she done?

* * * *

Claire stood up behind her camera and just stared in shock, her mouth dropping open. Colton did the same. What had just happened? While they stood paralyzed, watching Destiny writhe in pain, coaches and trainers were hustling to her side. Soon she was obscured from their view.

"What happened?" It was Mason. Claire shook her head.

"I don't know. One minute she is running toward us, winning the race, and the next ...," she stopped, just staring at the crowd that had managed to move Destiny out of the way of the incoming runners but still hid her from view.

"The next she was on the ground, grabbing her shin and screaming," Colton finished. "Well, sort of screaming."

"What happened?" Now it was Courtney. She was puffing hard, trying to catch her breath. Claire wondered how far away she had been to be so breathless. It couldn't have been *that* far.

"Destiny's hurt," Mason answered succinctly, "but no one knows what happened."

The four of them watched intently, waiting for any indication that might mean they would get an answer soon. Some people stood and moved away. A handsome black couple hurried toward the huddle.

Must be her parents, Claire thought.

Soon the crowd stood up and moved back, and the handsome man and another man, probably a trainer or her coach, put one of Destiny's arms around each of their shoulders and started walking her away from the finishing area and toward the parking lot. Claire watched, her camera all but forgotten. But what she would never forget was the look of total and utter despair on Destiny's face as she passed.

* * * *

Gabriel was crestfallen. His grand plan of taking Ruthie shopping and buying her a new outfit had failed miserably. He thought eighty dollars would go a long way, but after he had bought bread, peanut butter, fruit, soap, shampoo, and laundry detergent, he had only sixty-five dollars left. Since he didn't have a refrigerator, he could only buy a little meat at a time, which meant he would have to buy fresh every day. He thought about buying an inexpensive can opener so he could buy chicken and tuna, but he would wait a couple of days first and see how his money held out.

Then it was time for clothes. He hadn't wanted to waste money on the buses to get out to Walmart or Shopko, so they had found a little store near them. Though a shirt was only fifteen dollars, it was fifteen dollars too much, and Gabriel told Ruthie they would keep looking. He was so discouraged and tired he wanted to cry, but he couldn't. He couldn't let Ruthie know how defeated he felt.

"Where are we going now, Gabriel?" she asked expectantly. He tried to smile as he looked down at her, but he didn't know what to tell her. They still had to wash their clothes, and he had no idea how long that would take or what they would wear in the meantime. What a way to spend a Saturday. He shifted the shopping bag to his other arm, and then checked to make sure the contents were still okay. He looked back up but not in time to stop before he ran right into the back of a woman who was holding a bag of her own in one hand and a child in the other. She stumbled forward.

"I'm sorry," he said as he juggled his own bag, trying not to drop it.

"Should watch where you're going," the woman said, irritated.

"Yes, ma'am," he replied, seeing for the first time the line in front of her.

"What's going on?" he asked.

"Trading clothes," the woman said brusquely. Gabriel was confused.

"What?" he asked again.

"Trading clothes," she replied sharply. "You bring your children's clothes that don't fit anymore, and you trade them for clothes that do."

Gabriel was intrigued.

"Is it free?" The woman nodded.

"Yup."

Gabriel licked his lips in thought.

"Do you have to have some to trade?" he finally asked. "Or can you just get some?"

The woman moved forward with the line, which seemed to appease her a bit. "I think you are supposed to trade clothes," she replied, "but I don't think they keep people from getting clothes if they really need them."

Gabriel wondered who "they" were but decided it might be better if he didn't ask.

"Wait here, Ruthie," he said. "I just want to check it out." The last thing he wanted to do was to wait in a long line and then be told that he couldn't have any clothes. But if he could... he felt his spirits lifting already.

He walked toward the front. He could feel people watching him and could sense their disapproval. *I'm sure they think I'm cutting,* he thought.

"Just want to ask a question," he repeated as he walked to the front. "Just want to ask them a question. My sister's holding my place at the back of the line." That seemed to calm the crowd down.

When he was next to the door, he saw a huge poster of a man with long hair and a short beard, but very kind eyes, his arms outstretched. On both sides of him and in front of him were clothes, all kinds of food, and a lot of children. The picture was light so that the huge words printed over the clothes and food could be read. It said:

"Therefore I say to you, do not worry about ... what you will eat or what you will drink ... or what you will put on."[1]

Gabriel read the words again and then stared up at the man. He didn't know who he was, but he liked him already. As people came out of the left door, more people were admitted on the right.

Gabriel tried to squeeze through.

"Hey!" someone shouted. "Wait your turn!"

He was all ready to say that he just wanted to ask a question, but he had popped inside before he could reply. He stared in amazement at what he saw—a room the size of a gymnasium full of clothes *and* people. He swallowed hard. *And all this was free?* he wondered. Or did he indeed have to have clothes to trade? He looked around quickly, hoping to find someone to ask. He didn't want to leave Ruthie all alone for too long.

"Can I help you?" a kind voice asked. Gabriel turned toward it and looked eye to eye with a smiling woman his own height.

"Are the clothes free?" he asked.

She smiled. "Yes."

He licked his lips. Now for the hard one.

"Do you have to have clothes to trade in?" He waited. She looked him up and down very briefly, and if he hadn't been so desperate, he might have been annoyed, but he needed some clothes, badly.

"It helps," she said honestly, "but it's not necessary."

Gabriel felt his body relax for the first time that day, the tension draining out of him, and his whole face lit up.

"That's great," he said. "Do you have anything for a girl about this high?" he asked, and he put his hand out to his side to indicate Ruthie's height. The woman smiled.

"We certainly do. Where is she?"

"Oh, she's outside in line," Gabriel replied, his voice light. "She's holding our place. I just wanted to see if we had to have clothes to trade in. We'll be in in a little bit. We aren't too far back." He was babbling and he knew it, but he had not been this happy in a long time.

"I'll go pull a few things that might fit her," the woman replied. "When you come in go over there to the right," and she pointed to the far corner. "That's where her size is."

Gabriel smiled gratefully at the woman, shifted his bag again, went out the door, and headed back to where he had left Ruthie. But he didn't have to go far. Ruthie had used her natural charm to work her way into the hearts of the women waiting *and* up to the front of the line.

* * * *

Travis stared at his computer screen and then pulled out yet another file and started glancing through the numbers, comparing them to previous years. The screen showed a lot of red, which meant the school missed its targets, while green meant it met them. The Detroit schools on the whole had a lot of work to do, but Montgomery High was not at the bottom. In fact, it was yellow overall, which meant it had met some targets but not others. The science and technology magnet schools did the best, which made sense, but for a comprehensive school, Montgomery High was holding its own.

Travis wrote down the current figures and then went back once again to the previous years. Steady progress. That was good. Surely this had to count for something. He glanced at the other two schools also being considered for closure. They hadn't shown as much improvement. Travis felt a tinge of hope as he wrote those numbers down as well. He wondered if Maggie Graham and Josh

Edwards, the other two principals of schools in danger of closing, had given up their Saturday to pour over years of documentation and internet data to try and give their school an edge. It was not a comfortable place to be. He knew and liked them both, and he knew they were as committed to their schools as he was to Montgomery High.

Travis jotted down a couple more numbers, and a shiver hit him as he was thrown back fifteen years. *This is just like turf warfare,* he thought. *Kill or be killed.*

* * * *

Destiny had never been in such agony. She couldn't move her foot at all without searing pain shooting up the back of her leg. There was no comfortable position. Once her leg was secured so it wouldn't move, she was loaded into the ambulance and taken to the hospital. Her mother rode with her, holding her hand and stroking her arm, while her father followed in the car. No one said anything. There was nothing to say. Dazed, Destiny just stared at the roof of the ambulance.

The emergency waiting room was packed, so Destiny was placed in a wheelchair with her leg propped up, and they waited ... and waited. She looked down toward her left foot and could not see any definition in her ankle. Despite the ice, it had ballooned. The sharp pain had subsided somewhat and was replaced by a dull, throbbing ache, but even with her ankle immobilized she was still unconsciously able to make minute movements, each one sending another jolt of pain up her leg, forcing her to bite her lip and muffle a scream. Her parents could only sit, sympathize, and worry.

Finally, someone came and wheeled her in for an ultrasound and then wheeled her back out to the waiting room. Destiny wasn't sure which was worse, the pain or the waiting.

She tried to think back to what had happened. *What had gone wrong?* The race had been fine. Her muscles were loose and warm. She hadn't overexerted. It was only when she planted that left foot.

Though the waiting room never did empty, at least the would-be patients were being cycled through and, two hours later, a young nurse came out to get her.

"Destiny Williams?"

Destiny's parents stood up quickly.

"Right here," her father answered and maneuvered the wheelchair into position.

"Right this way," she said and led the trio through a maze of corridors, rooms, and equipment. Destiny only half listened to the buzzing and beeping and talking going on around her. Once in the room, the nurse efficiently took Destiny's vitals, carrying on a one-sided conversation and reporting results, hoping to put Destiny and her parents at ease.

"The doctor will be right with you," the nurse said when she had finished, and cast a kind smile Destiny's way. Destiny tried to return it but couldn't.

The doctor seemed younger than the nurse and burst through the door with more energy than someone at the end of a twelve hour shift should have, but his eyes were friendly though his face was non-committal.

"Destiny Williams?" he asked looking her way. She nodded.

He smiled. "I'm Dr. Stowell." Destiny didn't say anything.

"Good to meet you doctor," Destiny's father said, stepping forward and offering his hand. "Jared Williams. Destiny's father. And this is her mother, Tracy."

The two men shook hands, and Dr. Stowell acknowledged Mrs. Williams before turning back to Destiny.

"You're a runner?" he asked, taking note of Destiny's uniform. Destiny nodded.

"When during the race did you hurt yourself?" he asked. "At the beginning?"

Destiny shook her head. "No, after I crossed the finish line." Dr. Stowell nodded thoughtfully.

"Did you put your foot down abruptly?"

Destiny wagged her head back and forth and wrinkled her nose in thought before answering. "Not excessively," she said. "I was just trying to slow myself down a bit. I had come through the finish line pretty fast."

The doctor nodded and wrote something down on a form. Then he leaned against the door, resting the clipboard against the front of his thighs and looking at her thoughtfully.

"Had you been working out more rigorously lately?" he asked.

Destiny's eyes opened wide. "Yes," she admitted. "The last two weeks I started adding morning weight and treadmill workouts."

Dr. Stowell nodded thoughtfully again, and then jotted down more notes.

"The ultrasound shows that you have a ruptured Achilles tendon," he told her. "That's a complete tear of the tendon. It is usually caused by an abrupt start or stop in movement, but it is often preceded by extreme changes in the intensity of the workouts. I'm afraid your extra workouts probably put you at a greater risk. The sudden stop just ... well ... was the straw that broke the camel's back—only, in this case, the tendon."

Destiny listened, trying to make sense of it all. Her working harder had been a bad thing to do? It had caused the rupture? Now what? Could it be fixed? Soon? Fast? How long would it be before she could run again?

All these questions were bouncing around her head, but none came out of her mouth. It was again her father who stepped in.

"So what does that mean?" he asked. Destiny's eyes went from her father to her mother, who was biting her lower lip and looking down at the floor, then back to the doctor. He wasn't going to waste their time or his. There was still a full room of patients waiting to be seen.

"Surgery. A boot for about four to six weeks, and then therapy for approximately six months."

Destiny heard a small gasp escape from her mother and saw her father's face fall, but all she felt was a creeping darkness begin to envelop her.

* * * *

"What do you think of this?" the woman asked, showing Ruthie a yellow dress with ruffles along the waistline and bottom. Gabriel stared at it. It looked brand new. He turned to watch Ruthie. Her eyes opened wide, and her mouth dropped open.

"I can have it?" she asked, amazed that something so nice

could be hers for free. The woman nodded. Then Ruthie looked up at Gabriel for permission. He just shrugged.

"If you want it," he said.

"Oh, yes!" Ruthie cried excitedly. The woman smiled broadly.

"Well, let's just make sure it fits," she said. "Turn around." Ruthie obeyed, and the woman stretched the dress out and laid the edge of the sleeves up against Ruthie's shoulders. Gabriel watched. The seams went about an inch over on both sides. He frowned.

"Too big?" he asked quietly so Ruthie wouldn't hear. The woman smiled again. Gabriel liked her smile.

"For now," she replied softly, "but she's growing, so if she gets it a bit big then she can wear it longer." Gabriel saw the wisdom in that and determined to remember the advice.

"Is it okay?" Ruthie asked, her back still toward them.

"Yup," Gabriel said. He was about to say they should go now, but the woman wasn't finished.

"Now let's find a couple of pairs of pants, a couple of tops, some shoes, and a nice winter coat for her, and then we'll take care of you. Follow me."

Gabriel was about to object, but the woman had already started toward another table, and Ruthie was right on her heels. All Gabriel could do was follow.

It didn't take long to outfit Ruthie, and the woman put everything in a big plastic bag.

"Now for you, young man," she said. "We want you to look as sharp as your sister. Are you a twenty-eight inch waist?" Gabriel had no idea. He had never bought a pair of pants before, and he hadn't looked at these. He nodded mutely, hoping he was close. "Well, we'll get them a little big as well," she said and then looked at his current jeans, which were rising up above his ankles, "though I imagine you are going through a growing spurt of your own and might have to come back in a couple of months and trade them in for a bigger pair." Gabriel's eyebrows rose.

"You give away clothes more than once?" he asked. The woman nodded.

"Once a month," she replied, "and next time you will have some to trade in."

Gabriel chewed on this information for a minute.

"What's this place called?" he asked.

"The event is called The Neighborhood Hanger," she replied. "The building is Grace Community Church."

"This is a church?" Gabriel asked incredulously, looking around the huge, cavernous building. It didn't look anything like what he imagined a church to look like. Though he had never been inside a church, he had seen a couple around town and pictures of others, and they certainly didn't look like this. This place looked like a warehouse ... or a gymnasium. Suddenly another thought came to him. "Who is the guy on the poster?" he asked. The woman looked confused.

"Guy? Poster?" she asked. Gabriel tilted his head toward the front doors.

"When we walked in. There was a big poster with a guy on it with some food and clothes, and it said something about not worrying about what you eat or wear," he explained. Understanding dawned on the woman's face.

"Would you like to know who he is?" she asked. Gabriel nodded. If he was the guy who put all this together, then, you bet, he wanted to know him. "Then come tomorrow morning at eight thirty for something to eat, and then at nine you will learn all about him."

Gabriel nodded in assent and then thrust out his hand. "I'm Gabriel by the way," he said, "and this is my sister, Ruthie."

The woman took Gabriel's hand and smiled that wonderful smile of hers again, first at Gabriel and then at Ruthie.

"Very pleased to meet you," she replied. "I'm Mary Montrose."

Chapter 21

The early fall sun slid softly between the blinds and into Destiny's room, but Destiny paid little attention. Usually mornings were her favorite time of the day, when everything was fresh and full of possibilities. She would wake with a sense of anticipation, looking forward to what was in store, but today she felt nothing except a numbness—everywhere, that is, except in her lower left leg. The meds had worn off overnight, but she didn't have the energy to reach over and grab another pill. In fact, she didn't really have the energy, or desire, to do anything.

Her bedroom door creaked open, and Destiny could sense someone looking in. She closed her eyes to pretend she was still sleeping, and the door closed again. She opened her eyes and stared at the ceiling, not really thinking of anything. She didn't want to think right now, and she didn't want to feel. All she wanted to do was lie there. She felt listless and lethargic, and her eyes, heavy. It could be a result of the pain medication, but she didn't think so. She felt a heaviness deep inside as well. Despite having more than twelve hours of sleep, she had no desire to get up. What was there to get up for anyway?

* * * *

Gabriel picked up the bucket and headed for the door. After his brief shopping disappointment, he and Ruthie had had a wonderful day. Mary Montrose had made sure that they each had three sets of new clothes, well, new to them, and a coat, and then had given them something to eat. They then had managed to do their laundry, so now they had *six* different things to wear. If it weren't for this bucket, the day would have been perfect, but the bucket *was* here.

Gabriel didn't use it much. That was the advantage of being a boy. He could find places to relieve himself outside before he came in, and he used the school bathrooms when he could. But Ruthie didn't have that advantage, so each morning he would pick up the bucket and empty it as he always did except for one major difference. He no longer tried to take it down the five flights of stairs. Instead, he started dumping the contents down the open space under the stairs.

At first he felt guilty for doing so. It wasn't sanitary, but it did save him from having to put the boards back on, walk quietly enough not to be heard by the other occupants, and negotiate the timing so as not to meet anyone. Gabriel justified his actions by reminding himself that the building was abandoned and going to ruin anyway. In the end, however, his actions served yet another purpose. As the refuse began to accumulate, the lower floors began to suffer as the stench increased. First the ground floor was affected, then the second. The squatters on the third floor didn't wait for the smell to reach them and really weren't that interested in finding its source or fixing it. There were plenty of abandoned buildings in Detroit. They would just relocate. So Gabriel and Ruthie finally had the place to themselves again, which meant Gabriel really didn't have to keep removing the boards, but he saw no reason to tempt fate. The missing treads *plus* the creeping odor were two very nice safeguards.

* * * *

Claire stepped into the hallway and headed toward the kitchen but stopped short at the doorway and took a step back, hoping she hadn't been seen. Her mother sat in her rocking chair reading. Most of her back was toward Claire, but she was turned just enough so that Claire could see her in profile. The morning light rested gently on her mother's face, which had a peace and calm about it. Claire looked down at the book in her mother's hands and her heart dropped. The Bible.

Why did she always read that? Claire wondered. What good had it done her? She was living hundreds of miles from her home, had given up an exciting lifestyle, and now had to work a menial job and live with her own mother in a rundown neighborhood. Claire shook her head and vowed she would never be so duped. Sure, there was a time, when life was going just as she had planned, that Claire had liked some of the sayings of the Bible. They made a person feel good. It was the way things should be. But *this* was the *real* world, not an idealistic fairy tale. Hiding your head in some ancient book was the worst kind of denial a person could have.

She started to tiptoe back into the hallway before she was

noticed, but she was too late.

"Good morning, Claire." Claire froze. *How had she seen me?* she wondered. Her mom turned toward her and smiled softly.

"How did you know I was standing here?" Claire asked, and her mother's smile broadened.

"A mother always knows when her child is near," she replied.

That's not reassuring, thought Claire.

"Come over here and sit for a minute," Mrs. Middleton said, patting a chair across from her. Claire hesitated, not really wanting to be cornered but not having a good enough reason not to sit for a few minutes, so she reluctantly made her way over to her mother and sat down, keeping her eyes focused with unwavering interest on the rug at her feet. Her mother was neither deterred nor flustered by Claire's behavior but looked calmly and lovingly at her daughter.

"How's school going?" she asked. "I haven't seen much of you lately."

The subject seemed safe enough—for now—so she looked up at her mother as she answered.

"It's going fine," she answered honestly. "The work's not that difficult and pretty interesting."

"Are you making friends?"

Claire flinched involuntarily. Now how did she answer that one? Honestly, that is. Yes, she had made some friends. One, because a girl had sought her out: Destiny. Two, because Quintin and Violet had befriended her, and three, because all the lunch losers had met each other, and she hadn't been able to shake them, though she wasn't quite sure they classified as friends. She decided *not* to reveal all of this to her mother, so she just shrugged.

"A few," she admitted, and then thought it would be better to elaborate on her own rather than be cross examined. "Most through lunchtime, but a couple from my classes." She paused and then added. "It's only been a little over a month, so that's pretty good really," hoping to put her mother's worries to rest. "Junior year can be a bit tough to break in, you know."

The minute she said it, she saw the pain and guilt shoot across her mother's face, and she wished she could take it back. "But it's okay," she added hurriedly, offering a weak smile. "I'm meeting new people every day." That last statement was a lie, but Claire didn't care. She needed to erase that look from her mother's face. Her mother visibly relaxed, and Claire could feel the tension in her own body begin to subside.

Claire knew what was coming next and decided to take the offensive, so she stood up and clapped her hands on her thighs.

"Well," she said, "I guess I had better get to work. Just came out to grab some orange juice and a bagel before tackling my homework."

Now disappointment registered in her mother's eyes. Claire knew her mother wanted her to go to church with her, but Claire had absolutely no desire to go. Though she kept surprising herself lately with her concern for others—first the boy and his sister, then Destiny, and now her mother's feelings—she had to draw the line of sainthood somewhere, and this was it. Suddenly a thought crossed her mind that might make her mother feel better about her not attending church. She turned toward her before heading to the kitchen.

"My friend, Destiny, hurt herself at her cross-country meet yesterday. I thought I would go over this afternoon and see how she's doing, so I want to get my homework done this morning."

Her mother's response wasn't all Claire had hoped for, but it was enough. A slight rise of the eyebrows over her apparent concern for someone else, a brief smile of approval, but then the disappointment. Oh well, there was only so much she could do, and unfortunately she had now obligated herself to go visit Destiny in order to get out of church. Not much of a trade, really.

* * * *

Gabriel stopped twenty yards from the door of the church, held his arm out to stop Ruthie, and watched as a stream of people made their way toward the front doors. He looked down at Ruthie, who was wearing her new dress from yesterday's "shopping" experience, and then at himself. He had on a nice pair of black slacks and the black and white striped dress shirt that Mary had picked out for him. Both of them had on "new" shoes as well.

He gazed curiously at the church goers. Though neither he nor Ruthie had ever gone to church, for some reason Gabriel had thought they should dress up. Had he read it somewhere? Heard it? Seen it on television? Wherever he had gotten this notion, it was obviously wrong. Most of the men and boys were in jeans and T-shirts and so were many of the women and girls. He pursed his lips in concern. He already felt like an outsider; he didn't want to look like one too.

"Aren't we going in, Gabriel?" Ruthie asked. "I want to show

Mary my new dress."

Gabriel almost told her that Mary already knew what her dress looked like because Mary had picked it out, but he stopped himself. His heart was pounding, and he knew it was just his nerves talking. He licked his lips and summoned up his courage.

"Sure," he said instead. "Let's go." They worked their way into the stream of people, and Gabriel silently hoped they found Mary fast. He didn't want to be standing in that huge room looking as lost as he felt.

Gabriel hadn't needed to worry. As soon as he and Ruthie stepped through the door, Mary was almost on top of them.

"There you two are," she said exuberantly, and bent down to give Ruthie a quick squeeze. "That dress looks wonderful on you," she said. Ruthie beamed.

"I like yellow," she said and then fingered the ruffles along the waistline. "I like this dress," she added.

"I almost couldn't get her out of it," Gabriel admitted, and he felt himself relax a bit. "She would've slept in it if I hadn't told her it would be wrinkled for church today." His face turned serious. "I think we might have dressed up too much."

Mary followed his eyes as he took in the others milling about, then smiled.

"The early service is a bit more casual," she explained, "but there are still some who wear their nicer clothes," and she tilted her head across the room toward some boys and girls in attire similar to Gabriel's. "Now," she said, changing subjects. "I thought Ruthie would go to the third grade Sunday school class, and you might like to join the high school group."

Gabriel felt himself go cold. He thought he was going to be with Mary this morning, not have to venture out on his own.

"I want to stay with Gabriel," Ruthie said, moving closer to Gabriel and wrapping her arm through his. Gabriel was thankful for Ruthie's fear. It saved him from admitting his own. Mary smiled at Ruthie.

"Don't you want to show the other girls your new dress?" she asked. Ruthie wrestled with the idea, torn between her reluctance to give up Gabriel and her desire to show off her new clothes. Gabriel could feel her grip tighten and then ease, and he knew her fears were waning. Now what would he do? Finally, Ruthie gave him up completely.

"Okay," she said. "I'll go."

Mary smiled and then looked up at Gabriel. "What about you?"

Ruthie had left him no option. If she were brave enough to strike out on her own, then he could do nothing less. He shrugged his shoulders.

"Sure," he said weakly, trying to hide his lack of enthusiasm. "I'll go."

Mary smiled. "Perfect," she replied. "They will introduce you to the man you wanted to meet. The man in the picture."

* * * *

"You have to go. You promised you would be there."

Travis shook his head.

"Can't," he replied. "I have too much to do."

Cecile folded her arms across her chest and set her feet in a stance that always told Travis that she was going to win this battle. Travis sighed. Maybe he should just give in now. But the truth was, he *did* have a lot to do.

"What is so important that you had to miss church this morning and now you can't meet your family for our monthly Sunday lunch?" she asked.

Travis winced. Cecile had hit a nerve. Not only did the once-a-month lunch bring Travis together with Martha, Graydon, Danny, Grace, and the kids, but it also was the one scheduled event where he saw his own younger sister and brothers if they could make it. He never knew which ones would show up, all the planning went through Martha, but at least one always did.

She won. He was going. "You're right," he said. "I'll go get ready."

"Thank you," she replied, a note of victory in her voice and success gleaming in her eyes. But when Travis turned away, worry settled over her face. She knew her husband well enough to know the signs. Quiet became insular. Thoughtful became brooding. Work became obsession. Missing church meant retaking control. Something was weighing very heavy on her husband's heart and mind, so much so that he couldn't share it yet. Cecile pulled her lips into a tight line. Whatever battle he was fighting it was one that couldn't be won simply by her crossing her arms and standing her ground. This one required folding her hands and kneeling.

Chapter 22

Gabriel held Ruthie's hand as they walked home from church, half listening to what she was saying.

"And then after the story, we all got to color what we thought Joseph's coat looked like. This is mine. Do you like it?" She held up a picture that showed a boy in a coat of at least twenty different colors.

"Uh-huh," he replied absentmindedly.

"You're not even looking," Ruthie protested and held the picture up in front of his face, moving it back and forth.

Gabriel flinched slightly so as not to get sliced by the paper.

"Okay, okay, let me see it."

Ruthie ceased waving the paper and placed it in Gabriel's hands. This time he looked at it more closely.

"Wow. This is nice," he said sincerely.

Ruthie beamed. Gabriel studied the picture. Ruthie's colors flawlessly flowed together, each complementing the other. Gabriel knew nothing about art, and this was just a page out of a coloring book, but somehow Ruthie had made the two dimensional boy in the picture come to life. Sort of like the high school teacher did with the man in the poster. Gabriel had learned that the man, Jesus, had died over two thousand years ago but had miraculously come back to life. Hearing how they planned to prove *that* little conundrum was enough to get Gabriel to come back a second week.

* * * *

Claire stared at the girl sitting up in the bed and could hardly believe it was the same person who had befriended her so enthusiastically more than a month ago. *That* girl had been outgoing, full of life, and optimistic. *This* girl was anything but.

"So does it still hurt?" Claire asked lamely.

Destiny stopped staring out the window and turned toward her, and Claire braced herself for an angry retort. *Duh, of course it hurts, you dimwit,* she chided herself, but Destiny only nodded, her face never changing expression, her eyes still heavy with sadness or apathy or drugs. Claire wasn't sure which.

"Sorry," Claire said. Destiny shrugged.

"Not your fault," she said and turned back toward the window. Claire followed her gaze. Now what was she supposed to say? The silence was deafening, and the gaps in responses were awkward. If she were to be honest, this was hard work. Perhaps going to church with her mother would have been a better option after all. The thought of church spurred her into a new direction, hoping to brighten Destiny's day.

"Were you able to go to church today?" she asked enthusiastically. Despite her own aversion to it, she knew how important

Destiny's faith was to her. Surely, this line of discussion would open her up. But the question neither turned Destiny's attention back toward her nor elicited a response, only a shake of the head, and the awkward silence settled around the two again.

"Was it because you aren't supposed to walk?" she asked. Destiny shook her head. "Just too painful?" she continued. Destiny shook her head again.

"Just didn't feel like it," Destiny finally responded, and Claire couldn't fault her there. She herself never felt like going to church, and for someone who had just had both her senior year and her future pulled out from under her, well, she could understand. Destiny had the right to a little self-pity. Claire just didn't want to spend the afternoon being part of the party. She tried to glance at her watch discreetly. She had been here only fifteen minutes but it felt like an hour. How long did she have to stay before it was okay to go? Destiny saved her.

"You have things to do?" she asked.

Not really, thought Claire, but it was an out.

"Just some homework," she lied and felt her stomach twist in guilt. Destiny nodded.

"I understand. Not much fun sitting around watching someone lie in bed."

Got that right, Claire thought, but held her tongue. She wasn't sure what to say, but Destiny saved her.

"Thanks for coming by though," she said. "It was nice of you."

Claire took that as permission to leave so rose from her seat.

"Will I see you at school tomorrow?" she asked. Another shrug.

"Not sure." Another pause.

"Have they set the date for the surgery?" A shake of the head.
"Not yet."

Claire was getting frustrated with the curt answers, but again
kept her feelings to herself. After all, the race that ended everything
had happened only yesterday. Destiny was probably still in shock.

"Well, I'll stop by if I don't see you at school tomorrow,"
she heard herself say and wondered why in the world she had
said that. Now she was committed to another session of one-
sided conversation and sullen silences. She sighed. Well, maybe
tomorrow would be better. Maybe the shock of it all will have
worn off, and Destiny would be back to her old self. Claire hoped
so. One sarcastic, morose, cynical person in the room was enough,
and she already had dibs on it.

* * * *

Gabriel stopped abruptly. *What is* he *doing here?* He and Ruthie
had just crossed the street and started up the sidewalk toward
the picnic tables when he saw him—Mr. Johnson—the principal.
Gabriel swallowed hard and felt his skin grow cold. Was he in
trouble? Had Mr. Johnson found out about the flashlight, and had
Mr. Richards invited him to confront him.

When he failed to move, Ruthie pulled on his arm.

"Come on, Gabriel, I want to show Mrs. Richards my new
dress." Despite Gabriel's earlier protests, Ruthie had insisted on
wearing the yellow dress to the picnic.

"But you'll get it dirty," he had said. "You know how you like
to play."

"I'll be careful," Ruthie had countered. Gabriel had tried a few more tactics but then gave up. Ruthie was headstrong, and he really didn't want to fight with her anyway. A part of him wanted the Richardses to see the new dress, too. It showed he was taking care of his sister. But that was before he saw Mr. Johnson.

When he still failed to move, Ruthie let go of his hand and started running toward the picnic table.

"Ruthie! Come back!" Gabriel shouted, but he knew it was too late. Ruthie wouldn't come back, and his own yelling had alerted the family that they had arrived, and they all turned to look toward them. Even from this distance, Gabriel could see the young Mrs. Richards smiling and opening her arms to give Ruthie a big hug. Young Mr. Richards smiled as well and gave her hair a tousle. The older Richards couple was gathering around, too. Ruthie was suddenly the center of attention and loving every minute of it.

Gabriel felt his shoulders go limp. There was nothing he could do now but catch up. He walked reluctantly toward the small group. Besides Mr. Johnson, there were two other ladies there who hadn't been there last time. Both his curiosity and his suspicions were aroused. Within a couple of minutes he was at the table. Everyone smiled—except Mr. Johnson. He had a scowl on his face and didn't seem to notice Gabriel.

"Gabriel, Ruthie was just saying how you took her shopping and got her this beautiful dress," Grace Richards commented, and Gabriel could see the unspoken praise in her eyes.

"Well done, Gabriel," Danny said and gave the boy's shoulder a squeeze. Gabriel looked up. Danny's smile and look of pride made Gabriel feel warm all over and ease some of his fears. Maybe he wasn't in trouble. But then he looked at Mr. Johnson, who was still frowning and looking right through him.

"You know your principal, Mr. Johnson, don't you, Gabriel?" Danny asked.

Gabriel just stared at Travis, who for the first time seemed to notice him. Travis's eyebrows rose in surprise, and then he smiled.

"I'm sorry, Gabriel. I had something on my mind. Yes, Gabriel and I have met. He is one of our best math tutors."

Now Gabriel was both completely surprised *and* confused. Mr. Johnson knew all about him tutoring, and if Mr. Johnson wasn't here about the flashlight, then what was he doing here? He didn't have to wait long for an answer.

"Mr. Johnson lived with my family for a few years, so I guess you could say he is family," Danny explained. "This is his wife, Mrs. Johnson." Gabriel looked at the woman Danny was nodding toward. She wasn't a very pretty lady, but she had a soft face and kind eyes. Gabriel liked her immediately. "And this is Mr. Johnson's sister, Jasmine," Danny added. Gabriel turned to look at the other woman, who was a few years younger than Mr. Johnson's wife, and Gabriel felt his heart flip. While Mr. Johnson's wife was rather plain, his sister was stunningly beautiful and wore the most eccentric but exciting dress he had ever seen. It reminded him of a traditional African dress, with all the bright colors and folds of cloth. Only hers was uniquely different.

Gabriel nodded in acknowledgement. "How—" he began and then caught himself. Travis looked at him and grinned.

"My question exactly," he said, and Gabriel felt a flash of

warmth flow through him. Mr. Johnson knew what he was thinking. "Show him, Jasmine," he prompted. "Show him how you put it on."

Gabriel suddenly felt embarrassed. Surely, she wasn't going to take her clothes off here, was she? He panicked.

"That's okay," he said quickly. "You don't have to."

Jasmine laughed. "Don't worry. I have shorts and a tank top underneath. A lot of people want to know how I get in and out of this contraption." With that, she began weaving her arms in and out, fabric moving every which way, and in a matter of seconds, Jasmine stood before them in shorts and a tank top. "Now to put it back on," she said and started the process in reverse. Gabriel wasn't sure this was helping at all. When Jasmine was all put back together, he was just as mystified as when she had started. He looked up at Travis, his mouth open, and Travis let out a hearty laugh.

"Don't ask me," he said between laughter. "I am as confused as you are, young man."

"I think your dress is beautiful," Ruthie interjected, and Gabriel was glad for the reprieve.

"Why thank you," Jasmine replied. "I designed it."

Gabriel's mouth dropped open again. A person had to know geometry to create something like that with all those angles and folds.

"Jasmine went to college to study fashion," Travis explained, "and now is hoping to be a famous fashion designer."

"But in the meantime, I have to sell clothes at Penneys to make ends meet."

"I think you should be a model," Gabriel blurted, and then felt himself burn from embarrassment. Why did he say that? She would think him a foolish teenage boy.

But Jasmine let the enamored adolescent tone go right on by and chose to focus just on the compliment. "Thank you," she said smiling. "I have tried it, but it is a very demanding job, and a model has to watch what she eats *and* doesn't get to keep the clothes. Neither of those suits me. I love my food and my fashion."

Gabriel felt more at ease now. "Did you make the jewelry too?" he asked.

"I did! Thank you for noticing."

Gabriel smiled in spite of himself and relaxed even more.

"Can I take Abigail to the swings?" Ruthie asked.

"Yes! Yes!" said Abigail excitedly, and shoved her hand inside Ruthie's. Grace hesitated and looked at her husband.

"I promised Matthew I would be his goalie while he practiced his penalty kicks," Danny said, answering her silent question. Gabriel saw his chance to be helpful.

"I'll watch them," he volunteered. Grace looked at him, grateful.

"Thank you," she said and then added. "You'll need to keep a close eye on Abigail. She is a little daredevil."

Tell me about it, Gabriel thought, glancing at his own sister. *But I think she has met her match.*

* * * *

Travis smiled as he watched the two girls sprint toward the swings and Gabriel hustle to keep up with them. *That boy has his hands full,* he thought ruefully. He pursed his lips and furrowed his brow as another thought came to him.

"Where are Gabriel and Ruthie's parents?" he asked.

"They live just with their mother," Martha answered, "and she works on Sunday."

Travis chewed on this thought as he watched Gabriel slow Ruthie down and settle Abigail in the swing. "Didn't Ruthie say Gabriel got her the dress?"

Martha stopped setting the table and looked over at him. "She did," she agreed. "Why?"

Travis didn't say anything for a moment then shook his head. "Not sure, but you would think her mother would take her shopping, not her brother."

Martha laid the fork in her hand down and smiled.

"You would think," she said, "but I know *another* boy who was more likely to take *his* sister shopping than his mother was," and she looked right at him.

"Amen to that," Jasmine added and gave her big brother a hug.

Travis allowed an embarrassed smile to escape. "Okay, I get it," he said. *But my mother didn't work, and my mother didn't care,* he added to himself. If Gabriel's story was true, then this was just another piece that didn't make sense.

* * * *

"I said you would get your dress dirty."

Ruthie looked down at her yellow dress that had grass, dirt, and potato salad stains all over it.

"Sorry," she said, hanging her head, and Gabriel immediately felt bad for saying something, but he worried about the stains, not knowing if they would come out. Still, he didn't want to spoil Ruthie's day. The dirty dress was proof that she had thoroughly enjoyed herself. It was also proof that they had kept Gabriel on his toes. After the swings, the girls had run to the merry-go-round again, and Ruthie had insisted on pushing Abigail until Abigail was moving so fast that Ruthie missed her grip and fell to the ground. Gabriel was afraid Ruthie would get hit or Abigail would fall off, or both. He managed to slow it down, but now had bruises on both wrists from where the merry-go-round had hit him before he could grab hold.

Then the two started playing hide-and-go-seek with each other, and when Gabriel turned for just a second to see if lunch was ready, they both had disappeared from sight. He was frantic. Where could they have gone? He had taken his eyes off of them for only a fraction of a second. His heart pounded in his chest, but he didn't want to yell out their names. He didn't want Mr. and Mrs. Richards, nor Mr. Johnson, to know he had lost them. He turned a three-sixty as quickly, yet as thoroughly as he could. Nothing. Now his breathing was caught in his throat. He did it again, and this time, he caught a fleeting swath of yellow flutter from behind the trunk of red maple not more than fifteen yards away. He felt his breath come back and his nerves calm as he walked toward it. The trunk looked too small to hide both girls, but when he drew closer, he could hear whispering and giggling. Then a head popped out, saw Gabriel, and pulled back in.

"Ruthie!" Gabriel said sharply but under control and not too loudly. Ruthie came out from her hiding place. "Don't ever do that again! You scared me half to death, and if Mr. and Mrs. Richards had been looking for you two, I wouldn't have known what to say!"

Ruthie looked mildly contrite, but her mischievousness was still shining in her eyes.

"We fooled you, didn't we?" she said with glee, and he saw that Abigail was grinning from ear to ear and clapping her hands in delight.

"You did," he admitted, "but I don't think it's a good thing to be teaching Abigail to hide from people."

"Why not?" she asked. Gabriel pondered his answer before responding. Was it better to scare Ruthie into obedience or appeal to her sympathies?

"Because her parents would be worried if they couldn't find her," he finally answered. Ruthie's forehead creased in thought.

"They might think someone took her, wouldn't they?" she said sadly. Gabriel breathed easier. Ruthie understood.

"Yes, they would," he said simply. Ruthie nodded her head slowly.

"Okay," she agreed. "We won't hide anymore."

"Well, not without someone knowing you are playing hide-and-go-seek," he quickly interjected. "Then it might be okay."

A smile played on Ruthie's lips.

"Wanna play hide-and-go-seek?" she challenged.

Fortunately, Gabriel was saved from having to say no when the call for lunch came floating across the playground. The girls sprinted toward the tables, Ruthie inching up on Abigail and pretending to tickle her, and Abigail shrieking at the top of her lungs. Gabriel cringed, thinking the adults would think his sister too wild, but when he glanced their way, all he could see were smiles, except for on Mr. Johnson, who just looked at him curiously.

* * * *

Martha watched Danny watch Gabriel look for Ruthie and Abigail and a crease of concern formed on her forehead.

He is so vigilant, so protective, she thought. *What is he going to do when she is in high school? Driving? Going out?*

She saw him begin to rise in alarm, and she looked across the park toward the playground. Gabriel was looking frantically around him, and Martha's own heart skipped a beat, but all three—Martha, Danny, and Gabriel—saw the flash of color from behind the tree and relaxed. Danny settled back down but never let his eyes stray too far from his daughter. And Martha's never strayed too far from her son.

* * * *

Destiny lay in her bed and stared at the wall. She had been doing a lot of that today, but what else was there to do? The meds made her feel numb and lethargic, but when they began to wear off, the pain would shoot up from the back of her ankle into her hip any time she made the slightest movement. Even worse was that the heaviness and darkness that enveloped her was growing deeper and blacker.

Her mother had come in twice to see how she was and if she had wanted anything to eat, but Destiny wasn't hungry. How can a person be hungry when she doesn't do anything?

She closed her eyes, and even her eyelids felt weighted. She didn't care if she ever opened them again. Why should she? What was there to do but lay in this bed? She couldn't even move without pain. What was there to look forward to? Life now looked like a long, empty, dark hallway, and it scared her. She was a runner. She had always been a runner. She had worked hard to be the best high school runner in the state, and she was planning on being the best college runner. So who was she now if she couldn't run? Well, no one said she couldn't run—ever—but she couldn't run now and, after surgery, it would be another six months of rehabilitation. The cross-country season would be over, and she would never be back up to speed and ready for the track season. There was no comeback from this, not in time for the colleges to care, anyway. *Not in time for me to care either,* she thought.

* * * *

Claire placed a piece of bread on top of each of the three sandwiches, cut each in half, and then wrapped them in plastic wrap and stuffed them in the paper bag. She grabbed three apples out of the fruit bowl, washed them, and placed them in the bag as well.

"For someone who eats three sandwiches and three apples a day, you certainly look like you're losing weight."

Claire stiffened at the sound of her mother's voice. For the past week, she had wondered when her mother would question her on the extra sandwiches. Now she had, and Claire had to devise an answer quickly, for she *was* losing weight: three pounds this last week.

"Probably because I am doing a lot more exercise than before," she said with a clear conscience but not looking at her mother. "I am doing a lot of walking these days and the camera bag is not light." It was a true enough story, just not the whole story. Even with her back to her mother, Claire could feel her mother's eyes on her and waited, tense and expectant. Would she continue this line of questioning.

"How is Destiny?"

Claire let out a small sigh of relief. A bullet dodged once again, but this topic wasn't much easier. She turned to face her mother, then leaned against the kitchen counter, her hands gripping the edge behind her, propping her up. She shook her head and looked sadly at the floor.

"I don't know, really," she answered truthfully. "I think she's still in shock. She won't talk much, and she just stares at the wall. Maybe it's the painkillers she's taking, but she doesn't seem like herself at all."

"It's been only one day," her mother said. "I bet you are good medicine for her," she added in encouragement.

Claire shrugged.

"I don't know if I am or not. I really don't want to be there," she admitted. "It's hard work, providing all the conversation, trying to stay upbeat and positive." She found herself grinning in spite of herself. "Not the most natural of moods for me, you must admit."

Now Mrs. Middleton's smile broadened, and she laughed. As

much as she worried about the mental state of Destiny Williams, she was celebrating the breakthrough in Claire's. For the first time ever, Claire was truly seeing herself as she really was.

Chapter 23

Gabriel saw Ruthie off to school and then turned toward Montgomery High. He pulled his jacket around him a little tighter. The mornings were getting nippier. He was glad he and Ruthie had good coats now, but they would need something more at their apartment, some better blankets.

He took in a deep breath and felt himself puff up with pride. He had now received two paychecks and had been able to keep himself and Ruthie clean and fed. In two more weeks he would get paid again, and then he would buy the blankets. Mary had said there would be another Neighborhood Hanger in a month's time, so he and Ruthie could bring in their summer clothes and pick out some winter ones. He was glad they could contribute some clothes this time, though theirs were pretty tattered.

They had been to church a couple of more times and learned more about Jesus. Gabriel thought the stories were nice though a bit farfetched at times: Water to wine? Making blind people see? Even bringing a man back to life. Gabriel had listened politely but finally his need for facts and figures got the better of him, and he asked the youth pastor the question burning in his mind, "How do you know the Bible is true?"

The answer came in numbers, just the way Gabriel liked them. He remembered most of them. The sixty-six books of the Bible were written by forty authors from three continents over a period of fifteen hundred years and none of the books contradicted each other but instead they told one unified story of God's love and redemption. There were more copies of the Bible, over 23,000, still in existence than any other ancient document, making the Bible the most reliable of all the ancient documents by far. There were other things, too, such as archeological finds that supported Biblical accounts.

Though the data had been overwhelming, it had also given Gabriel a greater sense of peace. Maybe because of this Jesus he really *didn't* have to worry about what he was going to eat or wear. Look at him now. He had a job, he had a friend in Mary, he had someone leaving them food but not pursuing him. Everything was working out fine. He could feel the pressure of the last few weeks evaporating. He rounded the corner and saw his three friends waiting for him as usual. Gabriel joined them, the smile still on his lips.

"The police were at your house last night," Charles announced without warning, interrupting Gabriel's thoughts. Gabriel just stared at Charles, his smile fading.

"What?" he asked.

"The police were at your house last night," Charles repeated.

Gabriel did not speak. He was trying to wrap meaning around the words. He had almost forgotten about his life of a few months ago. Ruthie rarely asked about their mother, and Gabriel rarely thought of her. Now, suddenly, she might be back in their life.

"What did they want?" he finally asked.

"Wanted to know if any kids lived there," Charles said.

Gabriel pursed his lips. "Did they say why?" he asked.

Charles shook his head. "Nope."

"What did you tell them?"

Charles pulled himself up to his full height and puffed out his chest in pride. "I told them they had gone to live with their grandparents for the school year."

Gabriel just stared at him. "Why didn't you just say no?" he asked, irritated.

Charles shoulders and chest deflated at Gabriel's lack of appreciation for his ingenuity. "Because if they asked anyone else, they might say yes, which would be the truth. I thought it better to say you guys had left completely."

Gabriel was beginning to see the wisdom in Charles's answer. If the cops thought they were safely with their grandparents, then maybe they wouldn't keep looking.

"Did they say anything about my mom?" he asked.

Charles shook his head again.

Gabriel thought hard about the possibilities of what might be going on. His mother could have been arrested. It wouldn't be the first time. If she had been, then she could have told them she had kids, but he doubted she would have confessed. They would go harder on her if they could charge her with abandonment, too. Of course, they might have access to that information anyway. Would the police know they didn't have grandparents? Well, they must have them, but Gabriel and Ruthie didn't know who they were. Do police take the time to try and find that stuff out? What about the school? Would they go to the school? It would be easy enough to check to see if he and Ruthie were still going to school. The carefree feeling that had accompanied Gabriel to the corner was gone. His head suddenly ached from the weight of all the potential problems, and his stomach felt sick. He knew that the police talked to the social services people and some of them knew his mother and him and Ruthie. He had thought he and Ruthie were safe, but they weren't. Instead, they were being hunted.

* * * *

"Why can't I go to school today, Gabriel?"

Gabriel had caught up with Ruthie on the playground before school started and ushered her off the school grounds before anyone could see them. What should he tell her? What *could* he tell her? He contemplated different answers, some lies, some truth, some half-truths. He decided to go with as much truth as he could.

"The police were at our house last night."

Ruthie's eyes grew big. "When?" she asked. "I didn't see them."

Gabriel looked at her in confusion and then smiled wanly. Ruthie now thought of their place in the abandoned building as home, which was bittersweet at best.

"At our old home," he clarified.

"Oh," Ruthie replied without much emotion. "Why does that

mean I can't go to school? We didn't do anything wrong, and we don't live there anymore."

True on both counts, Gabriel thought, but knowing it didn't matter.

"They know that mom's not at home," he continued, "and so they're wondering where we are."

Ruthie mulled these statements over. "Does it matter where we are?" she asked. Gabriel nodded.

"They don't think we should be on our own. They will want us to be with adults."

"That's not bad, is it?" she asked.

"Not if they keep us together, but a lot of families who take in children only have room for one or only want a certain age."

Ruthie listened carefully and was beginning to understand the seriousness of the situation.

"So if they find us, they might not let us stay together?" she asked, and Gabriel thought he could detect a slight quiver in her voice.

"It's possible," he said. "I'm sure they would try to keep us together, but you never know."

Ruthie was silent. "For how long?" she asked. "How long would we have to be apart?" The quiver was graduating into a slight panic.

Gabriel shrugged. "I think until we're eighteen ... or until they think our mother can take care of us again."

Ruthie let out a snort. "Like *that* will ever happen," she replied, and her cynical tone caught Gabriel completely by surprise. She was only eight. He thought he had been shielding her from the harsh reality of their mother but obviously not.

Ruthie stuck her hand into Gabriel's and began walking away from the school with determination, and then she said with resolve, "Let's go home."

* * * *

"So what should we do?"

Three sets of eyes all stared at Claire.

Why are you looking at me? she wanted to ask. *I'm not in charge.* But she knew she was. She was the only one who really knew Destiny, and, for some reason, this little band of misfits had deemed her their leader and were now looking at her for direction.

"Do you think we should go see her?" Courtney's contribution.

Claire shook her head. "I don't think so. She doesn't seem to be up for company." *Now* that's *an understatement,* thought Claire. Even after two weeks, nothing had changed.

"What about flowers? Do you think we should send flowers?" This suggestion from Mason. Claire mulled this one over.

"That might not be a bad idea," she agreed. *It would show we care but save us from sitting in uncomfortable silence.*

"I think we should pray." Now three pairs of eyes stared at Colton.

"What?" he asked, his shoulders raised and his hands extended palms upward in a questioning gesture. "Isn't that what Destiny, Carla, William, and Jason are all about? Trusting God? Just sort of makes sense is all."

Claire felt a shiver run through her. It did make sense, and that's what bothered her. She didn't want to pray.

"Have you ever prayed before?" Mason asked. Colton pursed his lips in thought.

"Don't think so, have you?"

Mason shook his head. "Wouldn't even know where to start." The two boys looked toward the girls for direction.

"Don't look at me," Courtney said. "The only time God or Jesus is used around our house is for swearing."

Now all three sets of eyes were right back on Claire—where they had started. That was the other problem. Claire knew what prayers sounded like. She had even prayed aloud during her youth group back in San Juan, but it hadn't meant anything to her. They were just words to say. She didn't think that it actually constituted praying. For some reason, she figured you had to mean what you said.

"Have you ever prayed, Claire?" Colton asked.

What answer should she give? Yes, because she had said the words, or no, because she hadn't meant the words?

"Sort of," she compromised and waited for the follow-up questions that she knew were coming. "Well, that's a start," Mason said with relief. "So what do we do?"

Claire couldn't believe this group had so readily accepted the idea of prayer as the best option. Suddenly, Claire was thinking that sitting next to Destiny in awkward silence wasn't so bad after all.

"Do we have to get on our knees and fold our hands?" Courtney asked, and Claire could see the look of concern on her face. She knew what Courtney was thinking. She would never get back up if she went down. Without realizing it, Claire found herself smiling.

"I don't think so," she said truthfully. "I've seen a lot of people standing up and praying, and some of them have their hands outstretched or lifted up."

Relief washed over Courtney's face.

"Okay then. I'm in."

"Me too," stated Mason.

"Me three," added Colton. "So how and when do we start?"

Claire just sat there stunned. *Since when did praying become a ballot measure? And by the way, I never voted!* After a prolonged pause, she let out a defeated sigh.

"Tomorrow," she answered.

* * * *

Martha stood up from the cafeteria table, smiled at her colleagues, stretched her back, and said, "Once more into the breach." Her friends laughed.

"I'm going to go teach those seniors everything I know," Paul Stout announced.

"See you in ten minutes then," Glenn Wright countered as he moved to throw his trash away. More laughter.

"I'm thinking—" Carla Gabrielson began.

"Don't hurt yourself," Sarah Minor interrupted before Carla could finish her sentence. More laughter.

I will miss this, Martha thought. *I will miss these people, this lunchtime bantering and this camaraderie.* In their own way the friendships born out of teaching were like the friendships born in the wartime trenches. You were doing battle together:

battle against apathy, ignorance, complacency, low expectations, cynicism. Somehow sharing defeats made it easier and celebrating victories made it more rewarding. Leaving her colleagues would be hard, but she was looking forward to the long leisurely hours of retirement that stretched out in front of her.

She headed back toward her classroom, mulling over her mixed emotions, and before she knew it she was there, a small group already gathered at the door waiting for her.

"Good afternoon, ladies and gentlemen," she said enthusiastically. "Ready for English, I see."

As usual the replies were mixed, and she smiled. Nothing changed. She opened the door then held it as she welcomed each student with a smile and a greeting. She felt herself easing into her afternoon routine when it was abruptly interrupted. Claire Middleton, who in the last few weeks had become, if not an enthusiastic participant in fifth period junior English, at least a noncombative one, entered head down, shoulders hunched, and eyes averted. The first day of school she had sucked the life right out of the classroom. Today, it looked like the life had been sucked right out of her.

Chapter 24

*C*laire wandered up and down the main hallway trying to kill time. She glanced at her watch. Three thirty. She heaved a heavy sigh. Another hour and a half before she could drop the sandwiches off in the alley. She could go and visit Destiny now. She promised she would stop by today, but that would mean almost an hour to fill with one-sided conversation, and she would rather have an excuse to leave. Having to get home for dinner seemed like a plausible one. Hence, she was wandering the halls killing time.

She glanced at the display cases as she walked by but took little note of what was in them. When she reached the end of the hall, she did an about face and headed back the other way.

This is ridiculous, she thought. *Someone is going to see me and wonder what I'm doing. A delinquent looking to vandalize or a loner looking for a place to land?* Both thoughts were sobering, and when a door at the far end of the hall opened, Claire immediately turned and stared intently into the display case in front of her to avoid curious eyes.

At first she just stared at her reflection in the glass, and then slowly the contents came into focus. She had glanced at this one before. It was for the theater department. Claire looked more intently at the pictures, moving from one to the other, then to the big poster in the middle, and then finally back to the smaller pictures.

"These all have the same girl in them," she said softly to herself, and put her face almost to the glass to have a better look.

The black girl in the poster looked like she owned the stage, so confident and expressive. Even from where Claire stood—outside the glass box, many years later—she could tell this girl had been good. She stared at the caption under it. "Reba Washington starring in *Arsenic and Old Lace*." Claire now looked at the other pictures with more interest. She smiled at the one on the bottom left. The girl hardly looked the same. Though she wasn't beautiful by any stretch of the imagination in the poster, she was downright ugly in the small picture in the bottom left. "Reba Washington in *To Be Young, Gifted, and Black*," it read.

"She must have been a freshman there," Claire commented to herself as she stared at the bowlegged, bucktoothed, bug-eyed girl with unruly hair. *Whatever made her think she could be an actress.* Yet here she was.

An idea was forming in Claire's mind, and she reached for her camera, then stopped. It would be too difficult to take pictures through the glass. There would be glare. Maybe she could get someone to open up the case, or maybe ....

Claire smiled and hurried down the hallway just shy of a run. As she did, she checked out the other display cases, this time taking note of their contents, and her heart beat faster, and her excitement mounted. Ten minutes ago, an hour and a half weighed heavy on her hands. Now it wasn't going to be enough time.

* * * *

Martha sat back in her chair and released a long breath of air. This afternoon was reminiscent of one almost two months ago. Claire Middleton had once again managed to change the entire tone of the class, but whereas two months ago she had injected a poisonous venom into the classroom, today she had brought the weight of the world, and her heaviness of heart had somehow subtly affected the rest of the class.

Martha bit the inside of her lower lip in thought. She wished she knew Claire better, well enough to keep her after class or school and ask her what was wrong. But she didn't. The only contact the two had was in class, and Martha's influence had been limited to assignment choices and group selection. But something was weighing on the girl.

Martha shook her head. That makes two. Travis had that same look of distraction a couple of weeks ago at the park until Gabriel and Ruthie showed up, but even then he would slip in and out of something deep inside him. She knew Travis well, but that didn't mean she would be able to get any more out of him than out of Claire. She let out a deep breath of resolve. Well, even though she didn't know what was bothering either of them, she knew someone who did, and there was no better time to talk to him than now.

She laid her hands on her desk and then bowed her head. *Lord, you know the burdens Travis and Claire are trying to carry alone.*

Remind Travis that you have promised to help him share the load. Sometimes he forgets, Lord. He's a man, you know. She paused and smiled. Then the concern returned. *And Claire, Lord, I don't know where she is in her spiritual journey, but you do, and you know what and who she needs, so I leave her in your capable hands. Amen.*

Martha raised her head, a sense of peace washing over her. It had taken a long time and some difficult experiences for her to learn how to achieve that "peace ... which surpasses all understanding,"[1] but she had. It was now written in big letters on her refrigerator so she would never forget. "Let Go and Let God."

* * * *

"Do you have any old yearbooks?"

"How old?"

Claire pursed her lips. She had no idea. "Umm. The ones that might have Reba Washington in them."

"Definitely," said the school librarian. "All four years. Right this way."

She led Claire across the library floor to the far side where the reference books were and there in a far corner was a bookcase full of Montgomery High School yearbooks dating as far back as the 1920s. Claire was relieved to see the librarian lean over and select four near the bottom. She looked at the date and did a quick calculation in her head. The oldest was fifteen years ago. That would make Reba—another quick calculation—about twenty-nine now. She gave herself a mental high five for her ability to do higher level math.

The librarian laid them on the nearest table.

"She was a wonderful actress, even as a freshman," the librarian said. "The theater was packed the four years she was here. She's in New York now, did you know? Starring on Broadway."

Claire's eyes rose in surprise. No, she didn't know, but that could add another interesting twist. She needed to be careful. Her "project" was already morphing and growing each day, and could balloon way out of proportion. She wanted to show some continuity through the years, not pay tribute to one or two people.

Claire could see that the librarian wanted to keep talking, and she could probably learn a lot from her, but for right now, she just wanted to dig through the yearbooks and get some pictures, and time was ticking.

"Thank you," she said politely. "Should I put them back on the shelf when I'm through?"

A touch of disappointment crossed the librarian's face, but she quickly replaced it with a smile.

"That would be great," she said. "Enjoy yourself."

Claire nodded her reply, and as the librarian walked away, she quickly opened the yearbook nearest to her and started flipping through it. A football page caught her eye as it flew past, and she stopped and went back to it. A full page was devoted to a picture of a receiver stretched out full length, the football just touching his fingertips. But even though the receiver's face was obscured by his helmet, Claire could tell by the intense look in his eyes as they locked onto the ball that he had made the catch. The number on the jersey looked vaguely familiar, so she glanced down at the caption:

"Alex Kowalski grabs yet another pass on his way to setting a Montgomery High School and Public School League record for touchdown pass receptions in one season."

Kowalski. That was the name on the player in one of the display cases. The guy who was now playing for the Detroit Lions. Claire took out her camera, propped the yearbook up so she could get a straight shot without any glare, and snapped the picture. She was getting more excited all the time. *I wonder if they have any old game tapes that show Alex playing?* She found the team shot and ran her finger along the names of the players until she came to the name of the head coach: Lennis Bauer. She jotted the name down. Was he still the head coach? She had no idea. She hadn't cared a lick about football until now and had no idea who the coaches or the players were or how the team was doing. She looked for the names of the other coaches and wrote those down as well, just in case Bauer wasn't around anymore. Maybe one of these others was.

She glanced at her watch and then started flipping through the pages faster. She only had about twenty minutes before she had to get to the alley. The time she had been trying to kill was dead indeed.

Finally, she found the theater page and immediately saw Reba and read the caption: "Reba Washington as Elizabeth Proctor in *The Crucible.*" Claire had remembered watching a performance of *The Crucible.* Elizabeth Proctor was a virtuous, moral, principled woman who, though loyal and kind, had a coldness in her heart toward her husband. Claire looked at the photo more closely, and she could see that struggle being played out in Reba's eyes. She snapped the picture.

"I wonder?" she said under her breath. *Did anyone tape the performances? If so, would the tapes still be around?* She scanned the page looking for the faculty director and felt her breath catch when she saw the picture. She looked closer. The woman looked younger, but—. She glanced through the names in the caption, and sure enough, there it was: Martha Richards. Claire sat down in the chair nearest her. Well, at least she knew *this* teacher was still at Montgomery High.

* * * *

Gabriel wrapped his coat around himself a bit tighter. It was starting to cool off at night. He wished he had a watch so he knew what time it was, how long he had been standing there, and how much more time he had to wait, but he didn't have a watch, so all he could do was wait and hope.

It had been a long day, a really long day. After he and Ruthie had come home from school, there wasn't much else to do. They couldn't go out or to the park or to the store. They couldn't even go to the church because anyone who saw them would wonder why they weren't in school. So all they could do was huddle down in the building and do nothing. The hours dragged by, and time hung heavy on their hands. The only pastime was to eat, but Gabriel now knew that they were going to have to ration the food they had as well as the money he still had in his pocket. No longer did they have a free lunch at school. No longer would he have money coming in from tutoring. He silently cursed his mother. She had hurt them again—this time by showing up, not leaving, if that is indeed what happened.

Gabriel peeked around the corner of the recessed doorway where he was hiding and waiting. What if the person didn't show up? Then what would they do? He was counting on those sandwiches. A brief spasm of panic welled up in him, but just as it did, a figure turned the corner of the alley, barely visible in the waning light. Gabriel pulled himself back out of sight and held his breath. What if this wasn't the person? What if they just kept walking down the alley and saw him hiding in the doorway? He didn't have a knife, and he had left the flashlight with Ruthie so she wouldn't be scared. If he had had it, he could have slammed it over the person's head or hit them in the knee. Now fear started to run through his body as he heard the person come closer. He closed his eyes and held his breath and heard himself silently pray, *Please, God. Please, God. Please, God.*

He had no idea what he was praying for—safety? Perhaps this Jesus who promised food and clothing could protect him too. He *did* know that he had probably picked a doorway too near the trashcan because the footsteps sounded extremely close. Then they stopped. A shuffle. Then the footsteps started to recede. Gabriel waited until they were almost out of earshot before he peeked his head back around the corner. Despite the light at the end of the alley, the person was too far away to make out distinct features, but he could make out some, which told him two things: the person was a girl, and she was white.

* * * *

Claire hurried away from the alley as quickly as she could. It was unnerving stepping into the deep shadows. Once back on the street, she checked her watch. Five-fifteen. Just in time to catch the bus to Destiny's house. Since she needed to be home by six-thirty, she would be able to spend only a few minutes with Destiny. She was filled with both relief and guilt.

* * * *

"Destiny, would you like something else to drink?"

"NO!" came the sharp reply. "Can't everyone just leave me alone?" Claire didn't know what to do except look up at Mrs. Williams to see her reaction, which was a mixture of hurt and concern.

Destiny stared at the television's set. Claire wondered why she had even bothered coming.

"Your mom says your surgery is scheduled for Thursday," she said, trying to start some sort of conversation. Destiny turned from the TV to look at Claire and smiled weakly, and Claire could see she felt bad for yelling.

"Yes," she answered, and Claire breathed a sigh of relief. Her head was still intact. Destiny hadn't bit it off. She chanced another question.

"What time?" she asked and held her breath.

"Ten. I saw the surgeon this morning."

Claire exhaled and nodded. This was a good sign. Destiny was offering information.

"What did he say?"

"That I was having surgery on Thursday at ten in the morning.

And he's a she."

Claire felt like she had been slapped. She clenched her teeth together as her anger rose. She didn't deserve that. What had she done? She was just trying to be nice. She resisted the urge just to get up and leave right then and instead ventured one more question.

"Did *she* say anything about how long it would take for you to recover?"

Destiny didn't turn away from the TV this time, just stared at it, and Claire wasn't sure she had heard her question. She was about to ask it again when Destiny heaved a heavy sigh and without looking at her said, "Too long."

* * * *

Destiny wanted to cry. What was happening to her? Why had she lashed out at her mother? Since when had she become so sarcastic? Where were all these feelings coming from? What had Claire done to deserve such treatment? Yet, she couldn't seem to stop herself. The world seemed to be folding in on her, and nothing was making sense. Nothing seemed worth the effort. Nothing seemed worth anything. This "nothing" was frightening.

Of all the Bible verses she had memorized over the years, the only one that came to mind was "Meaningless! Meaningless! ... Utterly meaningless! Everything is meaningless. What do people gain from all their labors ...?"[2] Worthless. That's what that verse meant. All her efforts had been absolutely worthless. She had spent years developing herself as a runner. She was known by all her family and friends and everyone at school as a runner, and not just any runner—the best runner—the next state champion–the next full-ride scholarship to Michigan State. She had fashioned her whole future around running and for what? Nothing. "Meaningless! Meaningless! ... Everything is meaningless."

So, who was she now? Her whole body trembled under the weight of the question. She had no idea. And that not only scared the living daylights out of her, but it also added another layer of darkness around her.

* * * *

Claire watched her mother and grandmother guessing the *Jeopardy* answers. How was she supposed to go about this? Do you just walk up and say, "Hey, Mom, how do you pray?" That just seemed weird, not to mention she would feel stupid just asking. Her heart was thumping hard. Why the nervousness? She had always been able to weasel her way out of a serious conversation by using her secret weapon—sarcasm—but even that didn't feel right. In fact, she hadn't used sarcasm in such a long time that she had probably lost her touch. What was happening to her?

Her mother saw her standing in the doorway, and Claire's heart did a flip. Caught. Her mother smiled at her.

"Come join us," she said, patting the couch next to her. "I bet you know most of these questions."

Claire hesitated but couldn't think of a reason *not* to join them. Despite feeling a bit self-conscious, she went to sit next to her mother. They used to do this all the time.

"We used to do this all the time," her mother said as though reading her thoughts. Claire nodded, hoping they wouldn't venture too far down memory lane.

Let's just stay in the moment, Claire thought. *Nothing too sentimental.*

She focused on the television, hoping to stifle any urge in her mother to ask further questions. Soon, Claire was into the spirit of the game, and the three of them were rattling off answers, a few of which were correct. Bursts of laughter punctuated certain responses. Claire couldn't remember the last time she had enjoyed herself this much and felt herself relax into the softness of the sofa as she waited for Alex to reveal the final jeopardy answer. *No reason to ruin a nice evening by asking a stupid question about prayer,* Claire thought, hardly aware that her mother was watching her intently and doing exactly that—praying.

Chapter 25

Martha silenced the alarm then turned back over and lay in bed, eyes closed, listening to Graydon's rhythmic snoring. After thirty-five years of hearing Martha's alarm go off at five each morning, he was immune to it. Martha laid her arm across her eyes and felt a heaviness in her soul. She didn't want to get up. She didn't want to go to work. She wanted to lay in bed until about eight and then get up and have a leisurely cup of coffee with Graydon while they both read the paper.

She took a deep breath, hoping to instill some energy, but it didn't help. She was tired. Tired of working. Tired of grading papers. Tired of being "up" each day. If the truth be told, she felt fragile, as if she could break at any moment. She was emotionally spent, and each day required more effort to get herself going. *Lord, help me,* she prayed. *Give me the strength to make it through the day.*

With that she pushed back the comforter and felt herself shiver. The mornings had turned cold, but she wouldn't turn the furnace on. That would make it too warm for Graydon. Instead she headed for the bathroom to shower and turned on the small portable heater. Between the steam from the shower and the heater, Martha began to warm up, and as the temperature rose, so did her spirits. She knew that once she got to school and into the rhythm of the day, she would be okay, but she was already ready for the day to be over ... the week to be over ... and the year to be over. She was ready ... to retire.

* * * *

Claire stood in the hallway, slightly behind the threshold of the living room, watching her mother go through her morning routine. Her mom's back was to her, but she could see enough of her profile to recognize the Bible in her lap and her head bowed and eyes close—at least her left eye—so Claire knew she was praying.

Claire swallowed hard. She didn't feel like she had slept at all last night, but wondered why. Why was she so worked up over asking her mother how to pray? Why was she asking her anyway? The other three didn't have a clue how to pray, so she could make up anything she wanted. What would they know? Maybe if she just watched her mom, she could pick up enough pointers to satisfy their curiosity.

Pointer number one: bow your head and close your eyes.

Pointer number two: ... no clue.

What was her mother saying? Or was she sleeping? That would be a good one. But every so often she would see her mother's lips move, so Claire knew she must be saying something. But what? Claire strained forward to see if she could read her mother's lips.

Nope. She relaxed and leaned against the hall wall. Now what?

"Good morning, Claire."

Claire jumped, her heart stopping then starting again. The soft voice had come from behind her. She turned to see her grandmother standing there, her bathrobe wrapped around her, and her arms folded in front. Her eyes were kind. Claire glanced back to the living room to see if her mother had heard, but her head was still bowed, and her lips still mouthed silent words. Claire wasn't sure what to do next. She looked back at her grandmother. She had been caught ... caught at what? Eavesdropping? She hadn't heard anything. Watching? No crime in that.

"Your mother's incredible, isn't she?" her grandmother said quietly, breaking the silence and the ice. Without realizing it, Claire asked the question that had been on her mind for months.

"How does she do it?" she whispered, her eyes bewildered and sad. "How does she not get mad?"

Her grandmother smiled softly and moved closer to Claire, and Claire stiffened just a bit, but her grandmother didn't try to touch her or hug her. She just shook her head slowly and let out a sigh.

"Oh, she was mad," her grandmother replied softly, and Claire realized that she had moved closer in order to keep her voice low as they both watched her mother pray, "but she finally realized that the only person being hurt by her anger was herself. Your father was miles away. She knew in order to be free and at peace she had to forgive him."

Claire turned toward her grandmother—her eyes on fire. "How?" she asked, struggling to keep her voice down. "Why? He cheated on her!" *And me!* she thought.

"That's something you will have to ask her," her grandmother said.

Claire gritted her teeth, her blood boiling, and her breath coming in short spurts, but when she turned back to look at her mother, at that profile of peace, she felt her anger leave her and in its place was a longing.

"So what does she say when she prays?" Claire asked curiously, her eyes still on her mother.

Her grandmother smiled. "Just whatever is on her heart," her grandmother replied, and without fully realizing it, Claire now had the answers to her questions.

* * * *

Gabriel met up with the other three at their usual corner and went through the routine food exchange.

"So where'd you take off to yesterday?" Curtis asked.

"Just forgot something. Had to go back and get it."

"But you weren't at lunch," Thomas said, and Gabriel could detect a hint of suspicion in his voice."

Gabriel's mind was in overdrive. "Yeah, felt sick after first period and just left." But even as he dished out his second lame lie, he knew he couldn't keep it up. They would notice he wasn't at lunch again today, and he had science with Charles, who was already looking at him funny. Gabriel decided he needed to tell them something, but what? And how much? If he just disappeared, they would get worried and notify someone, and then people would come looking for him. He already had people looking for him; he didn't need more.

"I went and got Ruthie from school and took her home," he confessed. His three friends just stared at him, ignorant of the significance. He carried on. "If the police or social workers found her at school, they might take her away." He didn't have to add, "and I might never see her again." That part they got.

"So what are you gonna do?" Curtis asked.

"Hole up. See if we can ride it out. See if they stop looking for us."

"But won't they know Ruthie was in school Friday, but not Monday ... or today?" Thomas asked. "Won't they come looking for her anyway?"

"And why are you here today?" Charles asked. "Don't you think they will come to the high school, too?"

Gabriel's head was beginning to hurt. The complications were piling up, and he didn't quite know what to do. Why *was* he coming to school this morning? First, to go to the library before school and get some books so that he and Ruthie would have something to do. He would try to teach her and try to learn on his own as well. Second, he now needed the few food items they brought each morning more than ever. His self-sufficiency was a bust.

* * * *

"What was the name again?"

"Watson. Gabriel Watson."

Mrs. Green, the secretary, nodded and typed the name into the computer, and then stared at the screen.

"Looks like he's absent today," she said, and then stared at the screen more intently. "And yesterday as well. He could be sick. Have you tried his home?"

The woman nodded. "No one there. Adults weren't sure where they were, but some of the local kids said he and his sister went to live with their grandparents. Do you happen to have their name and address or maybe a phone number?"

Mrs. Green's eyebrows rose in surprise.

"We don't have any mention of grandparents or any next of kin. If Gabriel has gone to live with them, no one told us. You said he has a sister. Younger?" The woman nodded. "Have you tried her school?" Another nod and then a weak smile.

"Seems that she has been 'sick' a couple of days as well," she replied.

Now Mrs. Green's eyebrows inched upward.

"Now that is strange, isn't it?"

The woman nodded, then added, "It is indeed."

* * * *

Unless there was a reason for him to close it, Travis liked leaving the door between his office and the main office open. It made him feel a part of the activity, and, after three years, no one thought anything of it, and everyone talked as if he couldn't hear. But he could, and he often gleaned valuable information without having to dig for it: discontented parents voicing a complaint, needy students looking for a place to be accepted, teachers grumbling or celebrating. Mrs. Green was a godsend. If she was a football player, she would be invaluable. She was constantly running interference while handing off compliments and encouragement, and then tackling the tricky issues head on. One of the main reasons Travis had enjoyed the success he had was because Mrs. Green made him look good–very, very good.

The door was open this morning, so as soon as Gabriel's name was mentioned, Travis's ears perked up, and he started taking in the conversation. When it appeared the conversation had stalled, he decided it was time for him to get involved.

* * * *

Travis stared at the woman, dazed.

"Dead?" The woman nodded. "Are you sure?" Another nod.

"Very."

"And you're sure it's Gabriel's mother?"

The woman nodded again.

"As sure as we can be. She was in the system. Drug arrests before. The address matches Gabriel and Ruth's. The neighbors said a woman by that name lived there and identified her by a photo, and those who knew the family said that she had two kids named Gabriel and Ruth."

Travis sighed.

"What's a little strange is that only the kids said the two went to live with the grandparents. The adults were a bit surprised to learn they weren't there."

Travis agreed. "That is strange." Then added. "Though some of those parents have enough to worry about trying to keep track of their own kids." *And others don't even care,* he thought.

* * * *

Travis sat in his office, thinking about his conversation with the social worker. If what she said was true, and Gabriel's mother had been in and out of trouble, then it put Gabriel's actions and reactions into context, and they were now beginning to make sense. The food exchange in the morning, the anger over being accused of misdoings, the attempt to be discreet. Even the knife made sense. If he truly was his sister's protector, then he would want to be ready. Travis slid open his middle desk drawer and extracted the knife he had taken from Gabriel that first morning, remembering the anger and fight in the boy's eyes. Travis had disarmed him and had put him at a decided disadvantage. He wondered what the boy had been doing since then?

Travis thought back to his own childhood and teen years when he had to deal with his own mother's lack of involvement or commitment or whatever one wanted to call it, and he had taken over the role of parent to his three younger siblings. He knew the weight that must be lying heavy on Gabriel's shoulders. There was one difference though, and Travis's brow furrowed in worry as he thought about it. Travis and his brothers and sister had an apartment to live in. Their mother had been abusive at times, but the four had never had to live on the streets. Gabriel on the other hand had chosen to do just that.

So. How much did Gabriel know? Did he know his mother had died? Travis doubted it. He was sure the boy had left the apartment a while ago, when his mother had been gone for a period of time. Gabriel wasn't dumb. He knew he and his sister could possibly be split up if the authorities found them, and his sister was the only family he had. Travis was also sure that there were no grandparents. So where were they, and who were these kids who were covering for him, trying to lead the police and child protective services astray? Travis knew. Boys Number One, Two, and Three. Thomas, Charles, and Curtis.

* * * *

"Do you boys know where Gabriel is?"

Travis had decided to forgo pleasantries and small talk and get right to the point. He had also decided to bring in the three boys together rather than individually, which was the common practice when trying to discern the truth of a story. But these boys weren't in trouble, and he wanted to appeal to their common friendship.

Thomas and Curtis turned to look at Charles.

So he is now their leader, Travis thought. *A void must always be filled.*

"Charles?" he asked, looking straight, but gently, at boy Number Two. The boy's eyebrows rose in surprise.

"You know my name," he said. Travis smiled.

"And Thomas's and Curtis's," he added. "You'll remember we met the first day of school," he reminded him. The boy winced slightly at the memory.

"But that's the only time," Charles said. "It takes my teachers two or three weeks to remember our names or tell us apart."

"Remember, they have over 150 names to remember."

Charles pulled his lips together in thought. "Yeah. That's true."

Travis, pleased that the atmosphere now seemed to be nonthreatening, moved to put the conversation back on track.

"So do you know where Gabriel is?" he asked again.

Again, Thomas and Curtis looked at Charles. Charles looked away from Travis and at the front edge of the desk, his lips pulled tightly together. Travis waited and wondered how much to say at this time. He finally decided to bring the boys into his confidence.

"His mother has died," he said simply. All three heads shot up, first in surprise and then in wariness, wondering if this might be a trap. Travis understood all these thoughts and gave the boys all the time they needed to wrestle with both the situation and their consciences.

"When?" Curtis asked.

"A few days ago."

The three boys looked at each other, a silent conversation passing between them, and Travis knew a part of what was being said. *Now they really will take them into child protective services, and Gabriel's worst fears will be realized.* Travis watched as the mute conversation seemed to come to an end, and all three turned back to look at Travis. Travis looked at Charles.

"No," Charles said simply.

Chapter 26

"Well, whadya learn?"

Colton had asked the question, but Mason and Courtney had their eyes lasered on Claire, and all three had their forearms on the lunch table leaning forward. Claire instinctively leaned back a little, her personal space invaded.

"You just talk to God," she said simply. The three continued to stare.

"About what?" Mason asked.

Claire shrugged and licked her lips before replying. Her heart started pounding harder. "About what's on your heart." It sounded silly, even to her. The three pairs of eyes never left her. Courtney sat back up.

"That's it?" she asked, incredulously. "You don't have to use "'thees' and 'thous?'"

"I bet you have to close your eyes," Mason interjected, his head nodding up and down affirming his own statement. "At least that's what the pictures show."

Claire shook her head back and forth, implying that it wasn't a requirement.

"Not necessarily," she said, recounting her conversation with her mother earlier that morning, "though that does help you focus just on God. If your eyes are open, lots of things can distract you. But you can pray while you're walking down the hall to class." Claire was warming to her topic. The others hadn't scoffed or been embarrassed. They were genuinely interested.

Now the other two sat upright, eyes wide open.

"That's not what I was expecting," said Mason, voicing the opinion of the others.

It hadn't been what I was expecting either, thought Claire. In fact, the whole conversation had been a surprise. Her mother, at some point, had heard her and her grandmother and looked up. Already having her primary question answered, Claire was just going to bypass talking to her mother, but Grandma let the cat out of the bag.

"She was asking about prayer," Grandma announced, and Claire felt her face warm in embarrassment. Claire watched her mother's eyes move from surprise to hope before settling into their normal kindness.

"What did you want to know?" she asked. Claire shrugged.

"Just what you say ... and Grandma told me," she added, hoping to put an end to the conversation.

"I told her just tell him what's on your heart," Grandma said.

Her mother nodded and added, "Anytime, anywhere."

The atmosphere had been nonthreatening, so Claire had ventured a few more questions, which Mrs. Middleton had answered, and Claire was now sharing. All in all, it had been relatively painless.

"I think you have to believe in God first," Colton announced, bringing Claire back to the present.

"Ya think?" Mason asked. "Otherwise, what's the point?"

Courtney pursed her lips. "So do you?"

"Do I what?" Mason asked.

"Do you believe in God?"

Mason fell silent, and Claire held her breath, hoping the question wouldn't be forwarded to her. What would she say? Did she? She was sure mad at God, and how can you be mad at someone you don't believe exists? So she must believe he exists, just where? And what was he like?

"Not sure yet," Mason answered honestly, "but I'm willing to hedge my bets. Plus, what harm is there in giving it a go? If he listens and answers my prayer, then he exists."

"And if he doesn't answer your prayer, does that mean he doesn't exist?" Colton asked.

Claire listened intently to the back and forth, as all the questions running through her own head were being asked and answered by the others.

"Not sure about that one," Mason confessed. Then he abruptly redirected his eyes and the conversation back to Claire, and Claire felt herself freeze. "So what do you think we should pray for?" he asked.

Claire released a slight sigh of relief. Another innocuous question. She pursed her lips in thought, wondering how much to tell them.

"Well, Destiny's surgery is Thursday," she began. Courtney pulled out a pencil and opened her notebook and started writing.

"What are you doing?" Colton asked.

"Writing down what we're praying for. What do you think I'm doing?"

"Yeah, I get that, but why?"

Courtney took a deep breath. "Because I don't know if I believe in God, well, a God who actually cares about a person. I kind of believe in some big nebulous, out there in the universe, create an earth and some planets God, but not sure about this one. I'm going to keep track of what happens, here."

Colton nodded. "Not a bad idea," he said and took out a pen and wrote on the back of his hand. "Keep the big guy accountable."

Claire winced at the flippant remark. She didn't think it was a good idea to mock God if you were planning on asking him for things. Mason just shook his head, pulled out his phone, and went straight for his notepad.

"Archaic, both of you," he said, entering the information. "This is the digital age."

"Okay, surgery. What else?" Courtney replied, choosing to ignore Mason.

Amazed, Claire just watched the three of them. They were so willing to give God a chance, a God they weren't even sure existed, while she ... hmmm, she what?

"Well, she seems really down," she added.

"Understandable," Colton inserted and scribbled another note on the back of his hand. Courtney wrote, and Mason typed.

"Any more?" Colton asked.

Claire shook her head. "I think those two are enough to start with, don't you?" The three looked at each other and then back at Claire.

"Now what?" Colton asked, and Claire felt herself chill from the inside out. Now they should pray, but here? Now? In front of everyone? Her mother prayed in the quiet of her home in the early morning. That seemed a better time, but that might be too late for the surgery part since it was tomorrow. Did God need a day's notice?

"I think we pray?" Mason said before Claire had to respond. "That's what this is all about, isn't it?"

"Right," said Courtney. "I'll pray for the surgery, and Colton, you pray that she feels better. Then I think between each class and at the top of every hour we all should just keep praying for both." Courtney was like a drill sergeant dishing out orders to her troops. "We do that until we find out the answers. Make sense?"

"What about me?" Mason asked. "Don't I get to pray for something?" Courtney just looked at him.

"We only have two items," she explained.

"Well, we could divide one up," he said. "Like her surgery. You could pray that Destiny's okay, and I could pray for the doctor, since he better not mess up."

"Could be a she," Courtney countered.

"It is a she," Claire inserted.

"Yeah, okay, whatever," Mason said, "but does that sound okay?"

"Sure. That will work," Courtney agreed.

Claire sat there shell shocked, wondering when her world had spun so far out of control. In fact, she didn't even recognize the universe she was in. Before she knew what was happening next, Courtney's head was bowed, and Colton and Mason followed suit. Only Claire's eyes remained open.

"God," Courtney began, "if you really are up there, then we ask you take good care of our friend Destiny on Thursday during surgery. Fix her up like new." She stopped, and there was silence. "I'm done," she said. "Your turn, Mason."

"Okay," he said. "And God, don't let that doctor mess up. Give hi—I mean her—steady hands.... Next."

Colton didn't say anything.

"Colton, it's your turn," Mason said, and Claire saw him open one eye and peek up at Colton. Claire was looking at Colton as well. His eyes were sealed shut and his face wrinkled in intense thought.

"Colton," Mason prompted again. "Are you going to pray or not?"

"Amen," Colton said and opened his eyes. The others just stared at him. "What?" he asked. "I *was* praying. Claire didn't say it had to be out loud, right Claire?" Claire shook her head, not daring to say anything. "Plus, I had some other business I wanted to take care of with God, which didn't concern you guys, so I figured it would be better if it was just between him and me."

Claire felt her head swinging back and forth ever so slightly in disbelief. How did they do it? The three of them had never set foot in a church and yet they took Claire at her word that all they had to do was just talk to God, so that's what they did regardless of whether or not they believed in him. They probably could have been more reverent. Her years in church had taught her that God probably deserved a bit more respect, but they weren't afraid to give God a try.

She glanced around the cafeteria, looking to see if anyone had been watching. Nothing. No one cared what she and her little group did. She pursed her lips together in reflection. No one maybe but God.

* * * *

Gabriel took out the apple from his pocket. Without his knife there was no way to cut it into smaller pieces to share. He handed it to Ruthie. She could have it. He went over to grab the peanut butter and was dismayed to feel the lightness of it. When he unscrewed the top, his fear was confirmed. It was almost empty.

* * * *

Martha made her way back to her classroom, taking deep breaths then releasing them slowly. She felt a twinge of anxiety. *Now where did that come from?* she wondered. *Since when have I been anxious about talking to a student?* But the fact of the matter was, she *was* nervous. Though Claire had finally shed the passive belligerence a few weeks ago, Martha still wasn't quite sure which Claire would walk through the door. There had been the disinterested Claire, the aloof Claire, the silently engaged Claire, but never the approachable Claire. She had carefully and purposefully built a very impenetrable wall to separate her from everyone around her.

True, she had worked with her group well enough and had even warmed to Quintin and Violet a bit, but her defensive posture was still very much in place daring anyone to cross the invisible line.

She unlocked the door and stepped inside and within minutes the students started making their way into the room and to their seats. Martha greeted each one, waiting for Claire to make her entrance. She had no intention of talking to her before class or asking her to stay after class. No reason to give her something else to react to during class. She would wait till class was over to approach her.

The stream of students stopped, but Claire hadn't arrived. Martha went to the door and scanned the halls. No one. Martha wasn't sure if she was relieved or disappointed. One who liked to get things tidily in their place, she had hoped to talk to Claire today to try and make a few positive inroads. However, her absence meant Martha had a bit more time to develop a strategy. Martha started to pull the door closed when it abruptly stalled, pulling her slightly off balance and jarring her shoulder. She turned, and as she pulled again, she saw Claire pulling from the other side.

"Sorry," Claire said in true contrition, and Martha released her hold so Claire could open the door. "Didn't mean to be late," she added.

Martha watched her cross the room to take her seat and realized Claire had caught her off guard once again. Not because of the little incident at the door, but because today she had a completely different attitude spread across her face—perplexity.

* * * *

Claire sat in her seat not listening to Mrs. Richards start class. She was too busy trying to figure out her reaction to what just happened at lunch. Yes, she had been nervous to talk about prayer. Yes, she had been panicking when Mason, Courtney, and Colton had decided to pray right then and there because she kind of liked her nonexistent standing in the school, and if she was going to get recognized, she sure didn't want it to be for being a whacked-out spiritual weirdo. Both of those reactions made sense to her. It was this sense of excitement that didn't. This sense of anticipation about what might happen now. If she was to be truthful with herself, she was expectantly waiting to see what God was going to do. Now what was she to do with that?

* * * *

"Will you be here after school?"

Martha had been surprised to see Claire heading straight for her desk at the end of class. It saved her the trouble of asking her to stay after but pushed her curiosity to the next level. This girl continually kept her guessing. She looked at Claire carefully. The perplexed look was fading, and the more accustomed look of resignation was returning, but intermingled with ... Martha wasn't sure.

"I will," she answered.

Claire nodded. "Okay. Thanks. I'll be back." And then she left.

Now it was Martha's turn to be perplexed.

Chapter 27

*C*harles hadn't been lying. He didn't know where Gabriel was. Gabriel had never told them. But he did know where Gabriel would be in the morning—at their appointed corner to get his food.

Charles had only offered the information once Travis had convinced him that it was for Gabriel and Ruthie's safety and that he would try his best to work with Child Protective Services to keep the two children together. He knew in reality he had no influence in that placement at all. He was sure the agency worked hard to keep siblings together but that it often came down to the foster parents themselves. Could they, would they, take both of the children?

Travis glanced at his watch. One thirty. He had an afternoon, evening, and night to get through before he would be able to do anything about the situation. That was seventeen hours too many. He had never been a patient person. Even though his life in the gang and his dealing drugs had forced him to look the part of the calm and in control leader and dealer, he had always been churning inside. He was a man of action. Waiting wasn't his style.

But he was learning to wait. God was continually teaching Travis the importance of waiting on him rather than striking out on his own too soon. Travis took a deep breath, bowed his head, and silently repeated the verse that had steadied him through the years: *Be still, and know that I am God.*[1] Eyes closed, Travis again acknowledged God's sovereignty in all situations and now placed this one in God's hands as well.

* * * *

"May I ask you something?"

Always the English teacher, Martha silently congratulated Claire on correctly using "may" rather than "can."

"You may," she replied and watched the girl carefully.

Claire seemed nervous, shifting from one foot to the other, then licking her lips.

"You were the drama teacher here for awhile, weren't you?" she asked.

That question came completely out of left field and caught Martha unprepared.

"Yes. How did you know?" Martha asked. This was not the direction she thought the conversation would go. Now her own curiosity was piqued.

"I saw it in a yearbook," Claire answered. "In the library." Now Martha was really perplexed. "I'm making a short film," Claire continued by way of explanation. "I like film. I want to be a film director, and after our transcendental project I decided just to keep filming for fun. I was in the hallway and saw the poster of Reba Washington and then went to the library and the librarian showed me all the old yearbooks, and I took some pictures of the photos. Then I saw your picture in there as the drama teacher and thought maybe there were some DVDs or videos of some of the performances that I could splice into my film for effect."

Martha dropped all thought of her planned line of questioning. She doubted this film project was the reason behind Claire's anger or hurt, or her more recent concern, or even today's perplexity. Regardless, Claire had opened up an area of her life, and if this is the direction she and God wanted to pursue, then Martha would follow.

Martha smiled.

"I'm surprised you recognized me at all. That was about fourteen, fifteen years ago. But in answer to your question, yes, I was the drama teacher, and yes there are some DVDs of the performances. Anything that was on VHS has been transferred over. You are more than welcome to check them out."

Claire smiled, a small but genuine smile, and Martha realized that it was the first time she had ever seen her smile. As one would expect, it softened everything about Claire—her appearance, her demeanor, and her attitude. Martha hesitated but then decided to take advantage of the small crack Claire had opened.

"Do you mind my asking what the film will be about?"

Claire's smile disappeared, and her brow creased. Martha worried that she had pushed too far. She didn't want Claire to shut down now. She held her breath and waited while Claire bit her bottom lip in thought.

"I'd rather not say right now," she replied, "in case I change my mind on the direction I decide to take."

Martha nodded. "Fair enough. Would you be willing to let me see it when it's all done? As an old drama teacher, you know I love every type of performing art."

Claire's brow furrowed again, and the silence was heavy. Martha waited, holding her breath. Finally, Claire nodded slowly.

"Okay. But I can't really tell you when it will be finished."

Martha smiled and let out a small laugh, hoping to keep the atmosphere light.

"Oh, trust me. I know all about that," she said. "No pressure. You just tell me when you're ready. In the meantime, I will write a note to Miss Rogers, the new drama teacher, telling her you have my permission to check out any DVDs you need. You can probably find her in the drama room now. They're preparing their fall show."

Martha quickly wrote the note and handed it to Claire. The wisp of a smile had returned to Claire's face and this time made it to her eyes. She said a quick thank you and then hurried out of the room. Martha watched her leave, amazed at the transformation that a small smile could make.

She's a beautiful girl, Martha thought, surprising herself when she realized she meant both inside and out.

* * * *

Claire clutched the piece of paper in her hand and headed toward the theater, both relieved and excited. The interaction went better than she had expected. She had never given Mrs. Richards any reason to be nice to her. In fact, she had made classroom life difficult at times, so she was surprised to find Mrs. Richards so willing to help her.

The other surprise was that she hadn't asked Claire any personal or penetrating questions. Claire had been worried about that. "Difficult" students were ripe for the picking by caring teachers, and she had half—no three quarters—expected Mrs. Richards to take advantage of this little meeting, but she hadn't, and Claire had escaped unscathed.

She chided herself for talking so much. She wasn't sure why she had blurted out her plan without stopping once for breath. Perhaps it was because she had kept so much pent up for the first weeks of school and just needed to let something out. Or maybe she was afraid that if she gave Mrs. Richards an opening, Mrs. Richards would stop her midway with those clarification questions teachers were so good at, and then she would lose her nerve and drop the whole idea.

Claire made it to the theater, pulled on the door, and stepped inside. A teacher was blocking a scene, moving one student, then another, into position. Claire watched for a moment, then shoved the piece of paper in her pocket and pulled out her camera. Past performances could wait. She had a live one on the line.

* * * *

Gabriel waited nervously behind his usual doorway. The trash can was empty. Did he come too late tonight? Had someone seen the paper bag before him and taken it? Ruthie had complained about being hungry and his own stomach rumbled and twisted in response. He couldn't remember being this hungry.

The alley was growing dim, and Gabriel was beginning to panic. What was he going to do? He'd wait a bit longer, but he knew he couldn't let Ruthie stay by herself in the room. Soon it would be too dark to look in the trashcans for food. Now he cursed the girl, for she had ruined his chance at dinner in two ways.

He finally gave up, stepped out of his hiding place, and headed away from the school and back toward home, head down in despair, but thinking. He had to do something.

At the street, he stopped, looked first right, then left, then back and forth a couple more times, hoping for inspiration, his mind in a fog from hunger. Across the street, a man exited the local grocery store, stopping to check the contents of his bag before heading down the street. Gabriel watched him numbly before an idea sparked then ignited. He licked his lips and took a couple of shallow breaths. Then the breaths grew deeper as his eyes focused and his body tensed in resolve. He looked both ways once more, shoved his hands in his pockets, and headed across the street toward the store.

* * * *

It was past six by the time Claire secured the DVDs. She hadn't felt right interrupting the rehearsal to make her request. It wouldn't have done any good anyway since she was sure the instructor wasn't going to stop practice to run and get them for her. She thought about waiting till the next day, but once she started filming, she got lost in her world as she always did.

She moved closer to the stage and no one seemed to mind—or perhaps they didn't notice her. She was able to catch some of the crew working behind the wings and others up in the sound and lighting box. She took candids, some with different aperture and f-stop settings. Claire completely lost track of time.

When the rehearsal finally ended, Claire was hesitant to approach the director. Everyone looked exhausted. She decided to just introduce herself, explain what she wanted, and then set up a time to come back, but Miss Rogers was extremely friendly and helpful.

"They're in the drama room," she said cheerily, despite the fatigue in her eyes, "and I'm going there now so no time like the present."

Claire followed her backstage and then out of the theater, past the green room, out the door, and over to the arts building. Once in the classroom, Miss Rogers opened a large cabinet, which housed neatly organized scripts and DVDs.

"Which years were you looking for?" she asked.

"Reba Washington's years," Claire replied, mentally trying to calculate the year those might have been. What had Mrs. Richards said? Reba's freshman year was fifteen years ago? Before she could come up with a number, Miss Rogers had pulled eight consecutive DVDs from the shelf, efficiently noted their departure on the checkout sheet, and handed them over to Claire.

"I saw you taking some pictures of the upcoming performance," she said nodding toward the camera around Claire's neck. "Is this for the school newspaper?"

Claire shook her head, feeling bad that she might have given Miss Rogers the wrong impression and false hope.

"No, just a personal project," she said, hoping such an admission wouldn't ban her from the theater, but she needn't have worried.

"Ah," Miss Rogers said smiling, a twinkle in her eye. "An independent filmmaker. Good for you. Well, come back any time you like, and as long as you don't interfere with the rehearsal, you may move backstage as well. It's good for the students to have others watching." And then with a conspiratorial aside added, "Just don't give any of our secrets or surprises away."

Claire couldn't help but smile. Miss Rogers was being so kind. "I won't," she promised.

DVDs in hand, she said thank you and headed for the door, checking her phone for the time. Four messages from her mother were waiting for her. Each more worried in tone. Claire checked the time—six thirty. Hurriedly she called her mother.

"Where have you been?" her mother asked with a mixture of anger and worry.

"Sorry," Claire replied, and she was. "I forgot to take my phone off silent, and I was talking to Mrs. Richards after school and then filming a rehearsal for the fall play and lost track of time."

"You could have texted," her mother retorted. "I was worried."

In the past, Claire would have been incensed that her mother wanted her to check in, thinking her overprotective and hovering, but she could understand her mother's concern. The walk home, though not dangerous, was not necessarily the safest after dark.

"I am sorry, Mom," she said sincerely. "I should have."

She could hear her mother take in a huge breath, both a sign of relief and a prayer for patience.

"I'm coming to pick you up," she said, and Claire could almost hear her mother tense up, waiting for Claire's rebuttal.

"Thank you," Claire replied instead. "I'll be waiting outside by the sign."

There was a moment of silence before her mother spoke again.

"I'm glad you're okay," she said softly. Claire paused for a moment before answering.

"I know," she said. "I'll see you in a moment. Bye." The conversation ended.

Claire took her phone off silent and slid it into her pocket before opening her backpack to rearrange her books and put her camera away. Her breath caught in her throat, and she let out a small yelp, for there at the bottom of her backpack was a smashed brown paper bag, which still held three peanut butter sandwiches and a couple of apples. Her mom was probably not the only one who had been wondering where she was.

* * * *

Hands still in his jacket pockets, Gabriel stepped into the store and looked around. One teller to his right. He licked his lips and slowly headed down the first aisle, surveying the shelves.

On his left was the produce. He swallowed hard and then looked up to find a security mirror above the shelving. He could see the teller facing him, sliding the contents of a customer's basket across the scanner. Another look in the mirror showed the tops of heads in other aisles, some looking down, some looking in his direction. If he could see them, then they could see him. He swallowed again and moved closer to the apples. Another look up in the mirror and then two apples disappeared into his pockets. He clutched his hands over them, hoping to make it appear that he just had his hands shoved into his pockets.

He breathed a bit easier now, moved away, and started walking the aisle again, looking for other things he could slip into his jacket pockets. The boxes were too big, packages too noisy, and some things required cooking. He was getting discouraged. This was a lot of stress for just a couple of apples. He turned and started up the next aisle and saw cans and jars. They might work, if they were small enough. He would need cans with pull tabs. He looked both ways and then slid two cans of beans into his pockets. Another breath of relief. *One more,* he thought. *Just one more item and then I'm out of here.*

His heart was thumping wildly, and he thought everyone in the store could hear it. He saw the jars of peanut butter at the end of the aisle and headed for them. A small one was all he needed. He closed in on the section, pulling his hand from his pocket, when a woman turned the corner. He pulled it back. She stood next to him, gazing at the selection, and he knew his opportunity was lost. He would have to be content with what he had.

He shoved his hands deeper into his pockets, turned, and retraced his steps, exiting the way he had come in, hoping to stay as far away from the teller as possible. He kept his head down, never looking to his left, and exited the store. No alarms. No one running after him. No one calling the police.

Despite being safely outside, Gabriel's heart was still pounding against his chest and in his ears, but he withstood every instinct to run for it. Hands still jammed into his pockets, he tried to look nonchalant ... and innocent ... by stopping to look casually into a shop window before continuing down the street. Once at the corner, he crossed the street and headed back to Ruthie with his haul: two cans of beans, two apples, and what felt like a year off his life.

Chapter 28

"Destiny? Destiny? Are you awake, hon? It's time to get up. We have to get to the hospital."

Destiny could feel the gentle push of her mother's fingers on her shoulder. She tried to register what her mother was saying, her mind fighting its way out of a numbing sleep.

"Destiny?" Another push, this time a bit firmer. "Wake up, dear."

Destiny struggled to open her eyes. Her mind began to clear, and the room began to take shape. Her mother's face, a mixture of love and concern—as it had been since the injury—hovered directly above her. When their eyes met, her mother smiled.

"Time to get up, dear. We need to get to the hospital."

Hospital. The word fell with such force as to push the air out of Destiny's lungs, and she felt that heaviness, which she was only able to escape by sleeping, come crashing down on her again. Her legs and arms felt leaden. Though she knew she needed to get up, she didn't know if she could. She felt paralyzed.

Get up. Destiny started. Where had those words come from?

Get up, she heard again and she blinked. The voice wasn't unkind at all but clearly audible. Destiny looked up at her mother to see if she had heard anything, but her mother was just looking at her with that same mixture of emotions. *You can do it,* said the voice, and Destiny felt a falling away of some of the weight pressing down on her. As she started to move the blankets away, she could hear her mother release a breath of relief before moving in to help her.

Between the two of them, Destiny was soon up, dressed, and out the door to where her father waited by the car. Soon they were on their way to begin the long process of bringing her injured leg back to full health, but Destiny wondered who or what could heal the darkness that threatened to destroy her soul.

* * * *

Claire lay on her bed in the darkness, staring up at a ceiling she couldn't see and thinking about talking to a God she wasn't sure she believed in.

This was the morning of Destiny's surgery. In fact, she was probably on her way to the hospital now. Living with a doctor as a father, Claire knew firsthand that midmorning surgeries began with early morning preps. Even though it was only six and Destiny's surgery wasn't until ten, Claire knew she should be praying.

She stared at the ceiling. What should she say? Was it okay to lay in bed and pray? Her mother said you could pray anywhere, but she wasn't sure that included lying in bed. Did she *have* to pray? The others wouldn't know if she didn't. In fact, when she really thought about it, she didn't think she had to. Mason, Colton, and Courtney had made the agreement between the three of them.

Claire had just been the source of praying information.

She felt a wave of relief, followed quickly by flood of guilt. Semantics. That's all that was. Truth be told, she was kind of interested in seeing if prayer actually worked. Her mother seemed to think it did. But Claire wasn't sure what she was actually praying for. Yes, she wanted the surgery to go well, the doctors to do their jobs well, and Destiny to feel better and fully recover. But there was one thing more. Claire wrestled with her thoughts, trying to put into words the deep struggle Destiny was going through, until they came to her, and she closed her eyes to the darkness.

"God," she said aloud, and her own voice startled her so much that she stopped. *Was this all there was to praying? Just talking?* She swallowed and started again.

"God," she said again. "God, I'm not sure how to do this or what I'm supposed to say, but my friend Destiny needs some help right now." She stopped, gearing up for the big request. "She needs hope, God. Please give her hope."

Claire lay there a moment longer, her eyes still tightly shut, wondering if that was it.

"Amen," she added as an afterthought.

She opened her eyes, and as the dawn's light was beginning to take the edge off the darkness, Claire's eyes slowly adjusted. Shadows began to appear, and Claire could make out the corners of the room. Then she stared at the ceiling above her, pulled herself up slightly, and squinted. *What is that?* she wondered.

The room was growing lighter. Claire sat up in bed now and stared hard at the ceiling until it dawned on her what she was looking at. Two slash marks marred an otherwise pristine ceiling. Claire winced at the reminder of her anger, resentment, and rebelliousness. But then a slight smile emerged and a peace she had never felt before washed over her, and at that moment, she knew prayer worked, for there were only two marks on the ceiling. So someone—her mother or her grandmother perhaps—had been praying that same prayer of hope for her weeks ago, and it had obviously worked.

* * * *

Travis knew how to be invisible. He had spent much of his youth in the shadows, carefully watching the activity of the neighborhoods, evaluating moves, calculating motives, and planning retaliation. This was old hat. *Like riding a bike,* he thought.

What he hadn't expected was the return of that heightened sense of awareness that had always accompanied those potentially dangerous situations. Why would that feeling return now? This wasn't dangerous in the least. *But it is important,* came the inaudible reply. *There are lives at stake here.* Travis's mouth tightened in resolve as he settled against the building and watched the three boys take their positions, waiting for Gabriel to appear.

* * * *

Gabriel's stomach growled deeply as he made his way down the stairs. He hadn't slept well. It's hard to go to sleep when you're hungry. An apple and a can of beans didn't really fill a person up. Ruthie's stomach had been talking all night as well, and she had tossed and turned but never complained, which made Gabriel feel even worse. He wasn't doing a very good job of taking care of his sister. He thought a moment longer. And God wasn't doing a very good job of taking care of him either.

Well, all that would change starting today. He now knew what he had to do. He didn't like stealing ... didn't believe in stealing ... but his world was stacked against him right now and the forces out there weren't giving him many options. Originally, he had thought of using the daylight hours to try and keep him and Ruthie up to speed on their schoolwork, but schoolwork took a backseat to eating. What did it matter what you knew if you didn't have the strength to use it? No, he would focus his entire day on getting the essentials: food, water, some blankets—because it was getting colder and colder at night—toothpaste, soap, toilet paper, and anything else they needed to be self-sufficient.

He exited the building, headed up the alley to the main street, felt one of his legs buckle under him in weakness, and his resolve grew firmer. Get the food from his friends, feed Ruthie and himself, and then get out on the street. His breaths came quicker, and his chest firmed up.

He turned the corner and headed toward the morning meeting place but stopped short, surveyed the scene at the end of the alley, and then slid into the morning shadows. Something was wrong. He could see his three friends clustered together. That was the first red flag. They were never all three there at the same time. Gabriel looked up at the sky. He wasn't that good at telling time by the sun, but he knew it was early because he hadn't slept, and the sun was just now beginning to rise. Second red flag. Why were they all so early?

Gabriel watched them carefully from his hiding spot. The three were shifting nervously, peering down the alley and then ... what? Why did Thomas keep looking to his left? What or who was over there? A coldness washed over Gabriel, and he pulled himself completely back in the shadows. Had the police shown up as he had feared and cornered his friends? Was it someone from Child Protective Services? Who was over there?

Gabriel peeked around the corner and watched his friends carefully. When all three were looking elsewhere, he sprinted across the alley and then worked his way back the few yards to the main street. Then he walked another two blocks south and turned up that alley until he reached the main road. Now he could look back up to where his friends were gathered and see who was waiting in the wings.

He peeked his head around the corner. From this distance, he could see someone standing semi-concealed against the wall, but he couldn't make out who it was. But he was in no hurry. He had nowhere to go.

Another twenty minutes passed, and finally the three boys took one more look down the alley before Curtis raised his shoulders in question and started walking toward the figure. The shadow stepped into the light and for the first time Gabriel could see who it was: Mr. Johnson. His breath caught in his throat. He probably should have been wondering how Mr. Johnson found out where he and the guys met up or why Mr. Johnson was looking for him at all. But that wasn't what ran through Gabriel's head. All he could think about was this man had ruined his life not just once by taking away his knife, but now twice by taking away his and Ruthie's breakfast—forever.

* * * *

Travis glanced at his watch: a little after seven. He looked over at the boys and saw Charles peer down the alley again before turning toward him and shrugging his shoulders in bewilderment. That was enough. Travis pushed himself away from the building and waved the boys over.

"I don't know what happened, Mr. Johnson," Charles began. "He's usually here by now. This is the first time he hasn't shown up."

Charles did indeed look perplexed, as did the other boys, so Travis knew they hadn't warned Gabriel. But Travis knew what had happened. Gabriel wasn't a dummy, and when a young man is in survival mode, every instinct is heightened and on alert. Any— *any*—variation in the norm is reason to be wary, and obviously *something* this morning had tipped Gabriel off.

Travis smiled at the boys, gave Charles a comforting clasp on his shoulder, and then shook his head slightly.

"Don't worry," he told him. "We'll find him." *And Ruthie*, he thought to himself, concern settling a little deeper now. It was one thing for a fourteen-year-old boy to try and live on the streets, but an eight-year-old girl?

"Best we get back to school," he said, ushering the three ahead of him. They headed down the street but before he followed, Travis looked down the alley himself. Where was the boy? What was he thinking? How was he surviving?

Don't be afraid, Gabriel, Travis said silently. *Don't be afraid of me. I only want to help.* And then a slight smile tugged at his lips.

How many times had God whispered those very same words to him over the years?

* * * *

Claire headed toward third period glancing at her phone to see the time: nine fifty-nine. She kept it out until it turned to ten o'clock and then clicked it off. *Every hour on the hour,* she thought, somewhat chiding herself for being so precise about it. *Could have started at nine fifty-nine,* she thought, but something in her wouldn't let her. Something about the four of them all praying at exactly the same time heightened her anticipation.

She headed up the stairs, praying as she went. *God, I think Destiny might be going into surgery now. Be with her and the surgeons.* She stopped. Was that it? Was there anything else she should be saying? She couldn't think of anything. She breathed deeply. Well, then, that was it.

At the top of the stairs, Claire turned left and headed toward her third period class, passing Mason who was coming toward her. He gave her a nod, a knowing look, and a two-finger salute, all of which caught her by surprise, making her blush and feel a bit conspiratorial. She nodded back with a slight smile, and the two continued on their individual ways, yet Claire felt a bond between her and Mason that she had never felt with a person before, like they were on a secret mission together. In a way they were, she thought.

* * * *

"Well, did you guys do it?" Courtney asked, her face stern. All three knew what she was referring to.

"I did," Mason replied. "Like clockwork."

"Ditto," said Colton.

Courtney turned her attention to Claire, and Claire could feel the heat rise to her face, but she nodded. And she *had* too. She wasn't lying. Courtney relaxed and smiled.

"So did I," she said. "So now what? What time did you think the surgery was, Claire?"

"Ten."

One looked at his watch and the other two their phones.

"It's twelve fifteen now," Mason said. "You think it's over?"

Claire nodded. "I think so. Her mom said it usually takes about an hour, maybe an hour and a half, but I don't think she will wake up from the anesthesia for another two hours."

The three consulted their devices again, did mental calculations, and came to the same conclusion: it would be about another hour before Destiny woke up.

"You going by there after school?" Courtney asked, catching Claire by surprise. She hadn't thought of going by today. She had planned on working on her film and didn't think Destiny would be up for visitors. Plus, it was uncomfortable enough agreeing to pray, and Destiny had been less than civil the last time she was there. Claire pulled her lips into a thin line and felt her resentment grow. What had she agreed to?

"I'll go with you if you want," Courtney offered.

"Me too," offered Mason.

"Make that three," added Colton.

Though the three offers should have made her feel cornered,

Claire felt nothing but relief. Perhaps that was what was concerning her the most—not knowing what to expect and having to deal with it on her own. *En masse* they could share the burden—of talking, of deflecting cynicism, of encouraging her.

Claire nodded in acceptance. "That would be great. But let me call first to make sure that Destiny is home and that she can have visitors. Plus, I have a couple of things I have to do right after school, so could we maybe meet up about four?"

The others looked at each other and agreed.

"Could you text me when you know?" Courtney asked. "We have a lot of roses at home, and some are still producing. I will cut some and bring them if we are going by."

Claire warmed to Courtney's kindness. "I think she would like that," she said sincerely. Courtney smiled.

"Right then," Colton said. "Meet at four in front of the school. In the meantime ... we keep on praying!"

* * * *

Martha watched her fifth-period class file in, smiling and saying hello to each student, judging moods, calibrating breaking points. You could tell a lot about kids just by how they entered the classroom. Some came in full of life, happy to be a part of the flow of humanity. Others came in with heavy feet and faces. Others, withdrawn or pensive. Usually, their mood had absolutely *nothing* to do with a teacher's classroom but was affected by real life—or high school life, which many students interpreted as real life, but actually could often be much harsher.

Martha nodded and greeted a few more students, and then

Claire walked in. Martha watched her carefully, ready to take advantage of a "hello" or even a nod of acknowledgement to help build upon the fledgling relationship that had just poked through the frozen tundra, but Claire never looked her way.

Martha watched her take her seat and shook her head in wonder. Claire never ceased to amaze her with her chameleonesque demeanor. Today was not anger or scorn or perplexity, but once again another expression Martha hadn't seen on the young woman's face before: concern.

* * * *

Destiny could hear the low murmur of voices somewhere in the recesses of her mind but couldn't grasp any of the words. She felt chilled and shivered involuntarily, and then she felt hands working around her, wrapping her in something. Soon she began to feel warmer, and her shaking stopped.

The voices were now getting clearer and sharper, and words were becoming more distinguishable.

"—fine … soon … healthy—"

Healthy? She felt a twinge of excitement. Did she hear that right? But when she tried to move, her limbs still felt paralyzed. Nothing was better. Nothing was healthy. She felt herself slipping into the darkness again, and she let it take her down.

Chapter 29

Montgomery High has proven itself a quality school through its rising test scores, its strong academics, its respected sports programs, and its variety of clubs. But Montgomery High is more than a just a high school for its students, for it meets more than just its students' academic, athletic, and social needs.

For many students, Montgomery High is an oasis of hope in a desert of despair. For others, it is the needed lifeboat in an ocean of misdirection or uncertainty. For some, Montgomery High has been a much-needed reality check and the pathway to the future.

Travis paused and reread the words he had penned on the pad of paper in front of him. Montgomery High was fighting for its life, and he didn't know what more he could do to save it except speak from his heart. He smiled sadly. There was a time when Montgomery High didn't think he even *had* a heart. What was his nickname in the Mauraders? Stone-bone. No tears. No remorse. Therefore, no heart. And what had Montgomery High been for him? Turf. Contacts. Money.

But Montgomery High hadn't known him—at least not the real him. He had had a heart—a very strong, sensitive heart—but the world of the ghetto had struck at his heart hard, piercing it with fear, then anger, then revenge, and he had been forced to shield it from any feeling. But God had kept a part of his heart open through Travis's love for his brothers and sister and the love of the Washington family for him.

Now Travis's smile widened as he reflected on what he had once thought of as his lost and wasted years, which in retrospect were anything but, for God had definitely used those years. He had used an urban battlefield to develop a warrior for himself. And once Travis had started reading his Bible instead of just hiding his money and his poetry in it, he had not only discovered the wealth of God's promises and his tremendous love but also a man he could relate to: David.

In David he found a man just like himself: a warrior yet a lover of words; a man hardened by the circumstances around him but with a heart that could break; a man of integrity but one who could succumb to temptation; but most importantly, a man who loved God and wanted to follow God with all his heart.

Travis looked down again at the words he had penned, words from his heart. Then he opened his top desk drawer and pulled out a book he kept there for times like these—a book of the Psalms of David. Cecile had given it to him as a gift when he had become principal.

"The words of one warrior leader to another warrior leader," she had written on the cover page. Travis had argued with her that

David had been a king and he was only a principal, and that when he was on the streets, he was fighting for drugs not God, but Cecile would have none of it.

"Both David and you were responsible for the lives God put you in charge of," she had rebutted. "It doesn't matter the size of the domain. As for the other?" she shrugged and recited her favorite verse in the Bible, Genesis 50:20: "'[What was] intended to harm me, ... God intended it for good to accomplish what is now being done, the saving of many lives.'" She continued. "Our circumstances threw us into that world of gangs and drugs, Travis, but God in his mercy brought us out of it, and he has placed you where you can influence the lives of so many young people living in those very same circumstances."

Her words had touched him deeply, and the book had never left his office since, finding a home in that top left drawer. In the few years he had been principal, that little book had seen a lot of use. The leather cover still looked relatively new though worn where his fingers found their usual resting place, but the inside was a different story. Travis opened it now, and a sense of peace overcame him as his fingers ran over the pages. Yes, he agreed with Cecile that God had led him to this point, but now, with Montgomery High's survival in the balance, to what end?

He began turning the pages slowly, reading the words he had underlined, then double underlined, then highlighted, and then asterisked. And then the verses began to pop up at him. "Wait on the Lord; be of good courage, and He shall strengthen your heart; wait, I say, on the Lord."[1] Travis smiled. There was that waiting again. And then Travis saw the one that put his heart to rest: "But as for me, I trust in You, O Lord; I say, 'You are my God.' My times are in Your hand."[2]

They are indeed, Travis thought, *because they are certainly out of mine.*

* * * *

"So how are you feeling?"

Destiny looked up into three intense faces and one worried one. The question had come from Mason who was closest, his glasses magnifying both the blue-green irises and the whites of his eyes. Destiny had never realized how big his eyes were before, or was it just because of his nearness and intensity?

"Okay, I think," she replied and smiled. "I think I'm still on painkillers, so I really don't feel much at all."

Colton nodded in affirmation. "I hear you on that. Broke my leg, and they gave me some stuff for the pain and said I would feel *really* good for a couple of days, if you know what I mean." Now his head was going back and forth in the negative. "Made me feel completely out of it, like I was underwater and underpowered. No thank you."

Destiny watched Colton's animated facial expressions, amused by his passionate opposition to painkillers.

Funny, Destiny thought, *I have felt like I've been underwater since the day of the rupture, but I can't seem to get out. I want to. I really do, but every time I gasp a breath of hope, a wave of despair crashes down, and I go under again. It's a vicious cycle that only seems to be getting worse.*

"How long do you have to stay off your leg?"

That was Courtney, who had decided to fill the verbal void. Courtney had also chosen to go to the far side of the bed, whether to provide a sense of community or to have her own space, Destiny didn't know, but it did make her feel surrounded and a bit claustrophobic. Regardless, Destiny had to swing her head to the opposite side of the bed to answer her.

"Two weeks with no weight on it at all. Crutches—"

"Had to use those too," Colton interjected. "Get ready for your armpits to sting big time." Then realizing he might be coming across a bit negative added, "But it's a great way to build up your arm muscles."

Destiny smiled. Colton was making such an effort, as was Mason, and Courtney. She looked down at the end of her bed to where Claire stood. Only Claire remained silent. Destiny smiled weakly directly at her, and even though Claire smiled back, her eyes belied her sense of ease. Of the three, only Claire looked worried. The others looked expectant, of *what* Destiny wasn't sure, but Claire looked edgy. Destiny didn't blame her. Claire had been here when she had blown up at her mother and even now, Destiny could feel that same sense of despondency and hopelessness trying to rear its ugly head again. It was scary, because for some reason she had absolutely no control over her emotions.

* * * *

Claire watched the give and take between the three "friends" and Destiny. She could tell that Colton, Mason, and Courtney were all looking for something to show them that their prayers had been answered. Early recovery. Outright healing. Improved spirits. They had prayed and now they expected answers. But what did *she* expect?

She had prayed too, and she had felt twinges of expectancy walking through the halls while the surgery was going on, while Destiny was in recovery, even when she knew Destiny was home. But now, in this room, seeing her with her ankle in a cast and her lying in bed, nothing seemed to be any different.

What had she prayed for? Hope? She had to admit, Destiny seemed more upbeat, more willing to entertain visitors, but there was still something waging war against her and within her—fighting against hope. She could see it in her eyes—despair. But what else was it she was seeing? There was something else, something mingled with that despair, and then she knew it: fear.

* * * *

Gabriel glanced down the alley where a bag of peanut butter sandwiches and apples had awaited him every day for over two weeks. Until it didn't. That had cost him and Ruthie dinner. Now he had been burned again this morning—by his friends. Their betrayal had cost him and Ruthie breakfast. Oh, there was one more betrayal—Jesus, who had told him he didn't have to worry about food. But he did. He clenched his teeth and hardened his heart. He would have to do this on his own after all.

And he could. His initial—and successful—theft, despite the bone-deep fear it had generated, had emboldened him and given him confidence. He knew better than to keep going back to the same store. Having a teenager come in too frequently and leave without ever buying anything could only lead to disaster. No, there were plenty of small stores around that he could take advantage of. He would spend tomorrow canvassing the neighborhood both early morning and midafternoon, when it was natural for a high-school kid to be in a store.

He wanted to see which aisles were furthest from the registers, security mirrors, and cameras. Hopefully, each store offered something different for the taking. He would hate to have to live off of apples forever. Right now, though, he needed to get some dinner. He was back to his version of dumpster diving, but he would round it out with something else from a new market.

He hated leaving Ruthie alone but he couldn't risk having her with him. He did, however, need to find something the two of them could do in the afternoon to get away from that building. It was beginning to stink even to his accustomed nose.

He walked three blocks north of the first store and passed by another on the far side of the road to get a feel for it. It was about three thirty, and the store was mildly busy. That was the other problem. Even though the jacket wasn't out of place now, slipping something into the pockets while no one was watching was still tough.

At the end of the block, he crossed the street and walked back, allowing him to walk the whole length of the store before he came to the entrance. He stepped in and paused as he oriented himself. This store was set up similarly to the first with one major problem. The checker was right next to the door. To leave he would have to walk right by her.

He tried to calm himself as he headed to the far side of the store, which fortunately was away from the produce as well. Store number one could provide that. He turned at the end and found himself in the cooking area, disappointed, until he caught sight of two items: a knife and a hand can opener.

Gabriel tried to still his rapidly thumping heart as he casually looked around. He hadn't checked out the mirrors or cameras yet, so he left the aisle and wandered up a few others both to see what they might hold as well as to appraise the security setup. Mirrors only. Man he was beginning to love the ghetto. No money for high-tech stuff.

He worked his way back toward the kitchen utensils but not before picking up a can of beans, which he slid into his left pocket, and a small package of tortillas, which he shoved down the front of his pants. A few minutes later he had the knife and can opener shoved into his right pocket, trying hard to fold the cardboard packaging so that they wouldn't be noticeable. Then, as before, he nonchalantly worked his way along the back of the store and down the aisle leading to the exit. Again, he waited until there was a line waiting to check out and the teller was busy with a full basket. Then he slid by.

Once outside Gabriel released a huge sigh of relief and, despite the chill in the air, realized he was sweating.

* * * *

Claire pulled the paper bag out of her backpack as she walked toward the alley with purpose. She wasn't going to forget to leave the sandwiches twice. Her mother had stopped quizzing her on the extra sandwiches long ago. *She knows,* Claire admitted to herself. *She probably figured it out long ago and didn't say anything because she was happy I was doing it.* Then she squirmed a bit in her own skin. *Happy because I was doing something for someone else.*

If someone had asked her a year ago if she would anonymously make sandwiches for a homeless ghetto boy and his sister, she would have not only laughed but also openly scorned the idea of even being in a place that had homeless people. Such a place was too alien to the world of Fieldbrook Arts Academy.

She dropped the bag on top of the trash can and left, vowing to come by in the morning to see if it was gone.

* * * *

In the morning light, Claire stared at the paper bag sitting on top of the trash can. He hadn't come by. She turned and headed to first period, heart heavy with guilt and compassion—neither of which she was accustomed to.

Chapter 30

*D*anny strode into the tutoring center an hour late. Two unexpected sessions with new clients had cut into his Montgomery High time, but he didn't mind. He thoroughly enjoyed working with those who had been caught in the trap of drugs. It was definitely a challenge. Most wanted help ridding themselves of the beast until the hard part came, and then the lure of sedation or excitement was sometimes too tough to resist. But Danny had been there, right where they were, though perhaps not as deep as many of them. But the depth of the dependence really didn't matter, for once a person hit that pain/pleasure threshold, all bets were off. However, if the addict could just cross that barrier, the joy in the victory was sweet indeed. For many who resisted, their options were few: die and be free, or almost die and realize the need to be free.

So Danny prayed for his clients, for he knew that ultimate freedom—not just from the drugs but from the hook that drove them to drugs, could only come through knowing, trusting, and following Jesus. A person might be clean, but they weren't complete.

There really wasn't much difference between those clients he was paid for and these on Montgomery High's campus. Many here were just as hardened, just as cynical, and just as desperate. But if the stronghold of drugs was broken in high school, while a diploma was still within reach, then he could spark a flame of hope while there was still a future of possibilities awaiting. He could help salvage a life now, while life might still have meaning.

Danny smiled as he surveyed the tutoring center, checking out the activity. He knew many of the students now, some faithful in their pursuit of good grades, others still here in an effort by their teachers to keep them from failing. Two at the far corner he had talked to and worked with before. He knew both were on marijuana, and he was sure both were itching to move on to something stronger. He would work with them today, and see if he could make a bit more headway both in their studies and their lives.

Danny did a second sweep of the tutorial center and now a frown formed and deepened. He knew all of the tutors, and one was missing, again—for over two weeks now: Gabriel. Danny's gut tightened as his intuition kicked in. One absence was understandable. Two, a bit of a worry. Three, a cause for concern. But four? Four ... in the world these kids lived in ... could be life or death.

* * * *

"Do you know where Gabriel is? He hasn't been at the tutoring center for two weeks."

Travis looked up to see Danny filling the doorway of his office.

Travis shook his head and motioned for Danny to sit. Once he had, he filled him in on what he knew.

"So he's living on the streets?" he asked. Travis nodded. "With Ruthie?" Another nod. "Do you think he was when we saw them at the park?"

"I would almost bet on it. The timeline is right."

Danny shook his head, then raised his eyebrows. "That explains quite a bit though, don't you think?" Another succinct nod.

"No parents around," Travis offered. "Eating up a storm."

Danny raised his hand to stop him. "Whoa, he's a teenage boy. Even in a healthy environment he would be eating them out of house and home."

Travis smiled. "True."

"But the lack of a haircut," Danny continued, "the worn clothes, the deep dirt despite their efforts to stay clean." Travis nodded.

"And you say his friends said that he stopped showing up in the morning?" Danny asked. Another nod.

"I checked in with Charles again this morning. I think he caught wind of what was happening and now has abandoned the morning rendezvous." *And his food. And his friends,* Travis thought to himself. *His world is getting smaller and lonelier ... and probably more desperate.*

* * * *

"Look what I found?" Gabriel held up a worn but respectable backpack. Ruthie looked at it quizzically.

"What do you need that for? We don't go to school anymore."
Gabriel opened his mouth to respond and then realized he couldn't.
He had picked it out of a dumpster while looking for food, but he
couldn't tell Ruthie that he needed it to steal more food at one time.
What could he tell her? He opted for ambiguity.

"Just thought it looked pretty neat and might come in handy
some time is all," he said. Ruthie looked it over again and then
gave her smile of approval.

"It's a nice one, Gabriel," she said, and then tilted her head and
looked at her brother in appeal. "Can we go do something, Gabriel?"
she asked. "I'm tired of being in this room. Let's go outside."

Gabriel felt a pang of guilt. If the truth be told, Ruthie was
pretty much a prisoner in their little building. While school was in
session, she couldn't leave, and when he was out "securing" food
for dinner, she had to stay put, for her safety and his secrecy.

"Okay," he said.

"Can we go to the park?" she asked.

A sudden chill went up Gabriel's spine and he shivered
involuntarily. What if Mr. and Mrs. Richards were there—both
sets of them? Or Mr. and Mrs. Johnson. They would be caught. He
couldn't risk it, not today.

"Tomorrow morning we can go to the park," he answered.
That would be safe. The Richardses and the Johnsons would all be
at church in the morning.

"But aren't we going to go to church?" Ruthie asked. "They
have good muffins, and I bet Mrs. Montrose will wonder where
we are."

Another pang of guilt. Now what did he tell her? As much as he wanted a muffin, the last place he wanted to be was in that building with the picture of Jesus on the door. First of all, Jesus reneged on his promise. He and Ruthie *did* have to worry about what they would eat and wear. Second, he had been to church enough times to know that God knew everything about a person and could see him all the time, so he knew Gabriel was stealing. Gabriel was sure if he showed up in a church, God would strike him dead. So there would be no churchgoing again. Ever. But he couldn't tell Ruthie that.

"We haven't been able to wash our clothes in a while, Ruthie," he improvised. "It would be embarrassing." His sister pulled her lips together in thought, and Gabriel knew he had hit a nerve. Ruthie liked to look nice.

"Maybe we can go by there today and trade them in?" she suggested. "Get new ones."

This time he could answer her honestly.

"They only do that on the last Saturday of the month. I'm sorry," and he really was. There would have been food there, too. Ruthie hung her head in dejection.

"This is boring, Gabriel," she finally said. "I miss school. I miss my friends. I miss the lunches and recess and my teacher and the class rabbit." Gabriel could see tears welling up in her eyes. "How much longer are we going to have to hide here?" A few tears trickled down her cheeks, and she brushed them away rapidly, but Gabriel could see her body begin to rack with silent sobs until she started hiccuping, and yet there weren't many tears, which surprised Gabriel because Ruthie, though usually a very compliant and happy child, was a real gusher of a crier.

"I'll make you a deal," he said hastily, hoping to mollify her.

"Wh–what?" she choked, trying to bring her sobbing under control.

"If I can get us some muffins and orange juice for tomorrow morning, would you be happy just taking a walk this afternoon and then going to the park tomorrow morning?" Ruthie's convulsions were diminishing.

"So–so we aren't going to church and seeing Mrs. Montrose?" she asked once more, and Gabriel could see that she was on the verge of tears again so he needed to act fast.

"Next week," he lied. "I promise. The guilt tightened around his heart. "That will give us time to wash our clothes and get cleaned up."

The contractions were diminishing, and Ruthie was calming down.

"Cross your heart promise?" she asked. Gabriel swallowed his conscience and slashed his right forefinger over his heart twice. Ruthie smiled. "I can help wash our clothes," she said. "That will give us something to do."

"That's right," Gabriel said. "I'll go get the muffins and orange juice and some soap right now, and we can get started tonight."

"Can I come with you?" Ruthie asked, excitement over an outside adventure erasing her unhappiness. Gabriel felt his heart fall and the weight on his shoulders grow heavier as he rummaged around in his backpack, pulled out a long length of string he had salvaged earlier, and then embellished his lie.

"If we both go then it will take us longer to wash the clothes, and we won't get to take our walk. You get all our clothes together while I'm gone and put this string across the room. Can you do that?" Ruthie nodded. "Good, then we can get started right when I get back."

Gabriel could see the excitement return to her eyes, and she clapped her hands in glee.

"I can do it," she said. "Do you have enough money, Gabriel?"

"Plenty," he said, and he found that lying was becoming easier each time.

"Can you get me some candy, Gabriel?" she asked shyly. "I would really like something sweet."

Smiling sadly, Gabriel nodded as he put on his baseball cap, grabbed the backpack, stuffed his jacket into it, and then picked up the water bucket to leave by the front of the building. "See you in about an hour," he said. As he looked at Ruthie's smiling face, his heart was breaking. He knew he couldn't take this much longer. He needed to do something. As he closed the door to their tiny room, he knew he needed to close the door to his heart permanently as well if he was going to survive.

* * * *

This time Gabriel didn't even let himself think about the wrongness of what he was doing. He had to do it, and that was that. Right or wrong had nothing to do with it anymore.

He moved to the back of the store, opened his backpack, took out his coat, and put it on. Gabriel had thought his plan through.

Go into the store with a backpack that looked full and leave with one that looked full as well. The teller might not remember if he had been wearing a coat or not and would probably assume he had because of the coolness in the air, but he would remember an empty backpack transforming into a full one. He pulled his cap lower on his head to obscure his face.

He started his way up and down the aisles, found the muffins and stuffed them in the now empty backpack. But he wasn't reckless. He made sure the aisle was empty or attention was elsewhere before he lifted something off the shelf. He found himself crowding in closer, reading a label or two, and holding a product up to peruse while sliding another in close to his body. After two small juice containers, some lunch meat, a ready-made salad for later, soap, and two candy bars, he was heading toward the door. What was missing was his sense of fear.

He looked at some magazines until both tellers were diverted, and then he casually stepped out the door. This was getting a lot easier—too easy.

* * * *

Claire stared hard at the computer screen, working the mouse back and forth through the editing program: enhancing here, cropping there, inserting a video clip here, or embedding music there. The process was long and tedious, mostly because she was a perfectionist. The vision she had in her mind had to be matched on the screen before her.

What had started as a potential documentary about a homeless boy had morphed into something much bigger and completely unexpected—a tribute to Montgomery High.

She wasn't sure when her view of Montgomery High had changed, but it had. Perhaps it was when Destiny befriended her. As much as she hated being thought of as a charity case, Destiny had been nothing but honest and kind. Then there was that group project in Mrs. Richards's class. Though demanding, it allowed for creativity and collaboration, and working with Blake, Violet, and Quintin had shattered her assumptions that kids from poverty weren't interested in an education. In fact, if the truth be told, her classes at Montgomery High were proving to be more demanding than those at Fieldbrook.

Fieldbrook's arts curriculum was both thorough and interesting, and Claire learned a lot, but the foundational classes of English, math, and history, though solid, had not stretched her. In fact, now that she looked back, she realized there was one marked difference between Montgomery High and Fieldbrook. Montgomery High held its students accountable. Fieldbrook accommodated. If a Fieldbrook student complained about a grade loud enough and long enough, instructors often made adjustments, and Claire knew why. Money. Fieldbrook students felt entitled. Their parents paid a lot of money for them to go to the Arts Academy and thought that their money should pay some dividends, such as good grades and great references.

Claire felt a twinge of guilt. She knew all about how the game was played because she had played it—twice—during her two years there. Instead of working harder or, better yet, admitting that her efforts had been half-hearted at best, she complained that the guidelines hadn't been clear and then even more boldly accused the instructor of subpar teaching. That accusation had garnered such an immediate change in grade that it not only caught Claire off guard but had also revealed a bit of the dark underbelly of some expensive private schools. Teachers knew the power parents and money had over their tenure, so in the name of job security, many grades were "fluid."

Not so at Montgomery. At first, Claire assumed poor parents didn't care about their kids' education, and that was probably true for some, but she had already seen enough parents in the principal's office and in classrooms meeting with teachers to know there were both complaints and concerns, but so far she hadn't caught wind of a culture of coddling. And she could see the wisdom in that. If these students were to make it out of the poverty they were born into, then they needed an education, and not a nominal one but a strong, legitimate, demanding one. Some students realized that truth already, and those who didn't had either teachers or parents who did and made sure their charges couldn't escape their responsibilities.

So Claire's intended dark and stark documentary had morphed into a celebration. Still Claire had learned a few cinematic truths at Fieldbrook even if the school didn't adhere to them itself. One was "never sugarcoat the truth," so Claire included the boy scavenging for his food, and the meager, parentless abandoned building he called home. From her other classmates, she included close ups of tired shoes with open wounds, thin jackets, questionable handshakes, and apathetic looks. But all of that was balanced with what was more prominent: a teeming tutorial center, demanding dramatic rehearsals, and taxing athletic workouts, along with cafeteria camaraderie, busy and energetic classrooms, and hallways that honored excellence for Montgomery High students—past and present.

So intent was she on her project that she didn't hear her mother open the door nor see her peek in, smile, and close the door again. So involved was she in the world of fifteen hundred other students that she never realized there was one person—her mother—solely concerned about just one.

* * * *

"There. That should be the last of it." Gabriel hung up Ruthie's yellow dress on the makeshift clothesline and looked at their work in satisfaction. The clothes did look much cleaner. He had held off washing their cleanest set of clothes not sure if washing *everything* they owned at the same time would be a good idea. It was getting colder at night, and he was afraid the clothes might not dry by morning.

"You do good work, Ruthie," he said to his younger sister with a smile, and she beamed.

"Thank you," she replied, and Gabriel shook his head. *Always so courteous, so polite.* And then his mood sobered. *I hope she can keep it,* he thought. The life they were living was not conducive to positive attitudes. Look at him. Each day, each disappointment, each betrayal hardened his heart and made him a little more cynical and distrusting. He was hoping Ruthie could escape that. Ruthie coughed, and Gabriel's concern kicked in.

"You feeling okay?" he asked. Ruthie nodded as she wiped her mouth with the back of her hand.

"Just a tickle," she replied with a smile. "I'm fine."

Gabriel looked at her more closely. She was thinner than she was a couple of weeks ago, but then so was he. Living off of his "profits" was not the best diet. He hoped she was getting all the nutrients she needed. He would have to get some fresh vegetables, and his brow creased in thought. He had seen some outdoor stands. It would be a bit riskier, but he would do it.

He gazed at his sister again, and for the first time noticed how dry her skin was. Maybe he should pick up some skin lotion for her. He would do that next time as well.

The washing had taken a bit longer than he had anticipated, but there was still time for a walk.

"So how about that walk now?" he asked smiling.

Ruthie's face lit up but no words came. Instead she moved in and gave Gabriel a huge bear hug, burying her face in his chest. Gabriel wrapped his arms tightly around her and silently cried.

Chapter 31

"Good morning," Claire's mother said as Claire joined her and her grandmother in the kitchen. The two older women were each comfortably nursing a cup of coffee.

"Good morning," Claire replied. "Good morning, Grandma," she added, nodding in her grandmother's direction.

"Claire," her grandmother answered. Neither woman said anything as Claire went to the refrigerator to get the orange juice and pour herself a glass.

"How's the project coming?" her mother finally asked. Claire took a long, slow drink before answering.

"Good," she replied, "but still a lot of work to do."

The two older women looked at each other, knowing the statement was meant to ward off either of them from asking her to go to church with them. It was the definitive statement that said, *I have more important things to do than waste a couple of hours going to listen to a boring church service.* Neither obliged. Mrs. Middleton was the first to speak.

"Would you like to take a break this morning and go to church with us?" her mother asked. Her grandmother was right on her heels.

"It is such a beautiful fall day, I thought I would treat you and your mother to brunch down at the RiverWalk."

Claire felt her jaw tighten, and her patent refusal was on the tip of her tongue. She hated playing this game each Sunday, but for some reason today her rejection choked midway, giving her a moment of reflection before she answered. As much as she did not want to listen to a long-winded preacher, neither did she want to keep alienating her mother.

Ever since her grandmother's brief conversation with her when she had caught Claire watching her mother praying, Claire had paid more attention to her mother's actions, attitudes, and words. There was no doubt that Mrs. Middleton was now at peace, despite the chaos and rancor surrounding her life over the past year. Her grandmother seemed to have it too, though her grandmother's life had always seemed peaceful enough. Destiny had it before the accident, but not now. She wondered why. Wasn't that what this God thing was all about? Getting a person past the tough stuff? But then, her mother hadn't been this peaceful during the divorce. More than once she had heard her mother crying, seen a sadness she thought was permanently engrained, and witnessed bouts of depression and anger. So apparently, Christians went through the same stuff everybody else did. They didn't have a get-out-of-jail-free card, but they did have something that seemed to help eventually pull them through. Maybe she would get a brief whiff of what that was if she went—just this once though.

The fact that Claire had not immediately shot down the idea sparked a light of hope in each of the older women, and they waited. Claire did not disappoint.

"That sounds nice, Grandma," she said. "Thank you." And then to her mother. "I could use a little break, but we'll be back by one, won't we?" she added. "I do still have a lot to do." *Even if there is no deadline*, she thought, *I don't want them thinking my Sundays are now available.*

"We can," her grandmother said.

"OK. So what time do I need to be ready?" she asked.

"In about an hour," her mother replied, but all three knew it had taken sixteen years for Claire to finally be ready.

* * * *

"Ready?"

Ruthie nodded her assent to Gabriel's question, her eyes teeming with excitement.

"Ready," she said and started clapping her hands. It had been a wonderful morning already. Gabriel had brought muffins and orange juice like he had promised. Their clothes were almost dry, so Gabriel had said they would wash their other clothes and their sheets when they came back from the park, and they could take a bath then as well. Ruthie longed for a hot bath, but any bath would feel good.

"Did you brush your teeth?" Gabriel asked and Ruthie nodded again. "Let me smell your breath." He leaned in close, and Ruthie sent out a shot of foul air into the room. Gabriel reeled and recoiled in revulsion; his eyes started to water and he coughed violently.

"When!" he asked.

"Just a minute ago," she said, her eyes registering the hurt she was feeling. Gabriel managed to compose himself.

"OK. Well, open your mouth and let me take a look inside," he said. "Maybe you have a cavity."

Ruthie opened her mouth, and Gabriel took a deep gulp of air, hoping not to have to breathe during the inspection. He peered in and, though he saw some evidence of buildup, there didn't seem to be any rotting. He would need to be more diligent about her teeth brushing though. Her breath was offensive.

"Well, it doesn't look like you have any cavities," he mused. "Why don't you brush your teeth again and show me how you do it."

At first Ruthie gave him a "do I really have to?" look but decided to comply so that they could get on with their day. Gabriel watched her lather her toothbrush and begin vigorously brushing. Two minutes later she swished water through her mouth and spit it into the refuse bucket nearby. Then she pulled her lips back in a huge mock smile so that Gabriel could inspect her teeth.

"See?" she emitted through clenched teeth.

"And that's how you brush them all the time?"

She nodded, her teeth still bared. Gabriel was confused. Her breath shouldn't smell that bad if she brushed that thoroughly. Maybe it was because they had been eating the same things for so long. Perhaps he should try to vary their diet. But that was easier said than done.

He shrugged off the mystery and smiled down at her.

"Well, what are you waiting for? Let's go!"

* * * *

It had been almost a year and a half since Claire had sat in a church, and she felt very much out of place. Though she had been in church services before, she had never thought of it through a "me" and "them" mentality. In fact, she hadn't thought of *them* at all. Her previous stints in a church pew consisted of her thinking about what she was going to do later or if the cute boy in Wednesday night youth group would ask her out.

Now, suddenly it was *all* about them. She took her seat and looked around her. Some were greeting each other and talking. Many were in their seats reading the bulletin. A few teens in front were waving their friends over, and some people were just sitting quietly in their seats.

The worship team came up on stage and picked up their instruments, and the wanderers started gravitating toward their seats. Then on the count of three, the music started, and the service was underway.

It was very different from the church she had attended in San Juan. There was a lot of money in San Juan and that church had two huge screens at the front of the sanctuary, plenty of microphones and speakers, and lots of cushioned, individual chairs. Claire figured close to six or seven hundred people could attend the San Juan church.

She let her eyes sweep the sanctuary, did a quick calculation of the number who could squeeze into the dated wooden pews, and came up with about two hundred—max.

Claire listened to the singing, knew the words to this particular worship song but didn't sing along. Instead she was looking at each person individually. Why was that man here? Did he come because his wife made him or because he wanted to? What about that woman? Did she have questions like Claire did, or did everything make sense to her? And that young lady in the front row who wasn't singing either. What was she thinking? She didn't look happy. Was she checking out church to see if it made sense, or was something weighing on her mind?

Claire's eyes moved up and down the rows ahead of her, watching expressions, gauging involvement. Were these people happy? Some raised their hands, some sang with their eyes closed, and some stared silently ahead. A deep sigh escaped before she could contain it. She had all the questions. Now she just needed the answers.

* * * *

"So what do you want to do first?" Gabriel asked.

Ruthie didn't hesitate. "The swings!" she yelled and started running for them. Gabriel smiled and trotted after her, a warmth he hadn't felt for a while coursing comfortably through him. Ruthie jumped into the swing and started pumping her legs.

"Give me a push, Gabriel!" she called out, and he obliged, first a good strong one to get her started, then a second to keep up her momentum, until all he was doing was putting a cursory hand on her back as she flew by.

Ruthie pulled her legs underneath her, extended her chest forward as the swing made its way back to its apex and then shot out her legs. Then she threw her head back, opened her mouth and laughed, and Gabriel laughed with her in her freedom, now realizing that the cloister of their little room had been stifling their spirits as well.

I need to make sure we get out more, he told himself, though in the back of his mind he knew with the cold weather coming, going outside might be more difficult. He reprimanded himself. Already thinking of the negatives of tomorrow when they were having a good day today.

After fifteen minutes, Ruthie slowed herself down until she could hop off with a running stop.

"Oww!" she said and grabbed her left leg. Gabriel sprinted to her in concern.

"Are you okay?" he asked, worry written all over his face. "Did you land on your leg wrong? Did you hear a crack?" He could hear himself wittering away. *Worse than a mother!* he thought, but he also knew a serious injury would mean a trip to the hospital, and then what?

Ruthie shook her head while continuing to rub her left shin.

"My leg aches," she said. "Inside. So do my arms."

Gabriel listened in alarm.

"Was it from the swing?" She shook her head again.

"They ache at home, too. It's just that it hurt more when I landed." The look on Gabriel's face caused her to change direction. "I'm okay now," she insisted. "Let's go to the merry-go-round! Will you push me?" Gabriel stood there unsure for a moment, but Ruthie was already running toward the merry-go-round, so he had no option but to follow.

She positioned herself in the middle, spread her legs across the center circle to balance herself, and then grabbed hold of the bars on both sides of her.

"READY!" she yelled, and Gabriel started pushing until he got it moving and then pulled the oncoming bars to gather up speed. Ruthie squealed in the center. But ten minutes of that was enough, and she begged for him to stop. This time Gabriel noticed she stepped off a bit more gingerly.

"You still okay?" he asked. She nodded.

The bars, teeter-totter, and slides took up the next half hour, but after that Ruthie sat herself down on one of the picnic benches and looked around the park. She didn't say anything for quite some time. Gabriel grew worried again.

"Are you having fun?" he asked, and he held his breath.

Ruthie nodded, but he could see the wistful look on her face.

"It's just not as much fun without someone to play with," she confessed.

Gabriel felt his insides tighten then decided to take the lighthearted approach.

"So what am I?" he asked, jumping up and placing his hands on his hips in consternation. "Chopped liver?"

Ruthie laughed.

"Nooo," she said with a giggle, "but I wish Abigail and Matthew were here. Do you think we can wait to see if they show up? They might have a picnic, and then we can eat with them too."

Whatever warmth Gabriel had felt met with an instant flash

freeze, and he swore his heart stopped beating for a moment. Those eyes looking up at him were so hopeful. He wished he could say yes. He missed *his* friends, too. Life was becoming very lonely.

He smiled sadly at her then shook his head.

"Not today, I'm afraid," he said, and he could see her disappointed heart in her eyes. "We have to do the rest of the laundry today so that we can go to see Mrs. Montrose at church next week, remember? Maybe next week we can, after church?"

It was enough hope that Ruthie smiled again.

"Okay," she said. "Promise?"

Gabriel licked his lips. He had never broken a promise in his life, and now he was being asked to make another one that he knew with every fiber in his being he was going to break, and to the one person he cared about.

"Promise," he said.

* * * *

Destiny hobbled into the sanctuary behind her parents and tried not to react to the stares and whispered "Ooos" coming her way. She really didn't need pity. She had plenty of that for herself already. She would have loved just to slip in unnoticed into the back row because the crutches were unwieldy and difficult to get used to, but her parents insisted on sitting in their normal location—smack dab in the middle.

She still couldn't get her head around what was going on with her. The lethargy continued, the anger surfaced at odd times, the confusion reigned, and her thoughts just kept cycling over and over again.

Lord, isn't this where you're supposed to step in and help me? she prayed. *I don't want to be like this. I want to get out from under this fog, this oppression, this depression.*

Not until she had said the word did it dawn on her what was happening.

So this is what depression feels like, she thought, and she felt a new sensation—guilt. For years, she had silently chided those who had claimed they suffered from depression, labeling them as weak and unwilling to help themselves. When some had moved to medication, she had seen it as a cop-out.

Just get a grip! she had wanted to say. *Get over whatever is bothering you and get a life.*

But now she was realizing those were shallow and uninformed words. *She* hated living in this fog. *She* wanted to get out, but every time she tried to think of something else, her mind would cycle back to her damaged leg and her vanished future, and the hope that had wanted to surface would nosedive to the bottom of her soul once again, and the cycle would repeat and deepen.

But Destiny knew God was good, and in his infinite wisdom and perfect timing he had brought her here so that the pastor would deliver a sermon that would speak directly to her spirit and bring her back to health.

But the pastor didn't.

* * * *

Travis knew he should be listening to the sermon. Usually, when something was bothering him, God took the direct approach and spoke right through the pastor and into his heart. But today his mind was clouded by his own anxiousness, and he was just biding his time until the service was over and he could get to the park. But for what? Would Gabriel even be there? It was just a stab in the dark at best.

He hadn't moved a muscle. Years of gang activity had conditioned him never to give any outward indication of what might be brewing inside, yet he felt a cool, calming hand reach over, take his, give it a tight squeeze, and then hold it gently. Travis smiled. And years of loving him during those tumultuous times had taught Cecile to know when he wasn't at rest.

Her touch did what the pastor's words couldn't—it calmed him and reminded him of her nearness, her support, and God's sovereignty. If God wanted Travis to find Gabriel today, then God would bring him to the park. If he didn't, well …. But Travis really hoped God would.

God didn't.

* * * *

"I don't see him yet," Danny said, as they unloaded the car and carried the ice chest to the picnic table. Travis scanned the park, pausing at the various clusters of children to make sure he didn't miss anyone, then shook his head.

"No. I don't either," he replied, the disappointment evident in his voice. Danny watched him carefully. When Travis was his dealer, Danny had thought Travis was without heart or emotion. Their dealings had been strictly financial, and Travis never once wavered from his "you pay if you want to play" philosophy. But the subsequent years, the years as brothers, had revealed the real

Travis. Not verbally or through facial expressions, for Travis continued to be a man of few words and little visible emotion, but through his actions, his poetry, and his painting.

Danny had watched the softness with which he talked to his sister Jasmine, witnessed the relief when Travis's brothers were rescued from the gangs and given an opportunity for a fresh start, and admired the sternness with which Travis had challenged all three of them to take advantage of their new opportunity. Danny had seen Travis's love for the Washington family and his heart break over Jocelynn's near-death experience because of him.

Though resistant at first, Travis had finally relented and let Danny read the poems he had written. Angry and bitter poems about life's injustices. Desperate poems looking for answers. Then poems of gratitude toward a God who had saved him from despair and given him a family that showed him forgiveness and showered him with love.

The paintings were more straightforward, for those never ventured into darkness. They were of skies and clouds and light and displayed the hope that Travis had yearned for.

Now, as he watched Travis, Danny was seeing all of those emotions being directed toward a boy whom both had known for only a few months.

"God knows where he is," Danny said softly. Travis looked over at him and smiled wanly.

"That he does," he agreed, "but sometimes I wish he would let me know as well."

* * * *

Martha watched her two sons scan the park and then exchange a few words, and she could see the deep concern in both their faces and their body language. She pulled her sweater tighter around her. October in Detroit was always a bit iffy. It could still be muggy but the highs early in the month would slip from comfortable mid-sixties down to low fifties by the end of the month. October saw more rain as well. And late October accentuated all of them. Today was fortunately clear, but on the cool side.

The impromptu picnic had been Travis's idea. He had called all of the family together on Saturday to fill them in on Gabriel's disappearance, his mother's death, and his, most likely, dire living conditions. How could a fourteen-year-old boy with no money and no place to live support himself and his eight-year-old sister? It was imperative that they find him.

He had shared his hope that perhaps Gabriel had made a habit of continuing to come to the park even after he went into hiding, but Martha had been surprised by this unnatural naiveté on Travis's part. If the boy was determined not to be found, and he already realized something had not been right when his friends had led Travis to their early morning meeting place, then it was extremely unlikely that he would revisit the park, a place where he was sure to run into their family. But she had held her tongue and agreed to play her part. They all had.

"Maybe we could talk to some of the parents and kids and see if they have seen him here," Grace suggested. Travis nodded. The idea had merit.

"I'll go now," he said, but Cecile put her hand out to stop him.

"Might be better if Grace and I go," she said. "A man looking for a young boy is likely to result in more silence than answers." Travis stared at her, at first not realizing what she was insinuating. When it dawned on him, he pulled his lips together tightly. This was becoming a pattern: once again, he was forced to wait and watch.

* * * *

"Where's Abigail?" Danny looked around frantically. "Grace, have you seen her?"

Grace looked up from her packing. "I thought she was with you?"

Danny's heart raced, and his eyes scanned the playground. "She was. And she was here just a minute ago. All I did was take the ice chest to the car." He couldn't keep his voice steady. "Matthew, have you seen your sister?"

Matthew stopped dribbling his soccer ball with his foot and looked around the park before shaking his head. "No."

Now Danny was worried, scared, and guilt ridden. While the women were canvassing the area, he had been tasked with watching his daughter. The two had gone to the swing, played tag with Matthew, and then started a game of hide-and-go-seek. Danny's heart stopped. Hide-and-go-seek. That was Abigail's favorite game, and he was sure she was playing it now.

"I think she's hiding," he announced and then started giving directions. "Matthew, go over to the swings and see if she's hiding there somewhere. Grace, you check this side of the park, and I will head to the other side." He saw his wife's concerned face, and he smiled, hoping to instill confidence in both of them. "We'll find her," he said and then prayed. *Please, God, let us find her.*

Martha, Graydon, Travis, and Cecile split up as well, all calling Abigail's name and looking behind trees and trash cans.

"Abigail!" Danny yelled. "Abigail! Time to come out now! We have to go home. You win!"

His eyes darted from tree to tree, trying to pick up the blue-checked sweater that she had been wearing.

Please, Lord, just let her be hiding. Please let her be safe.

Ten minutes passed and Danny could hear the others calling as well, and with each passing second his confidence waned. Maybe she had been abducted. He felt like he had been kicked in the gut.

Then he saw it. A small flash of blue pulled back behind one of the park signs and Danny's heart leaped. "YES!" he cried with relief and started running in that direction, never taking his eyes off of the sign. Then he caught her peeking around it, and seeing him, pull back again.

"Abigail!" he yelled as he drew closer, and when she knew he was going to find her, she left her hiding place and started running across the park, laughing. Danny caught up with her, swept her up in his arms, and held her tight. She squealed and wiggled to get free. Danny didn't know whether to kiss her or spank her. He opted for the first one, setting his three-year-old daughter down in front of him, holding her tight, and looking straight into her eyes. She continued to wiggle and giggle. Danny held her firmer, shaking her enough to get her attention.

"Abigail! Look at me!" he said sternly, and she picked up on the seriousness in his voice and settled down, her countenance sobering.

"Abigail," Danny began again, trying hard to keep his voice steady. "Don't you *ever* do that again," he said. "Do you understand?" Abigail looked at him in confusion.

"I just playing hide and seek," she stated. Danny felt his heart returning to normal.

"But *I* didn't know you were playing. *I* didn't know you had gone to hide on purpose," he said. How much should he tell his young daughter about the potential dangers lurking about without creating an undue sense of fear? He opted for middle ground. "If I don't know you're hiding, then I think you might be hurt, and I won't know where you are so I can help."

Abigail's mouth drew into a pucker. "I won't get hurt," she announced, and Danny released a sigh. This was his strong, willful, independent child, ready to challenge anything he said. Will needed to be met with will.

"Well, do it again," he said, "and you will get a spanking, and the next time we come to the park, you will have sit at the table with Mommy and me and not play."

Abigail's whole face pulled itself into a grimace as she weighed the consequences. Danny knew the spanking wasn't phasing her one bit, but the potential lack of freedom was dire indeed.

"OK," she replied with a pout, her eyes showing her disdain for consequences she thought unfair.

Danny, his anger and patience spent, stood up, took his daughter by the hand and walked her back to the others.

One disaster averted. One child found, but two were still missing.

* * * *

Gabriel watched the entire scenario from his vantage point across the street. He had taken Ruthie back to their room and then had swung back to see if his assumptions had been correct. They had.

The entire Richards family was there along with Mr. Johnson and his wife. Gabriel had arrived in time to witness the women walking the park and talking to other families. He knew they were asking about him and Ruthie by their gestures. Hands raised to indicate Ruthie and his height. A motion toward him indicating the route the two might have taken.

He felt a sudden chill run down his back. Was this park now off limits? If any of these people saw them after today, they would know people were looking for them. Life was spiraling out of control. He stayed to watch the family a bit longer. Something they had he yearned for. Yes, he was hungry. He was starving in fact. The diet he was feeding himself and Ruthie may be filling a void in their stomachs, but it wasn't supplying the nutrients they needed. But he was starving for something else as well, a something he had never had.

He watched the family sitting together, smiling, talking—well, all but Mr. Johnson because he didn't say much—and laughing. He felt a pang of loneliness and desire. He saw them bow their heads in prayer, and now the emotions battled within him. Though the stories about Jesus sounded good, how could the Richardses believe in a God who broke his promises and put him and his sister on their own in a dangerous city? And Mr. Johnson, one of them, was the reason they had faced more and more hardship over the past few weeks. And now this. Their one place of fun and freedom taken away. Their world was growing smaller and bleaker each day.

He rose to leave when he noticed Abigail sneak off and hide behind a tree and then run to the sign by the park entrance when her parents were busy packing up. He wondered what she was doing. When she squatted behind the sign, peeking around every so often to see if they were looking for her, he knew she was playing hide-and-go-seek. He held his breath, though, and kept his eye on her. She was close to the road, and from his brief experience with the little girl, he knew she would run before she thought. Would she run into the street?

His eyes rotated from Abigail back to the family, and it soon became apparent that they were now aware that she was missing. Even from his hiding place, Gabriel could hear them calling for her. He looked back at Abigail to see if she would respond, but he could tell by her shaking shoulders that she was laughing and thought this all a game.

He wanted to come out of hiding, go to the girl, and take her back, but his self-defense mechanisms were in high gear, so he stayed put. Despite his confusion about God, he found himself praying softly, "Please, God, let them find her. Please, God, don't let her run into the street." When Danny moved in her direction, Gabriel quietly encouraged him toward Abigail's hiding place. "Yes, you're getting closer. Keep going. Abigail, stay put." Gabriel both willed and talked the two toward reunion, and when Danny finally caught sight of his daughter and started running toward her, Gabriel held his breath, clenched his teeth, and prayed especially hard. "Please, please, please, don't run, Abigail!"

But Abigail did run. Fortunately, she ran in the direction of the park, allowing Danny to catch up and grab her. When Gabriel saw him stoop down and turn his daughter toward him and give her the talk, he slid back behind the building and headed toward home. He was relieved that Abigail was safe, but knew his world had grown more dangerous.

Chapter 32

$\mathcal{M}$artha finished recording the last grade into the computer and hit return. She gathered the graded papers, straightened them, and placed them on her desk. She glanced at the folder holding the lesson, took out all copies but the original, and put them in the trash. She would save one copy in case a colleague might want to use it in the future, but experience had taught her that teachers liked to do their own thing, and this lesson would probably end up where she had just put the duplicates—in the trash.

* * * *

Travis stared at the attendance figures for the two months of school. They were good. Over ninety percent. And he realized that these numbers might help his cause. He scrutinized them more closely, looking at the various weeks.

First week was what he expected. The first couple of days had high attendance. Almost all students show up just to see each other, check out the new teachers or their classes, and see if this year was going to be any different than the last. Some even turned over a new leaf and vowed to do better in school.

But by day three, when the introductions to the classes were over, the homework was assigned, and the work involved in flipping that new leaf became a reality, there was a dip in attendance, and that was when Travis's new program kicked in. He had worked with his local church to set up mentors for some of the students. Retirees and individuals who had at least one hour a week to spare were asked to volunteer. Once the volunteers were in place, the process started. The first absentees were tagged, and the attendance office and vice principal went into action, hoping to nip the absences in the bud before they became habitual.

The minute the student was back on campus, Travis had them hooked up with a mentor. He had read a lot about the success of after-school mentoring programs, but most of those were for elementary kids who had less ability to leave school once they were there. High school kids were different, with a much more "fluid" view of attendance. If he had put the mentoring program after school, it was doubtful that the student would still be there. So he was willing to forfeit class time for mentor time. If the mentor could swing it, the two would meet a different period each week, so that each period was impacted only once every six weeks. Teachers were more than willing to excuse the student under this time frame as the alternative would be the student wouldn't attend class at all.

The mentors were given general guidelines. They weren't a counselor trying to solve problems. Nor were they a tutor. First and foremost, they were to be a steady, positive presence in the student's life, something many of these students didn't have. They were to show an interest in that student's life. Listen. Encourage. If they felt comfortable helping with homework or sharing life experiences, then so be it. Though they couldn't talk about Jesus in the public school setting, there was nothing to deter them from demonstrating the love of Jesus in very tangible ways.

Almost immediately, there was a change in the students' attendance. For some reason, just knowing there was someone in their lives who seemed to care about them brought the students back to school—at least for that particular day. But as the weeks progressed, overall attendance and grades improved as well.

Travis printed out the individual attendance reports of the students in the mentoring program both for this year and last, then shuffled the attendance reports together in a neat pile, putting the summary on top, followed by his description and success of the mentoring program. His arsenal was increasing.

* * * *

"How are you doing, dear? How was school?"

Mrs. Williams stood in the doorway of her daughter's room, testing the emotional waters.

Destiny worked hard to create a believable smile.

"Fine," she answered, nodding. "Good to be back." That was a lie, but she didn't want her mother to pry any further. She wasn't fine at all. She just couldn't get her footing anywhere, and that wasn't a pun. The loss of her dream had hit her like the death of a loved one and had created such a huge void in her life, she didn't know how to fill it. The minutes and hours and days and years just stretched out in endless sameness before her. Life just seemed pointless now. A weariness seeped then settled into her bones.

"Just a little tired still," she said. "Think I will take a nap."

Concern filled her mother's eyes, but she still smiled. "I'll let you get some sleep then," she responded and closed the door behind her.

Destiny fell back on her bed and closed her eyes. The darkness was comforting. If she were to fall asleep right now and never wake up, it would be a relief.

* * * *

Claire rubbed her eyes in weariness. It had been a long day—emotionally. Classes had been simple, but lunch had been challenging. Though Destiny had joined them again, it was obvious to the four that she was not okay. Mason tried to engage her in conversation, but her thoughts were fragmented and her energy low. Very quickly the lunch table had gone silent, and the uncomfortable awkwardness grew. Claire could sense everyone inwardly twitching. A few minutes before the lunch bell rang, Destiny excused herself, and four sets of lungs expunged the depressing air they had been holding. All four stared at each other. It was Courtney who spoke first.

"I guess praying doesn't work."

No one responded, but all were thinking the same thing. They had entered the experiment so hopeful, so excited. They had carried out their commitment so dutifully, so regularly. They had waited in anticipation to see God answer, and when he did, they were all ready to embrace him. Even Claire had found herself momentarily suspending her disbelief, willing to give God a second chance.

But the second chance warranted nothing. True the surgery was over and seemed to have been a success, so the doctor must have known what she was doing. Those were both answers to their prayers. But Destiny was still wounded, and what good is a successful surgery if the injured was still hurting?

The four had departed without any further word, and Claire had sat through her last two classes in her own thoughts. Mrs. Richards had called on her, catching her daydreaming, and when Claire confessed she hadn't been listening, Mrs. Richards had forgone her usual reprimand and only looked at her closely, told her the page they were on, waited till Claire had found it, and then moved on to a different student.

Quintin and Violet had waited for her after class.

"Are you okay?" Quintin had asked. Claire smiled weakly.

"Sure. Just a little distracted," she answered, fidgeting slightly. Claire wasn't concerned about Quintin. He was easy to appease. It was Violet she was worried about. While Quintin's eyes were filled with concern, Violet's were like lasers piercing through her. Quintin was all about feeling. Violet was all about truth.

"Well, you would let me know if anything was wrong, right?" Quintin asked as they walked down the hall. "You'd let me help?" Claire nodded, and Quintin sighed in relief, satisfied. "Alright then," he said, "I'm off to sixth period. You two take care." And he made a sharp right and headed down the stairs.

Claire wasn't able to shake Violet so easily. The girl matched her step for step but didn't say anything all the way to Claire's locker, and Claire felt a confusing sense of uneasiness and comfort by Violet's presence. Violet's eyes never left Claire's face.

"Is it Destiny?" she finally asked. Her discernment surprised Claire.

"Some," she answered honestly, but was unwilling to comment further. Right now her life was conveniently segmented into disparate compartments—class friends and "prayer" friends—Claire was loath to let them spill into each other. Quintin and Violet saw her as a capable student and a talented movie maker. Did she really want to blow that image? Did she want them to know that she was on a confusing spiritual journey with what they might see as three misfits? She didn't think so. Fortunately, Violet had left without demanding anything more.

Now, as midnight neared, Claire couldn't shake Destiny and God's apparent disinterest from her mind, and her feelings vacillated from anger to contempt to sorrow. She could see Destiny sinking.

She cleared her mind of all thoughts of Destiny and refocused them on the screen in front of her. Her film was nearing completion. Once she had edited the final few frames, she could add the music, and it would be finished. And it was good. Maybe God should take a few lessons from her on how to finalize a project.

* * * *

Destiny lay in the darkness struggling with her thoughts, searching for verses to sustain her, but the only verse that would surface was still Ecclesiastes 1:2: "'Meaningless! Meaningless!' says the Teacher. 'Utterly meaningless! Everything is meaningless.'" And that verse wasn't helping.

Chapter 33

*G*abriel woke up tired, stiff, and shivering. The days were getting cooler, and the nights cold. The two thin blankets he had found were now not doing the job at all. Last night he woke up not from his own cold, but from Ruthie shaking next to him. He had wrapped both the blankets and his arms around her and within a couple of hours she was sleeping soundly. But he wasn't. With his entire backside exposed, he had been a victim of the cold, and sleep evaded him.

Now it was morning, and the day stretched out before him. As always they needed food, and he felt that familiar pang of guilt slice through him, but it was quickly replaced with resolve. Stealing was now second nature. They needed food, so the ends justified the means. Plus, he had ventured far enough that he now had a cycle of stores he could visit, so at most he entered the same one only once every three weeks.

The problem was going to be the blankets. He couldn't steal those, and they wouldn't be in a garbage can, which meant he was either going to have to dumpster dive—something he utterly despised—or move closer to the freeway overpasses or downtown where the homeless congregated. There might be more options there.

The bigger problem had always been what to do with Ruthie. She couldn't go with him, and he often worried about leaving her alone in the building, but that was really his only option. But what was she supposed to do all day? He had finally devised a series of tasks for her—dusting the windowsill and their few bits of furniture, making their bed, and washing their dishes—but all of this would only take a few minutes. He had continued to worry about her schooling, so eventually he had stolen some books from a used bookstore that was so cluttered, the owner couldn't possibly know what books would be missing let alone who was in the store when they disappeared.

So their days and their stomachs were filling up, but Gabriel felt only a growing void in his soul.

※　※　※　※

Claire placed the DVD in a plastic cover and slid it into her backpack. Her project was finally completed, and she was glad Mrs. Richards had asked to see it; otherwise, she wasn't sure *anyone* would have ever seen it, for she certainly couldn't just go up and ask someone to look at it. Back at Fieldbrook, everyone would have seen what she had created since all projects were class assignments, and Fieldbrook believed strongly in peer and teacher critiques. Claire had reveled in them. Because she was so talented, her projects always received raves from her instructors with minimal constructive criticism. It was easy to take the few suggestions when they were doused in an abundance of praise.

She had silently mocked many of her classmates' attempts as juvenile or sloppy, but every so often she would condescend to offer a bit of praise or a snippet of advice. Such comments from some might be seen as a sign of humility, but coming from Claire they never had that feel. There was no misreading the arrogance behind her selective comments of others' works.

Claire winced just thinking about it. Yes, she had been good, for a tenth grader, but her developing eye and her growing artistic sense as an eleventh grader had already told her that she had much to learn. Still, she had worked hard on this documentary, and she was proud of it, and she wanted someone to see and appreciate it, and Mrs. Richards was the perfect person. She was an English teacher who had also been a drama teacher, so she would pick up on the allusions and subtle nuances while appreciating the artistic attempts.

Claire zipped up her pack and slung it on her back. One project was done, but unfortunately another was far from over—Destiny was still struggling.

* * * *

Martha finished her lunch, said her goodbyes to her companions, and headed back to her classroom. Fifth period would be arriving soon.

She mentally went through the afternoon's lesson, playing it out in her head, and then she switched tracks. She pulled her lips firmly together. She needed to talk to Claire today. For two weeks now, the young lady again had something troubling her, and Martha felt compelled to talk to her about it. She would ask Claire to stop by after sixth period.

The students filed in, exchanging hellos and smiles with Martha, who waited expectantly for Claire. She didn't have to wait long, and for the second time that year, Claire beat Martha to the punch, stopping in front of her and asking if she could see her after school.

* * * *

"This is the project I've been working on," Claire announced, holding the DVD case out toward Martha. Claire was surprised to find herself shaking slightly. "You had said you wanted to see it when it was finished," she added by way of explanation, hoping Mrs. Richards had remembered her request. Martha smiled.

"I certainly did," she responded enthusiastically. "Thank you." She paused, turning the DVD case over in her hand, then noticing the cover title Claire had created: *The Lives and Times at Montgomery High*. Martha looked up at Claire carefully, a wry smile pulling at her lips. "The title's not quite the same," she ventured, "but …" and she stopped to see if Claire had purposely intended the similarity. The smile playing on Claire's lips made her think it was a yes.

"Don't worry," Claire said. "The similarity pretty much stops there. But it did get your attention, didn't it?" Martha nodded.

"It did indeed, and raised my anxiety level a bit as well. You've been working on this quite a while now, haven't you?" Claire nodded.

"About six weeks."

"Well, I promise you I won't take that long to watch it, but it will probably have to wait until the weekend.

Claire nodded in acknowledgement but felt a flash of disappointment. She had hoped Mrs. Richards would have been excited enough to want to watch it that night, but she knew deep down that that was too much to ask. Teachers had a lot to do during the week. In fact, her class had just turned in an essay assignment yesterday, and Mrs. Richards always returned them, with multiple comments, within a week. No, she would just have to content herself with waiting until Monday for a response. Four days. Four long days. She frowned in thought, then heard Mrs. Richards clear her throat.

"Claire," she said mildly, and Claire looked up. Concern was written all over Mrs. Richards's face. "Is everything all right? You have seemed ... distracted lately, like something is bothering you."

Claire sucked in a deep breath. How much should she tell her? She had come to admire this woman and knew anything she might tell her would be safe, but still .... She decided just to stick to the physical facts.

"A friend of mine is having a hard time," she confided. "I think she's really depressed." Martha's eyes widened in concern.

"Who?" she asked. Claire thought about it a moment, deciding withholding the name wouldn't accomplish anything.

"Destiny Williams."

Martha's head began a slow nod. She knew Destiny. She had had her as a student her freshman year and had followed her running career, and knew that she was both a dedicated and determined student athlete. She also knew that she was a very real Christian presence on campus. Finally, she knew that Destiny had recently suffered a season-ending injury and potentially a career-ending one. It was no wonder she was struggling.

Martha smiled, trying to reassure Claire a bit.

"It's understandable, isn't it?" she said, and Claire nodded.

"But she can't stay that way," Claire blurted, and without thinking, she let what was really bothering her cascade out. "She's a Christian and people have been praying, but God isn't doing anything, and I don't understand why."

Once the words were out, Claire bit her lower lip, wishing she could take them back. She didn't know if Mrs. Richards believed in God or not, and she had seen many teachers at Fieldbrook verbally mock and ridicule students who asserted religious beliefs, implying those students were naive or stupid. Claire stared fearfully into Mrs. Richards's face, but the older woman only smiled.

"Oh, I think he's doing something," she said softly. "I think he has been working very hard."

* * * *

"Danny, I want you to talk to a student."

After Claire had left her room, Martha had headed right down to the tutorial center to see if Danny was working. Though he wasn't a clinical psychologist, if there was anyone who knew about depression, it was Danny. His spiral into drugs stemmed from his own depression. And his journey was not that much different from those he counseled every day. Drugs and depression seemed to go hand in hand, and just taking the drugs out of the equation didn't magically remove the depression. Even after his own secret had become public, and he had willingly sought help, the depression had lingered, and it had been a long, difficult journey back to full mental health.

Martha had waited until he had finished working with a student before she waved him over and delivered her question.

"What about?" he asked.

"Depression."

"Any idea what the trigger might have been?" he asked. Martha nodded.

"An injury that seems to have destroyed her hopes of a state cross-country title and perhaps her collegiate opportunities." Danny nodded somberly.

"Destiny Williams," he filled in. All of Montgomery High and anyone following Montgomery High knew of Destiny Williams. She was the next Montgomery High success story to make her mark. "How did you learn about it?"

"Through a student in my class who is kind of a friend with Destiny. Claire Middleton."

"Kind of?"

Martha took a few minutes to give Danny what backstory she had on Claire and her subsequent journey from an angry belligerent to a confused but concerned participant. When she finished, she realized that she didn't really know that much about Claire after all.

Danny didn't say anything. Finally, Martha broke the silence.

"So will you talk to Destiny?" she asked. Danny shook his head.

"No. But I would like to talk to Claire."

Chapter 34

"So Destiny is a friend of yours," Danny stated. It was Friday afternoon. It had surprised both Martha and Claire that Danny wanted to talk to Claire and not Destiny.

"Why does he want to talk to me?" she had asked when Martha had approached her Thursday after class. Martha had shrugged her shoulders. Danny hadn't confided in her, so she was as much in the dark as Claire was.

"Perhaps to get a better understanding of what's going on before he talks to her?" she had guessed. Claire had pursed her lips together in contemplation and furrowed her brows. She was getting more involved than she wanted to but maybe by talking to Mrs. Richards's son, she could hand Destiny and her problems off.

"Okay," she had relented, "but I can't today. I already have plans. Is tomorrow okay?"

Martha had texted Danny right then to see if Friday would work. The yes had come back just as quickly. So now here Claire was, sitting across from Danny Richards, wondering what would happen next. She nodded in answer to Danny's question. Yes, Destiny was her friend.

"And you think she's depressed?" he continued. Claire nodded again. "What makes you think so?"

Claire was a little irritated. Why did she have to go through this interrogation? If Mr. Richards would just sit down with Destiny and talk with her for five minutes, he would know she was depressed. Heck, she had just looked it up on the internet and connected the dots. Destiny's eyes were dull, her smile weak. She was first listless and then irritable. She didn't want to do anything. She didn't want to eat. There was no more excitement. No more joy. Bingo. Complete picture.

"She just lies around all the time," she said instead. "She doesn't want to do any of the things she used to like doing. She won't eat, and she snaps at people or doesn't respond at all." Claire stopped. That summed it up in a nutshell.

Danny listened, ticking off each point on his mental checklist. Classic depression, he agreed. He smiled at Claire.

"You are very observant," he said by way of a compliment, "and absolutely right. Your friend is depressed."

Claire could feel herself relax a bit. She had been right, and now help was on its way.

"Can you help her?" she asked, and there was no missing the hope in her voice. Danny shook his head.

"No," and Claire felt her heart plummet, "but you can," he concluded.

"Me?" she asked. "I'm not a counselor. You are. Why can't

you help her?"

Danny nodded slightly. "You're right. I could help her, but I don't know her, and you do. I believe it will be much more effective if you work with her." He paused, debating whether to continue, and then did. "My mother says you have been praying for her?"

Claire could feel herself turn red. This was going down a road that she really didn't want to travel. She shrugged nonchalantly. "A few others and I thought we would give it a try. Didn't seem to work though. He didn't answer them. She's no better."

Danny smiled. "I wouldn't be too sure of that," he said, and Claire looked at him quizzically. Mrs. Richards had said almost the exact same thing. "You're here, aren't you? I now know, and we are going to put together a plan of action. I would say God is moving, wouldn't you?"

Claire hadn't thought of it that way. She thought God just went in and cured people. She never really thought that he might use other people to do it. And she definitely hadn't thought he would use her.

"Can I share a story from the Bible with you? I think it will help explain what I am asking you to do."

Though skeptical, Claire nodded and Danny opened his Bible.

"The story comes from I Kings 18–19," Danny said, and he then proceeded to read about how Elijah had called forth a tremendous show of God's power, and fire came from heaven and burned up the offering, the wood, and the alter, while Baal's prophets could not get Baal to do anything. Elijah then thought that King Ahab and Queen Jezebel would repent and acknowledge the God of Israel as the true

God, but they would have nothing of it. In fact, Jezebel vowed to kill Elijah by evening of the next day. Consequently, Elijah ran and hid and fell into depression. He had followed God's orders explicitly, and experienced a commanding victory, yet—nothing changed. So he just lay there and slept. He wouldn't eat, and he wanted to die. Claire recognized the symptoms.

"So what happened?" Claire prompted when Danny stopped.

"God sent an angel to minister to him. In brief, the angel fed him to bring back his physical strength, then God listened to him, and finally God encouraged Elijah through his words." Danny stopped, and Claire waited. *And,* she thought expectantly, but Danny didn't continue.

"So … any idea where we can get an angel?" she quipped. Danny nodded and pointed his forefinger in her direction.

"You."

Claire sat there stunned. "Me?" she asked. "Why me? And how me?"

"You're one of her friends. She will respond to you more than others."

"Maybe we should get one of her church friends," Claire volunteered. "That might be more appropriate since this is a Bible story and all."

Danny looked at her calmly.

"Have you seen any of them around the house? Have any of them voiced their concerns about Destiny?"

In all fairness to the others, Claire really didn't know.

Danny smiled. "No worries. If they are, then good. She can't have too many friends right now. If they aren't, then you are needed more than ever. The first thing I want you to do is to get her outside. Get her to go for a walk. Make a picnic lunch and go to a park. Stay away from Belle Isle for a while as that might remind her of her loss. But minister to her physical needs right now. She needs sun, good food, and as much exercise as she can have with her leg in a cast. When she is ready to talk, she will. All you need to do is listen. You don't need to offer advice. Just let her know that you hear her and understand what she is saying."

Claire could do that, but it was the next part that scared her. The words of God. She didn't remember anything from the Bible.

"What about the last part?" she asked. "I don't think I know any Bible verses."

"When that time comes, and if God wants you to say something, he will give you the words, or he will provide them himself. Destiny knows her Bible. The verses will return.

"In the meantime, I'm going to call Destiny's parents, talk to them a bit, and see if they have been seeing the same things you have. If they have, I will let them know that I believe their daughter is suffering from depression, hopefully mild, and to watch her carefully. Then I will tell them what your role is. They are strong Christian parents. They, too, will know what to tell Destiny when the time comes."

Claire felt herself relax. So all she had to do was get Destiny to go for a picnic and listen. This angel business might not be so tough after all.

* * * *

"How about if we sit over here?" Claire asked, pointing toward a picnic table."

Destiny nodded in agreement. "Okay."

Destiny was ready and waiting for Claire when she arrived. Mr. Richards had called Mr. and Mrs. Williams right after he and Claire had finished talking, asked his questions, and explained what Claire was trying to do, so when Claire called later that evening to see if Destiny wanted to go to the park for a picnic, Destiny's parents had already been priming Destiny to accept.

Neither girl had a car, so Mr. Williams had agreed to drive them. Claire had opted for a park away from school, hoping to avoid people who might know them. She didn't know if this was a good idea or not and hadn't thought to ask Mr. Richards, but she figured on Destiny's first day out it might be better not to be bombarded by well-wishers. The downside of this was that that left all the work of carrying a conversation with Claire, and she wasn't relishing the idea. But it was only for two hours. Mr. Richards thought that would be enough for one day, and Claire thought she could hold up for that long.

Claire carried the picnic hamper while Destiny hobbled next to her on her crutches. Neither girl said anything and surprisingly Claire didn't feel uncomfortable like she thought she would. When they reached the table, Claire pulled out the tablecloth and laid out a few things. It felt good to have something to do. When she finished, she hesitated. She didn't just want to rush into eating.

"Want something to drink?" she asked. Destiny gave her a weak but appreciative smile.

"That would be nice."

"You have your choice of lemonade or ...," and she peered into the hamper, "lemonade. Seems like I forgot to pack the bottles of water I laid out. I wondered why the hamper felt light."

Destiny laughed, and Claire relaxed.

"If it had been me packing the lunch, we might not have had anything to eat. I'm not very domestic," Destiny said.

"Don't get too excited yet," Claire retorted. "You haven't seen what I brought to eat."

Destiny laughed again, a quiet laugh, but one that at least wasn't laced with despair. The two fell silent again as Claire poured the lemonade and handed Destiny a glass.

"Thank you," she said.

"You're welcome."

The autumn breeze picked up a bit, blowing a few leaves off a nearby maple. Destiny sighed, and Claire glanced over at her and noticed a mixture of joy and regret.

"You alright?" she asked.

Destiny paused before answering. "Yes. Fall was always my favorite time of year."

Claire felt a lump grow in her throat. Cross-country season. She didn't know whether to pursue the topic or just wait and see if Destiny wanted to say anything more. She opted to stay off that branch but decided to venture out on another limb.

"Do you feel like taking a walk around part of the park?" she asked. "I think our stuff will be okay, and we won't go far."

Destiny looked at the crutches in her hands and then the path that disappeared beneath a canopy of red and yellow oak and maple. She pushed herself up and adjusted the crutches beneath her arms. "Lead the way."

Claire breathed a silent sigh of relief. Things were going better than she had planned. Destiny was truly trying hard to enjoy herself and be pleasant. Once Destiny was on her feet and walking, Claire lifted her head to take in the scene as a whole. It was idyllic, what with the changing colors and the families enjoying the cool fall weather. Her eyes swept back to her right toward the playground, and her heart stopped. She squinted to get a better look. Was it? It was. She was sure.

There, pushing a young girl in a swing, was the boy from the alley.

* * * *

Gabriel gave Ruthie another push and she pumped her legs vigorously. It had taken Gabriel two days to find this park—six blocks in the opposite direction of the one they had been going to—the one they couldn't go back to because people were now looking for them there, thanks to the Johnsons and the Richardses. But here they were safe. The afternoon out gave them a chance to escape their room and forget their hunger. For Ruthie, it provided much needed exercise and the chance just to be a kid again. For Gabriel, it gave him some time to shed the weight of who he had become. So for a couple of blissful hours on a Saturday afternoon they were who they used to be—two kids with a future.

* * * *

Martha finished grading the last of the junior essays and pushed the recliner all the way to the flat position.

I could stay like this forever, she thought. The grading had worn her out, but the silver lining was not lost on her, and though her eyes were closed, she smiled. *That will be the last essay on* The Scarlet Letter *that I will ever have to grade,* she thought with pleasure. Martha's eyes were still closed as she realized she would never be giving that lecture or those illustrations again either, which brought a brief pang of sadness. She enjoyed instilling the relevance of literature and the English language. Sometimes the foundation of why they were asked to do or learn something was more important than the task itself. She let out a little laugh. Always the philosopher.

She turned her head to see what time it was. The DVD case holding Claire's video was right in line with the clock, and Martha couldn't help but see it. She sighed. She needed to watch it. She had promised Claire she would this weekend, and she *wanted* to watch it, but she wished she knew how long it was. She was tired and didn't want to have to think too much.

She took a deep breath and pulled herself upright, throwing her legs to the ground and resting her elbows on her knees. She glanced at the clock. Three fifteen. Almost two hours before she needed to think about putting something together for dinner. A plan was soon hatched. She would go for an hour walk, clear her head, then come back and watch the video. Martha pulled out her walking shoes and jacket and headed for the door. An ordered life was a happy life.

* * * *

Claire surreptitiously watched the boy as she and Destiny's route drew them closer to him. She wasn't worried he would recognize her. He had never seen her, and she had really seen him only once, but she had him on camera and had seen his image over and over and over again. There was no mistaking it. This boy was the garbage can boy. The girl was probably his sister. They both looked very thin—too thin.

The sense of relief Claire had felt only moments before began to fade. Perhaps one wounded person might be tenuously hanging on, but it looked like two others were slipping away.

* * * *

Back from her walk and a bit energized, Martha pulled the DVD out of its case, slid it into the player, then settled back on the couch and hit the remote.

"Alright, Miss Claire Middleton, let's see what you have done."

The screen remained black for a couple of seconds, and then Montgomery High School's main building appeared bigger than life, the columns and façade rising from the ground. From there, the footage took off in a montage of two-second shots. First the school sign, setting the location, then the hallways, next the stadium, and then various classrooms. The angles varied, keeping each scene unique, and the viewer engaged. The music was heavy on beat.

"Excellent start, Claire," Martha whispered.

Once the intro was over, a facing page swept across the screen introducing the upcoming section: "The Academics of Montgomery High." Now the tempo slowed as Claire moved her way first through science classes, taking closeups of students conducting experiments, and then on to a math class, filming students working with manipulatives. Next she took footage of students eagerly raising their hands in a history class or quietly studying in the library. Again, the music enhanced the studious mood. Then came the theater arts, and Martha witnessed practices, dress rehearsals, set building, lighting, blocking, and students practicing their lines.

The video continued, venturing through all that Montgomery High had to offer.

But the best was yet to come. When Martha thought that all of Montgomery High had been celebrated, "The Achievements of Montgomery High" slid across the screen and now Martha found herself stepping back into time. A close up of a former student would appear with their name inscribed beneath it, followed by photos and video clips from high school and then a current picture complete with achievements. When Reba Washington appeared, Martha's heart somersaulted. She looked so little and timid in the candid portraits, but the onstage photos revealed a very different young woman. Claire had pulled out exemplary clips and had also found a media shot of Reba in her current off-Broadway performance. Then came Alex Kowalski, and Martha couldn't help but smile. *Only fitting those two should be side by side,* she thought, for their successful journeys had been so intertwined in high school. Seeing him in his Detroit Lions uniform almost brought Martha to tears.

"Travis has got to see this," Martha said to herself as the final section was unveiled: "The Heart of Montgomery High." Now the camera zeroed in on individual students laughing, sitting in silence, looking pensive, chatting with friends. Martha found herself nodding in approval until one scene caught her off guard. She shot up from the couch, frantically searching for the remote.

"Where is it? Where is it?" she muttered, tossing papers and scanning the coffee table. She checked behind her on the couch, saw a bit of it peeking out between the cushions, grabbed it, and desperately tried to get it to rewind.

"C'mon. C'mon," she muttered impatiently, staring intently at the scenes flying by in reverse until she saw what she was looking for, paused the player and then hit the play button. She moved in closer to the TV to make sure. The scene ended, and she rewound it and played it again, moving in even closer until she was almost right on top of the TV screen. This time when the face appeared, she paused it, moved closer to the TV, and stared at it closely.

"Travis has *got* to see this," she said.

* * * *

"Travis, you have *got* to see this," Martha stated once Travis had opened the door and ushered her into the apartment.

Martha had wasted no time. She didn't even watch the end of the video but had called Travis immediately and said she was coming over.

"What's this about?" Travis had asked.

"You'll see when I come over," she had replied and hung up. Travis could do nothing but wait. But he didn't have to wait long. Martha was there within minutes, skipped straight to the scene, and hit play.

"That's Gabriel!" Travis yelled.

"Exactly," Martha affirmed. Though Claire had worked hard

to choose angles to keep most of Gabriel's identity hidden, Martha and Travis knew him well enough to recognize him.

"I can't tell where this is," he stated, rewinding and playing the scene again, taking in the alley, the brickwork, and trying to decipher clues from either. "Who did you say made this?" Travis finally asked.

"A student in my fifth-period class. Claire Middleton."

Travis pulled his lips tight. "Do you have her number with you?" he asked.

Martha nodded. She kept her students' phone numbers in her grade book. She had copied Claire's before she came over.

"What time is it?" he asked as he glanced up at the wall clock. "Five thirty. We have time now."

"Her family might be eating," Martha reminded him.

Travis's lips pulled into an even tighter line, and Martha could see his concern.

"I will call her around seven tonight," Martha offered. "Do you want me to see if she can meet with us tomorrow afternoon?"

"How about tomorrow morning," he suggested.

"You have church, and she might as well," Cecile, who had been watching quietly, reminded him, and when she saw Travis gearing up to object, she continued before he could speak, "and now isn't the time to leave God out of your plans." Cecile knew Travis's tendency to take matters into his own hands all too well. He had spent years fending for himself, his siblings, his gang, and her, and he had managed quite well. Letting go and letting God had been and continued to be the hardest lesson of his Christian walk.

She was now witnessing a new struggle. Finally, he let out a long sigh, looked up at her and then Martha, and smiled weakly.

"Okay, but we're going to the early service," he said, "so see if she can meet me at the school at eleven."

* * * *

"Yes, I can be at the school then," Claire said. "Why?" There was no missing the wariness in her voice.

Martha needed to put her fears to rest.

"I watched your video," Martha backtracked. "It is *very, very* good."

She could sense the change in Claire's silence. First relief and then waiting for the "but." Martha charged forward.

"The reason we want to meet with you is to talk about one of the students in your video."

"Which one?" Claire asked cautiously.

"The young man looking through the garbage." More silence, this one wary.

"Is there something wrong?" Claire finally asked. Martha went straight to the point.

"We think he might be homeless and in need of some help. He quit coming to school quite a few weeks ago, and everyone's been worried about him, Mr. Johnson in particular."

More silence. Finally, "I know he's homeless," Claire announced. "I know where he lives."

Martha hadn't realized she had been holding her breath through the entire conversation until a huge sigh escaped. "Would you be willing to show us where?"

Martha couldn't see Claire nodding on the other end so found herself holding her breath again.

"Sure," she finally stated.

"Wonderful," Martha said. "Mr. Johnson and I will see you tomorrow in front of the school. And Claire … thank you." One more long hesitated pause before Martha heard …

"You're welcome."

Chapter 35

"So are we really going to church this morning, Gabriel?" Ruthie asked, excitement and expectation in her eyes.

"We are," Gabriel announced. Though he had vowed never to step foot in a church again, he had run out of excuses. Now he had to go, but not without some anxiety.

Ever since he had started stealing on a regular basis, his heart had hardened, but he knew that once he stepped back inside that church building, he would not only feel the weight of his sin but also the wrath of a God who didn't really seem too interested in his well-being anymore.

Ruthie had already pulled her yellow dress off the nail on the wall and was getting ready.

"C'mon, Gabriel," she urged. "Get ready!"

"We have time," he responded. Did you brush your teeth?"

"Yes," she said. "See?" And she smiled broadly. Gabriel moved in to check. The teeth looked clean, but even from a distance he could detect the strong odor of Ruthie's breath. Even with the mouthwash he had stolen, it still stunk. He looked at her hands, arms, and legs. They were still dry as well, though he watched her lather herself in the lotion he had also lifted. What else could he do?

"Okay," he said deciding not to press the point. "I'll get ready," and he headed to the wall where his cleanest shirt and pair of pants hung, changed into them, and then attempted to settle his and Ruthie's hair into place. They both needed haircuts—badly. Ten minutes later they were ready. Gabriel took a deep breath, grabbed Ruthie's hand, headed to the door, and took one last look around their room, his last one ever if God decided now was the time to judge him for his sins and strike him dead.

* * * *

Destiny sat listening to the congregation singing, not really paying attention to the words of the song. Though her heart was still heavy, there was a small—very small—window of hope. Yesterday at the park with Claire she had felt a spark of life. She hadn't had to talk. Claire was content with just walking around with her. Something about just being outside, with the real world surrounding her, feeling the snap in the air and the breeze in her hair. That tangible concreteness had for those two hours given her tired mind a reprieve from its obsessive cycle. She was glad Claire suggested going down to the river tomorrow for a smoothie. It would be another chance to feel again.

While the congregation sang, Destiny busied herself by flipping through her Bible, not looking for anything in particular, just keeping her fingers and mind busy. One page had been bookmarked, and the pages fell flat when she flipped to it. One verse was underlined: Jeremiah 29:11, "'For I know the plans I have for you,' declares the Lord, 'plans to prosper you and not to harm you, plans to give you hope and a future.'"

Destiny looked at the date. Almost today to the date, but three years earlier. That was when she first realized that she had the ability to be a competitive runner. She had read that verse and took it as God's blessing and assurance that her future in running was bright. She smiled sadly. How naive she had been. She had since learned that that particular promise had been made to the Israelites, exiled as a punishment from God. In times of uncertainty God had promised them "a hope and a future."

Destiny shook her head. She, like so many others, had taken that verse out of context and believed it was God's assurance of personal security and a prosperous future. And yet ... her heart quickened. Though she didn't want to misapply the verse again, she knew that God loved her as much as he did the scattered Israelites. She also knew that now that her future was uncertain, he wanted her to have hope as well. He wanted her to know that he hadn't abandoned her.

* * * *

"It's in here," Claire said, pointing toward the door of the abandoned building.

Travis stared first at the dilapidated door, then stepped back to take in the whole building, and finally took a sweeping look at the entire alley. He was far too familiar with places like this. He didn't want to sound like a Bible-thumping street preacher, but they truly were dens of iniquity—and dangerous. It was in such an abandoned building that the Marauders and many other gangs had taken up residence. Without even looking at her, he could feel Martha's motherly concern.

Travis took a deep breath, then smiled at Claire. "Do you mind leading the way?" he asked. Claire shook her head and pulled the door open. An overwhelming stench accosted the three, and they all took an involuntary step back.

"Oh my," Martha whispered, placing her hand over her nose. Travis gritted his teeth, and Claire felt her eyes burn, her hand involuntarily covering her nose.

"It didn't smell this bad when I was last here," she said through her fingers, apologetically, hoping they wouldn't blame her for not saying something sooner. *If it had been, I would have told someone,* she assured herself, but would she have? "It's up these stairs," she added, hoping that moving might make the two adults forget her involvement.

As they headed up the stairs, the smell became less offensive. Finally, they reached the section where Gabriel had removed the treads.

"I think he did this to protect him and his sister. Make it harder for others to come up," Claire said by way of explanation, "but you can just hold onto the side and step on the support boards and keep going. You just have to be a little careful." She showed them what she meant, traversing the open space that once housed three steps and a portion of landing. Travis went first, then helped Martha up. At the top, he looked back to see exactly what Gabriel had done.

He bent over, stared down into the black cavernous emptiness, and took a big sniff. His suspicions were confirmed. This was their toilet. No wonder the bottom floor reeked.

"This is the top floor, isn't it?" he asked.

Claire nodded, then led the way to the end of the hall and stopped before a closed door. She looked back at Travis, pointed at the door, and then stepped away. Travis stepped in front of her, and Martha moved closer to Claire, placing a reassuring hand on her shoulder. At first Claire tightened but then she relaxed, secretly glad that something was finally going to happen.

After a brief pause, Travis raised his fist and knocked firmly on the door. Nothing. He waited, then knocked again, this time louder. Still no answer. He pressed his ear to the door, trying to discern if there was any movement inside. He shook his head in answer to Martha and Claire's questioning looks and then tried the door knob. It turned, and he pushed the door open and stepped inside. The two women followed. None of the three spoke as they took in the meager furnishings and the desperate attempt at cleanliness. Finally Martha broke the silence, stating the obvious.

"They're not here."

Claire didn't respond, but Travis did.

"Not now, but they will be. We'll wait."

* * * *

Ruthie was singing, and Gabriel was smiling as they walked back toward their apartment. The two had had their fill of sweet rolls and fruit, and Gabriel hadn't been struck dead for his sins. All in all, not a bad morning.

Gabriel had noticed Mary's shock when the two had walked in, and he knew it wasn't just because they had finally decided to show up again. Gabriel could tell by the looseness of his own jeans and the thinness of Ruthie's arms and legs that they had both lost a lot of weight.

He could also see the wheels turning in Mary's head. As the shock shifted to concern, he knew she was debating what she should do, which raised a huge red flag for Gabriel. While they could use better food, warmer clothes, and other amenities, they didn't need someone meddling. Now he knew they wouldn't return to the church. They couldn't. Catching Mary by surprise was one thing, but giving her a week to conjure up a plan of action and then walk right back into a trap was quite another. He would have to figure out something to tell Ruthie.

"Did you know Jesus loves little children?" Ruthie asked.

"What?" Gabriel replied, his thoughts broken.

"Did you know that Jesus loves little children?" she repeated. "They are special to him, and they are a blessing to parents. Jesus got mad at his friends for trying to tell the children to go away. There is even a song about it." She broke into a song about how much Jesus loved the little children.

Children, a blessing? thought Gabriel. Tell that to his mother. In her eyes they had only been a burden. But it made no difference to Ruthie, who was still belting out the words she remembered and inserting "la la la" for the words she forgot. Gabriel listened as she walked and then the singing stopped abruptly, and a question came at him without warning.

"What did you learn this morning, Gabriel?" she asked.

Gabriel thought about it a moment. What *had* he learned? "We learned about a guy named Jonah."

"What about him?"

What about him indeed? Gabriel mused.

"Well, he was supposed to go to this town and tell the people to repent, and they would be saved. But he didn't want to, so he took off in the other direction and got on a boat to get further away." Ruthie stopped and looked up at him.

"Can you do that?" she asked. "I thought God was everywhere? How can you run away from him?"

Gabriel thought about that. *How indeed? Hmmm.* "Well, actually, he couldn't run away. God caused this huge storm to come up so all the guys on the boat started throwing things overboard so the boat wouldn't sink. When that didn't help, and it looked like they were going to capsize, Jonah came forward and said he was the reason for the storm because God was mad at him."

"So what happened?" she asked, starting to walk again.

"They threw Jonah overboard."

"What!" Ruthie stopped again. "Why did they do that?"

"Jonah told them to."

"What!" Ruthie exclaimed. "Why would he do that?"

Good question, Gabriel thought. "I guess because he knew he was wrong, and he was going to hurt a lot of other people by his disobedience."

"Did he die?" Ruthie asked, and Gabriel could detect the

sorrow in her voice. Gabriel shook his head.

"Nope. He got swallowed by a whale."

"WHAT!" Ruthie's disbelief grew louder. "Are you making this up, Gabriel?" Her uncertainty was getting the better of her.

Gabriel thought about that one. "No. It's in the Bible."

"Well, then he had to die if a whale swallowed him." Gabriel shook his head again.

"Nope. He didn't. Three days later, the whale threw him up on a beach, and he headed straight toward that town he ran away from in the first place. Decided he had better do what God said after all." Ruthie shook her head.

"I don't understand that story," she said.

Gabriel thought about it as well: a story about a guy mad at God and thinking he could do his own thing and just hide from God; a story that suddenly had an all too familiar ring to it. He felt himself shudder.

* * * *

"What time is it?" Martha asked.

Travis looked at his watch. "Twelve twenty."

Martha pursed her lips. "We've been here an hour, and they haven't shown up. I know Claire has things she needs to do. Why don't we go, let Claire have her afternoon, and you can come back, now that you know where they're living."

Travis hated to waste an opportunity or an advantage, and he had both now, but he really couldn't keep Claire here any longer, and even though she had led them here and could probably just walk home on her own, he was responsible for her and Martha's welfare. He would walk them back.

"Alright," he agreed. "I'll come back. They should be here by then."

* * * *

At first Gabriel didn't notice the door ajar as he was too busy working his way through the Jonah story, but when he put out his hand to push the door open, he stopped. It was not just ajar; it was open a foot. Someone had come in.

"Stop Ruthie," he said as he held his arm out in front of her to keep her from entering the building. He held his finger up to his lips to silence her from asking any questions. "Wait here," he instructed. "I'm just going to step inside for a minute."

Ruthie obeyed, and Gabriel carefully slid inside the building without moving the door any further. Once inside, he stopped and listened. Nothing. He approached the stairwell, stopping at the bottom of it, closing his eyes and listening carefully. He held his nose, trying not to breathe in the overwhelming odor of human waste. He waited a moment longer and then heard it. What, he wasn't sure. But somewhere high in the building, someone was there.

He leaned in a bit further, straining to hear. He had never stayed on the bottom floor long enough to have to endure the stench, and he was beginning to feel nauseous, but he couldn't leave. He had to know more. Carefully, he placed one foot on the bottom stair, starting his own climb when the sounds became louder. Footsteps he was sure, and voices, and they were getting louder, which meant they were coming down.

He removed his foot and quickly but quietly exited the building.

Ruthie saw his eyes and forgot about being quiet.

"What is it, Gabriel?"

Gabriel grabbed her by the shoulder, turning her around and heading back the way they had come. "Shhhh," he instructed. His eyes surveyed the scene in a panic, looking for a place to hide, which would also give him clear sight of the doorway when the intruders left.

Please, God, he said silently, *let us find a hiding place and make them go the other way.*

He knew it was a prayer, but he didn't have time to evaluate whether he was worthy of getting God's ear. He hustled Ruthie in front of him and then saw the dumpster, the far end pulled slightly away from the wall.

"Back here," he instructed, and pushed her in front of him and behind the dumpster. He followed her. The end facing their doorway was tight against the wall, but there was enough space for Gabriel to see the door clearly. He and Ruthie were so wedged in, that should the intruders come this way, they wouldn't be visible unless the others actually looked behind the dumpster. Gabriel sighed in relief. God must not be too mad at him.

The two waited, and Gabriel wondered if he had been mistaken. Perhaps there were others living in the building again, and they weren't coming out. But as soon as he thought that, out walked a white girl Gabriel judged to be in high school and very much *not* like someone who would be interested in an abandoned tenement. Gabriel's curiosity was piqued. Then out came two more, and Gabriel felt every breath of air leave his lungs and his life deflate.

Mrs. Richards and Mr. Johnson. He had been wrong. God *was* mad at him.

* * * *

Claire walked back toward the school deep in thought. If someone had told her a year ago, make that six months ago, heck even three months ago, that she would be helping lift a girl out of depression one day and find a homeless boy and his sister the next, she would have laughed because Claire never helped anyone. Claire's concern was only for herself.

But something had definitely changed in the last few months, and try as she might, Claire hadn't been able to fight it. The anger she had felt when they had moved here had dissolved. She still hurt over the demise of her family, but the peace of her mother, the hand of friendship from Destiny, Quintin, and Violet; the kindness of Mrs. Richards; and the willing suspension of disbelief by her new lunchtime friends had all had a part in chipping away at the self-centeredness and cynicism that had consumed her.

And there was something else as well. A yearning? A pulling? The God she had been mad at when she first arrived in Detroit was revealing himself as a very different God. One that listened. One that cared. She pulled her bottom lip under her top teeth in contemplation. One that might be worth knowing.

* * * *

"So where are we going to live, Gabriel?"

It was the one question Gabriel didn't want to hear because it was the one question he didn't have an answer for.

"I'm not sure," he answered honestly. "Just put on as many

clothes as you can and cram food in the backpack. I'll figure something out."

His hardened heart was breaking, and he was fighting back tears. He didn't know what he was going to do. He was failing in every way, and the weight of responsibility was crashing down on him, but he did know one thing—they couldn't stay here. Mr. Johnson had made sure of that. He would be back. The thought wiped away the sorrow and replaced it with a growing rage. Gabriel's face tightened in anger. How many times would God let that man ruin his life?

* ** *

Travis watched Martha drive off with Claire in the passenger seat. Once they had turned the corner, he headed back toward the alley. He would not leave until he had Gabriel and Ruthie in his possession.

It didn't take him more than fifteen minutes to retrace his steps. He swung open the door, held his breath, and took the steps two at a time. No need to be quiet. There was no place the children could go. When he got to where the gap in the stairs had been, he stopped short. The treads were in place, meaning the two were back. Still something was wrong. If they were there, then why not remove them again? Gabriel had removed them for their protection, hadn't he? Something in Travis's gut tightened, and a sense of dread began to grow. He carefully maneuvered past the loose boards and down the hallway.

When he reached their room, he saw the door ajar and a sinking feeling overcame him. When he stood in the open doorway, his worst fears were realized. The room was empty. The kids were gone, and they wouldn't be coming back. He had lost them again.

* * * *

Gabriel held Ruthie's hand as they wandered up one street and down another.

"What are we going to do, Gabriel?" she asked, and he could hear the fear in her voice; his own voice choked as he tried to respond.

"We're going to find another place," he replied. "It will be alright."

Ruthie didn't say anything for a moment, then spoke. "Couldn't we go back to the church? Maybe we could stay there? It wouldn't be so bad if someone found us, would it?"

Gabriel thought about both questions. He was tired, discourage, defeated ... and hungry. Maybe they should go back. Maybe it wouldn't be too bad. Maybe they would try to keep the two of them together. He let out a sigh of surrender.

"Okay," he agreed. "But I'm sure there isn't anyone there now. We'll have to wait until next Sunday. But then I promise we will tell Mary everything."

For the first time in over a month Ruthie let out a giggle and jumped up and down in excitement.

"Maybe Mary will take us," she suggested excitedly. "Maybe we can live with her. I like her."

Gabriel liked her too, but he didn't think it worked that way. He didn't think you could pick your parents.

Chapter 36

*T*ravis sat in his living room, playing the DVD then skipping back to the scene and playing it over and over again, watching the boy pull garbage out of the cans, check it out, and then wrap it in a newspaper. *Why hadn't I figured this out earlier?* he berated himself. *The hand-off of food on the first day. The anger when the knife was discovered. The pride in getting the job in the tutorial center. And then the disappearance. It all made sense now.*

He shook his head in dismay. He had lived in these neighborhoods all of his life. He knew the signs. He recognized homelessness and neglect. But he had been too proud. Yes, he, Travis Johnson, had thought he had licked the ghetto and had built such a strong and safe school environment that none of *his* students suffered from ghetto side effects. He was a blind, arrogant fool. And he had been so wrapped up in trying to save a school that he had lost a life.

Well, the heck with the school. If the school board and the district administration decided to close Montgomery High, they closed it. It mattered little to him now. He had done all he could. What mattered now was finding Gabriel and Ruthie. He wouldn't be a man of God if he didn't sort out his priorities.

He felt a pair of soft hands slide across his shoulders and start massaging them.

"Do you realize that you have been watching that slice of video for over an hour?" Cecile said softly. Travis smiled weakly, put his hands on top of hers, and gave them a squeeze.

"I can't get him out of my mind. I have to find him." She kissed the top of his head.

"God knows where he is," she reminded him. "We've prayed for his safety. God will bring him to us in his perfect timing."

Travis squeezed her hands again, gave a quick sigh, and looked up at her. "You know better than anyone that God's timing and my timing are never quite on the same page."

Cecile laughed. "Yes, I do. But I think you know that as much as you fret and fume and try to rush things, it never turns out for you, so why don't you take Psalm 46:10 to heart and be still and let God be God. He's got it under control. In the meantime, there are thirty more minutes of that DVD that Martha said are also a must-see. So I think you should watch them before you go to bed." That said, she took the remote, started the DVD at the beginning, and sat down next to Travis to make sure he didn't move.

* * * *

"So how is everything going?"

Claire asked the question with a whole stomach full of qualms. She had no idea where this might lead, but Mr. Richards had given her a couple of questions to ask, and if Destiny wanted to talk, she would. If she didn't, she wouldn't, and Claire didn't need to press any further.

"Okay," came the pat answer.

Now what? thought Claire. Was that an indication that Destiny didn't want to talk, or did she think Claire really wasn't interested? She decided to press.

"What do the doctors say about how your leg is healing?" It seemed a safe enough question. Pretty objective.

"Okay," Destiny replied, and even though it was the same answer, it had more sincerity to it this time. Claire just waited, not sure what to say or ask next, but before the silence became uncomfortable, Destiny continued. "There's not much they can do until they take the cast off. That will be in a couple more weeks. Then the rehab begins."

Claire nodded, let out a soft sigh of relief, and decided to follow this thread. Destiny had given her an opening. "Do you know what the rehab will be like?"

Destiny nodded, smiling softly. "I've had plenty of time to read up on that," she said. "Plus what the doctor told me." She paused and looked down at her cast as though notes were written there. "Massage and mobility exercises first. No weight on it at all. Then add strength excercises and walking and then … after about four or six months, I should be able to try normal activities." There was no missing the despondency accompanying these last words. Claire pondered whether to ask her next question, then went for it.

"Will you be able to run again?" She held her breath.

"Uh huh," she said.

Claire could feel the big "BUT" just hanging in the air. "But?" she asked.

Destiny sighed. "But I don't know if I will ever get back to where I was."

Claire pulled back in surprise. "Well, why wouldn't you?"

Destiny looked over at her. "Well, I know I could, it's just ..."

Claire waited.

"Just what?" she finally asked. Now Destiny stalled.

"Just if it will be in time."

"In time for what?" Claire asked, feeling very dense. Destiny hesitated again, and Claire didn't think she was going to answer the question. Finally Destiny just let the words pour out.

"In time to get a scholarship," she said. "In time for Michigan State to want me. In time for all the years of hard work to finally pay off!"

The last word got hung up on a choked sob, and Claire could see Destiny fighting to restrain the tears working their way to the surface. Claire had always wondered if she would know what to say if Destiny were to share her deepest fear. But Claire did know—for one important reason. A flood of feelings rushed back over her.

"I think I know how you feel," she said.

* * * *

Claire hadn't meant to share her story as that wasn't in the plan, but for the next hour, she told Destiny how she had hated her father for the affair and divorce and her mother for dragging her to Detroit, and both of them for ruining what looked to be a promising career.

"That school had connections," she explained. "And all the teachers thought I had something special, so I just knew I was going to break into the industry ... which you can do from Southern California ... but not from Detroit."

Destiny had listened intently. "So what are you going to do?"

Claire shrugged.

"No idea. But I keep looking up stuff on the internet, taking pictures, and trying new things."

While she was talking, Claire watched her friend carefully and then remembered a part of their first conversation.

"Are you one of those people who believes everything happens for a reason?" Claire had asked her.

"I am," Destiny had responded.

But was she? Now would be the time to see.

"Maybe God wants you to wait a year," Claire suggested. Destiny pulled her lips tightly together and knitted her brow, and Claire thought she might be angry, but she was wrong.

* * * *

Gabriel held Ruthie close to his body and wrapped the blankets around them both. He could feel her shiver next to him. He hadn't found them a room they could stay in for the entire week. Each place had something that scared him, so he would wait till late at night, find a spot that looked safe, sleep fitfully, and then move out early the next morning. Such a system made it difficult to find food, to take care of bodily needs, and to keep some semblance of cleanliness.

The only thing keeping Gabriel from breaking down was

knowing that Sunday this journey would be over. He had lost. He was defeated. He was ready to surrender. Tonight, however, they had found no suitable room, so again they had tucked themselves into a doorway, and Gabriel had wrapped the blanket around them. Ruthie's breathing was coming harder these days. She didn't look well. Her skin was even drier, and her breath still rank. Gabriel was worried. Ruthie was another reason to give up and get to the church. She was sick and needed attention.

The rasp of her breath became more rhythmic as she drifted off to sleep. Gabriel envied her because he knew, as he listened to the sounds of the street, that he wouldn't sleep at all.

Chapter 37

*T*ravis looked at the clock. Two thirty, Friday afternoon. He shuffled the pile of papers filled with statistics and narrative into a neat pile, made sure they were all in order, and then set them aside to give to his secretary. He placed Claire's DVD on top with a smile. All his weeks of gathering statistics paled in comparison to what her film did for Montgomery High. It was amazing both in quality and content.

He placed his hands on top of the pile and bowed his head. "Into your hands I commit this issue, Lord. There is nothing more I can do. May your will be done."

He raised his head, took in a deep breath, and then picked everything up and walked to the front office.

"Margaret, will you make sure that these papers are bound properly and then have them sent with the DVD over to the district office?" He handed off the items to Mrs. Green, who took them carefully then looked up at Travis.

"It's in God's hands now," he said with a smile.

* * * *

Martha placed the last few copies of *To Kill a Mockingbird* into one of the cabinets and then closed the door, signaling yet another last for her. She would no longer take a freshmen class through the world and eyes of Louise "Scout" Finch as she curiously watched her father bravely and expertly avoid the landmines of a segregated and angry South.

She let out a soft sigh. Many things she *would not* miss when she retired, but class discussions where students had to critically question and evaluate their beliefs rather than just blindly accept them was one part she *would* miss. For what a person allowed to take hold in his mind would eventually find a way into his heart.

* * * *

Danny took the stairs two at a time until he reached the third floor, then bent over to catch his breath. These stairs were murder. Why hadn't his mother moved to the first floor when she had the chance?

"The further away from the office the better," she always said. Away from the office meant away from the noise, the public, and the interruptions. Even students who were tasked with delivering hall passes despised the stairs, so they would organize their deliveries to make sure they had to climb them only once, which in turn meant that her classes were interrupted only once as well, a rare occurrence if you were on the first or even the second floor.

Danny peeked his head in her room and saw her leaning against the cupboard, arms crossed, with her eyes staring out the windows across the room. He stepped in.

"You okay?" he asked.

She started a bit at the sound of his voice but smiled when she saw him.

"Yes, just reflecting."

"Having second thoughts?"

"Not one bit," came the quick reply, and the smile became playful. "I'm ready. But that doesn't mean I won't miss a few things." She straightened up. "So what brings you up to the third floor?" she asked, knowing his dislike for the three flights of stairs. Danny grinned.

"Personal delivery message. Grace has checked the forecast. Weather is turning on Sunday, possible rain, and then it looks like the temperatures will begin to dip. She wants to move our last picnic to tomorrow instead of Sunday."

Martha's brow furrowed. She had already laid out her Saturday, allowing her Sunday free, and she hated change, but sixty years of life, thirty-six years of teaching, and a son and husband who thrived on spur-of-the-moment decisions had taught her a bit of flexibility. The smile returned.

"I think that would be wonderful. What time?"

"Twelve thirty." Martha opened her mouth to speak, but Danny held up his hand, knowing exactly what she was going to ask. "And yes, Travis knows and has already agreed."

Martha smiled and nodded approvingly. Though Travis was not her biological son, his DNA was wired more like hers than Danny's was.

* * * *

Gabriel felt Ruthie's forehead. She was hot. Too hot. He looked at her lips. They were cracked and dry. Her eyes seemed to be sinking into her head.

"I have a headache, Gabriel, and I'm really thirsty," she complained. "I want some water."

Tonight they were tucked back in the remains of an abandoned factory. He could hear something scurrying on the floor behind him, and he hated himself. He wanted to cry. But he couldn't. He had to help Ruthie. Gabriel looked around him. The couple of plastic bottles they used for drinking were already empty. Where was he going to get water? How far would he have to go? He looked at Ruthie again, and he knew she was very sick. She needed more than water. She needed food. She needed help. Gabriel bit his lip.

"Don't go anywhere, Ruthie," he said, grabbing his backpack and kissing her forehead, the heat searing his lips. "I'll be right back." Like she had a choice.

* * * *

Gabriel could feel his heart pounding in his chest as he picked up first one box and then another, reading the labels, then checking the security mirrors to watch the cashiers. Ruthie needed medicine. Which one of these would cut her fever? Unshed tears were stinging his eyes making it difficult to read the information. A thought kept nagging him in the back of his mind: Would Ruthie die? The thought forced a sob to catch in his throat, sounding like a grunt. If she did, it would be all his fault.

He didn't have time to waste. He found one that said something about fever, looked around, and then stuffed it in his bag. Now the hard part. The convenience store was small and the customers few.

Gabriel had surveyed the layout when he came in and knew what he had to do.

He moved to the back of the store where the hotdogs were turning in the cooker. He pulled out two, put mustard and ketchup on both, wrapped them up, and then set them aside. He then went to the refrigerator and pulled out a large carton of orange juice. Finally, he found a large package of nuts.

Gabriel took his items and moved to the side of the store, checked the security mirror to make sure the teller was occupied, then placed the backpack on the floor, opened it wide, and, as fast as he could, put in the orange juice, nuts, and hotdogs. He glanced up again and now saw the teller looking at him. He quickly zipped up the pack, slung it on his back, and headed for the door.

"Hey! Kid! What do you think you're doing?"

Gabriel could see him slam the register drawer shut and start moving his way. At the same time, a man in line dropped his items on the floor and came after him as well. That was all Gabriel needed to see. His heart and feet were in full throttle, and he threw the door open and sprinted off, barely avoiding a head-on with a pedestrian.

Gabriel never looked back, but he could hear feet pounding the pavement behind him as he ran. He knew he wasn't running in the right direction, but he kept running, turning corners, then running again. He heard a siren and wondered if it was for him. He had never known the police to act so quickly, but he was afraid now would be the time. He turned another corner and shot into an empty doorway, pressed himself against the wall, and waited, not able to hear anything but his heart pounding in his temples.

He wasn't sure how long he waited, but he never moved until his breathing returned to normal and the alley was quiet. Then he poked his head around the corner, making sure all was clear before working his way carefully back to Ruthie.

Chapter 38

*T*he orange juice and medicine seemed to help, but Ruthie wasn't able to keep the hotdog down, and Gabriel was forced to find a way to clean up after her. It was almost impossible without any fresh water, so all he could do was take one of his shirts and wipe it up. Still the smell lingered.

Ruthie had finally fallen asleep, but her sleep was fitful, and, as always, Gabriel felt like he never slept, but he must have because when he finally awoke, the building was flooded with autumn light. But it was still cold, and Gabriel wrapped his jacket tighter around him.

He looked down at Ruthie, and he could hear her labored breathing. He leaned back against the wall and felt himself drift off to sleep again. Today was Saturday. Maybe they could just spend the day sleeping. Then tomorrow ....

He drifted off to sleep again, but Ruthie's coughing woke him from somewhere deep, and he felt completely disoriented.

"Mom. Mom, where are you?" Ruthie mumbled. "Mom, help

me. I don't feel good."

Gabriel forced himself up and over to Ruthie's side.

"Ruthie! Ruthie! Wake up!" he said loudly, shaking her and then feeling her forehead. She was still burning up. "Ruthie! Wake up!" he yelled and shook her harder. Ruthie, eyes still closed, continued to moan her response.

"Mom, don't leave. Help me."

"Ruthie! It's me, Gabriel!" he yelled, and he could hear the panic in his own voice.

"Mom, I don't feel well."

Gabriel sat back on his heels, his head reeling. He had to do something. He had to get help. But where? *The church,* he thought. But this was Saturday. Would anybody be there? He didn't know but he would have to try.

"Ruthie, stay calm," he said. "I'm going for help. I'll be right back. Don't move."

He doubted she would. He doubted she could, but it made him feel better to say it; it made him feel a bit more in control of a situation that was completely out of his control.

* * * *

Claire lay on her bed, a book by her side, and stared at the ceiling of her room. Two one-inch black marks stared back at her. As she stared at them, two names materialized. Destiny and Gabriel. A chill shot down her body followed by an inner urging to pray for them. *Where did that come from?* she thought. She had been sort of praying lately, what with Destiny's situation and Gabriel's absence, but she had never had this sense that she *had* to. *Pray now.* The urging was more intense and frightened Claire, but she obeyed, closed her eyes, and said a quick six-word prayer. "Please, God, take care of them."

* * * *

Destiny sat out on the back patio taking in the crisp sharpness of the late October air, her lunch by her side. Her mind was finally beginning to feel sharp. The dullness of the past two months was beginning to fade, her moods were balancing out, and life seemed more livable. She was grateful to Claire for just being there, forcing her outside where her mind could focus on other things, and her body could feel the tangible realness of the world.

Claire had challenged her as well. Not harshly, nor even knowingly, but nevertheless convincingly. Through her questions and statements, she had forced Destiny to reevaluate her faith, a faith that had been badly shaken when her injury had occurred. What Destiny had learned was humbling. She had realized that she had accrued a lot of head knowledge about God, but had never really learned to trust him. She had claimed Jesus as her friend, Lord, and Savior but had never had that tested. When things were going her way and lining up with her plans, it was easy to believe God had her back.

But when the floor of her life and dreams gave way, she fell straight into an emotional abyss, leaving her with a vacuum desperate to be filled, and, though it took time, God did not disappoint. Finally, more verses, ones she had memorized in Sunday school years ago, started coming to mind.

"When I am weak, then I am strong," 2 Corinthians 12:9-10,

because Christ's "strength is made perfect in weakness."

And then I Peter 5:6: "Therefore, humble yourself under the mighty hand of God, that He may exalt you in due time, casting all your care upon Him for He cares for you."

So, it was proving true just as God had promised in Isaiah 55:11:

So shall My word be that goes forth from My mouth;

It shall not return to Me void

But it shall accomplish what I please,

And it shall prosper in the thing for which I sent it.

... His word had not come back void, but had brought with it a new hope, and the start to a deeper, more personal relationship with God. She was now willing to rest her life and her future in his hands.

* * * *

Travis placed the ice chest in the trunk of the car and shut it. A Saturday picnic would normally have thrown him out of sorts as his weekend routine would have been completely disrupted, but it didn't today. Ever since yesterday, when he had bundled up his presentation to save Montgomery High from the chopping block and turned the results over to God, he had felt at peace about the outcome.

"Montgomery High may close," he had told Cecile, "but if it does, I will know it is because it serves God's ultimate purpose. I don't know what that is, but I don't need to worry about it. I have done my part."

Cecile had given his arm a squeeze and then kissed him on his forehead.

"Are you willing to do the same with Gabriel?" she asked, and his countenance had darkened immediately.

"I know I should," he said, "but I just can't sit on my hands while two young lives are in danger. But I don't know what to do. I don't know where to start. Plus, the police already know they're missing."

"And so does God," Cecile reminded him. "So does God."

* * * *

Gabriel ran straight to the church, praying that someone would be there.

Please, God. Please, let Mary be there. Let this be the day they give away clothes. Please don't let Ruthie die. I promise I will do whatever you want. I will be good. I won't steal anymore. I will let them split Ruthie and me up. Just don't let her die and let the church be open.

But the church was locked tight. Gabriel tugged on the door, willing it open, then banged on it with both fists. Perhaps someone was in there, behind the locked doors. He pressed his ear to the door to listen. Nothing.

He ran around to the back. Maybe that's where they were. Tomorrow was church, so surely someone would be here working to set everything up. But disappointment greeted him again as the small parking lot at the rear was empty as well.

Gabriel fought back the tears. *Now what?* He forced himself to think and then realized he had one other option. The park. Many of those parents knew him and Ruthie by sight, and a few knew them by name. Surely one of them would help him. A second later, he was running again.

* * * *

"Well, the weather is definitely changing," Martha acknowledged, pulling her sweater tighter against her. "You were wise, Grace, to get us all together today, as this might be it for the year."

The younger woman smiled. "I think *I* will miss it the most," she confessed. "Two very active children in the house over the winter is quite a challenge."

Martha smiled as she watched her son play with her two grandchildren. As usual Matthew had his soccer ball and was fastidiously practicing his dribbling and passing with his father. They were trying to include little Abigail, but her free spirit just wouldn't allow her to get pulled into routine drills. Instead, when the ball came to her, she would snatch it up and run with it—in any direction except toward her brother and father.

Matthew, ever the rules keeper, would yell that she couldn't use her hands, missing the entire point of Abigail's shenanigans. Danny would run and pick her up and bring her back, set her down, remove the ball from her clutches, and then place it on the ground in front of her, prompting her to kick it.

She would acquiesce, lulling them into a false sense of security, and then that sly little smile would reappear, telegraphing to anyone who saw it that more trouble was just around the corner.

* * * *

"Time to eat!"

Grace made the call and Matthew picked up his ball and ran for the picnic table. Danny made sure he had Abigail clearly in front of him as he made his way back to the others. When they all had gathered around the table that held the food, Graydon held out his hands, and the others followed suit, taking the hand closest to him or her until a unified circle had been made. Then, with heads bowed, he began to bless the food and their time together.

"Father," he began, "we thank you for the opportunity to gather as a family and to enjoy this food and this time together. We pray that you take care of those without family or food, and if there are some here in this park today who might need our companionship or our meal, then please make us aware and willing to share both as a demonstration of your love. In Jesus's name, amen."

"Amen," everyone chorused as the handholds broke and the plates were picked up.

"Abigail, would you like some fried chicken?" Martha asked her granddaughter as Abigail held out her plate. Abigail nodded. "What do you say?"

"Please."

Martha smiled and placed a leg on her plate.

"Thank you."

"You're welcome. Potato salad?"

Another nod and then the remembered please followed by the thank you. Martha placed a spoonful on her plate.

"Alright, you go sit down and if you finish it all, you can have some more."

Abigail took her plate, went back to the table where the place settings were, and laid it down at the end. Then she saw the soccer ball, and that small sly smile played on her lips. She glanced at the others and realized they were all working their way through the line, even Matthew. No one was watching her. Now was her chance. She grabbed the ball and ran to the nearest tree, peeked around, saw they were still serving themselves, and headed toward the park sign, which she had deemed her favorite hiding place. She had to hold the ball in both hands and it wobbled back and forth in front of her.

She had almost made it to the sign when her mother, having filled her own plate and Matthew's, realized Abigail wasn't at the table. One quick look up and a scan of the park, and she saw her daughter running awkwardly toward the far side of the park.

"Abigail! Get back here!"

When Abigail heard her mother's cry, she jumped involuntarily but then giggled and kept running.

"Abigail! Stop now!"

That was her father's voice, and when she slowed to turn and look behind her, she could see him already running toward her. She squealed, dropped the soccer ball, and turned back around and ran toward the sign, but then at the last minute changed her mind and made an abrupt right, heading for the cars parked along the street.

* * * *

Gabriel sprinted to the corner of the building and stopped to catch his breath as he surveyed the park. His eyes swept to the far side of the playground near the swings, as there he would find the parents who would be most familiar with him and Ruthie. He put his hand up to his eyes to shield the afternoon sun. His eyes scanned the play area, and he felt his hopes die. No one he recognized. Then he heard a laugh and looked to his left and there she was. Abigail laughing and running with Matthew's soccer ball. He felt a sigh of relief. The Richardses were here. Things were going to be okay. He was going to be able to get help for Ruthie.

He started toward the park when he heard Mr. Richards yell for Abigail. He looked left and saw him, and then his heart stopped. Right behind him stood Mr. Johnson.

* * * *

Danny's heart was in his throat when he saw his young daughter squeal, drop the ball, and then turn toward the street. His feet felt leaden, like he was moving in slow motion. His heart stopped completely when she slid between the two cars and peeked back at him.

"No! Please no, Lord. Don't let her—" but before he could finish his prayer, she was up and moving again.

* * * *

Travis had looked up when he heard Grace's shout for Abigail to stop, and then he dropped his plate when he heard the terror in Danny's voice and saw the scene unfolding before him.

"Dear God, no," he prayed under his breath and sprinted after Danny, almost catching up to him when he saw Abigail peek around the car, smile mischievously, and then head for the street.

* * * *

Gabriel watched as Abigail dropped the ball and make her escape. He stood paralyzed and his heart pounded in his chest. He watched her approach a car and duck behind it. His mouth went dry and his pulse quickened when he watched her peek around the car, see her father, and then stand up to run again, only this time her only course was onto the street itself.

In horror, he looked first to his right and then left, and there it was, a car coming from the left. Without thinking, he started running toward Abigail.

"NO!" he screamed as he approached the curb. By this time, Abigail was already in the street running toward him but looking back at her father. She didn't see the car. Gabriel didn't look both ways; he just sprinted straight for her.

He heard the screams from the family and the squeals of tires as he and Abigail reached the middle of the road at the same time, and then he leaped toward her in a flying football tackle, hoping to keep her in the far lane. He felt a severe jolt as something slammed into his leg a second after he crashed into Abigail, and he tumbled to the pavement. The next thing he remembered was an excruciating pain shooting through his body before he lost consciousness.

* * * *

"Ahhhhh," Gabriel cried out, his eyes shut tight against the pain.

"It's okay, son. I've got you," a deep, soothing voice whispered in his ear, and he could feel the strong arms cradling him. "You're going to be okay."

In his own darkness, Gabriel didn't feel like he was going to be okay. In fact, he could feel himself slipping away again.

"Abigail," he cried.

"She's fine, son. She's fine," came the voice.

Then only one thought remained, and it brought panic with it.

"Ruthie," he wheezed. "Please help her. Please. Concord." And then he was gone.

* * * *

Travis held Gabriel in his arms and felt the boy's weight double when he went unconscious. He stared down at the mangled leg. The driver had swerved to avoid hitting him, but the left front bumper had caught Gabriel's left leg squarely, snapping it instantly. Cecile had immediately called 911, and in the distance the sirens could be heard. The driver of the car had immediately pulled over and jumped out, crazed with concern.

"He just darted out from nowhere," he kept repeating. "I didn't see him coming. Is he okay? Is the little girl okay?" Graydon Richards had taken the driver aside, trying to calm and reassure him that it was indeed not his fault.

Meanwhile, Danny had snatched Abigail up and out of the street within seconds of the collision. She had scrapes and contusions from hitting the ground with such force from Gabriel tackling her, but Danny knew the screaming was more from being scared than anything else. She might have been dead had Gabriel not risked his own life to stop her.

Abigail was visibly shaking, and Danny did the best he could to calm her, but he was shaking badly too. Finally, Grace, after making sure Gabriel was okay, gently pulled their daughter out of her father's arms and into her own, whispering to her in an effort to soothe her, and then began to look at her wounds.

The ambulance arrived, and Travis stepped back as the paramedics went to work. Cecile moved in next to him, slid her hand through his arm, and pulled him close to her.

"He's going to be okay," she assured him. Travis nodded.

"But his leg is badly broken. I would be surprised if it wasn't shattered," he responded, and his face couldn't hide his worry. "Will you follow the ambulance to the hospital?" he asked. "I want to go and find his sister."

"Do you know where to look?" she asked, and he nodded.

"I have a place to start. He mentioned Concord. I am assuming that is Concord Street. Where on Concord I don't know, but I will start nearest to the park and just keep looking until I find her." Cecile gave him another squeeze.

"Why don't you take Danny and Graydon with you? Martha, Grace, and I will take Matthew and go to the hospital. Abigail needs to get checked out, and it will give Danny something to do." Travis nodded, turned, and gave her an uncharacteristic public kiss, which told her he was eternally grateful for both her and her wisdom.

"Good idea," he said, "but we will need you to pray," he added. "Pray for Gabriel and please pray that we find Ruthie."

* * * *

Concord Street ran over five miles, but Travis figured they should start on the north side of the park as that was the direction Gabriel was coming from.

"I don't see him crossing the road only to come back," he reasoned. "And there are more abandoned buildings on that side anyway. Just makes more sense."

So they had worked their way up the street, trying doors from the street side and then doubling back through the alleys in case they could gain access there. Block one had only one empty building, locked up tight. Block two was a bit more promising with three vacant houses, all open, and the men divided them between them to search.

They crossed Gratiot Ave and continued northwest.

Each block revealed nothing, and Travis was getting discouraged and thought that he had taken the wrong direction. They were far from the park now. Why would Gabriel have come to the park if he lived this far away? He looked at the options before him. A dangerously derelict house on the right and the remains of an old automotive plant on the left. He didn't move.

"What's wrong, Travis," Danny said. "Aren't you going to take a look?"

Travis stared at the abandoned plant again, and gave out a sigh.

"Yeah," he said. "But if she's not in there, I think we should go to the hospital and see if we can get more information from Gabriel."

"If he's awake," Graydon reminded him. "I'm betting they took him right into surgery. It might be awhile before he comes out from under the anesthesia."

Travis pursed his lips. True, he thought, the small thread they had to go on was proving to be very flimsy. *Lord, let us find her,* he prayed. *Let us find her soon.* He knew Ruthie must be in desperate need if Gabriel had run to the park for help, especially if he had run from here.

"Why don't you start on the left side, Danny," Graydon directed, "and Travis, you take the middle while I start on the right. I'm thinking if she is in here, she's on the bottom floor. It looks pretty hazardous to go any higher."

The others agreed and started their search, calling out Ruthie's name as they moved toward the back of the building, then waited, hoping for a response. Nothing. Travis reached the back end without success. No Ruthie. She wasn't here. Graydon moved toward him from his right, and Travis could see the disappointment on his face. The two walked toward Danny who had completed his canvassing as well and was turning toward them. No luck.

They wouldn't have found her if Graydon hadn't tripped on an exposed backpack strap. Travis turned to help stop his fall when he saw the pile in the corner. A blanket was all, but there was definitely something under the blanket.

"Ruthie!" Travis yelled, releasing Graydon. "Ruthie!" he yelled again, jumping over debris and around exposed posts to reach the bundle. He pulled back the thin, dirty blanket to expose a very tiny black girl, huddled in the fetal position.

"Ruthie, can you hear me?" he asked gently, and reached down to stroke her forehead. She was burning up.

"Call 911!" he yelled. "We've got to get her to the hospital! Now!"

Chapter 39

$\mathcal{T}$ravis, Danny, and Graydon followed the ambulance to the same hospital that Gabriel had been taken to, and the one where Grace worked. They caught up with Cecile, Grace, and Martha to exchange reports. There was nothing that Grace could do for Gabriel during surgery, but when she saw the state little Ruthie was in, she checked herself in to work. She followed Ruthie into the emergency room, got the okay from the doctor in charge, and took over Ruthie's care.

Gabriel was still in surgery.

"Did they say how long he would be in there?" Travis asked. Cecile shook her head.

"No, but Grace thought it would at least be another hour or so." Travis listened, turned an idea over in his head, then made a decision.

"I'll be right back. There's something I have to get from school," he said.

"Now?" questioned Cecile. "What could be more important

at school?"

Travis didn't answer. "I'll be back before he wakes," was his only reply. And with that he left.

* * * *

Gabriel could hear muffled sounds around him but nothing was registering. His head felt heavy and his body immobile. What had happened? Where was he? He tried hard to open his eyes but they refused to cooperate, and he began to feel a bit nauseous. He tried again, and this time they opened just a sliver. All he could see was an intense blue in front of him. He willed his eyes to focus and when they did, clouds appeared, their underbellies the color of cantaloupe.

Am I dead? Gabriel wondered. *Am I in heaven?* For the colors were so rich and peaceful. The heaviness and aching, though, caused him to reconsider. *No, I don't think people hurt or feel sick in heaven. So am I in hell?* The incongruity of the situation confused him, but his senses were sharpening with each second, and the scene was becoming clearer. There was a blackness beneath the clouds, a silhouette of a mountain range, and as his eyes returned to their normal focus, he realized he was looking at a large painting, one he had seen before.

"What?" he stammered. His voice caused the head next to him, one that had been bowed in prayer, to pop up, and the body attached to it leaned toward him.

"Gabriel?" came the deep, resonant voice, the same soothing voice he had heard not too long ago.

Gabriel turned toward the voice and saw the face it belonged to. The face didn't register. It shouldn't be here. Gabriel looked back at the huge painting sitting on an easel at the foot of the bed and then back at the face. The face looked concerned.

"Mr. Johnson?" he choked.

Travis placed his hand on Gabriel's head. "Shhhh," he said softly. "Just rest. You have been one very courageous young man today."

Travis's words sparked a memory in Gabriel. "Abigail?" he asked, worry written in his eyes. Travis smiled.

"She's fine ... thanks to you. Though you might want to think about playing football. That was a heck of a tackle you put on her." The words were out of his mouth before he thought better of them. Football was probably *not* in Gabriel's future. Travis hoped walking was.

Now it was Gabriel's turn to smile, weak though it was, and he seemed to rest a moment until another thought shocked him awake, and he looked fearfully back at Travis, afraid to ask the question. Finally, he mustered up the courage.

"Ruthie?" His eyes were a mixture of hope and trepidation. Travis nodded to Gabriel's right, and Gabriel turned his head to find a second bed in his room. Mrs. Johnson was on the far side and a doctor was on the near side.

"She's a very sick little girl," Travis told him, "but she is in good hands. I think you know Dr. Richards, don't you?"

Hearing her name, Grace turned around to see Gabriel looking at her, and she moved away from Ruthie to his bedside. She took his hand and squeezed it, then bent down to give him a lingering kiss on his forehead. Tears were in her eyes.

"Thank you for saving Abigail's life today," she said, her eyes deep with emotion, "and for saving your sister's as well," she added, nodding to the bed behind her.

Gabriel looked up, hopefully, expectantly. "Is she going to be okay?"

Grace nodded but did not smile. "Eventually, but she is extremely dehydrated, which has caused a few other complications. She will need to stay in the hospital for a few days until her body regulates itself.

Gabriel felt a stab of guilt slice through him, and his countenance darkened.

"She wouldn't be this sick if it weren't for me," he confessed, heaping the guilt on himself in truckloads.

Grace placed her hand on his arm and gave it a squeeze. "She wouldn't be here now if it weren't for you," she said, then added. "She's okay now. That's all that matters."

Travis listened to the interchange, but as he watched Gabriel struggling with his conscience, he knew that that wasn't all that mattered. Gabriel needed forgiveness.

* * * *

Danny sat with Abigail in a separate room while a nurse cleaned and tended to her cuts and scrapes. Grace had been with them, doing much of the work herself until Ruthie came in. Now it was just he and Abigail, the nurse, his thoughts, and a strong, unsettling realization: he could not absolutely, positively protect his daughter. Try as he might, he could not watch her or be by her side twenty-four seven. And what was becoming even clearer was that she had a will of her own. True she was only three, and he, as her father, had a responsibility to teach her how to make good choices, to discipline her when she didn't, and to instill good values, but there was only so far he could go. There would always come some point where she would be out of his reach. Out of his hands of protection.

But as today had shown, she was not out of God's.

* * * *

"What happened?" Claire asked. It was eight o'clock at night, and Mrs. Richards had called to tell her that Gabriel and his sister had been found but were in the hospital. Martha filled her in on the details, telling her that they would probably be there a week at least. Claire listened intently, mulling another question around in her mind.

"What time did all this happen?" she asked, her heart quickening as she waited for the answer.

"Around twelve thirty," Martha replied.

Claire's heart caught. Twelve thirty. She glanced up at the two black lines in her ceiling. The same time she was urged to pray.

Chapter 40

"I'll pick you up at after work, and we'll go down together?" Travis asked. Cecile nodded. and Travis smiled. "See you around three thirty then."

* * * *

Travis sat at his desk at loose ends. There was much he should be doing, but his mind wouldn't focus. His eyes scanned his office and landed on the verse on his desk—Psalm 147:4—"He determines the number of the stars and calls them each by name." That verse, reminding him of God's overwhelming love and attention, was the reason he worked so hard to learn every student's name—and many of their meanings. But as he read and reread the verse, he suddenly realized something: he wasn't God. True, he could learn the name of every person in his little universe just as God new the name of everything and everyone in his universe, but he couldn't truly *know* or *love* every one of them. Humans, in their finite form, were called to love intimately on a much smaller scale, and there were two names belonging to two children lying in a hospital that he realized he loved very much. Two names whose meanings rang true even if the children didn't know it. Gabriel–God is my strength, and Ruth–companion and friend.

* * * *

"Room 324. Third floor. Elevators are to your left. They are both in the same room."

Claire thanked the volunteer at the information desk and headed for the elevators. She wasn't quite sure why she had come. She didn't know Gabriel or Ruthie personally, but after three days, something inside kept telling her that this was a loose thread that needed to be tied.

She watched the room numbers as she worked her way down the corridor until she stopped just shy of the doorway of room 324. All of a sudden this didn't seem like such a good idea. What was she going to do? Say?

She took a step back, ready to make an about-face and head back out, when that inaudible voice out of nowhere said *Go in.* She stopped. She really didn't want to, but the last time that voice nudged her it was to pray, and look at what had happened. She stepped back to the doorway and looked in. Gabriel was lying in the nearest bed, his eyes closed and his left leg elevated in a sling and encased in a toe-to-thigh cast.

That can't be good, she thought, and looked past him to see his sister, but the curtain had been drawn. The closed eyes caused her to waver again, but before she could make her escape, the boy opened his eyes and turned toward her. *Caught,* Claire thought, and there wasn't much she could do now but continue.

"Hi," she said, entering the room and extending her hand. "I thought we should meet. I'm the bag lady."

* * * *

Claire hadn't known what to expect, but she certainly hadn't expected the reaction she received. Gabriel didn't answer right away, and she could tell by the working of his jaw and the flicking of his eyes that he was trying hard not to cry.

"You left the sandwiches?" he finally asked, and she nodded. "Why?"

Good question, she thought. What had possessed her to start leaving food for them? She thought back through the weeks to that day she had followed him to his hideaway and then had come back when she knew he wouldn't be there. It was his attempt at making a clean and tidy home for him and his sister, that desire to survive, that had prompted her to act.

"I guess I just wanted to help," she said.

"It did help," he said, leaving the unasked question lingering heavy in the air. Claire decided to tackle it.

"Sorry I missed a day," she apologized. "You probably thought I had abandoned you." She knew the answer because he had never returned, and she could see in the hard line his face now took that she was right.

"But I hadn't," she continued. "I was just late and missed you." Now his face softened.

"It's okay," he said. "It wasn't your responsibility to take care of us," and Claire saw both sorrow and guilt spread across his face. Then these, too, disappeared. "Mr. Johnson tells me it was you who found out where we were living." Now Claire sensed a suspended accusation—*forcing us out on the street.* But before she could respond, Gabriel did.

"Thank you," he said quietly.

* * * *

"Should we tell them tonight?"

Travis pulled his lips together in thought as he and Cecile walked toward the hospital doors. Gabriel and Ruthie had been in the hospital three days now and were recovering nicely, according to the doctors. Ruthie was gaining weight already, and her bodily functions were returning to normal. What Gabriel's leg might look like down the road was still uncertain, but he seemed to be out of pain. Travis nodded.

"They need to know. Now is as good a time as any."

As they neared the door, they heard laughter and looked at each other curiously. A moment later the mystery was solved. Ruthie was on Gabriel's bed, IV stand moved, courtesy of a kind nurse, and Claire was sitting in a chair next to them. Someone had said something funny, and the three were still enjoying it. Travis smiled inwardly. *Claire,* he thought. *Luminous and strong. She certainly has been a light in some dark worlds.*

"Well, this is pleasant surprise," Cecile remarked, smiling as she entered the room. Claire jumped up from her chair. "No, please sit," Cecile told her and then introduced herself. "I imagine you already know my husband."

"Hello, Mr. Johnson," she said.

"Claire," he replied, and the talking stopped.

Cecile let out a little laugh and looked at Claire conspiratorially. "Now, you know the length of conversations that take place in my home," she said, and Claire returned her smile.

"Gabriel doesn't talk much either," Ruthie inserted.

"We say more," Travis retorted in their defense, "when necessary ... right, Gabriel?" he added, hoping for a little male support.

Gabriel did not disappoint. "Right."

* * * *

Claire stayed only a few moments longer, complimented Travis on his beautiful painting—Gabriel had let it out of the bag—and then left. That left Ruthie and Gabriel together on the bed together. Now was the time.

Travis cleared his throat. There was no easy way to do this, and he knew Gabriel well enough now to know he would want it straight. Cecile moved to the far side of the bed, sat at the foot of it, and waited. Travis looked over at Ruthie and smiled softly then turned back to Gabriel and looked him straight in the eye.

"There's something we need to tell you," he said, and Gabriel waited patiently, never dropping his hold on Travis's eyes. Travis took a deep breath. "Your mother is dead."

Neither child said anything for a moment; then they could hear Ruthie breathing hard.

"What?" she said. "She's dead? What happened?" Cecile moved in next to her and wrapped her arms around the girl. Gabriel's eyes never wavered. Travis dropped his eyes in contemplation, debating whether to answer the question or not but when he looked back at Gabriel, he could see the set of his jaw and an ever so slight shake of the head. *Don't,* was written all over his face. Travis respected the boy's wishes. There would be time for details later—much later—when Ruthie could better understand the answers. He chose to be vague.

"No one's sure exactly what happened."

"Gabriel," Ruthie said between hiccups, "This is why she never came back for us. She didn't leave us. She died."

Gabriel smiled weakly and nodded at his sister, then touched her hand lovingly.

"Yeah," was all he said, before looking back at Travis. The hardness and hurt had returned, and Travis knew Gabriel was aware of the *exact* order of events.

Chapter 41

*M*artha gathered up her papers and put them in her bag. This had been a tough week, and none of it had to do with school. She smiled wryly. Retirement might not be so relaxing after all.

* * * *

Travis and Cecile headed toward the hospital doors for the umpteenth time that week, but they were nearing the end. Both Ruthie and Gabriel were scheduled to be released tomorrow. Both had heard the news the day before, Ruthie voicing the concern that they knew Gabriel was brooding over.

"Where are we going to go?" she had asked. "Is Mary going to take us home?"

Mary Montrose, after learning of their plight, had visited them every day, but had said nothing about taking the two children in, yet Ruthie's enthusiasm manifested her optimism while Gabriel's sullen silence testified of his skepticism. Only Travis and Cecile knew the truth.

Travis punched the elevator button and then reached out and

took Cecile's hand, giving it an encouraging squeeze, but remained silent until they entered the kids' room. Cecile immediately went to Ruthie and gave her a big hug, then turned back toward Gabriel and kissed him lightly on the forehead.

"How are you two today?" she asked.

"I'm much better!" Ruthie exclaimed, and it was obvious by her bright eyes and increased energy that she was. Gabriel merely smiled and glanced at his suspended leg.

"The doctor showed me my Xray today. I have a ton of rods and pins in my leg. I'm bionic." Then his face clouded over. "It's pretty messed up."

Travis reached out and squeezed the boy's shoulder. "Your healing's in the early stages," he said. "Don't jump to conclusions. There's a lot of time for growing strong again, and you're in good hands." Though Gabriel might only interpret this statement in light of his physical recovery, Travis knew there was a lot of emotional and spiritual healing that needed to take place as well.

Cecile glanced over at her husband and nodded, and Travis knew they couldn't delay the inevitable any longer. Cecile lifted Ruthie from her bed and placed her next to Gabriel, while Travis pulled over two chairs for Cecile and him to sit on. Travis looked first at Ruthie who waited expectantly. Then he turned his attention to Gabriel, who was watching him warily, and cleared his throat. "You are both going to be released tomorrow," he said, stating a fact both children knew.

"I know," Ruthie said, "but we still don't know where we're going to go."

Travis looked over at Cecile, who picked up the conversation. She looked first at one and then the other.

"We would like you to come home with us," she said.

Ruthie's eyes grew big. "Really? Forever?"

Travis inwardly winced. That was a tough question to answer right now. If it was merely up to them, it would be a definitive yes, but there were procedures and paperwork and bureaucracy to navigate. So much of it was out of their hands, that whether or not the children would eventually be in their permanent care was uncertain. Cecile, however, handled it beautifully. She laughed and gave Ruthie another hug.

"Well, how do you know you will want to live with us forever?" she asked. "Let's just wait and see. But you will be with us for a week or two at least."

Ruthie couldn't suppress her excitement. She was jumping up and down on her knees and clapping her hands in excitement.

Travis kept his attention on Gabriel who was watching his sister with a more tempered joy, for even though Gabriel knew all about government and paperwork and decisions, for the first time in his life he knew something else—someone actually wanted him.

Chapter 42

*D*estiny sat in the church pew next to her parents, her mind a thousand miles away from the sermon, but her heart very much at peace. Ever since she had let go of her shattered dream, a new one was beginning to take shape. True, she would no longer be able to win the high school cross-country state championship and most likely would not be earning a scholarship to Michigan State this year, but she had finally realized that neither of those necessarily meant her competitive running career was over. She would just need a bit of time to get back into shape, so she had two options: she could go to a community college and run for it or apply to Michigan State and try out as a walk on and hope to earn a scholarship that way.

Destiny had discussed both options with her parents, who were relieved that depression's hold was finally relenting and that Destiny was now looking at other options. The three decided that Destiny would apply to Michigan State. No decision had to be made until spring or even summer, and by then they would know where she was in the healing process. The community college would definitely be the more economical, but if it looked like Destiny was back to full strength and capable of earning a scholarship, then there was money in the college fund to at least get her started.

Destiny looked down at her folded hands. How long had she claimed to be submissive to God's will? To want only what God wanted for her? She shook her head slightly. When his will seemed to coincide with her plans, she believed she had been trusting him with her future. It wasn't until that dream had been ripped away that she realized she hadn't been trusting God at all. Now she had that opportunity. She wasn't sure where it would lead, and a part of her was still very nervous that her destiny might not be in running, but she was finally willing to put her future in his hands.

* * * *

Claire sat in the chair next to her mother, not hearing one word of the sermon. Instead, her mind just kept processing the past few months, trying to fathom how everything had come together as it had. Here she wanted to be a film director, to work in the world of the imagination, creating captivating stories and intricate plot lines, but nothing could match the stories she had just witnessed in real life. A director couldn't make this stuff up. If she did it would be considered so farfetched, so contrived as to be implausible, and yet ... they had.

For instance, she had wanted to hate everything about her move to Detroit and Montgomery High. She had wanted to make everyone around her pay for her life being upended. But those motivations had lasted only a few days before Destiny had befriended her, her English project had put her camera back into her hands, and something had opened her eyes and her heart.

Then, bad things, really tough things had happened to good people, threatening to destroy them, but they hadn't, and somehow, without her even knowing it, she had become a source of healing and rescue. So again, something had intervened, rearranged the pieces, tied up some loose ends, and opened a new window. Claire knew she was mixing a lot of metaphors, but that was how complicated the events and the subsequent results that were playing out had been.

Coincidence? Good fortune? Chance? Hmmm. Possibly, but she knew enough statistics to know the probability of all those pieces dovetailing like they did was high—incredibly high. So what was it? God? She squirmed in her seat.

Months ago, Claire had given him credit for personally ruining her life. Then she had chosen to discredit him and doubt his existence. So now was it time to credit God with working through her and around her—despite her?

Suddenly the pastor's words cut into Claire's thoughts.

"Are you tired of being angry? Tired of hanging on? Tired of trying to make everything work out the way you want it to? Are you finally willing to open those clenched fists of yours and accept the future God has for you? Are you finally ready to release your life into the hands of a Heavenly Father who wants to do 'immeasurably more'[1] than you could ever imagine, and have a peace which 'surpasses all understanding'?"[2]

Claire felt her heart race. Did she? The pastor continued.

"I want everyone to close their eyes."

Claire didn't. She watched, eyes wide open, as those around her closed theirs. Some had their heads facing upward, others had hands clenched tightly in front of them as they bowed low in their seats. Others sat quietly. The pastor's eyes surveyed the room. Claire maneuvered behind a body in front of her so she wouldn't be caught peeking.

"Now in the quiet of your seat, I want to ask you one more question. Would you like to know personally the God who will hold you in his hands each day as he leads you on the road he has planned for your life? If so, I would like to lead you through a prayer[3] that will bring you to that place. By a show of hands, who is ready to take that step?"

Claire listened to the questions and watched. Hands began to appear, and she felt her heart quicken. Did she want that? Was she ready and willing to give up her residual anger, doubt, and dreams for what God had in store for her? The pull on her heart was strong, and she sensed that the time to make a decision was running out. The pastor was closing the invitation, and a sense of panic enveloped her. Then, in a split second, she bowed her head … and raised her hand.

NOTES

Chapter 20
[1]Matthew 6:25 (NKJV)

Chapter 24
[1]Philippians 4:7 (NKJV)
[2]Ecclesiastes 1:2-3 (NIV)

Chapter 27
[1]Psalm 46:10 (NIV)

Chapter 29
[1]Psalm 27:14 (NKJV)
[2]Psalm 31:14-15 (NKJV)

Chapter 42
[1]Ephesians 3:2 (NIV)
[2] Philippians 4:7 (NKJV)
[3]A simple prayer of Salvation
Lord,

I know that I am a sinner in need of a savior. I believe that you were born of a virgin birth, that you were crucified for me as payment for my sins, that you were buried and rose on the third day, and that you now live forever. I accept you as my Lord and Savior and turn my life over to you.

J.E. Solinski

Other books by J.E. Solinski

Five very different people wrestle with the ultimate question—Who is in control?

Martha Richards is a high school teacher who prides herself on her efficiency in the classroom and her ability to solve problems. Three of Martha's students—Reba Washington, Alex Kowalski, and Travis Richards—and Martha's own son, Danny, find themselves entangled in a web of best intentions that Martha creates and then tries to control, but her intervention brings unintended consequences for everyone.

In A Matter of Control, faith is tested and illusions are shattered as each of the five comes face to face with the truth of who is really in control.

* * * *

Charlie Moynahan is happy that fourth grade is over and summer is underway... that is until a new kid, Rudy Roberts, moves into the neighborhood and disrupts Charlie's world.

However, when a robbery occurs around the corner at fellow fourth grader Sarah Morris's house, Charlie, with the help of best friend Harold Streeter, begins her own investigation, hoping not only to earn the reward money but also to put Rudy Roberts in his place.

Meet Charlie takes the reader on an adventurous journey of self-discovery as Charlie learns about prejudice, misunderstanding, friendship, and sacrifice.

* * * *

Though living for Jesus is always rewarding, it is rarely easy, and for teens, the pressures are often great: peer pressure, academic demands, the desire to fit in, the need to be appreciated, the pressure to conform to the world's values. The Battle Ready series is a six volume collection of short stories that focuses on encouraging teens to stay true to God's calling to live a pure life and on equipping them to be ready to battle a world opposed to God. Using Apostle Paul's description of the armor of God, Battle Ready Volume I reminds readers that before any other piece of armor can be donned, they must have God's truth securely wrapped around them.

* * * *

Available through booksellers, Ingram, Amazon.com and jesolinski.com
Ask about our fundraising opportunities.

www.ingramcontent.com/pod-product-compliance
Lightning Source LLC
Chambersburg PA
CBHW030650120726
47905CB00001B/145